SEVEN TEMPEST

SEVEN TEMPEST

by

VAUGHAN WILKINS

VICTORIA : 1839

'The late events in England distress me. How could
they let the Queen make such mistakes to the injury
of the monarchy?'

BARON STOCKMAR : *Denkwürdigkeiten*

'It was at this time that the King of the Belgians was
eagerly pursuing his scheme for marrying her to her
cousin, Prince Albert of Saxe Coburg. Although there
were rival candidates, and although Lord Melbourne
looked coldly upon Leopold's choice, the King was
obdurate and firm.'

LORD ESHER : *The Girlhood of Queen Victoria*

JONATHAN CAPE
THIRTY BEDFORD SQUARE
LONDON

FIRST PUBLISHED 1942

JONATHAN CAPE LTD.   30 BEDFORD SQUARE, LONDON
AND 91 WELLINGTON STREET WEST, TORONTO

PRINTED IN GREAT BRITAIN IN THE CITY OF OXFORD
AT THE ALDEN PRESS
PAPER MADE BY SPALDING & HODGE LTD.
BOUND BY A. W. BAIN & CO. LTD.

CONTENTS

BOOK ONE
SEVEN'S SEVEN YEARS

BOOK TWO
A PRINCESS IN REVOLT

BOOK THREE
ATLANTIC SEMINARY

BOOK FOUR
TWO KINDS OF ROMANCE

CONTENTS

BOOK FIVE

ANDROMEDA

BOOK SIX

PERSEUS

For
Two Williams:

MY FATHER
In Memory
and
MY SON
In Hope

SEVEN'S SEVEN YEARS

★

CHAPTER I

ARRIVAL OF A GENTLEMAN

MISS WIVERN paused suddenly before an open doorway, one worn step up from the muddy London pavement.

Once upon a time the doorway had been a handsome and imposing entry, with its carved side-posts and hood and much elegancy of panelling. It had been a doorway through which had undoubtedly passed great ladies with mountainous white wigs and hooped skirts, and gentlemen with cascades of fine lace at throat and cuff of their brocaded coats. Now its dingy paint was blistered and cracked: one of the many-paned windows that flanked it steamed from a tray-load of hot mutton-pies; in the other a dejected starling kept his wicker cage a-jiggling over a dusty row of multi-coloured bottles of barber's lotions.

The street number, painted on the lintel above the door, was barely discernible in the foggy light of a winter afternoon. Miss Wivern peered at it from under the precipice of her dark green bonnet — peered once; peered twice; fumbled under her dark green cloak, produced from beneath the folds a dark green reticule shaped like an Etruscan vase, extracted a paper; compared number with number; put the paper away; craned forward at the numerals over the doorway again, and repeated the whole business of verification afresh.

She looked down at her small companion —

'Well, here we are, Seven!' she said. 'Here we are!'

The boy stood for a moment in silence, gazing into the gloomy depths of the passage before him. The grey flag-stones reminded him of the church at home. He wondered if they, too, were incised with the names and dates of the dead who might lie beneath.

Then —

'Here we are, ma'am,' he echoed obediently.

'Here *we* are,' said Miss Wivern staring into the cold tunnel, and letting go his hand. 'And there *you* are!'

He knew then that the moment of parting had come. He doffed a shaggy rust-coloured beaver-hat, which sat low upon his head as though it were a candle extinguisher.

'Good-bye, ma'am,' he said, 'and thank you for all you have done for me.'

'Good-bye, Seven,' said Miss Wivern, shaking his hand. 'Remember that the coach-office is sending your carpet-bag *here*! The porter *has* been paid ... The *door* is at the end of the passage. It is labelled *Counting House*.' She broke off to scrutinize the upturned face. 'I could really wish that you had not got a black eye. It cannot make a good impression. *So* suggestive of combativeness — ungentlemanliness — ramping and roaring!'

'Bates's is a great deal worse than mine,' said Seven with simple pride.

'Bates has not got to meet his guardian,' said Miss Wivern, shaking her head so vigorously that the plumes on her bonnet were as agitated as a shrubbery in the wind. 'Now you must go! ... Whatever happens, Seven, be a *gentleman*! — Be a Christian — Be a *Daniel*, not a ramping lion! ... Good-bye! God bless you!'

Seven had an instinct that the invocation of heaven's blessing was one of the prerogatives of age, so he contented himself with wishing her 'good-bye' again.

When he reached the counting-house door at the end of the long bare hall, he turned and looked back.

In the entrance he could see silhouetted the gaunt figure of Miss Wivern waiting for him to disappear from view.

When he emerged she would be gone: he might never see her red face any more. The parting had taken place — that parting of which the prospect had clouded the coach ride from Rochester, had stolen the savour from the steak-and-kidney pudding at the Golden Cross, and dimmed the marvels of the London streets!

Seven Tempest was twelve years old: therefore he did not cry: he turned the handle resolutely, and opened the door to his new life. . . .

It was a dark panelled room lighted by one dusty window, and divided by a counter higher than Seven's head. On top of this barrier was a wooden grille painted green, with brass candle-brackets fixed to it at intervals. The candles were already lighted, although it was early afternoon. Behind the fortification three elderly clerks, perched on very high stools, bent their grey heads over ledgers. On either side of the window at their backs, shelves — crowded with large dingy books and portfolios — mounted to the ceiling.

One of the grey-heads turned over a page, wrote the date — November 16th, 1813 — in a copper-plate hand at the top of the new sheet;

ruled two beautiful lines — one thick and one thin — beneath it: raised himself up on his perch, and peered down at the visitor.

He saw a dark, good-looking child — with a long grave nose — dressed in his Sunday best. Dark blue tail-coat collared with velvet; buff nankeen trousers braced so high that they revealed a remarkable expanse of white sock; points of shirt-collar nearly up to his cheek-bones — Miss Wivern herself had arranged the folds and knot of the muslin neck-cloth. He carried a vast and baggy green umbrella under his arm, and his very tall and rather battered rust-coloured hat in his hand.

'Well, young man,' said Grey-head, 'and what do you want?'

'I want Mr. Fielding, please, sir!'

'Indeed!' said Grey-head. 'Does Mr. Fielding want you, do you think?' He raised his grey eyebrows so high in sarcastic inquiry that they seemed about to vanish into an extraordinary bush of hair that appeared to grow straight on end. He scratched the tip of his thin red nose with a quill pen . . . 'What may your business with Mr. Fielding be?'

'Mr. Fielding told Miss Wivern that I should . . .'

'What is the name?' interrupted Grey-head quickly, leaning farther forward on his elbows, and regarding Seven closely through the grille with faded red-rimmed eyes.

'Seven Tempest.'

At the sound of that name the other grey heads were lifted from their ledgers; craned forward to regard the visitor outside their wooden cage.

'Se-ven!' said Grey-head the First, pronouncing each syllable very distinctly. 'Se-ven! So *now* it's seven! . . . You said, "Seven", didn't you?'

Mr. Tempest assured Grey-head that he had said 'Seven', and that he had meant 'Seven', by a vigorous nodding of his dark head.

Grey-head exchanged a glance with his companions — one had a long snuff-stained upper lip, and the other a little shiny buttony nose, the tip being the colour and shape of a half-ripe cherry. They communed in silence. Then Grey-head abruptly vanished from his place behind the wooden bars — like a jack-in-the-box. His high stool grated on the bare floor: there was a sound of heavy breathing as he climbed down from the eminence; and he appeared suddenly — a shrunken little old goblin of a man, in a rusty suit, bony wrists projecting far beyond the frayed ends of his tight sleeves — on Seven's side of the den.

'Se-ven!' repeated Grey-head. 'Well, well, well! . . . You know the old proverbs, young man? — No! — You should study them! There's one that runs—"One father is enough to govern a *hundred* sons but . . ."'

A door crashed somewhere within, and Grey-head vanished again as if he had gone down a trap-door, or had been snatched up into a subfusc heaven above the grimy ceiling.

Seven remained in the middle of the room, clutching hat and umbrella forlornly aware of the surreptitious interest displayed in him by the inmates of the cage.

A porter from the coach-office — his bulging calves encased in blue woollen stockings — flung wide the door after giving it a resounding thump. He carried a large carpet bag.

His eyes fell on the small boy.

'Master Seven Tempest?' he said. 'And Master Seven Tempest it must be! Master Seven Tempest's baggage herewith! . . . A tizzy for the porter, Master!'

At each repetition of his name, Seven was conscious of an intensification of the regard of the Goblin Grey-heads from behind their bars topped by feebly flickering candles.

'Miss Wivern said . . .' he began in protest.

'Oh, she did, did she . . .' But no one ever heard what Miss Wivern had said or done, because at that moment Grey-head the First suddenly materialized out of space behind the porter.

'Put the bag down here,' he said curtly. 'You have been paid . . . Be off with you! . . . Master Seven, come with me . . . Master Tempest, I should say!'

They scaled the echoing well of a wide stone staircase, topped with a glass dome that made grey heaven even greyer; Grey-head, one step ahead all the time, clutching the handrail, and climbing with thin bent shoulders and thin bent legs . . . like a spider's. His knees were so bony that they looked as though they would push their way through his worn pantaloons.

'The carpet-bag is all, Master Seven?' said Grey-head, panting. 'Good! Good! Like Cicero, you can say, "*Omnia mea porto mecum*"!'

'I have only done some Caesar — and some Virgil,' replied Seven, addressing the bowed shoulders, as he laboured upward, considerably impeded by umbrella and hat. 'Dr. Wivern wanted me to learn more. But Miss Wivern said that classics wouldn't be much use to me. And Mr. Fielding, too, said something about it. I don't know what.'

'Miss Wivern was probably right,' said Grey-head, pausing for a rest. He swung round as he did so, clutching for support on either side to the hand-rail: poised thus spread-eagle, he scrutinized Seven closely once again, as if searching for a resemblance to someone, or for a remembered expression.

'No doubt Miss Wivern was right . . . in your case,' he went on at length. 'But the classics are a great comfort. A very great comfort! I read a little in them every night. A great consolation! Just a hundred lines or so . . . and fall asleep. I was at Eton . . . long before Keate or Goodall, of course. We paid more attention to Latinity in my day.'

He shook his head. They continued the ascent to an echoing landing under the glass dome — to an imposing mahogany door with elaborate moulding and pediment.

'Here you are, Master Seven,' he said. 'I wish you luck! . . . Remember, "*Palma non sine pulvere*" — which means, roughly, that you must sweat for success.'

He tapped with a bony finger at the door.

CHAPTER II

THE PASSING OF EXCALIBUR

SEVEN found himself in the longest and coldest-seeming room in which he had ever been. It was painted a light grey, and the tall windows opposite (each opening on to its little semi-circular iron balcony) revealed nothing but a view of grey and white sky. It was like being in a balloon above London — in a balloon in the clouds.

There were pale Persian carpets on the floor; many inlaid tables and cabinets were littered with papers — like the remains of dingy snow-drifts; and the glass of a multitude of prints in narrow black-and-gold frames shone as if there were sheets of ice along the chilly walls.

At the distant end of the room, back to a yellow fire, stood a very big man. He towered over the little group which confronted him: his cold big voice dominated the indefinite cackle of their speech: his great head crowned by a mass of iron-grey hair seemed twice as large as that of any ordinary man.

No one took any notice of Seven. He waited in silence by the door for several minutes, watching the gentlemen about the fire-place.

His attention wandered — was drawn to a queer little brass machine on one of the near-by tables . . . to a pink fruit-dish piled up with glittering lumps of ore, on another . . . to an oddly shaped metal bar — somewhat resembling a human thigh-bone — which lay atop a mass of papers on a serpentine-fronted commode . . . to the pictures. On his left hung a yellowed engraving, apparently a sectional view of a ship, as if cut in half from stem to stern.

The hum and clatter of voices continued at the far end of the room; so he turned to examine the fascinating thing more closely.

A cupid-garlanded title informed him that it was 'The Orthographick Simmetrye of a Ship, together with the Scenographic Appearances of each Part thereof'.

It was just like looking at a queer-shaped honeycomb, for the ship was divided into innumerable little cells by the bulk-heads. Some of the cells showed you port-holes with the cannon run up to them; some, elaborate cabins, or balustraded staircases; others a pile of round-shot, or heaped barrels — presumably of gun-powder. What made it utterly real was that forward, below deck, there was clearly limned a great

14

brick fire-place with a chimney and a monstrous copper. It was un-doubtedly a bricklayer's job, and it struck Seven as most intriguing that brickwork — a thing which seemed to him to be synonymous with dry land and immovability — should thus go to sea.

He was standing on tiptoe, trying to make out every detail, when his green umbrella slid from under his arm and clattered on to the glacial parquet. As he grasped desperately at it, his hat escaped from his hand and bounced on the floor with the noise of a muffled drum.

Scarlet with shame, he retrieved his possessions, and faced about, to see that the deferential court round the big man before the fire was deferentially filing out through a door at the upper end of the room.

'So you got tired of waiting, did you?' said the cold voice . . . 'Come here!'

The small boy nervously walked up the frigid length of the room, between crowded tables and print-hung walls. In one hot hand he held his hat firmly — very firmly indeed: in the other he clutched the baggy green umbrella about its middle — even more firmly. . . .

He halted two paces away from the big man, who leaned back, elbows on mantelpiece, regarding him.

'So you're Seven, are you?'

'Yes, sir!'

'Why?'

Seven was unable to answer that question. He himself had often wondered. He was, too, numbed by the frigidity of the voice, which was of a very different quality from the suave chill that had occasionally crept into Dr. Wivern's tones. For this frigidity was an integral quality — like the harshness and the uncultivated accent.

So he remained mute, head downcast.

'D'you know who I am?'

'Yes, sir!'

'Who?'

'Mister Fielding?' said Seven — doubtfully, because it seemed to him unusual to inquire your identity of a stranger. He stood bowed before the great figure, as though a sacrificial victim before some Northern Moloch who demanded frozen offerings instead of burnings.

'Why?'

This was another question that Seven was unable to answer. He did not even try.

Somewhere a clock ticked loudly with a quick brisk tick, as if at each stroke it snapped a piece of brittle ice.

'Let's have a look at you!'

Seven obediently raised his downcast face, and his dark candid eyes met those of Fielding — cold grey eyes under bushy eyebrows in a big countenance. He met inspection with inspection.

Deep lines were incised from the wide-winged nostrils of the straight nose to the corners of the tight-lipped mouth, and across the wide high forehead from which thick grey hair — frosted with white — was swept back. The square chin, jutting out over the folds of white neckcloth, had as deep a cleft in it as if it had been cut by a sabre stroke.

Whatever the result of his inspection, Mr. Fielding made no comment.

He walked to a table in the nearest window, leaving Seven facing the fire-place, over which was a lithograph of 'The Steamboat Comet' with an immense chimney smoking away for dear life amid the most romantic river scenery. He picked out a letter from a pile of papers, unfolded it, and returned to his station. He read it in silence, and very swiftly.

'The boy is capable of great concentration, but is inclined to daydream . . . Well advanced in geometry and mathematics . . . Great aptitude for mental arithmetic.'

He shot a glance over the sheet at the small attendant figure; demanded —

'How many seventeens in one hundred and two?'

'Six, sir,' answered Seven, after only a very short pause.

Fielding continued reading —

'Taught elementary chemistry in accordance with your instructions . . . Extremely intelligent and thoroughly gentlemanly lad.'

He looked up again —

'How d'you get that black eye?'

'Fighting, sir,' replied Seven; paused, and added, 'But I licked him, sir!'

Fielding displayed no interest in this important aspect of the affair: his chill eyes went back to the spidery writing which ended in the spidery signature 'Andrew Wivern', and in a long postscript. It was this postscript that held his attention longest. He read it twice with a bitter frown.

'I can tell you now that, after much prayer and thought, I deemed it my duty to over-ride your decision that Seven should have no sort of religious instruction. I have wilfully failed to inform you of this in my annual reports to you because it was my duty to God and the child to make certain that he should be brought up in the principles of Christianity.'

16

'So you believe in God, do you, Seven?'

'Yes, sir.'

'Why?'

Seven did not know why. He fidgeted beneath the gaze, rubbing one foot against the other, and black polish off shoe on to white sock.

'Why?'

'I d-don't know, sir.'

'You'll find few manifestations of the Almighty in the next stage of your education.'

Seven grasped the implication of the sentence.

'But God is *everywhere*,' he said in a shocked tone.

'He may be. But you'll find him remarkably indifferent — or inefficient!'

Fielding left the subject.

'Sit down! . . . There . . .' he said, pointing to a chair at the far end of a long mahogany table strewn with plans, scale drawings, and mathematical instruments.

As bidden, Seven sat down, on the extreme edge of a Chippendale elbow-chair, depositing his hat — brim uppermost — on one side of him, and the large umbrella on the other. Just as he did when he went to church.

He gazed fixedly and unhappily at the bunch of seals pendent from the fob-pocket of Mr. Fielding's iron-grey pantaloons.

That gentleman — hands behind back, chin sunk so deeply to his chest that the arching collar of his admirable iron-grey coat rode up behind his head almost as if it were a monk's cowl — spoke without looking at the boy.

'You have had twelve very good years, Seven. You have been — well fed; well clothed; well bedded; and well educated.' It was an unemotional recital of benefits bestowed. 'Is that not so?'

'Yes, sir. Thank you, sir.'

'All this has been at my expense. I have paid for your comforts. And your luxuries . . . Did you know that?'

'No, sir,' said Seven shifting his regard to an ivory foot-rule which lay on a large plan tinted red and green and blue, so that he should not possibly encounter the icy grey eyes.

'Your first twelve years have been good years. Very good years. Possibly too good years. We always have to pay for all we have had. And for what we hope to have. *You*, too, will have to pay. The next years will not be so good.'

He stopped for a moment as though considering whether he would offer any explanation: went on in even tone —

'My first twelve years were of a very different sort. When my mother was hanged I was sent to the poor-house.' — Seven was irresistibly impelled to snatch a quick peep at him — at a man whose mother had been hanged. He had never seen one to his knowledge before. 'I was hungry. I was ragged. I was thirsty. I was ignorant. I was verminous — I don't suppose you have ever seen lice!'

He told of incredible hardships and hideous brutalities in a few curt phrases.

The cold facts, the cold voice, the cold room froze Seven into a mental numbness. He did not appreciate what was being said. In his mind danced the memory of an old print he had once seen, showing the execution of Miss Mary Blandy. He wondered if Mr. Fielding's mother, too, had been hanged before a crowd from a transverse beam between two trees, petticoats and pointed toes a-dangle a few feet from the ground.

'And now you see what I am! A rich man. A very rich man — I that was a poor-house brat, born in the shadow of the gallows. And I owe no one thanks — except, perhaps, an old cobbler and his wife; and them I repaid a thousand-fold. I have done it all myself. I have battled with Fortune and beaten her. I have broken my enemies. Utterly. I have built up great industries. I give employment to hundreds — to thousands.'

His voice had grown louder. He flung his great head up as though challenging Fortune to retrieve what he had wrested from her.

'You have lived on my charity for twelve years,' he said — Seven's dry lips automatically shaped a 'Thank you, sir!' though no sound issued from them. — 'Now if you want me to continue caring for your future, you must prove worth your salt. You must show that you are tough enough, and determined enough to be deserving of help . . . See!'

Seven indicated silently that he saw.

'You will live as I lived. You'll sweat as I sweated. You'll work as I worked. You'll ache for sleep — and won't get it. You'll ache for food — and won't get it; and for warm clothing, and a soft bed, and a hundred other things — and won't get any of them.

'You've had twelve good years, Seven. Now you'll have six hard years. If you break — you break! If you don't — I shall have more to say to you.'

Fielding closed his mouth into a thin straight line, as if he were

18

snapping a trap upon speech; rang a little silver bell that sat on the mantelpiece under the picture of the *Comet*.

Seven — aroused by the silence from a profound speculation on the possible sensations of being son of hanged mother — perceived that the interview was at an end. He got off his chair, collected up hat and umbrella, and approached his guardian.

'What am I to do now, sir?' he asked deferentially.

'You are going to start work in a coal mine.'

At this instant a fat young man in black, with an inquiring expression upon his pale face, glided into the room.

'Book two outside seats on the night mail for South Wales,' said Fielding, his indifferent regard on the darkening cloudscape. A few heavy raindrops beat upon the window-panes. 'Arrange for Ollivant to accompany this boy. Send him to me. I will give him the necessary instructions.'

He swung back to a dazed Seven —

'What do you want with an umbrella? Men don't have umbrellas. Boys don't have umbrellas. Only old women! . . . Put it on the fire!'

Seven's jaw dropped at the sudden onslaught. None of the talk about God or his future had horrified him so much as the peremptory demand for the destruction of his umbrella. It even had a name. It was Excalibur — like King Arthur's sword. His grip tightened on it: it became in a split second a token — a last link with the vanishing days of Minerva House, and Miss Wivern, and Bates. Only last Sunday Batesy and he had fought a sabre duel with their umbrellas in the shrubbery.

He protested, politely, but firmly —

'But it's *my* umbrella, sir!'

'Put it on the fire,' reiterated Fielding.

He looked incredulously up at the cold face: looked, as though imploring aid, at the unresponsive countenance of the secretary.

It was no jest, then!

'I'm very f-fond of it, sir,' he stammered. 'Couldn't . . .?'

And saw so terrible an expression, that he stepped forward and tried to lay the victim lengthways on the blazing coal, as if it were a sword being dedicated upon an altar.

But Excalibur was too long to be disposed of thus across the grate. There was a strong smell of singeing.

Seven straightened himself: shot a swift glance to see if there was any indication of reprieve: took quick decision, and stabbed Excalibur upright into the heart of the fire. A little golden tongue of flame

19

licked at it. Enough! In that instant Excalibur passed, in a long stream of fire with white smoke pouring about the handle.

A bitter sense of injustice, of interference with the rights of property, carried him away. He stamped his foot —

'I am glad your mother was hanged . . . sir!' he said, and turned to the door before he should burst into tears.

CHAPTER III

ENDS IN MURDER

IT was not until he was nineteen years old that Seven saw the long pale room again.

The three grey-heads behind the counting-house cage had bobbed up as he said his name; and Grey-head the First — a trifle greyer, a trifle shabbier, and a trifle more spider-like in his ascent of the steep staircase — had ushered him up once more.

'If you will wait a little, Mr. Seven — I do not imagine that Mr. Fielding will be long!'

He assented curtly.

'You'll see but few changes, Mr. Seven. Although, alas! as Ovid says, "*et fugiunt fraeno non remorante dies!*" '

'Yes,' said Seven.

He stood squarely in the doorway — a tall dark lad, in the short blue jacket and calico trousers of a sailor, a black silk scarf knotted about his neck, a tarred round hat with low crown in his hand.

Grey-head, remembering the child of seven years ago, saw but few traces of him in the tanned face. There was little of youth there either. It was an unsmiling face, with deep-set eyes, aquiline nose and grave wide mouth.

' "... *Et fugiunt!*" ' echoed Grey-head regretfully, almost beneath his breath; and made a slow descent of the stairs to high stool and ledger behind the barricade. . . .

The room appeared to be unchanged.

The steamboat *Comet* still smoked away over the fire-place where Excalibur had burned those seven years ago, and — he looked to the wall by the door — there, too, still hung the 'Orthographick Simmetrye of a Ship'.

As before, the long tables and the inlaid commodes were strewn with plans and diagrams. He examined one or two with close attention and interest, and then walked slowly to the window, and looked out on to the smoky sky and the thin evening mists twining about the hazy outline of tree-tops.

Against that neutral background his imagination recreated the sordid

21

pageant of the intervening years — the pageant set in train by the man he was awaiting.

He saw the great wicker corve go swaying down into the darkness of the pit at Fychan, till its candle-light was swallowed in the depths. Knew again the horror of that twelve-hour vigil in subterranean night by the ventilation door which he must open and shut for the rattling coal trucks, eight hundred feet of solid earth propped up above him by crazy timberings. Saw again the desultory procession to whom he and other children were gate-keepers — a procession of hobgoblin women, trousered, naked to the waist, chained from their belts to the trucks they towed. In the glimmer of their lamps they straddled about the chains which passed between their legs, their bodies acrid with sweat and black with coal dust; their backs so bent that the sagging breasts hung straight down like the udders of beasts. For how many months had he watched them pass along that narrow dripping tunnel — old women, young women, and some far gone with child?

In the grey of the clouds before him, too, he saw the grey of the ravaged valley along which every day he had staggered three interminable miles to long hours of slavery at a blast furnace — a valley of smoking pyramids of brick and slag heaps and polluted streams, that was as a cancer amid the high hills.

Then the factory at Redditch where he had sorted needles — thousands, hundreds of thousands of needles — from a never-decreasing heap, so that their points were all in one direction! Two movements for the left hand, two for the right! Unless you were careful the needles stuck in the cloth stall on your right fore-finger, and went into the wrong heap. Oh, God! what a nightmare those needles had been!

Evening drew on. Somebody came in quietly, lighted the candle-sconces on the wall, and as quietly withdrew.

Such a kaleidoscope of jumbling memories! ... The battle with drunken Taffy Rees on the lip of a pool of molten iron — a pool burning with a violet-coloured flame ... The windowless cellar which was his home in Birmingham; where man and wife and two children slept in one bed, and a third child and himself (aged thirteen) had shared a mattress on the floor with the eldest daughter — a pale slug in her twenties, lecherously inquisitive ... The overseer at Manton's lashing Nellie Dawson with his thong across her scarecrow back until the blood browned the dirty smock that was her one garment ... A child that dropped dead in the cold dawn on its way to work, and lay spindle-shanked in the mud of an unmade road, while its companions hurried on lest they should be late at the factory gates . . . The thin crooked smile that Tod — his only friend — had given him when he left the dock to face a sentence of seven years' transportation for poaching . . . An obscene pool of viscid sewage filling the narrow court where he once lived — it was when he had been set to work at a Thames-side ship-yard. Under a brassy summer sky the pond had shone green, brown, irridescent; its stench had been that of death; the bearers who took the dead away had walked through it ankle-deep . . . Saw himself clinging for dear life over the fore-yard of the barque *Free Trader* (the foot-rope see-sawing under him) as the foresail was rent asunder by the roaring storm, and the jagged remnants whipped out — like a maddened washing-line — above a tilted deck that was hidden by night and the boiling torrents of the sea.

'Pleasant memories, eh! Seven?'

'No!' said Seven, and swung round.

Fielding had come in as silently as a cat; he stood now by the fire-place, elbows on mantelpiece, facing down the delicately-lighted room, great head turned slightly in the direction of the younger man. He was erect, unshrunken; but that his hair was now snow-white, there was no change in his appearance.

He offered Seven no greeting, and, after a casual glance, dropped his eyes to a brass-bound mahogany box on the long table in front of him.

'Why are you in that rig?' his harsh voice demanded. 'Spent all your money? Whoring — gambling — drinking? Come to whine for more?'

'No!' said Seven.

'Why, then?'

'Because I like it. Because I have just come from the sea.'

Fielding's heavy eyebrows rose: his indifferent gaze was still on the mahogany box.

Seven stood defiantly in an easy attitude, back to the dark oblong of the window. The soft glow of many candles had thawed that frigidity which, across the years, had been his most abiding memory of the long room. There were warm lights on shining furniture, reflections of small pointed flames in the gallery of prints along the wall, and a whole host of shadows — from dense black to the most tenuous grey — which loosed mystery about the distant corners of the room, made islands of the long tables in its centre, and flickered friendly-wise amid the litter of papers on polished surfaces.

Said Fielding —

'A year ago to-day you landed at Liverpool. You were handed six

23

hundred pounds to do with as you liked. One hundred pounds for each year in which you were . . .'

'. . . A slave!'

'My pupil,' he amended, unmoved.

'Pupil!' said Seven with a sneer. 'Pupil!'

'There were no conditions except that you should report here at the end of a twelvemonth.'

'Well, here I am!'

'So I perceive!'

There was a long silence during which neither of them stirred, Fielding's eyes on the mahogany box, Seven staring sullenly before him.

'Would it be too much to inquire,' Fielding asked at length, 'what you have done with the money?'

'Do you want it back? . . . I earned it, by God!'

'Just a matter of academic interest,' said the other, gently enough.

Seven brought out the phrases that he had rehearsed for weeks, and, as he spoke them, felt that they were stilted and unimpressive.

'I went to sea because I was told to. Just as I had done everything else — because I was told to. I went to sea a boy. I came back a man. I came back meaning to escape from you . . . I *have* escaped. I am never in all my life again going to do what you tell me.'

Fielding still lounged against the mantelpiece, but his regard had shifted to the young man. He watched him from under lowered lids.

'As you *have* escaped, there can be no harm in telling me *how* you did it. I imagine that the six hundred pounds helped!' he said.

It seemed a reasonable enough proposition.

Said Seven, continuing to look blankly into space —

'The day after I got the money, I bought a passage to America. A week after I landed there I started back again — in the *Savannah*. That's what I went for.'

'The *Savannah*!' mused Fielding. '*Very* interesting, indeed! And why the *Savannah*?'

'The first steam crossing of the Atlantic!'

'I know that. Well!'

'*I*,' said Seven with something of an air of condescension, 'believe in steamboats. And their future. I wanted the experience. I wanted to see how a steamboat would behave in *real* seas. . . . I knocked out one of the crew the night before she sailed, and was waiting on the quayside with my chest and ditty-bag next morning. . . Also I bribed the mate. . . . I signed on as fireman.'

An indefinable fleeting expression crossed Fielding's face.

'There wasn't much work for you in that case!' he commented.

'No,' agreed Seven regretfully. 'We only had eighty hours' steaming in a twenty-nine day voyage . . . But I learned her engine like the palm of my hand.'

'An interesting experience for those with time to spare. But where has all this got you to?'

Fielding, hands deep in the pockets of his grey pantaloons, had swung slightly round, so that his great body as well as his face was turned toward the young man, who was framed against the night and the square panes of the window.

'Escape . . .' answered Seven violently. 'Escape! . . . Did you think I was to be pushed about at your whim all my life? From one horror to another? . . . Did you?'

'No, oddly enough, I didn't,' said the other reflectively. 'I think I knew all along that *you* would be different . . . But I should be interested to hear a few more details of this wonderful escape. I haven't quite caught the thread of the story yet.'

Seven suspected sarcasm. It was obvious that he meditated whether to reply or not, and that youthful pride in achievement overruled antagonism.

'I bought books with *my* money,' he said stiffly. 'Books on engineering. On shipbuilding. I hired a tutor so that I should speak English as I once used to. So that I should get back some of the years you stole from me! . . . *Stole!* . . . STOLE! . . .' He emphasized the disgraceful word by beating his tarred hat on his thigh as he spoke. 'Every minute of my time I have employed. I did anything in any steamboat for six months. Irish Channel work in the *Hibernia*. Up and down the Thames, towing East Indiamen, in the *Majestic*. Then I went to Waterlow's and told them that I'd been in the engine-room of the *Savannah* — the only engineer in this country to have crossed the Atlantic under steam! They gave me their new boat, the *Fury*, on the spot. I've been her engineer for more than two months.'

He threw Fielding a look of triumph as he spoke, met his eyes, and was surprised by the intensity of the regard.

'The *Fury*! Ah, yes!' said the other in a dry tone, and shifted his gaze to the ceiling as if in concentration. 'The *Fury* — one hundred and six feet long. Seventeen foot beam. Thirty horse-power engine! *Mag*-nificent!'

And let a cascade of silver jingle down his breeches pocket, as though to signify that he had enough there to buy up the *Fury*, engine and all — to say nothing of her engineer.

'You seem to know a great deal about her,' said Seven, white with anger.

'I should. I built her.'

'Her engines were built by Finlayson of Birmingham.'

'*I* am Finlayson of Birmingham.'

Seven marched down between line of long tables and line of long dark windows, toward the door. He turned at the foot of the farthest table, and faced the great figure before the fire.

'I suppose you'll tell me next that you are Waterlow's, too!' he said thickly.

'Well, I am,' Fielding assured him smoothly. 'I am, indeed. . . . But I am sorry if you are annoyed about it.' He picked a large document from amid a crowd of papers, and sketched the gesture of offering it to Seven. 'By chance to-day I was checking a point in this contract Waterlow's are making for coal. You'll see it all here.'

Seven said, in a very low voice:

'So I can't ever get away from you?'

He stood with one hand on the door-knob, as though ready for flight. His face had grown more strained and yet more youthful, because the panic in it was almost that of a child and not of a man. In the candle-light the big brass buckles on his thick shoes shone like gold.

Said Fielding, down the room:

'Probably not, I should think.' And then, quickly, as Seven made a sudden movement, 'Just one moment before you go, Seven! . . . Do you remember me telling you, years ago, that my mother was hanged? . . . I see you do! . . . I did not add, as I might have done, that she was your grandmother?'

Seven had half-turned the door-handle as Fielding started to speak. Now he stood petrified, with frowning brows, as though he could not bring himself to believe the implication. When he spoke, it was with the bated utterance with which one speaks of some monstrousness too horrible to be discussed out loud.

'Then . . . you are my father?'

'I am,' answered Fielding. 'I will apologize if you like. But the fact will remain the same.'

Seven let go the door handle. He advanced a few paces into the room, fumbled unseeing with the drawings which he had examined on his first arrival.

He said at last, head downcast: 'What did my mother do, that you should revenge yourself on me?'

26

' "Revenge!" Nonsense!' — A new brisk tone, as if to say, 'Here's enough of melodrama for to-night!' — 'Your mother did all that was required of her . . .' He answered the faint inquiring lift of eyebrows — 'Gave me a son.'

'Why is my name Tempest, then?'

'It seemed to me as good as any other!'

'But your's . . .'

'My dear Seven, isn't it obvious to you that I am your father in fact, though not in law? . . . In other words, you are a bastard.'

Seven echoed the word, and raised his eyes to his father's face.

'But so am I! We are in the same boat in that respect. Like father, like son. On the other hand you have the pleasure — or the reverse — of knowing who your father is! Whereas I shall never know who was mine . . . He may have been any one of a dozen Jacobite officers who were quartered in the house where my mother was a maid. During the rising of '45. He may have been one of their servants. He may have been the Young Pretender himself. He may have mouldered afterwards in drunken exile. He may have died on the scaffold. He may have been massacred at Culloden. I don't know, and frankly don't care. It makes no odds. I am I!'

He did not raise his voice as he made that last arrogant remark. It appeared to him to be too obviously a statement of fact to require underscoring. It was this lack of emphasis, this assuredness, that checked the outburst on Seven's lips.

Surprised at his own calm, he met his father's eyes:

'You don't want to know who *your* father was. But insist on me knowing *mine*! You boast, "I am *I*!" But will not let me be *me*!'

'Think for a minute!'

'For a minute! . . . I have thought about it for seven years.'

'Well then, think again! Have you not had a year in which to be yourself, in which you have been at no one's beck and call — *and* six hundred pounds? A year in which to do what you would — to idle, to drink, to wench, to fritter your money away on horses or in gambling hells or the billiards saloons? . . . You might have done all these things, but say that you did not . . . Is not what you *have* done the answer? . . . You have been *you*!'

Seven meditated the problem with a frown. His essential honesty made him acknowledge the truth of what his father said. He suddenly countered:

'Did you know that I had gone to America? . . . That I came back in the *Savannah*? . . . That I am engineer in the *Fury*?'

Fielding pulled out the chair at the head of the table nearest the fire. He sat down. He looked along the line of tables that stretched the length of the warm twilight of the room — tables covered vaguely with papers, with books, with drawings; tables illuminated from silver candlesticks. He looked along them as the Sphinx might look across the desert. The curving white hair above his brow was as the opening wings of a great bird. His lips curved in the half smile of an Immortal — betwixt laughter and mockery.

'I own the Fychan Pit, Seven,' he said very quietly, 'but have never known the name of any "trapper" except of yourself and' — he paused to calculate — 'and half a dozen others . . . I own the Abercastell Ironworks — Johnston's Needle Manufactory at Redditch — Finlayson's Engine Works in Birmingham — Gregg's Shipbuilding Yards on the Thames — the Red Diamond Packet Line — *and* Waterlow's! . . . The names are all familiar? . . . Too familiar, perhaps! . . . That is by no means the entire list — but it is a list at any rate that you will know. . . . Perhaps you will believe me when I say that it is unlikely that I should know the names of any of the thousands of workers employed — unless I myself had ordered them to be taken on? How could I divine that you would seek work at Waterlow's? Why should I be told?'

Seven seated himself on a stiff-backed chair against the wall — under the 'Orthographick Simmetrye'. He spread his knees wide, and rested his hands upon them: he had dropped his round hat between his feet so that it lay, crown downwards, upon his ankles.

For the first time he realized what manner of a man it was whom he had challenged — not just a big man dominating a great room, but a big man dominating great industries; a man for whom wheels turned, for whom ships set sail, women sweated in coal pits, and puddlers stirred pools of molten metal.

On Saturday mornings he went to Waterlow's Wharf, and drew his pay, hat in hand — across a dented counter in an office grey with dust — from a supercilious young clerk. Mr. Waterlow himself had come through from an inner room once or twice as the silver was being told out — an elderly buck in drab tights and black gaiters; Mr. Waterlow who said condescendingly, 'Ha! What's your name? . . . Eh? . . .Oh! the *Fury*! . . . I remember now . . . Very young! . . . Well, well! . . . That's right, my boy! . . . That's right! . . . Good day to you!'

And then vanished, an antiquated Apollo, in a cloud of dust and a neat phaeton with bad-tempered horses, driven by a bad-tempered young woman of startling appearance, a cigar between her teeth.

This man made it possible for Mr. Waterlow to keep phaeton and young woman; provided the supercilious clerk with the where-withal to fill his horn snuff-box; supplied the coal and wood which sent the *Fury* fussing up and down the Thames. . . .

Said Fielding, breaking in upon his thoughts:

'You had better hear all that I have to say, Seven, before you stride dramatically from a father's presence.'

Seven said nothing; but he turned his head toward his father.

'I suppose you would say that you have had a hard time,' said Fielding. His voice carried icy clear the length of the room, although he did not raise it. 'But so did your half-brothers. And I had a far harder.'

'Brothers?'

'You have — you had — six, who survived infancy. Only one other came through the years of test beside yourself. And he — the final experiment was too much for him! . . . Six hundred pounds proved *his* undoing!'

'Brothers!' repeated Seven, endeavouring to absorb all his newly-found relationships.

'*Half*-brothers! You all had different mothers.'

'And mine?'

'An actress. Young, healthy, and good-looking. Intelligent, too. She found the proposal I made to her acceptable. After you were born she went away . . . What happened to her I cannot say. I have never inquired. I never even knew her real name.'

'She does not seem to have shown much interest in me,' said Seven after a pause.

'Why should she? She only saw you once in her life . . . And then for a few moments,' said Fielding, dispassionately. He rested his elbows upon the table, folded his hands almost as if in prayer, and tapped the finger-tips together gently. 'In every case I chose stock that was healthy and intelligent — so far as I could judge . . . Six of them have failed me.' . . . He directed a long glance at Seven from under his heavy brows . . . '*You* are the son of the seventh.'

'Have I failed you?'

He made no answer, but rose to his feet. He suddenly drummed with his fists on his great chest.

'*I* . . . Look at *me*! No one knows who *my* father was, or *my* mother — except that she was a foundling, and was hanged! *My* children had *me* as their father. *Their* mothers were chosen for them — for health, and looks, and intelligence. Yet *they* couldn't stand a tithe of what I had to undergo. They broke down utterly when they had to put up for just a few years with what I stood all my childhood.'

'*I*,' exclaimed Seven passionately, 'have not broken down!' He rose, too. He was nearly as tall as his father — though not so broad about the shoulders; and his face was not so square as the older man's. He looked him in the eye. 'I have got a job of my own without your help! I don't care a curse if you are the Abercastell Works — or Finlayson — or Gregg — *or* Waterlow's. I'll get another job — if need be! A better job! . . . I can!'

Fielding leaned forward on the table, pressing so heavily on his finger tips that the nails whitened along the edges.

'You have not broken down — so far,' he remarked. 'But you show every sign of making a fool of yourself now. An entirely unnecessary fool! . . . Listen to me, you bloody imbecile!'

The sudden use of invective by those chill lips kept Seven silent. That unexpected cursing brought his father into the plane of flesh-and-blood — metamorphosized him into a human being from a half-divine frigidity which toyed with mortal pawns like a careless chess-player. He said nothing.

'When my mother was hanged . . .' began Fielding.

'My grandmother?' interpellated Seven.

'Your grandmother, if you like it better so,' said Fielding, accepting the emendation. 'When she was . . .'

'Why was she hanged?' asked Seven, forgetful of personal crisis, and agog for lurid details of family history.

There flashed into his mind the memory of how he used regularly to read aloud to Tod accounts of the lives and lamentable end of notorious criminals, from tattered broadsheets, while they lay abed on a Sunday morning in Crane's-court. He could see now Tod sitting up, open-mouthed, on his straw palliasse whilst he read to him as dramatically as possible the gorier details . . . Perhaps he had, unknowing, recounted the story of his own grandmother! . . . All in a split second, too, he remembered that one of the poor sinners had 'suffered in a black bombazine sacque'. He recalled it because he had always wondered what a sacque was . . . Had his grandmother worn black bombazine for this important ceremony?

' "Why?" ' echoed his father.

He paused, still leaning on the immense table, looking down the long room. Then in a very quiet voice he went back to the beginning:

'When it was found that I was on the way, my mother's mistress turned her out of the house — the family had come back to London from the North. Out of *this* house! . . . I was born . . . My mother was nineteen and penniless. It was winter. She came back here, *here*, to appeal for charity. For me more than herself! It was refused her . . . She was left for a moment in a room downstairs. There was a little pile of guineas on the mantelpiece. She took two . . . They would have kept us both for more than a month . . . The theft was discovered as she left the house. She was arrested, prosecuted, hanged! Hanged for the theft of forty-two shillings!'

'Tod,' said Seven almost irrelevantly, 'was transported for seven years for poaching a couple of rabbits! He was caught: I wasn't!'

He saw with incredible clarity Tod's long thin face, long thin neck, hunched thin shoulders, tattered grey shirt (which he had worn for over a year without washing) and crown of fluffy thin hair.

'Ownership — even of rabbits — is the most sacred thing in the world!' commented Fielding ironically.

It was that comment, and its tone, that set Seven considering his father in a new light, although he said acidly —

'*You* ought to know something about ownership!'

Fielding ignored the remark; he continued his story, the echoes of an olden anger in his voice.

'After my mother — died, I was taken to a poor-house. I was starved — beaten — blackguarded — cursed — neglected. I was bound apprentice to your needle factory in Redditch. But they didn't provide luxuries like finger-stalls in *my* days. We sorted the damned needles one at a time! . . . Does that mean anything to you?' — Seven saw again that dirty bench with the dull pile of hundreds of thousands of unpolished needles to be drawn toward him and sorted in four movements of the fingers. So the big man had been through that, and worse! — 'I ran away. I went to the coal pits. I was caught a couple of months after and brought back. I ran away again. It was summer, and I tramped to London sleeping under hedges and eating the garbage of cottages. I got a job in a shipyard — *you* know that yard! . . . Are you listening?'

Seven was listening, and very conscious that every phrase he heard was a stroke at the wall of hate and suspicion which he had raised against his father, who continued —

'There's no reason why I should tell you how and where I first met with success. It would be wearisome for both of us. The fact remains — is obvious — that I did. I became rich. Very rich! Powerful. Very powerful! And the only debt of gratitude I owed in all the world was to an old cobbler and his wife with whom I lodged — who taught me to read, and saw that a growing lad never went hungry . . . I *paid* that debt . . . There was another debt of another sort — and I paid *that*, too. For I excavated the story of my mother from out the past. And then I broke the family that had murdered her. *This* was their London house. It is mine. Their house in Wales is mine, too. I have let their great manor in the North become a heap of rubble. I drove the heir to suicide. His mother died of a broken heart!'

'You revenged yourself on them,' said Seven. 'But why on me? Or my brothers?'

'On you, you fool? What had that to do with you?'

Fielding was silent for a moment. He was still bent slightly forward over the long table with its huddle of papers, and instruments, and despatch-box. He leaned farther forward so that his face was all but hidden from the young man. He appeared to be deciding how much he would tell. His voice was less harsh when he continued.

'I jibed a moment or so ago when I said that ownership was a sacred thing. There is little sacred about the hereditary ownership of rabbits, of miserable hovels, of titles, and rack-rented estates passed on from brainless father to imbecile son! But my kind of ownership *is* sacred. I have built up great industries bringing wealth and influence to Britain, giving employment to all manner of people. I do not gamble, or drink, or wench away the profits. I put them back into my businesses, or create new.

'Coal — iron — ships: that's where the strength of England lies. *I* am Coal, and Iron, and Ships: *I* am the Strength of England. It's a damned bad country — but it is better than the others! It's better than the pederastic impertinence of Prussia, the serfdom of Russia, the respectable immorality of France! My ownership is sacred. I have the strength of this country to hand on. Am I to hand it on by the fatuous law of succession?'

Seven found no answer. He sat there, under the diagram of a skeletonized ship, gently massaging his knees.

'Is what I have created, and nursed, and made strong, to be left to someone just *because* he is my son — to be squandered, to be lost by a rip or a fool? . . . I did not marry because I would not risk all on the ability of one woman to produce me an heir — the right kind of heir . . . Whoever succeeds me, succeeds to a sacred trust. He has got to be hardened and tempered and proved . . . *Now* do you understand?' . . .

It was more than an hour later that Seven left.

'You will be here at half-past eight to-morrow morning,' said his father. 'And come in Christian clothing.'

'Yes,' said Seven briefly, and departed.

As the door closed, Fielding drew the despatch box toward him, opened it, withdrew a folded document, sat down at the head of the table, and dipped pen in ink-pot.

With quill poised over a blank in the mosaic of closely-written words, he read one or two sentences: 'Make and execute this my last Will and Testament . . . executors of this my Will . . . the residue of all my property whatsoever to——' With a firm hand he filled in the gap — 'to my natural-born son, Seven Tempest.'

He rang the silver bell on the mantelpiece, gave a brief instruction, and was still drying the wet ink before the fire when Grey-head shambled into the room.

'I am going to the lawyer — to Mr. Peake,' he said, barely turning his head. 'Is my carriage here? . . . Yes! . . . I shall be back in less than an hour . . . I want you to wait for me. There is a good deal to be done before to-morrow.'

'Yes, sir.'

'You can wait for me here, Quilter. It is warmer than in your office, and it will save you the double journey up the stairs.'

He was gone.

From the tail of his shabby coat the old clerk produced a thin and battered volume of Anacreon's *Odes*, bound in grey paste-board with a faded rose-coloured back. He pushed the elbow chair at the head of the table up to the clear fire, lowered himself into it with extreme tenderness, and sat there — back to the door — mouthing the amorous philosophies of the Ionian poet.

He read the twenty-third ode, first to himself in the Greek; and then out loud. Afterward he leaned back, book on knee, eyes shut, and delicately gathered words for the translation:

> 'But since to purchase Life is not allowed to mortals,
>   Why do I make vain lamentation?'

And so remained there, sip-sipping at his book, savouring its music, and appreciating its paganism, by the mellow light of fire and candles. . . .

The well of the staircase was a dark unlighted pit. Not a solitary star twinkled in the glass dome whereon night pressed heavily. The shadows were so dense that they swallowed up the square figure which climbed the wide stairs, pressing against the wall, and pausing on each separate tread to hearken — a figure that halted at the topmost landing and flattened itself beside one of the pilasters of the doorway to the long room. . . .

> 'Since I was born mortal,
> To journey the road of Life,'

recited Grey-head, proceeding to the twenty-fourth ode — and with that came suddenly to a full-stop, and listened very intently for a repetition of the creaking that he thought to have heard without. There was no repetition.

> 'χρόνον ἔχνων, ὃν παρῆλθον
> ὃν δ' ἔχω ὀραμεῖν οὐκ δίδα,'

said Grey-head almost below his breath; meditated apt words for a translation; repeated the Greek a trifle louder; meditated again the best phrases for its meaning; heard once more what sounded like the faint remonstrance of an uneasy floor under a heel; rose to investigate, finger between pages.

> 'I know the time which is passed,
> But that which I have to run I know not . . .'

said Grey-head in a little more than a whisper. There was a good rise and fall in the language, he felt. He said it half aloud again, as he opened the door and peered out into the darkness —

> 'ὃν δ' ἔχω ὀραμεῖν οὐκ δίδα —'
> 'The time which I have to run, I know not . . .'

And with that fell face downward in the passage under the blow that shattered his skull. There was no more noise than might be made by an egg falling from a table on to a stone floor. Quilter died without a sigh; and though its manner may have been violent, yet his end was peaceful. He lay there dead, his hidden face half-smiling, bony fore-finger thrust between pages thirty-two and thirty-three of his Anacreon, and his lips formed to shape the music of a pagan poet.

The moon came out: the great glass dome over the staircase suddenly revealed the dense blue darkness of heaven. The thin light — pale ghost of sunshine — showed the dead man sprawled across the threshold of the long room and the clotting of his grey hair.

The man who had struck him down looked out of the shadows at the meagre body, and recognized it with anger and surprise.

*   *   *   *

The years slip by — hurry by — cascade over the rapids of succeeding crises.

The war that was to end war, and crush tyranny for ever, is almost forgotten. Victory has sown the seeds of fresh wars. Old tyrannies renewed have replaced that of Napoleon, the upstart, who has died in a little curtained bed in his lodge in an island prison, of cancer — and of boredom.

The returned heroes have found that they have won no freedom. They are even, perhaps, a trifle hungrier, a trifle more ragged, and a trifle more desperate. All over Europe there are conspiracies — and shootings, and sabrings, and hangings.

Women are no longer sinuous creatures, dampening thin petticoats to reveal delicate and dangerous outlines. Mode now demands of them sumptuous bosoms swelling above waists wasp-corsetted by Lacroix of Paris at five gold louis. Long slim legs must be hidden by a pyramid of underwear: shoulders must become hams decked in white and pink satin.

Mad, bad, and stupid kings have been replaced on the Throne of England by a girl — a very young girl . . . For the first time for many years there is no taint about the palaces . . . They are the fairy-tale palaces of the olden story . . . They are respectable palaces . . . They are — dull palaces.

England has been enchanted by its new monarch; it has adored Victoria's smooth, oiled tresses; it has guffawed to her childish giggle . . . It has become accustomed to her; grown bored — critical — irritated.

Mr. Secretary Greville, of Her Majesty's Privy Council, sharpens his quill pen. He writes for posterity, in his memoirs, of her who has been sovereign for but few months —

'Nobody cares for the Queen; her popularity has sunk to zero, and loyalty is a dead letter . . .'

Majesty, indeed, is shouted at in the streets, and hissed at on the racecourse.

Uncle Leopold, King of the Belgians, is in a sad taking about it all. He had hoped to rule England in its essential policies through a dutiful niece: but since she has become queen that niece is no longer as dutiful as he could have wished; she has practically ostracized her mother, the Duchess of Kent, and is capable of defying a prime minister.

Uncle Ernest, King of Hanover, rubs his hands and chuckles to himself. He is next heir to the Throne of England, until Victoria marries and has children; still hopes that the country will sicken of school-girl government and will call on him. He takes his morning airing through the streets of his capital in his glittering carriage behind his glittering greys, stiff old neck wrapped about with so many yards of muslin neck-cloth that the angry face with beaked nose and blind eye is cocked back like the head of a furious snake. The Hanoverian Press records that 'our revered Monarch enjoys excellent health'; declares reports that he is intriguing to dethrone his niece to be 'basely malignant' and 'almost idiotic'. But there are those who know better.

A PRINCESS IN REVOLT

CHAPTER I

TWO LADIES ARE DISTURBED AT BEDTIME

ANNE LOUISE ELIZABETH CAROLINE, propped upon an elbow, was reading by candlelight in the only place that was private to herself in all the world — her bed.

She had drawn the curtains of the four-poster tightly, so that she was enclosed in a cabin of glazed chintz, with pillars of dark mahogany at each corner. The candlestick with its cylindrical glass shade was established dangerously in a deep crease in the pillow against which her shoulder rested. Every time that Anne Louise stirred the candlestick stirred, and the little yellow flame within licked its glass cage in eagerness to escape, so that there was a long sooty tongue mark on the glass. The illumination, however, was sufficient to read by, and to show the posies of wild roses, pansies, bluebells, and other flowers which were congealed against a pale fawn background on the shiny folds of the bed-hangings.

Anne Louise was breaking every regulation; but she always did so — as soon as Miss Talfourd's frosty red nose, grey corkscrew curls, and wide-skirted, savoy-cabbage-coloured dress had departed.

Miss Talfourd had set a wax night-light in a dish filled with water on the distant washstand; had pulled the heavy curtains yet closer over tightly shut windows; had straightened the white crocheted lace cover on the chest of drawers; had swept the shadowy room with an all penetrating eye; had blown the candle out; sketched the sort of unwilling bob that Englishwomen present to foreign Royalties; remarked conventionally 'Good-night, your Highness'; and departed, closing the door behind her in the same decided way in which she was used to shut the cat out at night at her aged father's rectory in Nottinghamshire.

Anne Louise was alone at last.

She waited a precautionary interval, and then leaped from her bed; undid the top three buttons at the high frilled throat of her nightdress; untied the strings of her muslin nightcap and dropped it on the floor; lighted the candle afresh; pattered on bare feet to the casement, and threw open the windows wide to darkness, and to a wind with which the heavy curtains battled convulsively.

After this ostentatiously rebellious business Anne Louise went back to bed; hummocked snug sheets, blankets, coverlet and gay patchwork quilt about her shoulders; and immersed herself in the heavy calf-bound volume that lay beside her. Ringlets that were of every conceivable shade of gold fell about her intent face; the perilous candlestick in its crater on the pillow shuddered with each breath, and curtseyed more dangerously than ever each time a leaf was turned.

Anne Louise read on.

She had decided to implement the schema of instruction prepared for her long stay in England by Uncle Leopold with a much more general system of self-education. With all the determination of her family and race she was in process of reading, in their entirety, the one thousand eight hundred and eighty-three pages of that generally wearisome work, the British Cyclopaedia of Arts and Sciences compiled by Mr. Charles Partington, Professor of Mechanical Philosophy.

She reached page 345 on the long trail from Abacus to Zymosimeter: read with breathless interest the article on spontaneous combustion: read Surgeon Williman's account of the death in 1773 of Mary Clues, aged 50, who was 'much addicted to intoxication' and was found utterly burned to fatty cinders upon a feather bed which was unmarked by fire.

She lay there imagining the horrific passing of Mrs. Grace Pitt of Ipswich — burned by some internal flame after over-indulgence in spirituous liquors; picturing the transformation of the elderly dipsomaniac of Caen, Mdlle. de Thuars, into a mass of ashes after a foolish refreshment of three bottles of wine and one of brandy. Lay in her faintly-illumined cabin of shiny, shadowy chintz, head bent over the heavy volume, lips shaping unfamiliar words, pointed chin resting on palm.

Anne Louise read on.

She learned the meaning of *Come Sopra* and *Come Sta*; looked in the little English-French dictionary that was pushed under her bolster, to check the exact meaning of the word 'commensurable'; and plunged after the faintest pause, the merest hint of a sigh, into a dissertation on the Commerce of the World.

In former times (she read) commerce subdued the steppes of Scythia and the deserts of Libya —

With the wind that streamed through the distraught curtains, there was borne into the darkness of her room the lightly-accented clatter of quickly-moving hoofs, and the grinding of carriage wheels as they took the turn into the avenue a trifle too sharply.

Anne Louise Elizabeth Caroline sat up swiftly in bed — so swiftly that she was not able to prevent Mr. Partington's Cyclopaedia from thumping to the floor. The glass-protected candlestick, too, heeled over at the brusque movement, and the flame foundered utterly in the scurry at rescue which followed. A little of the hot tallow ran on to the tight pleated wrist-band of her nightdress.

With the extinction of that friendly wick her gay cabin was submerged in the general darkness: its chintz hangings were no longer walls against the world, but the sides of a shadowed cage in which she was held, awaiting the coming of some crisis. For Anne Louise knew, with utter certainty and with the egotism of youth, that no one would come to that house at ten o'clock of night with such a clatter of hoofs and rattle of wheels, except about the business of a Duchess of Limburg who was also a royal princess and ward of a king — even if she were but seventeen years old.

Then she suddenly realized that, through a knife-edge chink in the curtains, she could see a small circle of pale radiance cast on the ceiling by the night-light on her wash-stand. The discovery of that faint flame gave her confidence. She slipped out of bed with a careless display of slim, naked legs; scurried across the bare floor; closed the windows; restored the ship-wrecked candlestick to its accustomed table; collected the abominated nightcap; pulled open the bed-curtains; and was back again in an instant, pushing Mr. Partington's Cyclopaedia out of sight, far down between the sheets, where it lay — angular and resentful — against her toes.

To anyone entering a moment afterward, Anne Louise would have appeared to be asleep — eyes fast shut; breathing deep and slow; quilt (with all its little triangles of green, russet and yellow silk and velvet) spread over her like a sort of bird's-eye view of a Devonshire hillside....

The bed-going of the mistress of Severall, the Lady Augusta Wentworth, was a ritual — solemn, almost royal, reminiscent of the ceremonial couching of the late venerated Queen Charlotte, to whom she had been Woman of the Bedchamber for nearly a quarter of a century.

The room was as big as a field — a very green field. The four-poster bed was as big as a barn — a green satin, gold-fringed-and-tasselled barn, walled in by folds of curtain except for the main entrance at the side by which Lady Augusta entered its privacy up a portable staircase (consisting of two shallow tapestry-covered steps) and except for an aperture at the foot whereby Lady Augusta could watch the flicker of the fire and perceive the good-night reverences of her housekeeper. The green of the enormous carpet, the green of the terrific hangings, the flower-bed upholstery of the sarcophagus-like sofa, were given all the shades and shadows of a stage garden by the light from a scattered multitude of silver candlesticks, and from the fire that blazed in a greyish marble fireplace large enough for the entrance to a mausoleum.

Amid the monstrous splendours of this apartment Lady Augusta looked like a wizened monkey.

She was disrobed, and — so to speak — dismantled, ensconced in a high wing chair before the fire, and enveloped in two or three layers of the softest white shawls imaginable. Then her face was sponged with lavender-scented warm water by her elderly woman, Perkins, whilst a rosy-cheeked deputy stood by holding pleasantly warmed towels of fine cambric ready for the drying ceremony.

After that came the Rites of Hair-Brushing, of Powdering the withered face, of the Assumption of the Yellow Kid Gloves, and finally the almost sacramental Presentation of the small Round Table, on which were set a glass of mulled claret (piping hot), a Bible with shiny black cover, two thin biscuits on a silver platter, and one clean handkerchief upon a silver salver.

At that moment an unseen clock chimed the quarter before ten; a discreet tap sounded upon the panels of the distant door. Junior attendant tiptoed across the field of bright green carpet, and peeped out and whispered and returned, and whispered again to senior attendant; and senior attendant stepped towards the bent figure that was swallowed up in crimped nightcap and voluminous shawls and colossal chair, and whispered in her turn —

'Mrs. Day waits upon your La'ship.'

And then Mrs. Day sidled in, as shiny black in her silk dress as a slug, and attendants sidled out according to inviolable rite. And Lady Augusta, warming her ancient bones by the fire, dipping that thin beak of a nose into the wide-mouthed glass of hot wine, breaking crisp biscuits in her long fingers with swollen joints, heard the news of the day. Heard the official gazette on household supplies and meals— heard of the movements and morals of staff — heard of the gossip of steward's room, servants' hall, and kitchen — heard a faithful chronicle of events in house, and manor, and the meek villages that lay about them in the smooth Suffolk countryside.

Mrs. Day, standing exactly a yard and a half from that almost-sacramental Round Table, plump hands folded over plumper abdomen (as shiny and curved in black silk as a beetle's wing-case) looked like a bonze in reverential duty upon a God. An amphigamous God with fierce eyes under the halo of a frilled nightcap, and with a hooked nose presiding over a long and snuff-stained upper lip.

Lady Augusta had dusted her fingers of biscuit crumbs, cast off her shawls, risen and walked (upright as a poker) to those altar steps by which she gained her bed, when Mrs. Day decided — after an internal debate that had lasted all the afternoon and evening — to tell her best story.

'I *think* you ought to know, m'Lady. I am *sure* you ought to know, m'Lady . . . I *know* you ought to know, m'Lady,' said Mrs. Day, piling up a crescendo of conviction. 'The girl Lovell . . .'

Lady Augusta never displayed any sign of interest beyond the merest twitch of a muscle. Now, as she proceeded in her long white nightgown to the sanctuary of white sheets and grass-green hangings and gold cords and fringes and tassels, she conveyed her permission for the narrative by the very faintest inclination of the head — the movement of a fraction of an inch.

'The girl Lovell,' said Mrs. Day slowly, wondering if she had been altogether wise, and accentuating her adjectives as she broke the news, 'is, I fear, a *designing* young party, m'Lady! A *dangerous* person, m'Lady! A *most* dangerous young person, m'Lady!'

'Has she got to let her stays out?' asked her Ladyship indifferently, preparing to mount the tapestry-covered steps. She might have been merely inquiring about the approaching maternity of the stable cat.

Mrs. Day was not prepared to make such an asseveration — in words at any rate. She implied her belief in future stays-letting-out by a grave and dubious inclination of the head which was a sort of cross between a respectful nod and a respectful shake.

'Send her home,' said Lady Augusta.

'She is an orphint, m'Lady.'

'Send her back to the orphanage!'

'Gaol is what she wants — the designing hussy!' amended Mrs. Day, pressing her thin lips together, in token of irrevocable and considered judgment, so tightly that they practically vanished, and her mouth became a straight slit, with an enormous wrinkle at each corner running down to her chin and up to her nose.

'Well?'

'I saw,' began Mrs. Day, and paused. 'I am certain I ought to tell you, m'Lady. Indeed, m'Lady . . .'

'Saw? . . .' commanded Lady Augusta, placing her left foot on the first step, and the shiny Bible upon the pillow.

'. . . Saw,' repeated Mrs. Day slowly, watching the old lady drag herself up one foot at a time, her gloved hands resting for support on the bed. 'Saw', said she in a great rush, 'My Lord come out of her attic! Last night — long past midnight!'

She breathed her horror at the inveiglement of my Lady's nephew heavily through her nose. A snort it would have been, had she not been in that grass-green room, and in the Very Presence.

Lady Augusta had reached the top step: one long yellow foot was nuzzling forward into the warmth of nicely aired sheets: the primrose-gloved hands were sunk into the downy hollows of the feather bed: she was bent, inelegantly, so nearly double that her hind-quarters (decently draped in the thick folds of her night-wear) were almost as high as her head.

She turned a swift regard that was full of menace down the green cavern of her bed to her henchwoman at the foot.

'And why not, indeed?' said Lady Augusta in her most freezing voice. 'And why not?'

And just then — although every window was tightly shut and shrouded in curtains of thick green velvet — they, too, heard the quick beating of hoofs and the grinding of carriage wheels. . . .

A minute before, the striking-train of Uncle Leopold's travelling clock, which lived in a sort of narrow red morocco tray under the front window of the carriage — with a silver-knobbed brandy flask, a vial of eau-de-cologne, a container for two packs of patience cards, and a series of slim mysterious note-books — had given its premonitory cluck before announcing the hour.

As it did so Uncle Leopold's carriage swung out of a main road that was faintly illuminated by stars and a watery moon; was swallowed up, with its satellite vehicle, for a few moments — but for the yellow glimmer of the lamps — in the restless shadows of an avenue of great elms; emerged at last before the lofty portico of a house which fronted dim park-land across a wide dark lawn.

Uncle Leopold had not said a word during the last sixteen miles of the journey from Colchester.

He had sat in chilly abstraction, staring through the mud-speckled window before him into the night, strong cleft chin propped on the folds of black satin neck-cloth, and the delicate curves of the whiskers under his cheek-bones resting on the gills of his incredibly high collar as though they sprouted from it. He had swayed, with the swift poise of the bubble in a spirit level, to the jerks and jolts of the carriage over uneven country roads, his restless fingers playing all the time with a tangle of string.

His companion preserved a deferential silence; furtively watched the twining fingers in the hazy light of the carriage-lamps; furtively glanced at the cold mask which hid — he felt — not the ordinary emotions of the human heart, but the formulated movements of a precise and almost soul-less intelligence.

The chariot came to a halt. Uncle Leopold cast one bleak look at the unwelcoming face of the house, where only showed a subdued radiance in the semi-circle of the fan-light over the hall door.

'It would appear,' said he in frigid tones — as though holding his companion responsible — 'that WE are not expected.'

The second carriage came clattering up. Hühnlein, his favourite servant, leaped out, and ran to open the door for him: another bustled up the steps before the portico, fumbled a moment in the gloom, and set a bell jangling wildly in the distant recesses of the house.

Uncle Leopold prepared to descend.

'Not expected!' he repeated in a voice that held restrained and displeased astonishment. . . .

There were thirty bells hanging in a row in the flagged passage between the vast deserted kitchen and the warm intimacy of the house-keeper's room. That single one of the company, being jerked into violent life at the end of a long wire, set its mates quivering into a thin ghostly tinkle.

The violent proclamation of the bell, and the trembling chorus that accompanied it, aroused old Woodrow, the butler, drowsing over a half-full decanter of Madeira and a seed-cake, before the fire in the silver pantry.

It flustered him into his tight blue coat; flustered him into dusting the cake crumbs from the starched pigeon-breast frill of his shirt; flustered him into the shoes he had kicked off to ease his gouty toes.

It announced the arrival of a King.

CHAPTER II

UNSEEMLY CONDUCT OF A NIECE

Anne Louise came into the saloon where Uncle Leopold had just finished the cold supper hurriedly prepared for him.

He sat now very formally in an elbow-chair drawn up to the fire, contemplating with unmoved expression a large portrait by Sir William Beechey of his first wife, the Princess Charlotte of Wales — roguish, bland, smiling, in billowing muslins and cherry-coloured sash and ribbons. The picture was the only modern thing in a room which otherwise had been left unchanged for over a hundred years — a room of faded tapestry, walnut furniture, and Chinese cabinets lacquered to the delicate tint of the silver-green outer rind of an almond.

A decanter of wine and a plate with a half-peeled apple — apples were good for the teeth! — were on the small table at his elbow.

Anne Louise entered so quietly that he did not hear her, and she stood by the door for a moment studying, in anxious silence, the brother of her long-dead mother.

She had not seen him since she had been suddenly summoned to Brussels from her remote valley in Provence nearly two years ago, to hear the fate that he, as her guardian, had imposed upon her.

She remembered vividly the violence of her rebellion, which had left Uncle Leopold as unmoved and as icy as the chill magnificence of the vast mirrored room in which he had announced his decision. He had worn then — she recalled — a blue dress coat with a star upon the left breast, and had sat picking his teeth at her across the length of an enormous table whose reddish marble top was supported by gilded sphinxes.

She was to go to England for a year or so (he had said) to 'complete her education' — to leave dear Lecques where her long orphanhood had been spent.

She had faced him with a stony countenance, eyes seeing, not the young green of plane trees through the tall windows behind him, but the surging ocean of pines that rustled and sang in the wind about the battlemented walls, the grey towers, the dark red roofs of her far distant home. She had closed her eyelids: she was climbing the wide worn steps from the courtyard into the cavernous dimness of the great entrance-hall: she was in the Long Gallery where a line of faded portraits stared from dark panelling out of mullioned bay-windows over the sea of trees: Aunt Sophia — as faded as any of the pictured beauties — was knitting in a high-backed chair before the fire, her thin frame sheltered, from the draughts that roared about the tunnel of a room, by a black lacquered screen studded with mother-of-pearl.

'I won't go,' she had said violently, at last.

Uncle Leopold had shrugged his shoulders.

'Your opinion is not invited,' he had replied.

And she had countered in a voice pitched high by anger and fear, 'But I won't!'

He had raised supercilious eyebrows — 'That is not the way to address your elders. Go to your room, Anne. I am afraid that you are out of hand.'

It all came back to her now.

Since then — she knew well — she had grown up. They were no longer the eyes of a child that looked on that slightly *passé* hero of a fairy-tale — the younger son of a Saxe-Coburg princeling who had been shot out into the world to seek his fortune . . . and had achieved it; who might have ruled England, if his wife, the Queen-to-be, had not been so unwise as to die in child-birth; who had rejected the Throne of Greece, and now was King of a brand-new kingdom, that of the Belgians.

She took in the perfection of his dress: dark green coat with high collar of velvet; sprigged satin waistcoat; stone-coloured trousers strapped under the lacquered boots which had such astonishingly thick soles — for Uncle Leopold was always afraid of damp feet. She took in the careful-careless manner in which the shiny black locks of his 'wind-swept' wig were brushed forward to hide the growing baldness of the forehead: noted the lines that had engraved themselves beside mouth and deep-set eyes under the dark straight brows: remarked the faint blurring of the romantic beauty of the face which had won him fortune — and was maliciously glad at those signs of the approach of age.

It was his endeavour to shape her destiny — for his own purposes, she was sure! — that she resented, far more bitterly than his annexation of her miniature state directly her father died, when she was a small child.

She advanced into the room.

'Uncle Leopold! How do you do?' she said in English, and swept a curtsey that set her wide lavender-grey dress rustling upon the polished floor.

He removed the quill tooth-pick with which he had been exploring his strong white teeth; turned his cold black eyes upon her; reminded himself that she was going to be useful — very useful — and so rose with a courtesy that was almost discourteous in its casualness.

'Ah, Anne!' said he, approached a step, bent, planted an icy kiss upon her forehead. 'I see you well? . . . You have grown . . . You are getting very tanned: that is an English habit you must not adopt.'

'Yes, Uncle Leopold,' answered Anne Louise comprehensively, and immediately hostile.

For a very long moment he said nothing, but stood with his back to the fire, looking at her with an air of detached and scientific appraisement, toothpick in hand: stood inspecting her narrowly and frigidly as if she were a family possession — a jewel, a horse, a piece of porcelain.

Anne Louise supported the examination with chill disdain. She stood at some little distance from him, beside a high lacquered chest surmounted by a Nanking vase. Her grey unsmiling eyes fixed their regard on the carving of the gilded frame behind him.

Uncle Leopold took note of the fair hair — with its golden and silvery lights — which curved from the parting into two clusters of shining ringlets; of pointed chin and wide cheek-bones; of the white shoulders revealed by the bodice that was cut so low and so straight at the top and tapered at the waist. He even appeared to debate within himself on the taste of her dress with its short puffed sleeves and bows of violet down the front; whether he would himself have chosen the same shade of grey silk for her shoes; and whether he could altogether approve the faint inquiring twist to the delicate eyebrows she had inherited from the father she could barely remember; whether he thought the short straight nose sufficiently royal; whether a member of his race ought to have even two freckles; and whether the mouth was not just a trifle too wide for one so close to a throne.

'Sit down,' said Uncle Leopold at length.

He divided his coat-tails precisely, and seated himself with studied elegance. He placed his long white hands along the arms of the chair, and turned his head very slightly as though regarding the fire, so that (his niece felt) she should see his profile at the best angle.

Anne Louise fancied that these actions were codified and performed according to a schedule which was probably drawn up in an exquisite angular handwriting in a green Russia-leather-bound book with gilt edges and an index.

Deliberately she remained standing where she was: deliberately she refused to look at that celebrated face, and cast her regard downward to the pointed toes of her shoes.

Leopold gave no sign that he had observed those small portents of rebellion.

'Apparently,' he said rather acidly, 'my visit was unexpected, although I wrote from Claremont three days ago.'

'We have had no letter, Uncle,' said Anne Louise in her high, clear voice.

'These English posts! I never trust them. I have never used them except in cases of absolute necessity. *I* should reorganize them. *I* should . . .' he broke off, and then continued with a fresh grievance. 'And Lady Augusta is abed with the influenza!'

He spoke with the faintest hint of questioning in his voice, as if he suspected that once Lady Augusta had retired for the night she would not rise again to greet a King — even himself. Which was the fact.

'Is she?' asked Anne Louise, with malicious intent to confirm him in so humiliating a belief.

He cast her a quick glance, and then resumed his study of the fire. After a pause —

'I have travelled considerably out of my way to see you, Anne. I must leave to-morrow morning. The British Government have a steamboat waiting for me at Harwich. I must be in Brussels at the first possible moment . . . I have a great deal to say to you . . . Sit down, Anne!'

She did not dare disobey his command a second time. She seated herself in the high-backed tapestry-covered chair behind her — seated herself with eyes downcast, and hands folded on pale lavender lap.

Uncle Leopold threw himself back in his chair, cocked one immaculate leg over the other, regarded indulgently a particularly fat cherub (tied with a pale blue ribbon) who disported himself on the painted ceiling; and then took on the appearance of a fatigued Apollo, an extremely weary Ganymede, and a relentless but jaded Grand Inquisitor.

'Your English?' asked Uncle Leopold, and did not stay for an answer. 'No, I need not ask. It is good. Very good! I congratulate you, Anne! . . . Have you kept up your reading of political history? Has Miss Talfourd followed the course I laid down? Have you finished your Hallam? . . . I think you had better read Robertson's "Disquisition" on Ancient India, and his history of Scotland in two volumes. There was a good edition published about ten years ago. I will have it sent to you. You cannot read too much of anything that relates to

England and its possessions . . .' he paused, '. . . or about Hanover.'

Here Uncle Leopold coughed slightly — just twice: a fact which obviously caused him great concern, for he rose out of his chair, sought in his tail-pocket, produced a small gold box, and extracted therefrom a greenish comfit, which he sucked very slowly. Meanwhile he rambled elegantly about the room, diffusing a gentle aroma of horehound and liquorice. When he spoke again it was in a low voice as if he would save his throat from as much wear and tear as possible.

As he walked, he picked up the trifles of porcelain and silver, the miniatures, fans, pouncet-boxes, and carved ivories, that were scattered over serpentine-fronted bureaux, walnut commodes, and chests of tulip-wood; ran his finger approvingly over the satyr-masks carved on the mahogany legs of a table which supported nothing but a large Chinese covered-bowl wheron crawled five-clawed dragons of bronze.

He shifted the position of a Dresden shepherdess with hooped skirt, powdered hair, but excessively naked bosom; admired the rearrangement; and continued his inquisition — and disquisition — whilst he found fresh homes for every ornament, studied each change, and admired it.

'What about Hume — a most philosophical historian?' said Uncle Leopold, questioning within himself where he would place an ivory tusk carved to tell of a round-up of wild elephants in the teak forests of Mysore. 'Not too impartial, perhaps! But impartiality can be a serious nuisance. Ve-e-e-ry!' — He shifted the carving by half an inch — 'Ve-e-e-ry serious . . . I should like you to read Machiavelli's *Il Principe* . . . How is your Italian? I was passably good when I was twelve years old.' — He examined disapprovingly a circle of embroidery studded with the irridescent wing-cases of some South American beetle — 'I spoke Russian, French, and English extremely well by the time I was fifteen.'

Anne Louise made no comment. She was extremely angry and extremely afraid. She felt that, like the Dresden shepherdess, she might be taken from her accustomed station by this meddlesome man; dusted with a lace-fringed handkerchief, held up to the light, examined for a flaw, approved or disapproved, and set down where she would not be.

She prayed that one of those delicate and precious things would drop from the long white fingers, and crash on to the shining oak floor . . . But nothing did.

'You may think it curious,' said Uncle Leopold, 'that I should have travelled so far out of my way to talk about history and education.' —

He paused as if requiring acknowledgment of a King's self-sacrifice. Anne Louise said nothing. He went on — 'My questions, however, have an intimate bearing on your future.'

He said '*your* future', but permitted the phrase to sound as if that future was a personal gift from him to her.

He stood facing her across the hearth, twisting between his fingers a small gold object which he had taken from his waistcoat pocket — a clamp which was screwed to his back teeth at night so that he should not injure their enamel if he ground them in his sleep. His head was bent a little toward her, a faint smile curving his beautifully shaped lips, as though expecting — and deprecating — words of stumbling gratitude.

Anne Louise felt no gratitude: she was certain that '*your* future' meant '*my* future — the future which I have arranged for *you* to suit *me*.' His use of the words told her with deadly certainty that her suspicions of coming danger had been correct.

In that short thanks-anticipating pause she formulated her policy. No more open childish mutiny, but the rebellion of an adult — planned, effective, and secret until the time was ripe.

So it was, that, while Uncle Leopold only saw one Anne Louise, two sat facing him. One the respectful and dutiful niece who bowed her sleek head in assent at intervals : the other a daring termagant of a rebel.

'Yes, Uncle Leopold,' said Anne Louise number One.

'No! No! No! . . . Bloody bitch!' said Anne Louise Two — but not out loud. She had been rather taken by the lilt of the expression when she had heard Lord Henry Wentworth stammer it out last night to an unseen someone down a dark corridor.

Then in a most disconcerting manner Uncle Leopold suddenly changed his tactics. He drew the chair nearer to the hearth : seated himself : and leaning forward, elbows on knees, talked to her while he made a succession of little old-lady-like jabs with the poker at the fire of cherry logs and coal.

'How would you like,' began he without preamble — paused whilst he broke a golden-red chip off a flaming ember, and then continued, 'to be a — Queen?'

He did not even turn his head as he spoke.

'Queen?' echoed Anne Louise, utterly lost at the turn the conversation had taken.

'It is not necessary to repeat my words. I said "Queen",' said Uncle Leopold.

'Queen! Queen! Queen!' repeated the invisible Anne Louise defiantly.

The other Anne Louise permitted herself to give the King a glance that hinted at deprecation of stupidity.

'Queen,' said Uncle Leopold again, in a sarcastically explanatory tone — 'the consort of a King!'

He emphasized every syllable of the sentence with a stab of the sharp point of the poker into the heart of the fire.

Queen! Uncle Leopold was the only King she knew, now that funny old King William — to whom the Duchess of Kent had presented her — was dead. Old William the Fourth, who had taken her slim hand in his gouty paw, and said, 'Pretty lass! Very! Danger to the lads one of these days!' Adding, 'Honester face than the rest of your tribe!' while the Kent had snorted and gone maroon-coloured.

Queen! . . . For a horrified moment Anne Louise fancied that Aunt Louise-Marie had died, and that he was now proposing to marry her, himself. She knew it was not an impossible thing, for his brother, the unpleasant Uncle Ernest, the Duke of Saxe-Coburg and Gotha, had wedded a niece after his divorce.

'I have never thought about it, sir,' she said in a prim maidenly tone, although her lips were trembling and she felt that she was about to be sick.

Uncle Leopold — Husband Leopold, with his trebly-soled boots, and wig, and romantic mask of a face! She did not blench, however, but sat in silence, looking at the left-hand bottom corner of the portrait over his head.

Leopold continued in a stately tone, poking away with much dignity the while —

'It is a great and high honour to be a queen, Anne! A world-figure! An influence on the policies of nations! Consort of the head of a State! Arbiter of Society and Fashion! *Mother*' — said Uncle Leopold with a theatrically emotional lift to his voice — 'of Kings!'

A new and worse horror seized on Anne Louise, for the word 'mother' connoted to her the end of everything — the degradation of a reasoning, forethinking woman into a farmyard creature in the breeding season; a bitch in whelp scratching up the straw, a sow with sagging dugs, a ewe stamping her foot and peering round foolishly for her own amongst a crowd of lambs. She recalled Aunt Louise-Marie in Brussels, heavy with child, bloated, lethargic, plaintive.

Almost instinctively she looked down at her lap, visualizing for an instant a day when it might be nearly hidden from view by a swelling belly. At the age of seventeen, the preliminaries to child-birth seemed to Anne Louise most horribly indecent.

The secret Anne Louise burst through restraint.

'I don't want to be a mother at all,' she said quickly and fiercely.

Leopold turned his face toward her. By the very absence of all expression it seemed supercilious beyond endurance.

'You are pleased to be extremely childish,' he said. 'I am talking to you very seriously. You cannot remain a child for ever. You are now practically grown up. You are even old enough to marry.'

'I . . .' began Anne Louise.

He raised a long compelling hand.

'I must ask you not to interrupt. I have a lot to say to you. Of extreme importance. Serious decisions have to be taken — and quickly. I have little time: I have the affairs of My People to consider, as well as yours.'

With that he launched into a discussion on the dynastic affairs of Britain, emphasizing each essential point with a vicious poker attack on the fire, which gradually wilted under the assault from a golden blaze into a sullen glow.

When King William the Fourth, a nasty rough half-witted old fellow, died (explained Uncle Leopold) the heir to the English throne had been the daughter of the next oldest of his brothers — Anne's cousin, Victoria, child of her Aunt Kent. She understood that?

Anne Louise understood.

She had herself under control again: the rebel was pushed out of sight by the obedient niece. She signified comprehension by the faintest squeak of a 'Yes'. Personally she thought very little of Cousin Victoria, and still less of Aunt Kent. The daughter (she considered) had a meaningless face and meaningless eyes and a never-quite-shut mouth that was also meaningless: the mother, that type of countenance which comes from over-indulgence in port, new bread, and rich meats with richer sauces — in other words, a thin red nose with small purple veins straggling about it, and greying hairs sprouting here and there on a chin that had the colour and texture of underdone roast beef.

Victoria — said Uncle Leopold, examining the poker, as if he had never seen it before — was to marry Cousin Albert, Uncle Ernest's son. He had arranged that himself. A very suitable and desirable match! A highly satisfactory match! . . . She understood that?

Anne Louise again signified comprehension — 'Yes, Uncle!'

The other Anne Louise challenged him wordlessly — 'I won't be one of your stud farm! I shan't be one of your stud farm! I'm not afraid of you, even if they are!'

Uncle Leopold paused. He spoke very slowly. The jabs at the fire grew more frequent: in fact they punctuated the sentences he formulated.

If — *jab* — by any chance — *jab* — anything — *jab* — happened to Victoria — *jab; very long pause* — the next heir was — *jab* — King Ernest of Hanover, the Queen's eldest surviving uncle.

At this point Uncle Leopold attacked the fire so furiously that she felt that he was picturing himself digging a bayonet into King Ernest's vitals, instead of a poker into a despondent grate.

When Victoria (said Uncle Leopold, granting an armistice to shattered log and powdered coal) came to the English throne, Ernest, then Duke of Cumberland, had succeeded to the Kingdom of Hanover. Salic law prevailed in Hanover. Women couldn't inherit. Anne knew that?

Anne Louise did. She said a timid 'yes', and gave a confirmatory nod at the broad green back stooped over the wrought-iron grate within the marble hearth.

'The position, therefore, is this,' said Leopold ... He leaned back in the chair, thrust his long legs out before him, and folded his hands together — wrists on sprigged waistcoat, fingers pointing upward — in what would have been an attitude of prayer if he had not perpetually tapped the finger-tips together, with a small dry noise like the tit-tupping of very distant hoofs ... 'King Ernest has one son — George. He will be King after him in the ordinary course of events. Of Hanover, certainly. Of England, possibly. He is an excellent young man. Most amiable. With no sign of any of his father's gross faults ... for I will not hide from you the fact that King Ernest has committed may gross *bétises* in his time ... You perhaps realize why I am talking to you about Prince George?'

He looked round at Anne Louise. She schooled herself to meet the regard with one of polite attention. She realized what was coming — that they had planned a perpetual exile for her; marriage; motherhood. Every nerve and muscle in her body ached with the strain she put on herself to prevent the furious and determined rebel from peering out of her eyes, from bursting into mutinous speech from her lips.

'Yes, Uncle Leopold.'

'Serious *bétises*,' reflected Leopold, satisfied as to the perception of his niece, and harking back in his mind to his own enjoyable misdemeanours, which had been so pleasant, because so private. The King of Hanover, on the other hand, had rushed into sin with the noisy abandonment of a bull in a china shop. His brothers, too, of course, had all been like that.

He cast another look at his young niece, whose gaze was now fixed on the buhl clock upon the mantelpiece.

The gilded pendulum, visible through a glass panel in front, was fashioned in the likeness of a hoop-skirted lady, who rode forward and backward in a golden swing. Anne Louise formulated the situation to the movement of the little lady.

Ún-cle: Léo-pold: wánts to: máke me: már-ry:

Geórge of: Hán-o :vér and : háve ba : bíes, tick : tóck, tick:

You had to be careful about the dissyllables, and plan very quickly, so that the stresses came with the beat.

She continued telling the story to herself to the faint chatter of the little clock, while Uncle Leopold went on —

'You are an eligible young person, Anne. You ought to do well. You are an orphan; you've got looks; you've got wealth . . . *I*,' said he with the emphasis and reverence of great egoism, 'had only two hundred pounds a year, but *I* married the daughter of George the Fourth. *I* have become a King. My second wife is daughter of the French King! Your Aunt, Victoria Kent had no money and none of your looks. *She* married a son of the English King. *She* might have become a Queen. Her daughter *is* Queen. Your Cousin Albert has looks but no money: *he* is to marry your Cousin Victoria — he will be virtually King of England. Your Cousin Ferdinand has none of your looks and little money: he is already King-Consort of Portugal . . . I hope you are going to be a thoroughly sensible girl, Anne?'

'Yes, Uncle Leopold,' said his niece, staring at the swinging lady, hands so tightly clasped that the top joints of her fingers became crimson and the nail-tips the colour of old ivory. 'Yes, Uncle Leopold,' said she, meaning — 'No, Uncle Leopold . . . No, Uncle Leopold! . . . No, Uncle Leopold!'

She will be even easier to handle than Albert, thought Uncle Leopold, and ambled gracefully on. He droned a sort of Coburg family epithalamium. He talked of family pride; of duty to family; of ambition; of the vast estates she had inherited from her grandmother; of Power (with a capital P) and of Influence; of the concurrence of all her uncles and aunts in the desirability of the match; of King Ernest's concurrence. How pleased her dear mother — his sister — and her father would have been!

He harked back again to Ambition — to Influence. What influence (said Uncle Leopold, toying once more with the little gold object that had its home in his waistcoat pocket) a woman could exercise, if she were careful! 'What a power for Good! . . . Especially in — in the circumstances!'

'Cír-cum-stán-ces,' ticked the gilded lady on the gilded swing. 'Cír-cum . . .'

'What circumstances?' asked Anne Louise suddenly.

Her uncle rose to his feet; pushed away the chair; stood towering before the hearth, blotting out clock and swinging lady as he faced her.

'You have been brought up as a woman of the world, have you not, Anne?'

'Yes, Uncle Leopold,' answered Anne Louise, staring at the hands folded in her lap, and listening for the tick-tock of the invisible lady.

'Speaking as a man of the world to a woman of the world, I frankly think, Anne, that a wonderful future awaits you. Wonderful! Your attitude shows that you have good sense — sound sense. You have realized that we don't live in a fairy-tale, where princesses are lovelier than other ladies, and princes the pink of physical perfection . . . George of Hanover is — blind!'

She caught the faint tick-tock.

Tíck — blind! . . . Tóck — blind! . . . Tíck — blind! . . . Tóck — blind!

A blind husband whom she had never seen; who would never see her! If her uncle had not continued speaking, she would have raised her slightly bent head, shown him the hate and horror blazing in her eyes, and screamed — and screamed — and screamed! She saw herself at the elbow of a blind man who walked uncertainly between ranks of lackeys to the vast folding doors of State bed-chamber. She. . . .

'You see, Anne' — he bent an all-knowing, wise, benevolent regard on her, whilst his fingers twisted that tiny glittering object about — 'we of royal birth do not *mate*, like brute beasts and the populace, for passion. We *marry*. We marry for reasons of State . . . You have no romantic ideas, I trust?'

No: Anne Louise had no romantic ideas: although she could barely shape the word 'No', for the other Anne Louise was wrenching at her lips, impelling her tongue with other words — words of furious renunciation and refusal.

'We marry on a business basis. Influence put in the balance against riches! Great position balanced by an unblemished family! You will be a Queen one day, Anne. Against that, you are the richest heiress in Europe. Ernest can't, and don't, complain. You will have enormous influence — the more so, because you will have to deal with a man who is utterly dependent upon you. Against that you bring an un-sullied name and lineage to a family that sadly needs respectability . . . *Quid pro quo!*'

Qúid-pro: Qúo-tick: Qúid-pro: Qúo-tick: said the clock.

Anne Louise lifted innocent-seeming eyes to her uncle. In her mind she was pummelling the beautifully shaped nose — battering her fists against red lips parted to show even teeth — throwing the romantically-dishevelled wig into the fire. None of that was apparent as she said —

'Yes, Uncle Leopold.'

'Sensible girl,' commented he warmly. 'You are a *very* sensible girl. You have improved greatly. We will forget that silly outburst of yours in Brussels ... We are only thinking of your good — and of *The Family*.' (He always used a sort of vocal italic when speaking about them.) 'Romantic ideas about love are dangerous and idiotic nonsense. Love is just an appetite. Any good cook will give you a satisfying dinner ... I suppose I shouldn't say this to you, now. But you will certainly realize when you are older that you can have love entirely apart from marriage — especially marriage with a blind man!'

He shook his head, and energetically twisted the little gold object, in a sort of passion of envy of Anne Louise's prospects as the wife of a blind king. What fun she could have — said Uncle Leopold's head-wagging — as the wife of a blind man! What fun, indeed!

'Beast! Horrible beast!' cried the rebel Anne Louise, but not out loud.

The buhl clock chimed the hour. Midnight. The silver strokes roused Uncle Leopold from his head-wagging.

'Twelve? ... It is late for you, Anne. You must be off to bed. We will discuss details some other time ... I shall want you to come with me to Brussels to-morrow. Miss Talfourd will accompany you. I must superintend the later stages of your education myself.'

Anne Louise rose: her skirts rustled on the floor like fallen leaves dancing on a flagged terrace.

She made her supreme effort.

'Brussels? With you? That *will* be nice!'

He came toward her. He towered over her. Suddenly he stooped, and before she could even flinch, kissed her on the forehead. There was a smell about him of lavender-water, and liquorice ... and rotten-ness!

She wanted to cry out — to rub away the stain upon her skin — to turn and run. Instead she smiled at him: she curtseyed very low — very low, indeed, to that most High, Mighty, and Excellent Prince, her uncle, Leopold, King of the Belgians, Duke of Saxony, Prince of Coburg-Gotha; to that tall man with the weary beautiful face, and the cleft chin, and the long eye-lashes, and the cupid's-bow lips ... and the bad breath. He was not to know that it was a mocking curtsey — such as a mistress sweeps to a discarded lover when she gives him his congé.

'Good girl,' said Uncle Leopold appreciatively. 'That's right! Good girl! . . . God bless you!'

She had made less fuss than had Albert about matrimonial arrangements. Less even than Ferdinand.

He had brought a bribe: it should now be a reward. He took up a shallow case of worn purple leather that lay on the little table beside his chair, with the decanter and the half-peeled apple. He opened it.

A diamond necklace lay within, upon a bed of black velvet. It sparkled in the radiance from silver candelabra and wall-sconce as if it were moonshine caught in a thin spray of water, its colours blurred and merging rainbow-wise. Sunset and sunrise upon shining ice were held within it.

'Good girl! God bless you!' said Uncle Leopold again: and in the next moment Anne Louise felt the frigid jewels slide about her neck and trickle downwards to the warmth of her bosom.

She steeled herself to the chill — and to the hate.

She curtseyed again. Very low. Another mocking curtsey.

'*Dear* Uncle Leopold,' she said — but not out loud — 'if you think you have got me at the end of a string like all the rest of the family you are mistaken. *I* am not going to dance to your tune: or marry at your proposal. *I* am not going to do anything you want me to do.'

Actually she breathed the words, 'Oh! Uncle Leopold!' with grateful emphasis. She could not bring herself to thank him. She *would* not thank him in so many words.

She backed to the door: curtseyed once more to ineffable Majesty — and so escaped into the dimness of a passage lighted by a single candle on a pembroke-table.

She took off the necklace and held it up between finger and thumb as if it were something unclean. In the faint yellow light, which battled so hopelessly against the shadows, it looked as dead as a fillet of raw fish.

Anne Louise regarded it for an instant. She brought it up close to her lips — just close enough not to touch . . . And then she spat on it . . . And watched the spittle bubble slowly down from stone to stone.

Leopold remained for a little standing with his back to the fire.

A table whose slim fluted legs were inlaid with thin lines of malachite stood against a wall. Upon it was a tall porcelain jar with a delicate pattern in the colour of an unripe peach. He walked to it; stood by it, with one long white hand resting on the table-top; remained so poised against the background of dim tapestry. In his imagination he saw himself thus standing. He raised his chin a little so that the attitude should be yet more one of lofty and wise command.

Yet another link forged between himself and the great ruling families of Europe! Yet another channel along which he might thrust his influence! And if the old plotter of Hanover succeeded and supplanted Victoria, Uncle Leopold would be little worse off. Anne Louise would eventually become his mouthpiece in the Councils of England. He saw himself guiding, directing, instructing half a dozen dynasties from the study at Laeken; secretly master of the fantastic puppet-show of Europe — a very viceroy of destiny.

He poured himself out a glass of port, and realized with some disgust that the knife-marks on the half-peeled apple on the dish had turned dark brown. He felt that apples peeled by princes should not tarnish thus. It was as incorrect as if blossoms were immediately to wither upon a virgin's bosom.

There was a knocking at the door.

Little Hühnlein, with his round rosy face and fat lips, appeared: closed the door behind him with the suaveness of the server to a priest at Mass.

Uncle Leopold raised his dark level brows.

'I was able to arrange it with the young lady, your Majesty,' said Hühnlein.

Uncle Leopold asked another question without uttering a word.

'I have explained here that she is the English wife of one of your valets going out to join her husband under your Majesty's protection,' replied Hühnlein.

Uncle Leopold said nothing. There was no flicker of expression on his face; but Hühnlein answered the question that was never asked — from ten years' experience.

'She was extremely reasonable. She appears to be extremely discreet . . . She shall be in your room in ten minutes' time, your Majesty?'

'In a quarter of an hour,' amended Leopold, and poured himself out another glass of wine . . . and yawned. He had no affections — only an acute realization of chemical necessities.

CHAPTER III

ANNE LOUISE IN SEARCH OF TROUSERS

MISS TALFOURD had not waited for the reappearance of her charge. Nor had anyone attempted to repair the confusion created by Anne Louise's hurried toilette.

Anne Louise closed her bedroom door, and bolted it.

A pair of candles glimmered on the old-fashioned narrow mantel-shelf, and another pair before the mirror upon the chintz-petticoated dressing-table.

The bed-clothes were as disordered as when she had leaped from them; and various garments were strewn upon chairs and the narrow sofa at the foot of the curtained bed. Her nightdress lay, a puddle of white linen, on the dark carpet, where she had stepped out of it.

Carrying the diamond necklace as if she held a dead mouse by the tail, she crossed to the hearth, and dropped the precious thing with a crash amid the fire-irons before the empty black-leaded grate.

A plan was already crystallizing in her mind.

On the chest-of-drawers was her travelling writing-desk, a sleek wine-dark box edged and inlaid with brass. She unlocked and opened it out. At the top of the writing slope of green leather, between the well in which the ink-pot lived and the sockets for the candlesticks, were two small black lids with ivory knobs. From one recess Anne Louise took a little heap of gold coins: from the other a number of bank-notes, each folded up into a neat square.

She spread out the notes, and counted them, and placed them on her dressing-table, under the pile of sovereigns.

There were eleven pounds in gold—the remains of her usual allow-ance; and one hundred and ten pounds in crisp paper, representing birthday and Christmas gifts from dear Aunt Sophia in far-away Lecques.

Lecques!

The paper rustling under her fingers spoke to her, hinting of its magic spell. A magic spell that would send horses a-canter down winding roads, and bring her over a hill-crest to a grey sea. A magic that would send a ship bowing and curtseying for her to the breeze — that would bear her across the length and breadth of France; across an arid plain under the lea of purple mountains, and so to the jumble of stony hills which slanted upward into heather-covered slopes and then into a windy forest! A magic that would at last bring her to the mountain gap, whence first could be seen the red roofs of the castle rising from the dark green tide of pines and looking down a long steep valley toward the shimmer of another and brighter sea! A magic compounded of discs of yellow metal and of oblongs of crinkling paper!

Was it a strong enough magic to do all that?

Seized by grave doubts, she picked the string of diamonds gingerly out of the fender, regarded it quizzically for an instant — it seemed poetic justice that Uncle Leopold's gift should be made to aid her escape! — and dropped it upon the pile of money.

Then she threw a grey silk shawl over her bare shoulders; lighted the glass-shaded candlestick; undid the ribbons of her shoes, and crept from the room in stockinged feet. . . .

At the top of the steep stairs her candle merely emphasized the immense gloom of the long floorless attic before her. The rafters and the beams cast shadows the denser the more distant they were. The rain scrabbled at the tiles: the boards of the small strip of landing at the stair-top creaked beneath her. She did not dare risk knocking at the door on her right, although a line of light showed faintly beneath it: the only other door — which faced her maid's — jittered on its hinges in the wind.

Anne Louise pulled down the latch with vast caution — and entered the smallest possible room, a mere cupboard, crowded by a truckle bed, a washstand with a basin no larger than a soup-plate full of soapy water, and a stool. Clothing and bonnets hung from nails along a wall.

A girl in a wide grey serge dress lay face downwards on the bed, her face buried in her arms, and a candle on the stool guttering away within an inch of one slender elbow.

'S-st!' said Anne Louise.

And again —

'S-st!'

At that second breath the girl on the bed raised her head, and looked swiftly round. An incredulous, welcoming smile faded in a split second into an expression of astonishment. She twisted to a sitting position upon the sagging bed; rose to her feet.

'Lovell!' said Anne Louise in a whisper. 'I want you. At once!'

Even in that moment of crisis she realized how lovely the creature was — slim, tall, black-haired, blue-eyed, with a quick colour in her cheeks flushing a skin that was faintly golden.

'Yes, your Highness?' said Lovell.

'I want you to get some men's clothes. *Immediately*,' said Anne Louise, with the utmost composure, as though asking for a chemisette, spencer, or polonaise.

Lovell raised her downcast eyes. They were clouded with tears. Even in the pale flicker of the candles in that whitewashed garret, a plum-coloured bruise showed on her right cheek-bone.

'Men's clothes?' repeated Lovell, almost mechanically.

'Yes,' said Anne Louise. 'And quickly. Get me whatever is necessary from Lord Henry's dressing-room. Breeches. Boots. Coats. Neck-cloth.'

'But ...'

'Don't argue ... Bring them to me. Then come back here and dress as quickly as you can. Bonnet. Cloak. Bring anything you may need for a journey — a long journey. I want you to come with me.'

'My Lord's dressing-room? ... I can't, your Highness,' said Lovell in a low voice. 'I can't, indeed!'

'You must.'

Against the grey of her frock Lovell's fingers writhed together. Her head was bowed; she could have seen nothing but her shoes and the dingy floor-boards.

The shadows of the two girls, cast by the candles tilted on the rush-seating of the bedside stool, danced furiously (in a sort of distorted fantocini-show) upon the bluish-white wall which, a foot after it left the ground, bent inwards, and so became a slanting ceiling.

'I can't, your Highness!'

Anne Louise stood so close that she was able suddenly to put out her hands, and shake Lovell by the shoulders. Fiercely.

'Lovell! ... You've got to! ... You must! ... I order you to!'

The maid was unresistant. Her downcast head nodded to the shaking like a rain-drenched flower in the wind ... and in the end she raised such candid tear-filled eyes that Anne Louise knew defeat: knew, too, that it was 'Can't!' that Lovell said, and not 'Won't!' That it was collapse, and not mutiny.

She did not pause further to analyse Lovell's refusal. What had to be done, must be done — at once.

'Will you come with me, then, when I go ...' she asked, adding from honesty the qualifying phrase ' ... a very, very far journey?'

For a long moment they stood looking at each other. Lovell's eyes seemed to be saying something, to be explaining some tale that her lips could not tell.

'Yes, your Highness,' said Lovell.

'Can you help me to harness a horse?'

'Yes, your Highness.' She stopped, caught her breath. 'Anything, your Highness! . . . But I can't go — *there*!'

'I must go myself,' said Anne Louise disdainfully. 'Be dressed and ready in my room in ten minutes' time. Take your shoes off when you come. Make a bundle of what things you need, and bring them with you. And be as quiet as a ghost!'

Lovell curtseyed as the princess turned to make her way down those precarious stairs into the black depths of the house; along passages whose thin carpeting barely disguised the harshness of the floor-boards — down a winding staircase with rough deal hand-rail — through a baize door that swung to, with a clatter, after her — along a lofty corridor where deeply-recessed mahogany doors shone in the candle-light, and the pile of the carpet was as deep and soft to tread upon as a century-old lawn.

At the end of the corridor two doors faced one another, and the dark outline of a giant fir was printed within the frame of a tall window against the blue-black darkness of the night-sky.

Anne Louise waited for a moment before the window. Her breath came very fast, as if she had been running. She found herself astonishingly frightened.

Then, in some way, she absorbed courage from the dim silhouette of the tree without. The slant of its boughs resembled the pattern of the forest trees about her home so far away; was unlike the trim orderliness of the tamed beeches, and oaks, and elms of this foreign countryside.

Very silently, and very slowly, she turned the handle of the right-hand door, and listened: but there was no sound save the tick of a clock.

She put her head through the opening: held up the candle.

The dressing-room was empty, and the door at the far end fast shut. It smelled vaguely of cigar smoke.

She crept in.

One side of the room was almost entirely occupied by a vast wardrobe of indeterminate-coloured mahogany. It seemed to her as long and as dull as a terrace of mean-street houses. Shelves opposite held rows of boots, from varnished elegancies to riding-boots with rose-coloured tops.

A pair of black stockinette pantaloons lay upon a stool before a long cheval glass, and a dressing-table in the window at the far end was littered with toilette articles.

Anne Louise tiptoed into the room; set her candle down upon the dressing-table, amid the litter of pomatum pots, handkerchiefs, combs, letters, money, gold chains, and pearl-studded breast-pins — beside a red morocco razorcase stamped with golden bees and the mystic initial 'N', which Lord Henry's uncle had looted from Bonaparte's travelling-carriage after the flight from Waterloo.

She made directly for the pantaloons; held them up; meditated on them; folded them; added to them a white shirt and a most complicated looking collar (with dangling tapes and a neckband studded with slots) which were strewn upon a chair; found a wadded black satin neck-cloth; meditated again; placed it, too, upon the pile; and then with caution opened one of the enormous portals of the enormous ward-robe.

Within she saw a closely packed rank of coats suspended on hangers from a brass rail, lapels and front buttons (gilded, bone, and silk-encased) nuzzling immaculately smooth backs. A green coat — she noticed — with darker green collar of velvet; a dark blue coat; a wine-coloured coat with a collar of burgundy red; a dress-coat in midnight blue, with square tails; a knee-length coat of something very thick, the colour of wet sea-weed, with pleated, capacious pockets.

Without any hesitation she took down the shooting-coat — it would unquestionably be less revealing than any of the others! So, too, she took a voluminous black cloak (with emerald green lining, flat fur collar and short shoulder-cape) from one of the cupboards.

For ease of transport she shrugged herself into the coat: put the cloak about her slim shoulders — although it swept the floor, she felt certain that it could be pinned up satisfactorily.

With pantaloons, shirt, collar and neckcloth over one arm under the cloak, and with the candle in her hand, she proceeded to explore the shining rows of footwear.

The lightest and the smallest appeared to be a pair of riding-boots of very thin patent lacquered leather and of a blackness that was as glistening as a pool of ink.

She had taken them up by the tops with her disengaged hand, when there was a slight noise at the far end of the room.

Her heart missed a beat. She turned in panic and defiance, and stood at bay, still holding boots and candle, her face very white above the wide dark collar of the all-enveloping cloak.

A slender young man, in a dark velvet dressing-gown, had entered, and was watching her from the inner door. A tasselled nightcap was cocked rakishly to one side of his head. He carried a flat candlestick: by the light from it Anne Louise could see the blank astonishment on his pink-and-white face fade and give way to an expression of condescending amusement — the sort of amusement with which the antics of a precocious child are observed.

He advanced a few steps; and for a moment they silently confronted one another in an islet of faint light amid the vast shadows of the room.

'I came,' said Anne Louise, speaking in low tones and very quickly, 'to borrow some clothes . . . I tried not to wake you.'

'Chahmed, your Highness!' said the young man. 'Vewy chahmed!'

From the tone of his voice you might have thought that he found it the most normal thing in the world for the Duchess of Limburg to invade his dressing-room at midnight. He took in the riding-boots, the cloak, and guessed vaguely at the obvious bundle hidden under its folds.

'I beg you to say nothing about this,' said Anne Louise.

'Of course not, your Highness. I . . .'

Suddenly he burst into uncontrollable laughter — not loud, but so violent that he had to lean against the dressing-chest for support.

Anne Louise regarded him with frozen dignity. She turned to go — in her most stately manner.

'I beg your Highness's pardon,' he said, and preceded her with quick strides to the door.

Fingers on the handle, he suddenly paused, and studied her for a moment questioningly.

'May I venture to ask your Highness for what purpose you need these — er — garments?'

Highness, treading on the trailing folds of that too-voluminous cloak, hesitated before replying.

'I — I — find I need them,' she said in cold non-explanation.

'Natchwally! Natchwally!' assented my Lord. 'Quite! But, if I knew for what purpose, I might even be able to help your Highness . . . You appear — if I may say so — to have a wather odd assortment, for *any* occasion!' He tore off his nightcap, flung it to the floor by the long tassel, rumpled his hair that was so fair as almost to be white, regarded her in his most boyish manner, and added — 'Tell me the twouble. I'll keep it secwet. I swear it! . . . 'pon my liver and lights!'

Anne Louise, boots and candle still in her hands, again hesitated. It did not occur to her to doubt his discretion: she debated whether or not he might be useful: decided that he would.

'I must leave here at once,' she said. 'I must go home. I thought it would be easier in disguise.'

'Running away?' he commented, and whistled beneath his breath . . .

'But, Good Lord! You would be spotted for a woman in a minute if you went in that vewy odd get-up! Dwess pantaloons — shootin' coat — widin' cloak — and pawade boots!'

'A woman can't go across Europe by herself.'

'She certainly couldn't go in the vawiety of clothes that you have chosen . . . Beside, they won't fit you.'

Still facing him, candle in hand, but the 'disguise' fallen in a heap at her feet —

'What can I do then? I must go to-night. To-morrow they will make me go to Brussels . . . They want me to marry some one — and I won't.'

She looked at him very anxiously.

Lord Henry Wentworth took the boots from her unresisting hand, restored them to their position among their fellows, removed the candlestick and placed it on the dressing-chest, locked the outer door, lighted some more candles, and delicately lifted the heavy cloak and coat from her shoulders.

Whilst he did this in a sort of lazy hurry, his mind was revolving her problem.

She was one of the greatest heiresses in Europe. She was Royal. She was, equally unquestionably, good-looking.

'What are your plans?' he asked at length.

'I shall go to Lecques. I shall shut the gates . . . We could stand a siege! . . . *They* will not dare do anything. The country-people would not let them.' She was very certain of the loyalty of the peasantry who had protected from the fury of the Revolution that branch of her family which had ruled there from the days of Raimond de Berenger, Count-Regnant of Provence.

Lecques! — Somewhere in the most distant corner of France, he reflected. At least a week's journey! More! Anything might happen on such a journey — in such a week! In a quick flash he summarized his own position — the stream of duns at his chambers in Regent-street; the stream of duns (wine merchant, horse dealer, milliner, mantua-maker, bonnet-maker, tailor, butcher, baker, and carriage-builder) at the little laburnum-surrounded villa in St. John's Wood where he had established Fantine: saw his father cursing the Reform Bill, the late King William, Sir Robert Peel, and himself in the very breath in which he had refused to advance another penny — saw the short white whiskers (so astonishingly silvery to have sprouted from that scarlet face) against an enormous bookcase of unread volumes bound in olive-green, with the ducal coronet stamped in gold above the title. Saw, too, the quick suspicious glance his aunt had levelled at him, when he had arrived, unheralded, three nights ago on a begging expedition. Reflected that the business about Lady Weston had taken a particularly ugly turn. Reminded himself of another minor complication.

He ruffled his hair again.

'Has your Highness enough money for such an adventure? ... If I may dare to ask!'

Anne Louise, sensing a possible ally —

'I've got a hundred and twenty pounds. *And* a diamond necklace — as well as other jewellery. It must be worth hundreds.'

It was then that he began to see a journey across Europe very clearly: saw post-chaises swinging on their long springs over dusty roads — landlords bowing at the passage of the Great to a fairy-tale castle a week and more away from Fantine and the duns: visualized a dozen romantical incidents: prided himself on his way with women: pictured himself as the Consort of a Princess — cousin of monarchs, and standing among the privileged few about the fireplace in the draughty galleries of royal palaces.

All this; and he turned a flushed face toward the Giver of the Opportunity; smiled at her in the simulation of a youthful enthusiasm.

'You can't go alone,' he said. 'I will come as your escort — if I may ... I can twavel as your gentleman-in-waiting — or as your brother. Whichever you think wisest.'

It did not occur to her to doubt his good faith; or to think for one instant that few men offer to travel across a wide continent for the sake of chivalry alone.

'Can you — will you? ... I'll be ready in half an hour,' said Anne Louise.

'They'll think we'll go to Harwich, or try to get a boat from London,' meditated Lord Henry, thus accepted forthwith as an ally. 'But we won't! Oh, no! We'll have 'em guessing!' He rubbed his hands gleefully. 'We'll toddle down into Wales and charter a small boat to the Continent from one of the Welsh ports. May take a bit longer but much safer. Hundred per cent safe! ... That's the ticket!'

Anne Louise, hearing this matter-of-fact programme, also thought that it was the 'ticket'. It was clever of him to have thought of that way of putting the pursuers off the track. He had justified her confidence.

'You will want a maid?'

She nodded.

'My woman will come with me. She is getting ready now.'

'Get her to bring your baggage — as little as you can — to the stable-court ...' he glanced at the clock ticking upon the mantelpiece, and in a new brisk manner — the confident manner of a man who can handle difficult and dangerous affairs ' . . . within the half hour. Less if you can. The sooner we are gone the better. We'll take Aunt Augusta's travelling chariot — the yellow one; it's light and fast. *And* the bays. My groom shall be postilion and I'll ride.'

He flattered himself that he might have habitually planned the vanishment of princesses: might frequently have plotted such an escape in the small hours of the morning in his dressing-room, with a great lady, in wide lavender-coloured dress, hanging intent-faced upon his words.

With the arrogance of youth and royal birth she thought of him but as a sort of courier. All that she knew was that the road to Lecques had been made easy; had become a triumphal progress: horses, chariot, attendants, ship awaited her pleasure and need.

She acknowledged her indebtedness —

'You are very good, my Lord.'

He had gone toward the door to open it for her. He now took her hand in his, bowed low over it, and kissed it in courtly fashion.

'You *are* a pretty creature!' he thought, and visualized the romantic scene as if he were a spectator, and not a participant; saw himself and her, as in a picture, painted in pale colours and posed against the white panels of the door, which faintly shimmered in the golden candlelight. Visualized, too, in a flash other and even more exciting and romantic scenes on that long journey which they were about to undertake.

She withdrew her hand.

'In half an hour, then!'

He opened the door. She stole out into the corridor, conscious not of his good-looking face or his romantically ruffled flaxen hair — but of the absurd jumble of the discarded disguise which lay in the middle of the room, collar with straggling tapes and black pantaloons crowning the heap.

How did one adjust those tapes, she wondered.

CHAPTER IV

BEGINNING OF AN ODYSSEY

THE yellow travelling-carriage was in the middle of the stable-yard, the glimmer of its feeble lamps the only light in a rain-filled darkness. The baggage had already been strapped on under a tarpaulin, and the horses were being backed up to the swingle-trees by a shapeless figure who 'Whoa!'-ed them and 'Steady!'-ed them under his breath.

Iron-shod hoofs and the trailing hook of a trace clacked most alarmingly on the wet cobbles. Anne Louise prayed that the high wind which moaned round the house and sang in the tall trees would mask the clatter.

There was no vestige of light, however, in the sombre mass of the buildings that enclosed the yard: only a deeper darkness showed where the open doors of the coach-house yawned.

Lovell, cloaked and bonneted, stood waiting in rather drooping fashion beside the high step of the chariot.

Anne Louise climbed quickly into the padded gloom which smelled vaguely of leather and damp — an odd smell, something like that of stale biscuits. In the light of the lanterns the windows were black oblongs seared by the silver trickle of rain-drops.

She dropped the two volumes of Mr. Partington's Cyclopaedia on the floor with a bump. At the last moment she had felt that that great work alone could keep her in reading matter on a week's journey.

'Get in,' she commanded Lovell, who still stood without, in the rain.

Together they waited in silence. To Anne Louise's anxious ears every sound of preparation was magnified a hundred-fold, until she wondered why rough voices did not challenge them, and why lights did not appear in the black bulk of the house which loomed over the stable-buildings. With clenched hands and set teeth she anticipated a vast burst of illumination and the clangour of the great fire-bell in its belfry over the stable-yard arch.

The door opened. A wet red face appeared in the gap. A forefinger went up to a dripping hat-brim.

'Goin' now, ma'am,' said a husky voice. 'I'll lead the cattle till we're clear of the yard.'

Husky-Voice sensed an unspoken question.

'Them's my h'instructions, ma'am . . . But there's no one to 'ear us h'actually. Nobody sleeps in the stable but Evans. 'E's as drunk as a — Juke . . . We're goin' down the Lower H'Avenue . . . My Lord'll join us by the Lodge plantation.'

The door closed, and almost at once the carriage moved.

' "My Lord"?' said Lovell in little more than a whisper. 'My Lord?' and half-rose from her seat.

'I am not running away with him, you fool!' said Anne Louise — and chided herself at once for deigning any explanation.

'But . . .'

'Do I have to explain my actions to you?'

'No, your Highness. I beg your pardon, your Highness,' said Lovell humbly, and shrank back into her corner, and sat nervously pleating her cloak into folds.

As they turned out between the lofty iron gates by the porticoed lodge, Anne Louise became aware that someone on horseback had come up from behind, and was passing them. She caught for one moment the pallid blur of Henry Wentworth's face above the collar of his cloak. It seemed to her that he smiled reassuringly as he went by and preceded them to the high-road.

After that, interminable hours journeying through the night and rain-swept countryside — carriage swaying on its high C springs — hoofs clattering — pebbles crunching into the wet road beneath swiftly turning wheels — harness faintly a-jingle — once the crack of a whip as the horses were urged back into a trot at the crest of a hill.

Somewhere they halted, and, after a long delay, secured fresh beasts. But Anne Louise did not realize it. When Wentworth opened the door and peered in, there was no answer from the inner darkness to his questionings, for she was fast asleep — her head against Lovell's shoulder.

It was a little after dawn when she awoke.

The windows were so wet without, so steamed over within, that they were translucent to the grey light but not transparent, like clouded ice.

Anne Louise straightened an aching back; regarded the sleeping Lovell. The girl's head lay pressed for support into the corner. Under the wide bonnet, even in that unflattering light, the contours of her face, her long black lashes, and her skin stained with the flush of a rose, were exquisite.

Anne Louise sighed a little, enviously.

From the curved hand-bag with heavy gold tassel, which lay on the seat beside her, she took a flat and padded case that held a square mirror; examined herself.

Her high-crowned bonnet had been pushed awry. There was a dent in the wide brim — which was lined with dark grey silk and bordered with green ribbon — where it had been crushed against Lovell's shoulder. There was, too, a rather crumpled dusty look about the long pelerine of dark green velvet edged with swansdown — which clung closely to her figure as far as the waist, and then billowed out, swallowed her spreading skirts, and fell to her toes.

Before she rectified these matters she wiped clear a circle in the front window . . . There was nothing to be seen but the sodden coat of the postilion and the steaming flanks of the near-side horse which he rode. They jerked together in unison, up and down — up and down.

She made herself a peep-hole in the glass beside her. Through the blurred look-out she saw the thin interlacing of a low hedge, against which their wheels brushed; along it glistering tree-trunks, black against the banks and fences of the opposite hills like the stems of crotchets and quavers on a stave of music. The green drenched meadows beyond the hedge sloped sharply downwards, and at their foot a river, whose waters were as dull as the steel of a dirty knife, lay motionless — or so it seemed.

Anne Louise, spitting on her handkerchief, then perpetrated a slight toilette.

The carriage came to a grinding halt, and she had only just enough time to tuck the moist handkerchief into her bag before the door beside her opened, and the head and shoulders of Henry Wentworth appeared against the background of dripping hedge and leaden sky. His black cloak was silvered with the wet, and the nap of his tall hat was all towsled by wind and rain.

'Good morning, Lord Henry,' said Anne Louise leaning forward, and speaking as primly as if she were greeting him at the breakfast-table.

'Good morning, your Highness!' — And Lord Henry smiled at her in his most boyish manner, showing beautifully even and white teeth. 'I hope you have had some sleep . . . I thought you might like a snifter to keep your couwage up till bweakfast time.'

' "Snifter"?'

'Aha!' said Lord Henry gaily. 'That's another word for what Dr. Wentworth pwescwibes! What the faculty weccomend for escapin' pwincesses!'

He fumbled under his cloak; produced a large leather-covered flask; poured out a tot of pale yellow fluid into a silver cup.

'This'll put new life into you!'

Anne Louise — feeling extremely cold, rather depressed, and certain that the single curled bird-of-paradise plume in her bonnet had been badly battered by the night's journey — was conscious that she greatly needed new life being put into her.

Highness took the cup from his hand; tilted something fiery and rather disgusting into her mouth; swallowed furiously; gasped; felt all the better for it.

Wentworth had taken back the container and appeared to be meditating whether a dose of the same potion might not be extremely palatable to himself, when Anne Louise suggested —

'I think that Lovell had better have some too.'

At that he shot a swift startled glance into the carriage; realized for the first time the identity of the girl who was stirring into wakefulness.

For a second his light-blue eyes were held by Lovell's. Then he dropped his regard; poured out more brandy, and advanced the silver cup into the carriage without looking at her.

Lovell made no effort to take the cup. She shook her head, looking straight before her, lips shaping a refusal that they did not utter.

Anne Louise grasped the little vessel.

'You've got to drink it, Lovell,' she said, and held it toward her. 'I insist! . . . It will do you good.'

Meanwhile Wentworth remained at the door with averted face. His reins were over his arm, and his horse poked forward a heavy head and snuffled gently and inquisitively at the opening. Anne Louise, sensing some change in his manner, looked at him again — found him paler than she had thought.

'I am afraid you must be very tired. You have had a good many hours in the saddle.'

'It's nothing,' he assured her, leaned in, and took the cup awkwardly from Lovell's extended hand without looking at the girl. 'I am used to it. We'll have a long halt later on — not just now.'

'Not now' — the phrase seemed to hold an implication that it was not yet safe to stop.

'You don't think that we are being followed?' she asked.

'Not a bit! They'll never guess we've come this way. What time are you called of a morning? . . . Eight! . . . Well,' — he extracted a watch from under the folds of cloak and coat; glanced at it — 'the hunt won't have yet begun. It's barely seven. They won't have even wealized that we've gone, much less got on our scent.'

'But . . .'

'We'll be turning off the pike in about half an hour. Then we'll be as safe as houses. Can loiter or huwwy, just as we please.'

He shut the door, nodded reassuringly, raised his hat. The carriage rolled on. . . .

In three days of arduous journey they had left the smooth contours of Eastern England far behind; had reached the grey beauty of Oxford, passing under the lee of the Chiltern Hills, those uttermost bastions of London; had crossed the windy Cotswolds, to stare for a moment from the steepness of Birdlip on to the valley of the Severn, where smoky mist and yet smokier night dimmed the lights of Gloucester spread far below; had laboriously climbed into the Welsh hills, and as laboriously descended them, with the drag on the rear wheels of the carriage grinding into the ill-made road so that a wide wake of muddy spray foamed up behind them.

Their flight had been so swift and broken only by such short pauses for sleep and refreshment that Wentworth had made no progress toward his personal aims. Indeed, he had not attempted any: he had been content to bide his time for the opportunities that were bound to come. . . .

It was now the morning of the fourth day. They had journeyed all night through streaming darkness.

Only with the dawn did the rain cease its patter on the glass.

Anne Louise opened a window. They were travelling along the ridge of a wide valley of pasture-lands studded with slate-roofed white farms. The further slope merged at its crest into one yet higher; that, in its turn, made a faint wash of faded green against the sunless iron-grey wall of the mountains, which rose beyond and were emphatic only where their outline was etched (as if in ink) against a monotonous sky.

Anne Louise picked up from the floor the first of Professor Partington's fat volumes. She had been using it for footstool. As the carriage swayed and jolted she continued to read in its narrow double columns, that dissertation on the Commerce of the World which she had begun days . . . and days . . . and *years* ago.

They went down a steep and winding hill; paid toll at the smallest possible octagonal turnpike house, which so swarmed with children that you might have thought it a parrot's cage inhabited by a family of white mice. Thence they laboured up a long incline cut through a dark woodland, swerved into a still deeper side-road, and forthwith came to a halt at a low grey inn which stood at the corner, pressed back under a canopy of leafless trees.

Wentworth spoke to his weary man: came back to help Anne Louise descend.

The open door of the inn gave directly on to a large and darkish kitchen with a stone flagged floor. From iron rods along the low ceiling was festooned a vast quantity of bacon and ham — legs, sides, hocks, shoulders, and indeterminate sections. Off most of them slices had been pared, and the fat, barely streaked with lean, was candle-white against the brown rind and the smoke-stained beams.

There was a lustreless oak table in the centre, a curved low-backed settle by the hearth, and on the mantelshelf a row of dusty plates alternating with tarnished brass candlesticks of various sizes. A sooty kettle hummed to itself upon the fire, and was answered from the low window by the chirrup of a bird in a wicker cage that was much too small for it.

A man appeared in an inner doorway as they entered. He wore a seaman's jersey and a black apron, and was extremely short and broad: in fact his body seemed to be perfectly square. His head — tied up in a black handkerchief — was so sunk between his shoulders as to lead Anne Louise to speculate whether he had any neck at all. Some thin wisps of grey hair escaped from under the handkerchief on to the low forehead of his huge yellow face, which was dominated by a pro-portionately huge and very battered nose.

'Yes-s?' he asked.

Anne Louise felt that something very hostile brooded in his regard.

'Yes-s?' he repeated sharply.

' "Yes-s"!' said Wentworth querulously. 'Is that the way you always greet patrons? "Yes-s?" — A fine way to promote business! Do you think we've come here at bweakfast time for anything but bweakfast? ... To buy baboons or cockatoos, or a yard of bombazine? ... Bweakfast is what we want, Mr. Yes-s!' and he slapped a black riding-boot with his riding-crop in a most peremptory manner.

The Square shuffled one step nearer, and Anne Louise found herself meeting the angry stare of reddish eyes, and thought for an instant that some violent rejoinder was about to issue from the straight mouth that was almost lipless — a slit with narrow bluish edges.

She sank down on the settle and endeavoured to warm her slender ringless fingers at a sullen fire. The inn-keeper's eyes travelled quickly from her to Wentworth's pale arrogant face and slim cloaked figure, to the gold-mounted crop.

'Bweakfast — and plenty of it!' said Wentworth, letting his cloak fall onto a chair-back. Bacon: eggs: tea: bwandy! . . . A woom where this lady can put herself to wights. Somewhere for me to wash and shave. We have had a long journey.'

The man swung on his heel without reply. In a high, almost falsetto voice, he called into the dusk beyond the doorway —

'Llinos!'

'Breakfast, too, for Lovell and your man . . . I think Lovell is ill,' said Highness, and undid the ribbons and let that wonderful green-grey bonnet fall casually upon the settle. She rose and stripped off the swans-down-edged pelerine.

'Llinos!' called the Square again.

A thin girl with dark red hair emerged from the gloom: exchanged with him a few quick words in a sing-song tongue that was strange to Anne Louise: turned, with a gesture, obviously to lead the way.

'I shall be ready in about a quarter of an hour . . . Henry,' said Highness.

'I shan't be longer . . . Anne,' replied he.

They had breakfast together in the dim kitchen under the canopy of bacon. An enormous blue dish, filled with pink ham rashers and delicately fried eggs resting upon a thin golden-brown film of molten fat, was flanked by an enormous and shapeless loaf — by an enormous oblong of yellow butter, by an enormous brown earthenware tea-pot full of a dark and scalding liquid, and by a very large jug holding milk that was still warm from the cow.

They talked desultorily at their meal — very desultorily; for Anne Louise found that waves of fatigue surged over her, that she was taking short naps between sips of the hot strong tea, and dozing off with her mouth full of warm new bread that soaked up the yellow butter like a sponge.

'I said,' repeated Wentworth, faintly hinting by his tone distress at inattention, 'that we must set to work on our — our — plans. We must have evewything cut and dwied.'

' "Plans!" ' echoed Anne Louise, recalling a wavering consciousness by a stern regard of the eight finger-tips on the edge of the table, by which she kept herself propped upright.

'There are a lot of plans to be made, now we are almost in sight of the sea,' said he, pouring out a strong lacing of liquor from a black bottle into the tea-cup at his elbow. 'We have had no time to talk seriously before this. Plans! The secwet of all success is — plans!'

' "Plans!" ' echoed Anne Louise, again, nodding.

'While I was widing through the wain last night,' said Lord Henry, 'I planned . . . Planned!'

' "Planned!" ' echoed Anne Louise once more, in a despairing clutch at consciousness.

'I thought — What are they going to look for? Why, a vewy young lady and a young gentleman! Who is going to suspect a middle-aged gentleman with gwey hair, accompanied by his daughter? Why exactly nobody! . . . Gwey hair! Gwey hair! Gwey hair! That's the ticket!'

He sat back chuckling in triumphant merriment at the scheme; became grave; outlined the next stage of their adventure; told of an inn among the mountains near the sea where they could remain hidden — for weeks, if need be. But, of course, it wouldn't be a matter of weeks. Pwobably it would be only a day or so before he could find a ship!

'There's only one thing that bothers me at all . . .' he began, and paused.

But Anne Louise evinced no desire to press him for explanation, and he had to continue un-urged —

'I'm vewy nervous about your maid . . . What's her name — Lovell? Is she dependable? Is she twustworthy? There've been odd . . .'

He came to a halt, realizing that although Anne Louise was sitting bolt upright, with the shreds of an air of polite attention still clinging to her attitude, yet she was fast asleep, the gold-dusted curls faintly trembling about her face as she nodded.

His expression changed as he rose to his feet. It was no cheerful boy who watched her speculatively through narrowed eyes, but a man. A young-old man!

It would be rather amusing, he thought, to awaken a sleeping princess with a kiss on the enchantingly curved cheek; but was taking no risks, for this was a serious matter of business in which he stood to win a great deal if he played his cards correctly, and if . . .

He opened the door to the inner house and called softly —

'Lovell! . . . Lovell!'

She appeared in the doorway a moment later. He forced himself to meet the direct regard of her very lovely eyes. It was for the first time since the beginning of their Odyssey.

'Her — your mistress is too tired for us to go on at once. Take her upstairs. She can rest for an hour.'

He followed the girl's glance at Anne Louise. She still slept.

'Afterwards,' he added in a low voice, 'I must speak to you here.'

She did not understand or catch, perhaps, his last sentence, for she came a little into the room, and looked at him questioningly. He realized then what he had once or twice suspected, that she was more than a little deaf.

He repeated what he had said, irritably, and a trifle more loudly whilst she watched his lips.

He saw her mouth shape the words, 'Yes, my Lord!' although it did not utter them aloud.

Very gently he shook sleeping Highness by the arm, and, as she woke, said with the utmost sympathy —

'You are vewy, vewy sleepy! I am *so* sowwy. You've had a fatiguing journey. You must lie down for an hour. We can quite safely risk that. Lovell shall see you're comfortable upstairs.'

Over her head his eyes warned Lovell, and warned her again.

He hurried to the door, and held it open for her, and bowed very low, and permitted himself the ghost of a smile that was almost tender. The bow and smile of a devoted and respectful courtier to a queen in exile.

'Isn't he a nice man?' thought Anne Louise sleepily as Lovell, kneeling beside the bed in the small dark room under the roof, untied the ribbons of her shoes. . . .

My Lord stood by the little window sunken in the thick wall, looking out at the rutted muddy road and, beyond it, the dense tangle of a leafless wood that shadowed the interior of the inn into twilight, even at high noon.

'Shut the door,' he said harshly without turning his head, as he heard the light tread; and not until the latch clicked did he swing round.

She stood very humbly some little way from him, eyes cast down, hands clasped before her. He was not an imaginative man, but in the faint light, with her wide grey dress and the sudden pallor of her face, she seemed to be almost something disembodied — the wraith of a dead love, perhaps.

'Well?' he said; and then, 'Come nearer!' accompanying the words with a gesture, so that she should understand even if she had not heard.

She approached him very slowly — as slowly as if she feared physical violence once she was within his reach.

Now that she fronted him near to the window, he was shocked — as he had been shocked before — by the bruise that still stained her cheek. He put his hands upon her shoulders.

'Little fool, why did you make me angry?' he asked.

She shook her head without raising it. Tears were trickling down her face.

'You have not said *anything*?'

'N-no!' The merest whisper.

'To *anyone*?' he insisted.

'N-no!'

'And you will not?'

'I won't! I won't — Only don't . . .'

'Swear it!'

At that she lifted her head, and gave him such a look that any but he would have known the secret to be safe with her.

He tightened his grip on her shoulders.

'Listen! If you breathe a single word, I'll break you! I'll leave you to the workhouse and the streets! . . . By God, if I thought you would, I'ld smash you — smash you — smash you! Do you understand? . . . Do you?'

The fury of his vehemence distorted his face. It was not the gay lad who escorted escaping Highness that confronted Lovell: it was a face yellow as ivory where the skin was tautened over the bones.

'You know that I should never tell, my Lord!' said Lovell.

'Don't say "my Lord", you bloody fool! Don't say "my Lord", you bastard bitch!'

'Don't strike me — *again*,' she appealed, and shrank from him, and looked away from him — anywhere but at the threatening face advanced toward her.

' "Again"?' And he released her.

'Why did you hit me before?' she asked in quick low speech. 'Why did you? I told you nothing but the truth . . . You know it is the truth.'

He turned his back on her and stared out at the mournful palisade of wet trees. Perhaps he had already frightened her enough!

'How do I know?' he flung at her over his shoulder.

'You do know. How can you ask? You *know* you know . . . I made no threats. Indeed, I couldn't — and wouldn't . . . I asked for nothing but help — when the time comes!'

'Oh, don't start it all again, for God's sake!'

She fell silent, and he meditated.

It was the most infernal luck that a damned abigail should have it in her power to wreck him at this present juncture; that the ghost of a dead love-story of two months ago — should gibber and mow at him when he needed all his wits about him. He had no illusions as to the reactions of a seventeen-year-old princess at the revelation that her escort was the father of her waiting woman's child-to-be. It had never occurred to him at the time to enquire of the girl what part she played in the domestic economy of his aunt's enormous home. He wished to God that he had known that she was Highness's woman. He wished to God that he could commit murder without any consequences — could pound with his fists against that tear-stained face whereon the colour ebbed and flowed ... He restrained himself.

When he faced the slim grey figure again he was as grave and sad and elegant as an erring Apollo might be — were he clad in a plum-coloured riding-coat with dark green stock. As benevolently apologetic as a Deity toward some mis-shapen human of his creation.

'Penny!' he said. 'I am sorry that I struck you. Very sorry.' — It was not worth the trouble to mal-pronounce his 'r's' for her — 'I have never done such a thing in my life before. I dreamed about it afterwards ... I was overwrought. What — what you told me was the climax to a month of troubles! I must have been mad, Penny! Won't you believe me?'

But Penny remained silent, twisting her long slim fingers before her. He remembered well how roughened from sewing had felt the tip of the left fore-finger upon his palm when first he had taken her hand in his.

'Penny!' he appealed. 'Just think of that as a moment's madness! You help *me*, and I will help *you*. I promise it by all that's holy. I promise — promise — promise! All you have to do is to keep silent about me. Never let h— anyone know ... Any name will do.'

A sudden thought struck him —

'I suppose you are quite sure?'

'Quite, quite sure,' said Penny.

'I'll see you through. I'll see to everything. But you must swear to keep silence.'

In the urgency of his need he seized her by the hand and drew her toward him; but again she drew away — not fiercely, but with an even and continuous resistance.

'Is it a bargain?' he asked.

She stood as far from him as his grip of her hand would permit, straining her head back, so that he found himself once more admiring the long line of her slender throat, the delicious slant of her chin.

'You don't mean any harm to *her*?'

He found it an offence that this discarded mistress could question his intentions toward a great lady, the neice and cousin of monarchs: an offence that the waiting woman should constitute herself protectress of a — what was the terminology? — High and Mighty Princess. But again restrained himself.

'Don't you understand that I can only avoid ruin by escaping from England — that I can escape most easily by helping *her* escape? ... Can't you understand that, Penny? That we are going away from all our troubles together, you and I, and helping *her* at the same time?'

She raised her dark-fringed eyelids for an instant, revealing the violet eyes that had first attracted him: looked at him doubtfully: could read nothing in the glance that he bent on her.

'Is it a bargain?' he asked. 'Is it a bargain?'

Still contemplating throat, chin, and curving lips, he stooped to her face, meaning to seal that bargain with a kiss which should be not merely the official stamp to a business deal, but a token of appreciation, and, possibly, a promise of favours to come.

But Lovell wrenched her hand from his grasp; threw back her head to avoid the unwelcome embrace — he even thought that horror looked out of her eyes — and was gone. . . .

For a little while he paced restlessly about, revolving a dozen schemes: came to a halt before the only picture in the room. He stooped the better to see it in the dim light.

It was a coloured etching of the great battle at Thistleton Gap between Cribb and the negro Molineux in 1811. Molineux wore pale green breeches and was the blackest black man that there ever was; and the whites of his startled eyes, as he reeled back under a blow to the jaw, were the whitest that ever were.

Studying the brutalized and battered face of the champion, Wentworth at once realized what had been the former profession of their landlord.

Wondering vaguely what sort of career the fellow had had, he flung himself down in the low window embrasure. He lounged with crossed legs, contemplating alternately his mud-sparked boots and the handful of shabby books which shared the seat with him.

There was a 'Time's Telescope' for 1815 in battered grey pasteboard, leaning against a Welsh Bible in worn leather cover from which the clasps had been torn; half of the 'Innocent Adultery' supported by the wreckage of a 'Week's Preparation for the Worthy Receiving of the Lord's Supper'; and one volume (in a faded beetroot-coloured binding) of the 'Cabinet Bible: embellished with Engravings by James Fittler from the Works of the Great Masters'.

This last book opened brightly — Wentworth discovered — with the representation of a muscular Adam and a superbly plump Eve, about whose nudity climbing plants had wound, in an apparent desire to preserve the decencies.

He was still rapidly searching through the volume — and in vain — for further matter of interest when he realized that he was not alone.

The red-headed girl was clearing the table.

CHAPTER V

SEQUEL TO AN ENCOUNTER WITH A RED-HEAD

ALTHOUGH she was tall and astonishingly thin, the red-headed girl moved with great grace — moved with the sway of long grass in the wind.

Wentworth kept his eyes upon the disappointing Bible, but he was well aware of her and of her constant watch upon him.

He timed a quick upward glance to catch her in the act of espionage. He succeeded. She did not, however, lower her lids or look away, or indeed do anything but hold him with the slightly mocking regard of her green eyes.

Wentworth became very interested. He studied as a connoisseur a face that was broad at the temples and pointed at the chin; eyes green and clear as glass under thin brows; smooth hair looped about the ears — tresses that were not the red of gold or copper, but held, rather the generous depth of colour of dark and shining mahogany.

Although it was winter, she wore a printed cotton dress of green and grey which revealed such sharp angles to her body that he felt her breasts should have been angles, too, instead of slight and exciting curves.

He rose to his feet.

She did not stir, but stood still, fronting him across the table, her hands grasping the rim of a large blue dish. Her eyes never left his; only a faint smile seemed to tremble at the corners of her wide red mouth.

He approached her: but she did not retreat, or even quiver.

He was at her side: she gave him a swift sidelong look; her hands dropped from the dish which they had been about to lift.

He put an arm about her waist and slid it upward. Beneath thin dress and under thin flesh he could feel the sharp ridges of her ribs.

She was as tall as himself. Even as his mind registered the reaction that it would be pleasant and convenient to kiss someone of his own identical stature, he found that she was held in his arms, was straining most passionately against him, was demanding caresses with a ferocity to which he instantly responded.

She was so thin and so ardent in his embrace that he felt he must be aware of every bone in her body. Somewhere in the recesses of his consciousness there jingled very absurdly the maxim — 'The nearer the bone, the sweeter the meat . . . The nearer the bone, the sweeter the meat!'

Not a single word had been exchanged between them.

He took his lips from hers —

'My lovely . . .' he began : and was torn from her on the instant by an irresistible force ; was swung to and fro by the collar of his impeccable coat ; was flung against the table wherefrom blue crockery cascaded and crashed upon the flags ; was then sent reeling into the window embrasure.

Quick-footed as a cat he recovered himself, and leaped round to face the unseen assailant. His hands had fallen on the crop which lay in the window seat, had grasped it ; and as he leaped round, so he lashed out.

The square inn-keeper had thrown the red-headed girl violently onto the settle ; was approaching on dancing toes, with fists milling like the claws of a giant crab. The huge yellow face, sunk deep upon an enormous chest, was yellower than ever : the thin grey curls on his forehead were dark with sweat. He mouthed a babble of incomprehensible words. He was murder incarnate.

The leather loop of the whip struck full across that yellow face, across the almost bridgeless nose with wide nostrils.

The blow staggered the man so greatly that he nearly fell — that he hurtled back against the settle which rocked at the impact. Those few seconds of his bemusement were enough for Wentworth to put the table between them.

The older man was up in an instant, however, and gave chase to Wentworth round the table, blood streaming from his nostrils, curses streaming from his lips. Once he feinted — made as if to pounce on one side, and, instead, came charging round the other at terrific speed for one of his bulk. Wentworth avoided the rush very narrowly, and only by thrusting the heavy table sideways at his opponent as he fled out of reach.

They faced one another again across the check cloth that was stained with overset milk and tea and dishevelled with scattered crockery.

'Stop it, you fool!' said Wentworth, one hand resting upon the table-edge, the other questing almost frantically for a pocket under his coat-tails. 'Stop it! I've done the girl no harm!'

The other made no reply. He leaned upon the table, crouched like a gorilla with huge bent arms. With tight-shut mouth he ground his teeth : he breathed quickly and fiercely through distended nostrils, and at each snort there shot out a little spray of blood.

The red-headed girl had risen and stood watching. Her attitude was that of an impartial and critical spectator — a trifle excited, perhaps, because her teeth showed very white between her slightly parted lips.

'Stop it!' said Wentworth again, watching between panic and fury the slow menacing sway of the other's head and shoulders. Often had he watched, from the ring-side, a heavy-weight boxer come swaying in that manner across the sawdust, as he advanced like Fate itself upon a staggering adversary.

'Stop it! What's the harm in a kiss?'

Perhaps it was the sibilants in the word 'kiss' that penetrated to his opponent's slow-reacting consciousness.

He came to an utter standstill: leaned forward on his great clenched fists so that the table juddered beneath his weight.

He broke into speech — a speech made difficult of comprehension because his 'd's' sounded like 't's', and the 's's' hissed like serpents, and his voice rose and fell in an alien rhythm and tune.

'T'you know who I am?' he asked, and snapped his lips together. 'T'you know who I am, you barsstard? T'you know I'm Saul the Dreadnought? . . . That knocked out Deaf Burke in thirteen rounds! . . . That stood up to Cribb himself! . . . "A kiss!" . . . "A kiss!" . . . I'll gif you a kiss!'

'Don't be a fool!' reiterated Wentworth. He had found what he sought. He stood now at his ease, both hands behind his back, legs slightly apart. 'You struck me first!'

Saul the Dreadnought paid no heed to the interjection. He leaned still further forward, so that the table tilted beneath his weight, and the crockery travelled jerkily toward him — a rolling milk-jug hopped onto a plate, spilt its last dregs, hopped off, and smashed on the iron-grey flags.

'T'you know,' said the ex-pugilist, 'that I — I — knocked out Spring? That I mashed Langan in sixteen rounds? That I've fought Bendigo?'

'Balderdash!' commented my Lord as if in weary amusement. His pallor had been succeeded by an almost feverish flush. He had recovered his poise. He jerked back a lock of hair that had fallen across his forehead, and permitted himself a slight contemptuous smile. 'Balderdash! . . . Balderdash! You couldn't knock out a half-baked rabbit! . . . You're a million years old! . . . You ought to be in your grave, and marigolds or turnips sprouting out of your guts!'

Said Saul the Dreadnought —

'Firsst you'll be in your grave, my kitscatgewhoram! . . . You —'

and he gave the word the sound of an explosion of steam ' — barsstard! You lily-livered toad! . . . You'ld pinch my girl, would you? . . . You'ld pinch old Dreadnought's tart, would you? . . . You'ld do the Corinthian on me, would you, you spawn of a sea-cook?'

The Dreadnought closed his great hands on the edge of the table, which he grated upon the stone as he spoke. Instead of swaying from side to side, now he swung slightly to and fro from the hips. It was obvious that in a moment he would launch the table and himself upon the younger man.

Said Wentworth again —

'For Christ's sake . . .'

But Saul the Dreadnought had already wrenched the table toward himself; was leaning over the tilted glacis of blue cloth, down which the breakfast appurtenances slid; had reached the very second of frantic assault.

Wentworth leaped back.

In a high voice he called once more —

'Stop it, you fool!'

— And, since his cry did not halt the preliminary to attack, he brought up, from behind his back, a hand that was armed with a small pocket pistol.

The inn-keeper did not appear to realize his danger, or to have seen the round iron eye of the pistol that stared across the room at him, although it was fully in such light as the window gave.

He was stooped low with wide-stretched arms over the table, which he had caused to rear up toward Wentworth like an angry horse. In another instant the heavy oaken thing would have been projected at the young man with the violence of a rocket.

'Have it, you fool!' cried Wentworth, and fired, and leaped sideways as he did.

His arm was jerked violently in its socket; his nostrils were filled with the acrid scent of gun-powder; his ears rang with the roar of the explosion.

The table clattered back to the level. Saul the Dreadnought stood swaying over it: one great arm threshed the air, the other hung useless at his side: the shoulder of his blue jersey was suddenly dark with blood. He gave a prolonged scream — a strange high cry to come from so massive a frame; clawed at the sopping wound; and then crashed headlong on the table, and thence rolled onto his back upon the floor.

Wentworth's eyes sought those of the thin girl, who had not moved

83

from her position by the settle. She seemed interested, but not concerned by events.

'I call you to witness,' said he, rather pinched about the elegant nostrils, 'that I fired in self-defence!'

She nodded vigorously.

'Serve the dirty dog right!' she remarked. 'That's put paid to him for a bit.'

They stood together looking down on the fallen man as he lay amid a clutter of crockery between table and window. The trickles of blood still ran from his nose, and a dark shining puddle spread over the grey stone floor from his shattered shoulder. He lay there with his head slightly bent to one side, so that an enormous cauliflower ear was folded over and presented for inspection upon a broken willow-pattern saucer. He breathed stertorously through his open mouth. He appeared to have but one yellow tooth in his head, and for an instant Wentworth questioned how and what he ate.

'Well, he ain't dead!' said the thin girl. 'More's the pity!'

'Bloodthirsty little devil!' remarked Wentworth. He flung the pistol into the window embrasure, took the pointed chin between his hands, and kissed her with appreciation. 'Considering everything,' he added, 'it was a good shot. Lots of damage and no danger! *He* won't throw tables about so lightheartedly again!'

He waited, listening tensely in silence for a moment. There was, however, no sound of hurrying footsteps — of alarmed voices. From a distant stable came the stamping of horses and Brown's loud objurgations. Anne Louise had apparently slept through the uproar which had not penetrated, either, the dulled ears of Lovell.

He raised an eyebrow at the thin girl.

'There's nobody in the house,' she said, 'except me. His brothers went to Morriston for a fight last night . . . Their girls went with them . . . And now *I'm* going . . . Back to Bristol! . . . Back to Silas! . . . Unless . . .' She paused; regarded speculatively the slim graceful figure in riding-coat and shining boots; put from her mind whatever idea had crossed it; continued, 'I'm going back to Silas! Wish I'd never left him! . . . Blast this dirty scum!'

She dropped on her knees beside the senseless hulk of Saul the Dreadnought; explored under the black apron; withdrew a greasy leather purse. It jingled very cheerfully. She opened it, and tilted the contents out on to a pink palm. There were twelve sovereigns and five half-sovereigns.

'Bristol!' said the thin girl triumphantly. 'Bristol! Bristol' — and flung the empty purse with great accuracy upon the fire; pulled up skirt and petticoat, and dropped the coins into a sort of pocket in the top of a green stocking above tightly knotted garter.

'I shall take his pony and ride to Llangadoc and catch the coach,' said the thin girl. 'And he'll look for me in Newport; and he'll look for me in Swansea. And all the time I'll be in Bristol! . . . I'm Welsh, but I've had enough of Wales. . . . *And* enough of him — the bloody swine!'

She kicked the human log in the ribs viciously with a pointed toe.

'We'd better shift him — I'll get Brown — while you clear up this mess,' said Wentworth.

He went out into the sharp freshness of the morning, and stood still, listening to the soughing of the forest trees, appreciative of the glint of cold light in the runnels of rain-water in the deep ruts, of the glistering upward climb of the road and the sudden bend that it took into an unknown beyond as if to escape the dark sentinelship of the wood. He was glad to have come out-of-doors from that low and shadowy room where the ceiling seemed to press downward, and violence to be far more violent because confined within so small a space.

In the muddy yard alongside the inn Brown was coaxing recalcitrant horses back into the yellow chariot.

'I want you, Brown,' said my Lord with an air of indifference; and Brown (after an interval spent in hitching those recalcitrant horses to rings in white-washed walls) came nonchalantly to deal with my Lord's requirements — nonchalantly to drag the battered Dreadnought along a stone passage into a small room entirely occupied by a bed and a tall chest-of-drawers of golden oak and lighted by one small window that appeared never to have been opened — nonchalantly to strip back coverlet and blankets and to hoist the senseless body on to the swollen feather-bed in which it sank so deeply that you might have thought that it would be drowned in down — nonchalantly to plug and bandage the wounded shoulder with strips torn from a shirt — nonchalantly to remark that he thought the fellow had 'bruk' an ankle when he fell.

' 'E looks a fair old comic, my Lord,' said Brown in his hoarse Cockney, looking with a certain proprietary interest at his patient. 'A fair comic! . . . And wot an ugly customer — my woord!'

Wentworth studied a most lady-like little watch. Having recovered from the urgency of the crisis he found time once more to lose his 'r's'.

'Bwown,' said he, 'this muck's all out!'

' 'Deed 'e is, my Lord!'

'So we'll go — before there's any more twouble!'

'Very good, my Lord! . . . Very wise, my Lord! . . . They sez 'is brothers are a lot worse nor 'im!'

My Lord was accompanying his man back to the stable-yard. He suddenly stopped —

'Who said?'

'Feller wot was out in the stables . . . 'E mizzled like a rabbit when — when 'e 'eard trouble!'

' "Heard trouble"?'

' . . . 'Eard the pistol shot, my Lord.'

'Oh, so you heard the shot, did you?'

'Yus, my Lord! But it was, in a manner of speaking, nothing to do with me! . . . The feller wot was out 'ere, the minute 'e 'eard the shot, 'e said in that sing-song lingo of theseyere Welsh . . . 'e said, "That's murder! . . . Murder again! . . . They're allus having murder 'ere!" and with that 'e was gone! Gone like a ginger-snap down an orphint's throat!'

Said Wentworth coldly —

'Have the cawwiage wound in ten minutes!'

'Yus, my Lord!'

'And there's no need to mention this — this business to her Highness or to her woman.'

'No, my Lord!'

'And no "Highnesses" and no "my Lords" in future! Not a dam one.'

'No, my Lord.'

He picked his way over the wet stones of the yard to a back entrance to the inn — a black oblong in the whitewash, wherein stood the thin girl with a bright green cloak swirled about her.

She said as he approached —

'I'm going! . . . I'm going now! . . . You'd better go, too! . . . His brothers are devils. . . . Far, far worse than him! . . . Three of them — dark dangerous men!'

'When'll they be back?'

She calculated —

'Not before noon, at the earliest.'

'Two hours to go!'

'And I'll be on the coach at Llangadoc long before.' A little triumphant laugh bubbled from her wide red mouth. Her eyes were even greener than he had thought. A small brown mole near the corner of her lips was as emphatic as a beauty-spot against the clear pallor of her skin.

'It's a pity,' said Lord Henry Wentworth, 'that we've had all this trouble . . . for nothing!'

'I must go!' she answered.

'. . . In an hour?'

'Now!'

'In ten minutes!' He thrust his arms about her under the green cloak as he spoke; and bore her, unresistant and laughing under her breath, into the darkness of the inn. . . .

For hours — it seemed to Anne Louise — the carriage laboured upward along a narrow road that was but a muddy furrow through the woods.

The chaise swayed, jolted, rolled; once Brown dismounted to ease the ridden horse, and led the sweating beasts for more than a mile. The windows were yellow-grey with mud; it was hardly possible to see out of those in front. There was, too, a stronger smell than ever of damp biscuits about the claret-coloured cabin, for the rain had found weak places and the fine cloth upholstery of the roof was stained with wet.

Directly they had left the inn, Anne Louise had tried to settle down to her Partington; to continue harvesting information about the world's commerce, bent over the heavy volume open on her knees.

Self-education was, however, a strain in the circumstances. It was difficult to absorb such facts as 'In Bohemia, far the greater portion of the trade is in the hands of the Jews who are numerous in the country,' when you were bumped to and fro; when the book bumped to and fro; when the carriage lurched — as though it would capsize — at a sudden corner made by a buttress of wet rock projecting out of a dank thicket.

They passed only one or two miserable cottages on the climb upward — cottages with thatched roofs the colour of mud, windows stuffed with rags, and whitewash peeling in great blisters from the walls.

'. . . To Iceland it exports rye-meal, rye, barley, brandy, and other spiritous liquors . . .'

Definitely travel along a mountain bye-road in Wales was not con-ducive to an appreciation of the great Partington! Anne Louise shut the book. She turned for entertainment to Lovell, who sat upright in her corner, apparently regarding with lowered eyes the grey-gloved hands lightly clasped on her grey lap. The girl appeared to show no interest whatever in the adventure, to partake of none of the excitement with which Anne Louise was still filled.

A PRINCESS IN REVOLT

'Lovell,' said Anne Louise in her clear voice, 'have you ever been on a long journey before? A really long journey?'

The girl looked up — not at once, but after a little, as if it had taken a such time for her to realize that she had been spoken to, and the purport of the question.

Anne Louise saw the angry purple bruise on Lovell's right cheekbone: its stain was spread to the eyelids. She had seen it many times before, but had never thought to inquire about it. Now a new relationship between her and her maid was in the process of springing up. She asked —

'How did you do that?'

Lovell would never be a good liar.

She stammered, flushing —

'I . . . I . . . hit myself, madam.'

'Hit yourself,' echoed Anne Louise incredulously.

'With . . . with . . . with a broom-handle, madam,' said Lovell extemporizing unhappily.

'It was very careless of you, Lovell! It was very near the eye. It might have been quite serious,' remarked Anne Louise severely. She harked back to her first question. 'Have you ever been on a really long journey before?'

Lovell had not.

What was the furthest Lovell had ever been?

From Stowmarket to Severall.

But that was only twenty miles — if as much.

Lovell had no reply to that statement of fact. Anne Louise found conversation difficult, yet persevered.

'You will like it very much, Lovell . . . Very educative! . . . Not this, of course; but when we get right away. Ships! Sea! Great cities! Strange people! Forests! Mountains! Real rivers — wide rivers! Castles! And then dear Lecques! . . . You will like Lecques!'

'Is . . .' the girl made no effort to pronounce the strange word '. . . where we are going, madam?'

'It's my home,' said Anne Louise, her eyes lighting up, already viewing those fairy-tale turrets shining above the surge of dark forest. 'It is the loveliest place. You shall stay there with me. I shall live there always — and always.'

The girl's hands clasped and unclasped.

'Perhaps,' she said at last, 'you . . . you . . . won't want me, madam! Perhaps . . .'

'Don't be absurd! You have come with me. It will be my duty to look after you.' A sudden idea struck the princess. 'Or is it that you will miss your mother?'

'I have no mother, madam,' said Lovell in a low voice.

'Your father, then?'

'I . . . I . . . never . . . had a father.'

Anne Louise was pondering upon this interesting piece of biological information, when the carriage, breasting a rise as steep as a camel's hump, emerged from the woodlands, and came out upon a bare mountainside under a lofty sky. Everything was grey in various degrees — road, moor, and heaven; grey in all shades from lavender to iron. Even a brief and sudden scurry of rain was grey.

They rounded a shoulder of the hill, and found themselves in thin sunshine and upon one of the high ramparts of a valley several miles wide — a valley of white villages and farms each sunk deep in its bed of trees, with a river curving between smooth pasture-lands, and a highway bordered by poplars. The farther battlement of the valley was a line of mountains with jagged crests. The violet sides of the great hills were stained with patches of golden-brown — of jade-green — of black — of amber: so that they looked like nothing so much as an immense billow of an immensely stormy sea, frozen in the very act of breaking over the valley beneath.

In a dip immediately before them was a cross-roads, flanked on the left by an unkempt copse of stunted pines behind a tumble-down stone wall. A battered sign-post gave almost indecipherable directions.

They halted under the lee of the copse. Wentworth, who had ridden ahead, dismounted, read the wording on the post, and came back to Brown who waited at the horses' heads. He looked puzzled.

'What was the name of the place where we stopped — the inn?'

Brown's round unshaven face glinted with the beginnings of a reddish beard, as if it had been powdered with gold dust. There were dark rings of fatigue about his eyes.

'Pont — something, my . . . sir!' he answered.

'Pontefengylydd?'

'Summat like that, sir. Summat.'

Said my Lord —

'We've just come from there. And yet that damned post's got a sign pointing up to the left!'

'It'll be a bridle path — a short cut — across the mountains . . . Nout more!'

Wentworth looked at his watch. It was nearly twelve: there could be no pursuit from the inn yet! The Dreadnought's brothers — 'those dark dangerous men' — were not due to return until midday, and in half an hour, threequarters of an hour at most, they could be in a populous district, and in refuge at some quiet and well-conducted inn. There could not be any pursuit yet; there might not be any at all. Or could there, or might there be? . . . Supposing the thin girl had miscalculated! He thought of his pistol, and clapped a hand to his pocket; but it was not there: he remembered then tossing it on the window-seat after he had dealt with the Dreadnought. Fool! And double fool!

The winding track up the mountain took on a sinister aspect. A short cut! He gazed up it, as though he expected to see riders emerge at a dogged canter round any of its bends. He was almost sick with fright: he had never cared for a battle against odds, or indeed any sort of battle except of the wits.

He took a quick decision.

'I shall ride on. And make arrangements for fresh horses . . . Fix up dinner, too. No good me keeping pace with your nags — they're nearly foundered.'

He went back to the carriage. Anne Louise had lowered the window, and was looking out at the friendly open country spread far below, and the distant town that rose up from the river and many-spanned bridge — a town that shone white and grey upon its ridge like a bank of wet pebbles upon the sea-shore.

He explained his programme to her, quickly — for he was anxious to be gone. He saw the security of inn-yard and streets and houses so near at hand.

He swung off to the right, sharply down to an archway of trees, and so into the steep slanting tunnel of a tree-lined road that overhung a rushing stream. When he was out of sight of the carriage he put spurs to his wretched horse, and knocked it up into a dreary canter.

'Nothing can happen to *them*,' he assured himself. 'It's only I who run any risk.' . . .

He had vanished into that dark tunnel; the carriage, too, had begun the downward journey when three quickly-moving specks came in succession over the sky-line . . . precipitated themselves down the breakneck mountain path from Pontefengylydd . . . and swept into and out of the shadows of its dips and bends.

'Travel is *very* educative, you understand, Lovell! You learn without knowing it . . . languages . . . history . . .' Anne Louise was saying; and Lovell, violet eyes fixed on her mistress, was punctuating an aphoristic speech with nods of comprehension, when the chariot came to a sudden halt.

The door was wrenched open.

A square mud-stained figure leaned into the carriage. Between shapeless broad-brimmed hat and green handkerchief tied about its face, no feature was visible except a pair of black eyes.

'Come out!'

Anne Louise's heart missed a beat: she was astonishingly frightened. She stiffened in her seat: she held her chin very high: she barely looked at the creature without.

'Shut the door!' she commanded in an even tone, and called, 'Drive on, Brown!'

But Brown could not drive on: he lay in the wet road, hatless, eyes shut, mouth wide open, and a trickle of blood upon his forehead, near the heels of his frightened horses. Another vizarded man, with a cudgel in his hand, stood over him. A third flung open the other door, and waited by it, holding a cocked pistol. Three sweating ponies, their reins knotted together, circled in the road behind.

'Come out! . . . Come out!' said the harsh voice.

Anne Louise did not stir. She could not decide what a princess should do in such circumstances. Princesses were not given orders by the lower classes — except in revolutions. This (she decided) was, in a sense, a revolution — at any rate a revolution personal to her. In revolutions — her memory obliged her — princesses either successfully defied the mob, or disdainfully complied with their will.

She was deciding on her course of action, when a large hand seized her ankle — her royal, untouchable ankle! — and obviously purposed to extract her from the chaise by it.

'Please to let me go! I will come!' said Anne Louise, non-resistant, rigid; and regarded the foot that was in the clutch of a hairy hand as if it were something contaminated and divorced from the rest of her.

She rose; was released as she did so; and stepped with the greatest deliberation down on to a road so little used that it was carpeted deep with the dank oak leaves of the autumn fall. She decided that correct royal conduct in such a predicament was to ignore the representative of Multitude — to pretend that for her own royal pleasure she had emerged from her carriage to breathe fresh air, and stare at the spider's web of bare black boughs and twigs which had been spun overhead.

The niceties of royal behaviour were lost on the man with hairy hands. He seized her by the shoulders of the admirable dark green velvet pelerine, and shook her so that not merely the tinted plume in her

bonnet danced, but so that the wide-brimmed bonnet itself threatened
to tilt at a most undignified angle over the royal nose; so that even her
teeth would have chattered, had she not clenched them hard — for a
princess's teeth did not chatter!

'Where's the man?' said Hairy-hands. 'Where's the man, you bitch?'

Anne Louise opened her admirable mouth. He loosed his clasp, to
hear what she should have to say.

Anne Louise closed her eyes, and permitted herself to yawn . . . She
drawled at her slowest —

'What man?'

'The man in the green coat!'

'Oh, the *gentleman*!'

'Chentleman!' Hairy-hands spat — and Anne Louise had no idea
that the human frame could eject so much saliva in a single burst.
'Where iss he?'

'I don't know.'

'You musst!'

'I do not know,' said Anne Louise coldly. She drew herself up; she
did her best to look through the man before her, as if he were no
obstacle to her view of the tree-lined vista of the road. Somewhere
beside her, far down through the dark leafless thickets, a stream sighed
and gurgled and rushed.

'You know! Yess, indeed! You know, and I shall make you tell.
There are many ways of making women tell!'

He took her right hand in his. It flashed through Anne Louise's
mind that they stood there beside the travel-stained yellow chaise, in a
queer parody of affectionate greeting.

'Many ways!' reiterated Hairy-hands; and his breath smelled of
strong spirits.

Anne Louise did not shift her regard from over his shoulder. She
ignored him utterly: she prayed that someone would come up toward
them through the tunnel of the trees; prayed that she might hear the
thudding of rapidly approaching hoofs on the carpet of dead leaves.

'Do you understand? Yess?'

He suddenly twisted the slim royal wrist reverseways, until the palm
of her green-kid-gloved hand came uppermost. She stood thus before
him, feeling the jarring strain on every tensed muscle of her arm.

Anne Louise said nothing. She still stared over his shoulder into
the archway of the trees, but she knew that under the torture her hand
had opened, and that the dark-green fingers of her glove were spread
wide, most inelegantly, like a duck's foot.

'Where . . . iss . . .?'

From the pain of that new and sudden wrench she almost screamed — almost, and only almost! She even endeavoured to remain confronting her torturer, but the agony of sinew and bone and muscle forced her to swing away from him until the shoulder of the tormented arm was toward him, and she was gazing blankly and unseeing down the ravine.

'Where iss that man?'

Anne Louise clenched her teeth: her beautifully shaped mouth (too wide to be a cupid's bow) straightened itself into a thin line, and the lips whitened at their outer edge.

She said not a thing.

'Where iss . . .?'

She thought then that under this new brutality her arm must snap, It was no longer a limb, but a red-hot pain. Although she could refuse to speak or struggle or cry, she could not refuse the plea of her agonized body for relief, and she turned — with the twisting of her arm — until her back was to the man, and she was looking into the empty carriage, with the *British Cyclopaedia* on the floor, and her tasselled handbag lying derelict upon the claret-coloured seat. Lovell had got out of the other door; was staring, as though mesmerized, at the double-barrelled pistol that nuzzled at her breast.

'You *will* tell me,' said Hairy-hands, 'where that man hass gone. You *will*!'

So violent was the force he used that her lips parted automatically to a scream to which her will refused utterance. Such was his violence that her body arched away from him in the agony — as if it would escape him — while her shoulders were drawn irresistibly back until they were pressed against his chest. It was no longer a localized pain that she endured; but a pain beyond thought, that travelled from wrist to elbow, tore at her shoulder, ached at the base of her neck, and even wrenched at the muscles of her breast.

Her face became clammy with sweat. She knew that she must cry out — must struggle; no, must do nothing of the sort!

Then suddenly the carriage appeared to sway, and — as it swayed — to swell to such an enormous size that it blotted out everything else. It filled the whole range of her vision; darkened, became a great mass of blackness that shuddered, surged forward . . . and swallowed her up in a dizzy abyss.

Anne Louise crumpled to her knees. For an instant she remained kneeling upon the wet carpet of leaves; was held up by the twisted arm behind her back; and then, with its release, fell into a small, neat, and senseless heap at Hairy-hands' feet.

The man was obviously taken aback by her collapse; stood looking down on her for some little time, as if a fragile piece of porcelain had surprisingly shivered into bits from out of his hands.

Then he called to his colleague by the farther door of the carriage, in rapid Welsh.

'The servant knows nothing,' answered the other. 'I think she speaks the truth.'

The third, meanwhile, in bitter malice had loosed the horses, and, with a couple of buffets, had sent them ambling down the road, the traces dragging and jingling at their heels.

Lovell came round the carriage: kneeled in silence beside her fallen mistress, and, sitting on her heels, took the golden-brown head upon her lap.

Anne Louise's bonnet had dropped off, and the face turned up toward Lovell's downward regard was that of a child.

Lovell smoothed the scattered ringlets; took off the wonderful green gloves, and caressed the cold hands with hers. Somewhere in Lovell's soul there flowered a wonder — a thing ever to be remembered — that she should thus nurse a princess, she that was a nameless child. With that comprehension she bent a little further over Anne Louise, curved her arm about the small head a trifle more protectively, clasped the small hand a fraction tighter. Her lips moved as though she were telling Highness of her affection and other secret things that she had never dared to say before.

Regardless of them — and disregarded by them — the three men methodically ransacked the carriage and its contents. They broke open the trunks strapped to the back, burst the Bramah lock of the red Russia-leather despatch-case, violated the tasselled handbag, even gutted the sage-green carpet-bag in which Lovell's few possessions were enclosed.

The derelict carriage, so mud-stained now that its yellow panels were fog-coloured, rose from a sort of swamp of clothing. A pair of my Lord's black silk dress pantaloons draped a step; his tortoiseshell-backed brushes lay, bristles uppermost, like dead insects, upon a heap of shirts that were as white as summer clouds.

One of the three square men found Uncle Leopold's diamond necklace. He put it round his neck: he capered in elephantine imitation of a gleeful girl: he pranced absurdly while his brothers screeched with laughter. They parcelled out Anne Louise's golden sovereigns between

them; and discussed swiftly the eleven tidy small squares into which
the bank-notes had been folded, decided that they were identifiable
and therefore dangerous, made a loose heap of the crumpled paper,
and set fire to it with a phosphorus match.

It was the man in the trailing greenish great-coat, with a purple
scarf bound about the lower half of his face, who slashed the upholstery
of the chariot to ribbons; slashed it with one of the razors from the
Emperor Napoleon's travelling case — slashed it so that the horse-
hair came curling out on to the claret-coloured leather; and then
broke the glass of every window with his cudgel — joyously like a small
boy breaking thin ice upon a puddle . . . With that they departed as
swiftly and silently as they had come — a shabby, sinister cavalcade of
large men on small ponies.

CHAPTER VI

UNCIVIL BEHAVIOUR OF A HOST

A MINUTE or so later a large, fat woman breasted her way out of a thicket a little way ahead — to the accompaniment of as loud a snapping of twigs as though she were a travelling bonfire.

She had an immense red face shaded by a vast straw hat, which — in the fashion of twenty years before — was fastened securely to her head by a faded handkerchief knotted under a chin well sprinkled with grey hairs. She was enveloped in a stained red garment of indeterminate character, and projected before her so huge and shapeless a bosom that it was impossible to imagine that she had merely the ordinary human quantum and had not been provided, by a bounteous Providence, with a sufficiency of breasts to nourish sextuplets at least. These wonderful organs formed a ledge a little below her chin, and descended in large bulges and knobs to her bulky waist.

She held tightly in one hand an enormous green umbrella so swollen in the midriff that it might have been about to give birth to a whole litter of little umbrellas.

'Hey, my girl! Ho, my girl!' said the large lady in a large voice, approaching Lovell. 'That ain't the way for faints. Head down — feet up, my girl! Hartshorn — wet handkerchiefs — burnt feathers, my girl! Yes, my girl! That's the way!'

She spiked the umbrella into the soft earth of a grassy bank by its ferrule. Being thus cleared for action she loosened her garment at the throat, and then plunged a questing hand into her astonishing bosom, assisting the mysterious operation by thumps, dabs, and pushes in the same region from without: appeared to wrestle for a moment as if with some guardian of its secrets, and then produced, like a conjuror, a package wrapped in an old handkerchief. She gave herself a vigorous wrench from the hips; brought to light a medicine bottle apparently full of milk — a paper twist — a short clay pipe, and finally (after a most complicated acrobatic, in which her bosom appeared to give battle to the intruder) a small phial.

She unstoppered it, snuffed the contents with much pride and satisfaction.

'Hey, my girl! Don't say that old Sarah Liddell don't carry things handy-like! Give the poor dear a sniff of that . . . It'll soon put her to rights!'

She watched the operation, leaning on her umbrella, and radiating benevolence.

But more than the spirit of hartshorn was needed to bring a flutter to Anne Louise's long lashes.

'What shall I do? Oh, what shall I do?' moaned Lovell, looking up from the pale face below to the red face above.

Mrs. Liddell was equal to the emergency.

'Joe!' she called — and Lovell became aware for the first time that someone else was standing beside the violated carriage; a little shrimp of a man with a wizened face, shrouded in a voluminous black cloak that nearly reached to his heels. Perched on the top of his head was a small foraging cap with tarnished gold braid — such as his late Majesty King George the Fourth had fancied very greatly for travel and pleasure excursions. A large bundle done up in a cloth, and a carpenter's bag full of tools, were at his feet.

'Joe,' called Mrs. Liddell, 'get the tinder-box!'

Joe advanced, stooped, picked up the bottom of his wife's dress, and extracted the tinder-box from the hem of a grey flannel petticoat.

'I'm not a one for stooping,' the large lady explained to Lovell. 'I'm not a stooper, and I'm not a stoopid!' She laughed very heartily in deep rumbles at the joke: then in a sharper tone to Joe — 'Hey, man! Ho, man! Bustle up, Joe! What do you think you want a tinder-box for, but to get a light? . . . Take the feather out of the little dear's bonnet . . . At your feet it is, stoopid! . . . Don't stand with it like a drumstick, Joe! Singe it, man! Singe it!'

The gay curled plume was accordingly plucked by Joe out of the grey-green bonnet — singed — handed to Lovell — held close to the nostrils of its afore-time wearer, diffusing the foulest stench possible.

'That'll do the business, or my name's not Liddell,' said that lady surveying progress with the very greatest interest. 'Hey, Joe! Ho, Joe!' she continued without turning her head. 'You go and see whether that fellow's come to, yet. Instead of standing there gaping.'

Brown had risen to his feet, was supporting himself by the muddy spoke of a high rear wheel: he was sick — very loudly and then stared in a dazed fashion, first at the ruin of the equipage, and then at the queer small figure that came to him round the carriage.

'Did *you* do this?' he inquired swaying.

'Indeed, sir — no, sir!' said Joe backing away. '. . . I think, my dear, this gentleman would be better for a little brandy. A very little.'

'Very little, indeed!' said Mrs. Liddell, not removing her intent regard from the pale face to which a faint flush had come — from eyelids which even then quivered. 'Very, very little!'

Still watching, she plunged her free hand into her bosom, wrestled again awhile, and eventually produced from that interesting store-cupboard a very small bottle full of brandy, and a cup that must have come from a doll's house.

'Hey, my little dear! Ho, my little dear!' said she in a voice of enormous caress. 'Now you're feeling better! Now you're coming nicely round! . . . Handy old woman, Sarah Liddell! Very handy! . . . Now my duck, you stay still a bit! Just a bit! . . . Joe, the littlest drop of brandy ever — and don't you dare take a swig at it!'

Anne Louise, recovering consciousness, found the range of her vision limited to a tender down-bent face with tear-filled eyes, and, high above it, a mystifying tracery of black lines upon a grey background like a fishing-net strewn upon a stone jetty.

She raised her head a little, and realized that she was pillowed on Lovell's lap under the lofty vaulting of leafless trees; realized the wonderful shape of Mrs. Liddell outlined against the bulk of the chariot; felt the throbbing of her injured arm; began to remember; tried to rise.

'You lay down, there's a ducky! Lay down for a bit! There's none'll harm you . . . Ho, girl! Keep the ducky down a bit! . . . They there Davieses . . . ' she muttered darkly '. . . shan't hurt you no more! If old Sarah Liddell had her way, she'ld scalp them! She'ld pull their legs off like flies!'

'Who are the Davieses?' asked Anne Louise in little more than a whisper.

'The Davieses! "Who are the Davieses?" . . . Ho, ducky! They are spawn of Hell! They're the curse of these parts! There's no constable dare arrest them. There's no jury that dare convict them. They're above the Law. They're wicked through and through. They're devils!'

Anne Louise pushed aside Lovell's restraining hand; she sat up; she tried to pat into order the disorder of her ringlets.

'Help me up!' she commanded, and rose shakily to her feet, and surveyed the scene of disaster — derelict chariot, jumble of scattered clothing, empty trunks, despatch-box with wrenched-off lid, tasselled hand-bag with its blue silk lining hanging out as if it had been evis-cerated, Brown sitting on the carriage-step with his blood-stained head held in his hands. The completeness of the calamity was obvious and overwhelming. She wanted to burst into tears: would not — princesses did not: clutched Lovell's supporting arm the tighter; swayed a little: asked —

'What can I do?'

'What can you do, ducky? . . . Hey, Joe, bring back that brandy! . . . Why you *can* go to the Justices — and a lot of good it'll do you! You *can* go to Squire Tempest for help. And that's what old Sarah Liddell would do. That's what she'ld do! Yes, indeed! . . . Ho, Joe — the brandy!'

'But all my money's gone! My necklace!'

'And gone for good, too!' said Mrs. Liddell in a rumble of sympathy. 'But I couldn't swear it was the Davieses , ducky! No, ducky, and what's more I wouldn't swear it was the Davieses — not if it was ever so! No — we shan't be sailing for Ameriky for a week's time, Joe and me, and they'ld find us afore then. They'ld find us afore then! And where would Joe and me be then? — Ah, where, indeed?'

'But . . .' began Anne Louise, and then fell silent. She could not explain to this woman that not merely had gold, notes, jewels been stolen from her; but also the means of escape — that Lecques had been stolen from her, too, and that she had been sold back into the captivity of Uncle Leopold and a blind bridegroom.

She thought furiously while Lovell adjusted the desecrated bonnet, brushed the desecrated pelerine with one of Wentworth's tortoise-shell brushes. If she were to apply to the Justices, she might regain her property, but she would undoubtedly lose the secret of her journey. If, on the other hand, she sought immediate aid at a near-by house, she and Wentworth might have time wherein to evolve some new pattern of campaign.

She drew herself up.

'Madam,' she said with a little inclination of the grey-green bonnet, 'I am exceedingly obliged to you. . . . Brown, you will stay here' — the man was, indeed, obviously incapable of doing anything else — 'and inform my — Mr. Wentworth of what has happened. I and Lovell will go together to fetch help.'

'Hey, ma'am! Ho, ma'am! Old Sarah Liddell is always glad to help. Handy-like, old Sarah Liddell is! . . . Squire Tempest — and he's a rum 'un, if ever there was! — lives half a mile down the road. You'll see his lodge where it joins the 'pike. Joe and I are going that way, ducky — Hey, Joe, where's that brandy? — for it's all on the way to Ameriky!'

'On the way to America?' questioned Anne Louise, conscious amid her troubles that princesses should always display interest in the doings of those of the lower orders with whom they came in contact; conscious that the wounded traveller in the Parable must have politely questioned the Good Samaritan about his destination.

'In a manner of speakin', yes,' said Mrs. Liddell, dropping the medicine bottle of brandy into her bosom, after examining the level of the liquid with a very critical eye and seeing that the cork was secure. 'In a manner of speakin', yes,' continued she, shaking herself so that the bottle sank to the right depth, and then fumbling and clutching at her person until she had clawed the little vessel into its proper nesting-place somewhere under the left-hand bolster of flesh — 'We're walkin' to Rhosmaen, where we take ship for Ameriky, Joe and me . . . They say there's great openings for coffin-makers in Ameriky — great openings! And Joe's a good coffin-maker, though I says it as shouldn't . . . Hey, Joe, you know a coffin when you see it, don't you?' — Joe, trailing behind them, bleated some unintelligible remark — 'Oak coffins! Elm coffins! Deal coffins! They're all the same to Joe. Prince or pauper! Silver handles, brass handles, iron handles — it's all the same to Joe! . . .

'These Welsh,' rambled on Mrs. Liddell, 'love a funeral. They lap up a funeral. They rejoice in a berryin' of the dear departed. But they will *not* spend money on their coffins — Hey, Joe! Will they, Joe? — No real chanst for a good craftsman as loves his job . . . Told I am, that they used to eat their dead — like them dirty Irish! . . . Now in Ameriky I hear . . .'

They walked very slowly down the steep wet road, Mrs. Liddell talking all the way, her discourse punctuated by an occasional vigorous thrust of her enormous umbrella, by an occasional clank of the oddments that were stored in her enormous bosom.

All the several parts of Sarah Liddell's anatomy shared, individually and separately, in that walk. While the main mass of her body lumbered forward with the movement of her feet, her vast buttocks surged gently and synchronously from side to side, and her still vaster bosom rose and fell like a buoy — like a lot of buoys — on an ocean swell. She thus moved forward, and sideways, and up and down, very noticeably and all at once. 'Twenty miles we've walked since Monday,' said Mrs. Liddell. 'Old Sarah will be that thin by the time we reach port that she'll pass through the eye of a needle easier than a camel.'

They came at length to a point where the road poured out over a hump-back bridge; between a small white forge with a dark entry — from which came the dull clangour of beaten metal — and a small white inn, with a creaking sign, and a gig at the door; and so into a broad highway.

Opposite the road junction was a wide bay of smooth green grass, with a stone wall behind it and open gates — rather rusty — giving onto a long avenue of lofty and leafless trees: at the end of the vista gleamed faintly the grey walls of a house.

'Here's where we part,' said Mrs. Liddell coming to a halt, and speaking in her most thunderous voice. 'Us — Joe and me — for Ameriky. You for Judgment!'

'Judgment?' said Lovell before Anne Louise could speak, fixing her eyes on the large lady, her conscience suddenly envisaging the revelation of guilty secrets.

'Judgment!' asseverated Mrs. Liddell. 'Old Mr. Fielding foreclosed the mortage he held on the house. He said it was judgment — a judgment on the family what had owned it for donkey's years. So he called it Judgment when he came to live here. Very bitter against them he was! They say . . .' She brought herself so violently to a verbal halt that her body quivered under the effort of suppression. ' "Speak no scandal! No, nor listen to it." That's old Sarah Liddell's motto. Always has been: always will be. . . Caer Afon Abbey is what this place used to be known as.'

She bobbed a little nod of farewell to Anne Louise. It set her all a-quiver — even the ancient straw hat that was fastened so securely by faded orange handkerchief.

'Good-bye, ma'am,' said she. 'Good-bye, girl — remember, in faints: Heads down! Tails up! Always. Always . . . Glad to have been of service, ma'am! Old Sarah Liddell comes in handy-like sometimes.'

'Thank you, indeed, madam,' said Anne Louise with a grave little bow. 'I wish I could . . .' and finished the sentence with the merest sketch of a gesture, as if to show the emptiness of her hands and purse.

'Hey, ducky! Ho, ducky!' replied the large lady, getting even redder in the face than before. 'Money isn't everything. Money isn't human charity. No, ma'am. What's a sniff of hartshorn — a lighting of tinder — advice — a teeny droplet of brandy? Is it money, ma'am? No, it's love.'

'I am sure, madam, I can only wish I could prove my gratitude.' — Princesses were never under an obligation to their inferiors!

'Human kindness is paid for only by kindness, my dearie,' said Mrs. Liddell vehemently, and changed the subject. 'Joe, up with them bags! D'you think you're a monument? . . . Ma'am, when you see young Mr.

Tempest — young, says I, but he's well into the thirties — when you see him, please to give him old Sarah Liddell's love. Old Sarah that washed the blood off his face when he was born! Old Sarah that saw his poor mother in her pains! He'll remember old Sarah well enough! Good-bye and God bless you, ma'am! . . .'

At the end of the avenue there was a gravelled space, and — sentinelled by a clump of green-topped pines that were as tall, and straight and bare as masts, except for their shivering summits — the grey hulk of some portion of an ancient church; a chapel, perhaps, or one of the aisles of a great choir. Beyond, a drive-way ran, under the lee of the high wall of an enclosed garden and evergreen bushes, to a long low house with a steep roof facing a wide smooth lawn.

The seas of time had swept over the ruin for so long that, at first sight, it seemed an almost featureless mass of rubble. The centuries had well nigh washed away in their tides the great buttresses which had once supported the crumbling pile — had set ivy hanging like sea-weed from the upper walls — had smoothed away the moulding over a door, and obliterated the saints who once lived within niches that now were only faint dints in the masonry. Two of the great windows had been roughly filled in with brick and plaster; windows that gave neither light nor air; fossilized windows. The stone tracery of the third did not enclose chapters of violent scriptural history told in glass of green and blue and red, but rectilinear panes of plain glass holding within their depths no more light and colour than does a duck-pond at twilight.

Then suddenly, as Anne Louise approached, the window lost its lifelessness, and for a second was violently illuminated from within, and shone with a curious yellow light — like the reflection of very pale sunlight in water — that was quenched as abruptly as it had sprung up.

The door opened. A tall man in shirt sleeves looked out through the arch; surveyed Anne Louise for a moment without any sign of interest; said a few words to an ancient person in a long smock and battered tall hat who was raking over the gravel; withdrew, slamming the door with a tremendous crash.

Anne Louise addressed the ancient person, who regarded her with rheumy eyes, and touched the ruffled brim of his hat with a trembling hand that was as twisted and as dirty as the root of a shrub.

'Do you know if Mr. Tempest is at home?' she asked.

'Eh?' said the ancient, cupping the root to an ear.

'Is Mr. Tempest at home — do you know?'

The old man gave a succession of jerks that shook ancient hat and ancient face in marionette-like spasms: he pointed shakily to the doorway in the ruin without a word.

'In there?'

Methuselah nodded again.

Tapping was of no avail against the heavy timbers and the mixture of noises that came from within — a dull roaring as of flames, accompanied by the sound of constant shovelling. 'Br-r-r' said something continuously: 'Cr-r-runch' said something else: 'Cr-r-rash' was the response: and then the something-that-purred appeared to snarl for an instant, and then purred more loudly than ever. Mingled with it all was a loud hissing.

Anne Louise pulled the latch and peered through the opening.

She saw, across the stone-flagged floor, under rough roof and ruinous vaulting, a sort of step-pyramid of dull red brick with openings in its base that revealed furnaces glowing like liquid gold: a pyramid about ten feet high with round iron doors at various levels, and culminating at its apex in a cistern with a huge tap from which something trickled into a funnel and feed-pipe. Pipes sprouted from all over this strange altar so that it bore a sort of obscene resemblance to a tentacled octopus or a many-armed Indian god. On either side of it stood two or three minor deities — iron cylinders, most of them man-high — ranged along the wall under blind arches which had once been open to the stained light of a great East window, to the swell of an organ, to the rich perfume of frankincense and myrrh, to the echo of boys' voices flung back from a lofty roof, and to the low drone of a priest intoning the solemn mysteries of the Mass.

The floor was black with coal-dust, and against the bricked-in transept arch was an enormous pile of coal.

A pair of men stripped to the waist, their torsos shining with sweat as if they had been varnished, were shovelling fuel into those golden, gaping mouths.

A third stood watching them. His shirt sleeves were rolled up to the elbow: his collar, without the restraining influence of a cravat, and sodden with sweat, sagged in Byronic fashion away from his neck.

'Mr. . . . .' began Anne Louise, addressing the backs of the high priest and the satellites of the furnaces.

She was answered by a snarl.

'Shut that damned door!'

A royal lady who had refused to be intimidated by the torture of a blackguardly highwayman, refused equally to be intimidated by the churlishness of a potential adjuvant; refused even to consider that such a remark could be addressed to her.

'Mr. Tempest?' said Anne Louise to the back, in — and she could not help it — her very coldest tones.

But Mr. Tempest did not turn to pay homage to a princess in distress. He addressed himself first to the grimy figures who shovelled coal into the gaping orifices —

'How much have we got on board now?' — pause for calculation — 'That'll make the chaldron ... Pipe down for a bit!' ... He did not turn or even look over his shoulder at her Highness, the Princess Anne Louise Elizabeth Caroline, Duchess of Limburg, niece and cousin of Sovereigns, who stood rigid and furious in the doorway behind him. All that he gave utterance to, was a bellow —

'For God's sake, get out! And *shut* that door!'

It was fortunate that Lovell was so deaf that she did not comprehend her mistress's humiliation; that Anne Louise could remove herself before either of the grimy figures turned to grin appreciation of their master's rough welcome.

Anne Louise withdrew with immense dignity. She retreated the bare three steps to the outer air with an assumption of great calm.

She did *not* shut the door.

She halted irresolutely outside, looking through the grey pillars of the pines, across the green turf toward the house. It was so very friendly a dwelling! — Long and low, with many shining windows, with a steep roof of tiles that were lichen-stained, and more brown than red, and with a porch supported by two glittering white columns.

Anne Louise, regarding that happy house, felt no longer a princess — but a beggar whose appeal for charity had been scorned. She had forgotten herself and forgotten Wentworth: all she knew was that she was responsible for Lovell — who stood respectfully two paces behind — for Brown with the blood-stained head, for a derelict carriage, for runaway horses. She nerved herself to a fresh effort.

Round the far corner of the house there appeared, on the instant, a rapid procession.

First came the Ancient, proceeding at an extremely fast shuffle aided by the rake — so that he looked like a caricature of Neptune with his trident. Then a very short square red-faced gentleman without a hat, in a wide-skirted shooting coat of an unbelievable tartan of bright green with red and yellow lines, and fawn-coloured leggings with blue buttons that came well above the knee; with a pair of tortoiseshell-rimmed spectacles tilted to the end of a very short nose, an enormous spectacle case in one hand and a pair of enormous scissors in the other. Then a plump young maidservant in mob-cap and dark blue apron over a raspberry-coloured dress; with a flat gardening basket full of laurestinus blossom on her arm. And, finally, a small boy with his hands in the pockets of peg-top check trousers, and a blue tasselled Cossack cap very much on one side of his head.

It was, in its way, an extremely noisy procession.

The Ancient was mumbling and mowing, every dirty wrinkle in his dirty wrinkled face working as he did so. The square red-faced gentleman in the tartan — his hair was as stiff and grey as a badger's bristles — was swearing loudly, but without anger. The maidservant was giggling, and the schoolboy whistling.

'David,' said the tartan-clad gentleman, 'you are a fool! . . . David, you are a dom'd fool! . . . David, you are a bastard!'

All this was said in a most rapid manner, and in the most matter-of-fact way possible.

The procession, having navigated the house, crossed the angle of the lawn, came to a halt under the pine-trees, and formed up in a semicircle in front of Anne Louise.

'Madam', said the badger-haired gentleman, 'I apologize for David. He's a . . . a fool. Always has been. He shouldn't have sent you to the gas house. He knows that quite well. Dom'd idiot! I apologize for Sep! He was rude . . . d — very rude! I'll stake my life on it! He always gets upset over this gas business. Becomes unbearable. Dom' — very unbearable. Always. I apologize for everything — and for everybody!'

'Mr. Tempest's reception,' said Anne Louise coldly, remembering the phraseology of a favourite novel, 'left a good deal to be desired!'

'I'll bet it did! I'll swear it did, by God!' said the tartan-clothed gentleman.

On closer inspection, his pockets appeared to bulge with string and crimson handkerchiefs: his grey eyes were so bright that they did not seem to need the aid of his very foggy glasses: his face was the beautifully mottled red of nicely underdone cold roast beef, garnished with very short iron-grey whiskers; and the stiff points of a snowy-white collar projected up on either side of his square chin half-way to his cheek-bones.

'Togarmah Smith,' said he, pointing to his tartan chest and spotted blue neckerchief with a stubby forefinger. 'Togarmah Smith, madam — and very much at your service! David — big fool! — on my right! Prudence — Prue! — on my left. . . . And Daniel the Dom'd, a bit farther off!'

With this wholesale introduction he paused, obviously awaiting a reciprocal gesture.

Anne Louise hesitated whilst she endeavoured to remember what name it had been decided that she should adorn.

In that pause Mr. Togarmah Smith recollected the claims of hospitality.

'Prue,' he commanded, 'the madeira and seed cake in my room at once! . . . Togarmah Smith, madam, is the name! Housekeeper at Judgment, madam, is the station!'

'I'm Anne Louise Wentworth,' said Anne Louise. 'And this is my maid . . . We were waylaid by highwaymen . . .' and so swung into a staccato and restrained account of the encounter on the road from Pontefengylydd, an account punctuated by interjections of 'Bloody swine!' 'Oh God, the villains!' from Mr. Togarmah, and occasional prolonged whistles from the wide-open-eyed Daniel.

'Leave it all to me! Leave it all to me,' said Mr. Togarmah Smith in a most soothing manner, and seized Anne Louise by the arm, and marched her rapidly toward the house, throwing instructions over a thick tartan shoulder to Prudence, to David, and to Daniel.

They entered a hall of bare scrubbed boards, without a picture and without a chair. They passed through swing doors into an inner hall that was equally nude, and from which uncarpeted stairs mounted to a pillared gallery. Somewhere in its further gloom a door gave on to a little room which seemed to be mostly full of a round table with a red serge cloth with a woollen fringe. A large fire burned in a very small grate. The wall-paper was almost entirely hidden by sporting prints in wide black frames.

'Here we are! Here we are!' said Mr. Togarmah, throwing his shears and his spectacle case upon the table. 'We'll get your man. We'll haul in your carriage. We'll find your horses. We'll collect your baggage. We'll tell your brother. Nothing whatever to worry about! Nothing at all! . . . You drink your madeira — Where is the dom'd madeira, by the way?'

He pulled a red cord beside the fireplace with great violence; put a large hand on Lovell's arm with a fatherly admonition — 'We'll find you a spot of comfort, too, my pretty!' Cursed the late arrival of Prudence, and eventually left Anne Louise in a saddlebag chair over the fire, with the madeira decanter and a wine-glass on a silver salver on the table at her elbow, as well as a magnificent carroway seed cake which must have at least weighed six pounds.

'Hi, Tog!' called Daniel the Dom'd to the departing figure. 'I'm going to have — *moi, j'aurai* — a *morçeau* of *votre* seed *gâteau*!'

Without waiting for a reply, he proceeded to cut an enormous slice of the cake, and removed it and himself from the room, casting a shy but appreciative glance over his shoulder at Anne Louise as he did so.

Left to herself she sank back into the depths of the shabby but comfortable chair. She suddenly felt certain that the entire load of her responsibilities had been lifted from her shoulders by Mr. Togarmah Smith. That bustling gentleman — she was sure — would see that everything was put right; for he radiated efficiency, even if it were as startlingly noisy as his stunning tartan suit.

She poured out a lady-like ration of madeira — wincing as she tried to raise the heavy decanter with her injured wrist; sipped it; found fresh fortification in the rich sweet wine; drained the glass; meditated upon a second; decided against it.

She found that the small dark room, with its one window looking on to a flagged courtyard, was even friendlier than she had thought.

The mosaic of colour prints — black frames, wide white margins, and mainly bright reds and greens and browns — was, too, less revolting than it had first seemed. Even if Alken's 'Fight between a Bull-dog and a Prize-Monkey' jostled lovely aquatints of field-sports by Samuel Howett; even if a Rowlandson 'Milling Match' was cheek by jowl with the supernaturally exquisite race horses of J. F. Herring, and a bull-baiting print neighboured an engraving that showed his late Majesty King George the Fourth, when Prince of Wales, enjoying the pleasures of the chase in a most condescending manner. Anne Louise decided that violence of treatment was largely excused by variety of interest.

On one side of the fireplace was a cupboard with a two-three square bottles on top. On the other side — that nearest her — was a low bookcase. In a hurried review Anne Louise realized that the uppermost row was devoted to works on cookery, gardening, and horse management. The others carried a most remarkable collection of romantic tales and novels of fashionable life — to judge by their titles. Lying open on the floor beside her chair was Dr. William Kitchener's immortal *Cook's Oracle*.

Anne Louise would have conducted further investigation had not, at that moment, footsteps sounded on the bare boards without.

When Mr. Togarmah Smith entered, she was sitting meditatively before the fire, her magnificent pelerine and sadly damaged bonnet thrown upon one of the red plush-covered chairs.

CHAPTER VII

PROFESSOR TEMPEST'S ACADEMY

'AREN'T we in luck's way?' said Mr. Togarmah without preamble. 'Lady visitor to dinner — And it's three o'clock sharp, my dear! Very sharp! — on pork-and-onion pudding day! Pork, onions, suet crust! Smashed potatoes with lots of butter! Turnips! Marvellous!'

And he smacked his lips and shook his head in such an ecstasy of pleasure that his spectacles travelled down his short nose and were in imminent danger of falling off.

With this remark he opened a door at the end of a bare and resounding corridor, and ushered Anne Louise, with a polite little bow, into the best bedroom — a room so well scrubbed that it smelled of yellow soap and that silvery ribs showed along the grain of its floor-boards. There were no curtains and no carpet. A big bed with a patch-work quilt and a semi-circular canopy of green serge at its head — like the baldachin above a throne — faced three tall windows that were full of a view of high white clouds. A small shield-shaped mirror stood on a battered chest of drawers. That was all the furnishing, except for a mahogany corner washstand carrying a willow-pattern jug and basin little bigger than those used at a tea-table, a rush-seated chair beside the large clear fire, and an astonishingly prominent stoneware chamber-pot.

Mr. Togarmah surveyed the apartment proudly.

'I hope — I am confident — that you will be comfortable,' he said; and then his face fell.

'How did I come to forget the dom'd flowers?' he demanded, and pulled fiercely at the long cord suspended from a sort of metal question-mark high on the wall by the bed.

Anne Louise did not think that a posy of laurestinus would do much to alter the shocking emptiness of the room, but she gave him a smile —

'Please don't trouble!' she said.

'Trouble!' replied Mr. Togarmah. 'Trouble be dom'd! Nothing is too much trouble! It's a reflection on my housekeeping! A pretty young lady visits us — and it's not often that that happens — and I forget to have flowers placed in her room! Horrible! Monstrous!'

Prudence appeared in the doorway.

'The slate!' commanded Mr. Togarmah ominously.

The girl apparently had divined his need in advance; for, with a broad smile, she produced a large slate from behind her back.

As she handed it to Togarmah, Anne Louise saw that on its wooden frame were inscribed in ink in very large characters, the notifications, 'No. 7' and 'B.Spare R.' A slate pencil was attached by a string.

Mr. Togarmah read rapidly down the items which were written in a round hand on the lines incised across the slate.

' "Dusting" . . . h'm . . . "Windows" . . . h'm . . . "Fire" ' — he glanced at the grate — ' "Clean linen" . . . "Towels" . . . "Hot water" . . . "Warming-pan" ' — with extreme speed he ascertained that instructions had been complied with — '*And* flowers, dom it, Prue! . . . It *is* down! . . . Why no *flowers*, Prue? What d'you think you were taught to read for?'

He took the pencil, licked it, and underscored the word with a hideous squeaking of slate against slate.

'Flowers! Flowers! Flowers!! . . . Order, you see, my dear young lady! Order and organization! A slate for every room! A household slate for every day of the week! But what's the use of order and organization and slates, when you have a dunderhead like Prue? A fat-head — a feather-head — an empty-head! . . . Think of nothing but the lads, do you, Prue?'

He spoke very fiercely, scrubbed his iron-grey stubble very noisily as if he were a human rattlesnake about to strike . . . and then grinned in the most disarming fashion.

Anne Louise was undecided about the part she ought to take in such a conversation in her bedroom. She desired most furiously to undo the silk ribbons of her shoes — to loosen those elegant and abominable stays made by the fabulously expensive Monsieur Lacroix of Paris. The visibility of the chamber-pot embarrassed her.

But it was with a calm face expressive of the exactly correct amount of correct gratitude, that she uttered the formulae instilled into her —

'You have been most kind. I am greatly indebted to you . . . Flowers are beautiful — but quite unnecessary!'

She paused a moment, and then gave Mr. Togarmah a bow of polite dismissal — as she had been taught.

Wentworth — a self-exculpatory Wentworth, breathing fire and vengeance — was found at a hostelry in the town; horses recovered; yellow chaise brought into the refuge of a roomy coach-house; scattered baggage (as far as possible) restored to order and its owners; and Brown put to bed in one of the attics.

Before dinner Anne Louise had a long talk with her escort in Mr. Smith's little sitting-room, where the chill light of the winter afternoon drowned the bright colours of the crowded picture gallery in the blur of glassy reflections. The cold sheen contained within those countless black frames, indeed, gave Anne Louise the sensation that she was in the midst of a collection of small aquariums.

Amid that frigidity there was something almost indecent in the vehement gestures of my Lord. He stamped about the hearth-rug before the little fire, in his shining black riding-boots, tight-fitting buff breeches, plum-coloured coat with square tails and black satin lining, and low-cut waistcoat with an opening full of dark green neck-cloth arranged in the most sophisticated folds.

Anne Louise watched and listened for some five minutes. She told herself that he looked like an enraged fashion plate. Then she broke in on the fire-breathing —

'They've got the necklace! . . . They've taken all my money!'

She paused to let the implications sink in — implications which she herself had not thoroughly realized until she had thus voiced the sources of them: for she knew — once she had spoken — that it was as if she had said — 'They have put Lecques beyond my reach! . . . They have not merely robbed me, but delivered me into the hands of Uncle Leopold — delivered me to a blind bridegroom, and queenship, and babies by an unwanted husband!'

She added then, very quickly —

'Have you any money?'

'Money?' he echoed, as if the word were new and incomprehensible to him. '*Money?*'

'Money — for the journey,' explained Anne Louise impatiently. 'I have nothing left. Nothing at all!'

Only then was it borne in on him that the great adventure was at an end almost as soon as it had begun. He stood before her, uneasy and fiddling with the folds of his neckcloth, aghast at the situation in which he was involved. If that adventure had succeeded his father and aunt would have been cynically amused and secretly proud of his share, but most certainly neither of them would forgive failure accompanied by scandal. There would be no help forthcoming now from them when his creditors closed in on him. Escape was as urgent for him as for her.

'Have you no money?' repeated Anne Louise.

He shook his head —

'A few pounds only!'

'Can't you get any?'

'I can't ask my father or my aunt. That's obvious.' He paused — 'And all my fwiends are as hard up as I am.' There was not one, he knew full well, who would even trust him to the tune of a five-pound note. Nor any money-lender who would so much as look at his signature.

'We *must* do something! ... Can't you suggest anything? ... How much do we need?'

He calculated for an instant —

'If we found a boat in Swansea — *if!* — I suppose it would cost thirty pounds at least to get to Marseilles. Expenses here, and from Marseilles to Lecques — thwee people — post-horses, porters, ostlers, inns, incidentals — say ... well, say another fifteen pounds. Allow five pounds for emergencies, and call it fifty pounds, all told! ... If we have to charter a boat ...' He ended in a doleful whistle.

Anne Louise sat very still in her red plush chair, hands folded on grey silk lap. She stared through the window onto the small flagged yard and the whitewashed wall with the open door that revealed a constant bustle of plump maidservants. She was angry — with herself, for having been robbed; with Wentworth, for having permitted that robbery, for his over-much protest, for his failure to produce an immediate scheme of succour.

'Surely I could borrow?' she said at length. 'You know, I really am rich — very rich! ... Aunt Sophia says ...'

She paused. She remembered Aunt Sophia's very words, uttered during one of those delicious confabulations when she drank her early coffee (from a chalk-white handless cup, with cherries painted on it) in the old lady's bedroom — ensconced in a great elbow-chair, and wrapped in a crimson eiderdown beside the old lady's bed. She could savour that hot, strong, sweet coffee; hear that old thin voice reciting the list of great possessions: see through the stone mullions a tiny triangle of sea in a gap in the encircling hills — a triangle of deep blue sea which sparkled in the early sunshine as if it had been dusted with gold leaf ... She came back to the damp yard and the wall from which the whitewash was flaking off.

'Aunt Sophia says I've got a million francs a year. I *must* be able to get money *somehow*!'

A million francs — forty thousand pounds a year! Henry Wentworth looked at her appraisingly through his sandy lashes. There was something rather boyish about her, he felt, despite the delicacy of the profile that was outlined against the neutral background of the window, despite the long ringlets which held as many shades of gold as a field of ripening corn. She would need more careful handling than he had thought — he told himself — if the adventure survived the present crisis. But forty thousand pounds a year was worth some trouble!

'You aren't of age,' he said. 'You could not bowwow, except through your guardians. You certainly could not get any money without wevealling your identity.'

'I *won't* go back,' said Anne Louise with sudden violence. She rose and confronted him, hand on the mantelpiece. 'I *will* go on . . . Even if I have to walk . . . Alone! . . . Besides, we may recover our things!'

'I'm afwaid not!'

'Sell the carriage! . . . Sell my fur cloak — it's worth a lot of money! Why don't you make some suggestions instead of standing there saying "no" to everything? If you had been . . .' She broke off, walked to the window, stood there beating a light tattoo upon a pane.

'Oh, Anne,' he said reproachfully, and leaned in elegant dejection against the mantelpiece. 'Let me think for a moment!'

Over the fireplace, level with his eye, there was a lithograph showing a batsman in blue shirt and very neat pumps in the act of sending a cricket-ball crashing to long-leg. An umpire in top-boots and beaver hat was complacently regarding the mighty stroke. Something about his square figure reminded my Lord of Togarmah Smith.

Anne Louise turned. My Lord buried his romantic flaxen locks in his hands. He was ostentatiously in deep concentration. An idea had struck him.

His thoughts ran: Bare boards . . . pork-and-onion pudding for dinner . . . curtainless windows . . . whitewashed walls . . . camp-beds! True! — But, on the other hand, to all that Spartan simplicity some contrasting extravagance . . . a private gas plant such as old Lord Normanby's . . . carriage horses better than anything Blessington had in his hey-day . . . finest stables he'd ever set eyes on . . . And then the green chariot! —

In the coach-house he had seen it — a travelling-carriage which (he reckoned) must have cost all of seven hundred pounds bar the small change. Seven hundred pounds? Every penny of it! The carriage he had bought when Fantine and he had gone on their fantastic Continental tour had cost four hundred guineas in Long Acre, with three imperials and brown holland cover; and it was not in the same class; equally, it was not yet paid for.

He raised his head and, staring at the picture of the cricketer, he visualized the luscious vehicle in the coach-house at Judgment — lighter, and better sprung than any he had ever seen before; spokes of

wrought iron, dished alternately inward and outward; long springs
damped down, in some way which he could not fathom, so that they
should not drag against the horses; coachman's box protected from
the weather by a folding hood of leather with side-screens into which
were let circular glass port-holes.

A stableman had shown him with pride how a table unfolded from
the panel under the front windows; how its lid lifted up and revealed a
silvered wash basin; how a section of the seat could be pulled out so
that the owner of the fairy-car could travel reclining as upon an elegant
settee — all of button-studded green morocco leather.

'A mint of money it cost his Honour!' had said the stableman with
pride, rubbing off an imaginary spot from an immaculate panel with a
damp leather.

'A mint of money!' he had repeated. 'All 'is own design! . . . London
built . . . The lightest, fastest, comf'blest travelling carriage h'ever
made! With relays arranged his Honour reckons to go h'anywhere at
eleven miles an hour — day h'and night! . . . H'anywhere!'

'Eleven miles an hour! . . . Hey?' said my Lord.

' "Hey", sir? No, sir!' responded the stableman in high dudgeon.
'Supper here at eight . . . Breakfast in Brummagem at eight! Non-stop!
Through Brecon — through Hay — through Tenbury — through Kidder-
minster! H'eleven miles per *hour*! . . . Beat the coaches! . . . Damn the
turnpikes! . . . Blast the roads! . . . That's his Honour!

'Oncet a week reg'lar. Leave 'ere Wensday night — Brummagem,
Thursday! Leave Brummagem same night, and 'ere for breakfast on
Friday! . . . Wot a man!'

'Birmingham! Once a week? Every week?' commented my Lord,
dubiety in his tones.

'H'every bleedin' week,' had asseverated the stableman. 'H'every
blinkin' week! . . . Rain — hail — snow — or shine! H'every Wensday
night the same. After supper, at eight-thirty percisely, "Where's my
blarsted shay?" And then — "H'up, 'osses! H'u-up!" And away they
go, full tilt!'

Thinking things over, Henry Wentworth fancied that perhaps he saw
how something could be done. He faced round to the room. Anne
Louise was standing in the window looking at him. He spoke in a tone
of courteous assurance, whilst permitting his demeanour (he considered)
to imply deferential reproach for her lack of confidence in him.

'I believe I see a way out.'

'How?' demanded Anne Louise.

But he had no intention of sharing with others her gratitude for a flight successful. It was essential that he, and he alone, should take all the credit. Again he registered realization, with a twinge of annoyance, that she would have to be handled carefully.

'Leave it to me for the moment,' he said. 'And don't wowwy! It will be all wight!' . . .

They had dinner in a lofty room, so bare and of such desolated magnificence that Anne Louise felt as if they were a party of travellers who had halted by the wayside to picnic in an abandoned mansion.

Five tall mirrors — two of them cracked — stared bleakly out of tarnished rococco frames, across the width of the room, at five tall windows that were curtainless. The panelled walls might once have been delicate harmony in gold and white; now they were yellowed with age.

At the far end of the room a small and unimposing table was laid for dinner before a vast carved chimneypiece of stained marble, which reached up to the lofty painted ceiling — a ceiling so discoloured by time and smoke that Anne Louise could distinguish no one complete figure amid the obscure tangle of plump limbs and dim draperies. An iron gasolier thrust its way down uncompromisingly through the elegancy, and sprouted above the table into two arms with a naked burner on each.

The floor was carpetless, the chairs rush-seated, and the table spread with all sorts of oddments of clumsy crockery.

Anne Louise did not find her lean dark host to improve on further acquaintance. He had acknowledged his presentation to her with the briefest of nods. He showed no sign of having ever encountered her before, or of having caused her deep offence, or — indeed — of caring if he should have done so. He dropped into his place at the head of the table, and ate what was set before him in silence.

Togarmah, however, kept up a continuous flow of conversation on every possible topic — from the cooking of mackerel with onions and beef suet to the comparative merits of the two Pittmans at rackets, and the epic run of the Pytchley as recounted in the current number of 'Bell's Life': went off at a tangent about shooting, and enticed Wentworth into argument on the rival claims of flint-lock or copper-cap.

'I tell you, sir,' said Mr. Smith — raising his two-pronged fork and squinting along it as if it had been a fowling-piece — 'I tell you, sir, I saw old Osbaldeston bring down ninety-seven grouse with ninety-seven shots! *Nine-ty-se-ven!* With a Manton flint-lock! Beautiful! . . . Lovely . . . Show me the copper-cap-firing abortion with which you could do that! Show me!'

'It would have been a hundred if he'd had a modern gun,' said Wentworth.

'What did he want with ninety-seven grouse?' suddenly asked the master of the house. 'Was he employed as slaughterer by the local poultryman?'

Anne Louise, surreptitiously watching the saturnine face of Mr. Tempest, had imagined him withdrawn from his surroundings and the dinner-table discussion into a world of his own. She had been aware, a little before, of a quick glance that had assessed her indifferently, had passed on to Wentworth, weighed him too in the balance, and then returned to a further study of herself, as though the problems offered by the two faces had some close relation. After that, his interest had apparently lapsed. He had, in the intervals of service, drawn diagrams on on the cloth with a thin silver pencil — capped by an octagonal green bloodstone flecked with red. She noticed that he had long strong hands, very much scratched, and not — she thought — meticulously clean. There was no vestige of linen at his wrists, and his dark-brown coat was shiny at the seams.

'Now, Sep!' said Togarmah hurriedly, resting his knife and fork on the edge of his plate and mopping up the gravy with a crust of brown bread. 'Now, Sep! Are you going to be Radical *or* humanitarian this afternoon?'

'The man sickens me,' continued Tempest, disregarding the interruption. ' "Osbaldeston! — England's greatest sportsman!" All that that means is that he has massacred more birds, more foxes, and probably more horses than anybody else! The bloodier the record, the greater the sportsman!'

The Duchess of Limburg, eating — and much misliking — pork-and-onion pudding, was suddenly enlightened about the incident that had occurred earlier in the day. The man was a Radical! That was why he was so rude! All Radicals, she had gathered from Uncle Leopold and Aunt Sophia, were rude and revolutionary. She had not previously met a Radical. She studied him surreptitiously afresh.

Seven Tempest sat — or, rather, lounged — with his back to one of the mirrors, long legs crossed, and an arm hanging over the back of his chair. He half-turned his head at this moment and met her gaze directly, and Anne Louise recognized the strength latent in the long face with the cleft chin — a face that would have seemed even longer than it was but for the width of the temples and at the cheek-bones. Something of the sinister was added to its darkness by a lock of his black and ruffled hair falling upon the forehead in a curve that suggested a question-mark.

In the same way his nose had the faintest twist to it, as though it were interested in things that should not concern it; and his eyes appeared to be half-veiled so that they should give no hint of their secrets. Here — she realized — was a dominating personality. She imagined him to be old — in the mid-thirties!

'But where would the country be without sport?' asked Lord Henry, bending toward his host deferentially. 'Now, weally, where?'

Tempest had dismissed Anne Louise as a child, and a girl-child at that. Wentworth seemed to him to be the perfect example of hereditary uselessness. He let a cool appraising stare linger for an instant upon exquisite coat, marvellous cravat, breast-pins, rings, and gossamer-like watch-chain that encircled my Lord's neck and slid down to pocket in champagne-coloured waistcoat.

'The country would be without *sportsmen*!' said Seven. 'Noble or otherwise! Without bookmakers ... racecourse touts ... swindling jockeys ... horse-copers ... brutalized prize fighters ... and all the riff-raff that they keep about them.'

'There's other kind of sport beside hunting, shooting, and wacing,' protested Wentworth, fiddling with the folds of his neckwear. 'Games, y'know! Waterloo "was won on the playing-fields of Eton"!'

'Eton! Playing-fields!' said Tempest explosively. 'The devil it was! Waterloo was won *in spite* of the playing-fields.'

'Sep!' said Togarmah, turning to him so urgently that his spectacles travelled down his short nose and only brought themselves up with a jerk at the tip. 'Sep! ... Keep yourself to humanitarianism!'

Tempest took a small rosy apple out of the dish before him, and started to eat it — Anne Louise had never before seen an apple eaten unpeeled. He went on — 'Waterloo was won by men who had never seen Eton ... or a playing-field. By men who had never shot pheasants, unless they had poached them. By men who had never hunted, except for vermin in their shirts.'

It was not part of Wentworth's policy to fall foul of his host: he remained silent.

Said Anne Louise —

'But, after all, the generals and the officers had *something* to do with it!'

'Very little,' said Seven conclusively.

'I don't see how you can say that,' persisted Anne Louise, flushing at his manner — a manner only to be expected from a man who stuck pins into his coat lapels. What did he want with pins, she wondered.

'But I do,' remarked Seven dryly.

'Sep!' said Togarmah, rapping on the table with a black-handled knife. 'Remember your manners! Dom it! Remember your manners! I'll swear, ma'am, he gets more ill-conditioned every day.'

'I won't inquire very deeply into your knowledge of military matters, Miss Wentworth,' said Seven suddenly, after a pause in which Tog had spilled the salt — thrown it over his left shoulder with his right hand — and endeavoured to start a discussion on the hot-house growing of early lettuces. 'But I'll ask if you can tell me of any reasonable explanation, for instance, why the death-rate in the army in peace-time should be twice as great as that of the civilian population? In *peace*-time!'

Anne Louise could not.

'Does it not strike you as curious that this should be so? Very curious . . . considering that troops are men in the prime of life. Under discipline. Amenable to every kind of health and medical regulation.'

Anne Louise disliked his sarcastic tone. She disliked the pins in his lapels. She disliked his method of eating apples. She disliked his earlier rudeness. She made no remark, but did her best to look as if she knew the answer to his conundrum, but did not choose to tell. Her chin went up — a little: her nose went up — a little. She was about to address herself to Wentworth, who sat opposite her, the long dimming room behind him, when —

'I'll answer my question myself . . . It's because those in command know nothing whatever about the life of the common soldier. Have had no experience of it, and haven't enough brain to imagine it . . . Do you know how an officer gets his commission in the British Army? . . . He buys it! *Buys* it — just as if it were a plot of land, or a grocer's shop or an annuity! . . . If the young gentlemen who parade in corsets, frogged tunics and gold lace, had to sleep four in a bed; had to feed on stewed beef every day, every week — year in and year out — had to eat, sleep, live their private lives in one overcrowded barrack-room, and were flogged for misdemeanours, you'ld soon see a change . . . I'ld make every officer serve for a year in the ranks before he got a commission.'

'Great God!' ejaculated my Lord thoroughly startled.

A picture flashed before Anne Louise's imagination — of Wentworth sleeping four in a bed. She smiled faintly at the thought of that elegant head resting on such a crowded pillow.

Tempest saw the smile; misunderstood it. He drove on, expanding his theme, with wilful desire to irritate.

'And why not?' he asked. 'Why should one man be thought fit, automatically, to govern his fellow-creatures, just because he's been born to

117

wealth or rank? Why shouldn't a would-be officer be made to know what sort of life his men lead: a manufacturer's heir do a spell as an ordinary mill-hand: the landlord's son live in one of his father's slums, and a king-to-be go incognito to a charity school or have a week as a chimney-sweep?'

'But . . . '

'There's no "but",' said Seven. 'It's sense. If you've got to have the hereditary principle, then you ought to insist on an heir — whether it's to a throne or to a business — being made fit by practical experience to enjoy his privileges . . . Why shouldn't a monarch know intimately the common people he — or she — rules? There are many more than there are fellows with gold braid and yard-long titles, or fashionable "naughties" . . . I'ld have given Victoria a month in a cheap boarding-school, and a month as lodger with a washerwoman, and a week as seamstress in a Bethnal Green attic. She wouldn't be making such a hash of things if she'd only learned something about real life.'

'Hey!' said Tog, looking anxiously from one to the other of their guests. 'That's treason, Sep! You don't mean it!'

'Every word of it!' said Seven. 'You can't tell me that she hasn't lost the popularity she started with. Because she has. She's arrogant. She's obstinate. She's inconsiderate. She's ignorant . . . Can you tell me why she was hooted as Ascot? . . . Answer that!'

The short winter afternoon was closing. In the half-light the lofty room became yet colder, yet more grey, as though it were its own ghost. The fire in the cavernous chimney-place had sunk to mere red embers. Mr. Tempest sat at the head of the table, face and shoulder turned casually away from Anne Louise. He appeared to be staring through the chill oblong of a window at a colourless world.

'And did you undergo the tests you suggest?' asked Anne Louise caustically.

'I did,' said Seven without emphasis.

'Your father must have been a most unusual man,' she commented.

'Most.'

'Were you an only son, may I ask?' inquired Wentworth.

'There were six others that I know of. But of course there may have been more.'

The reply greatly intrigued Anne Louise. She turned it over in her mind without coming to a satisfactory conclusion.

'You see,' said Tempest in a tone of courteous explanation, 'one can't be sure of the total. We were all what you politely term love-children . . . My father was one, too.'

Togarmah, who had been pulling in a worried fashion at the astonishing spotted neck-cloth that lapped his shirt-collar, completed its ruin: he leaped to his feet —

'My dear young lady, Togarmah's my name, and Togarmah's my nature . . . You know . . . "They of the House of Togarmah traded in thy fairs with horses and horsemen and mules". Ezekiel twenty-seven! . . . Know more about horses and horsemen than young ladies. But I'm certain the right place for you is — bed. After all these adventures! Hot bath first . . . to ease out the bruises! . . . Hip bath shall be sent up right away.' He was pulling with immense energy at the bell rope. 'Then, by-and-by, a little hot supper in bed . . . and a night-cap of bishop. Last thing. Piping hot. Just one small glass. Made with a roasted lemon stuck with cloves. And port . . . *good* port. Splendid! Magnificent! Make you sleep like a trivet. To-morrow as right as rain. Righter!'

Anne Louise found herself being gently propelled toward the door where a smiling old woman with grey corkscrew ringlets and a rustling grey dress to match awaited her.

Much as she misliked Mr. Tempest, yet she would have been glad to hear more about this hereditary tendency to illegitimacy.

Tempest rose, as the door closed behind her. He took a lucifer match from a brass box, ignited it, and lit the hissing gas jets.

By the flaring greenish-yellow light, the desecrated room seemed to withdraw farther from them — as if it would escape their presence. Reality alone was about the table with the untidy litter of the meal. Wentworth had risen too, and was looking rather wistfully at a decanter of port that had just arrived. Seven permitted himself a moment's inspection of the romantic flaxen head and milk-and-white complexion of the young man.

He said with a brutal directness —

'That young woman is not your sister. Your skull structure is entirely different . . . Are you eloping? Or is she your mistress?'

Togarmah had returned from bowing Anne Louise to the door. He scrubbed a stubbly chin with a rough hand. His red face became purple — even in the gas-light.

'Now, Sep! Sep!' he remonstrated. 'That's a charming little gel! . . . It's none of your business.'

Wentworth drew himself up to his full height. He inclined his head slightly to Tempest in a sort of restrained remonstrance. He spoke in his most affected voice —

'I'm afwaid, sir, that my tale was not quite true! Your suppositions, however, equally are incowwect! . . . The young lady is — Her Highness, the Pwincess Anne Louise, Duchess of Limburg, niece and ward of the King of the Belgians. A cousin of Queen Victoria and welated to the Fwench King . . . I am in attendance on her! . . . I must ask you to wespect my confidence.'

The announcement was greeted with no display of interest whatever by the person to whom it was addressed. He did not even comment on it; nodded merely in the curt acknowledgement of reply to question; left the room without a word.

Not so Togarmah.

He was enchanted by this unexpected revelation of royalty and romance; beamed appreciation through the moons of his large and rather foggy spectacles; rubbed his hands with delight; poured out two brimming glasses of a port that was almost black; took up his stand, short legs wide apart, back to the fireplace —

'Now, my boy,' said he, 'you mustn't mind Sep! Don't mind Sep! His bark's much worse than his bite. Much worse! Tell me what all this mystery is about . . . Dom it, I *must* know! Lovely princesses . . . highwaymen . . . handsome cavaliers . . . just like a romance by Scott! Now you've said so much, you may as well spill it all! . . . Good stuff, this port! The veritable *black strap*! Real grip of the gob, mark my words! . . . Now tell me, What is Her' — and here he lowered his voice as one who speaks of Sublime Mysteries — 'Highness doing in these parts? It shan't go any further — not a syllable of it; not a comma!'

Wentworth's opportunity was thus handed to him; and he took it. He described graphically Highness's flight from undesired husband and unwanted throne. A colourful story of court intrigue, night escape, galloping horses, and chivalry.

He came to a stop; took a long sip of port as if to steel himself against the finish of the tale: concluded with a shrug —

'Well, there is no more to be said! It's the end.' — Put down glass with air of utter finality — 'Our goose is cooked! . . . It's all U-P! . . . *Poor* lady!'

'What do you mean?' asked Togarmah who had listened with the livest attention and (literally) an open mouth.

My Lord pushed a long slim hand into his breeches pocket — brought out a purse of red netted silk with tasselled ends — tossed it on the table, where it fell against the edge of a plate with a feeble clink.

'You can't,' he commented, 'go far . . . on' — slid the gold ring about its middle, and poured the contents onto the coarse table-cloth — 'on five sovereigns. Not eight hundred miles! Or escape from a King! . . . Those devils looted us of every other stiver.'

With unlighted cheroot revolving between his teeth, hands thrust deep into side-pockets of tartan jacket, stubbly chin couched between high points of collar, Togarmah cogitated in silence. Chuckled internally at his astonishing luck in being involved in such a happening of high romance. Gasped internally at the catastrophe which had befallen the heroine of this melodrama that was being played for his benefit — a heroine you saw close, instead of from the distance of the theatre boxes — a heroine with faintly inquiring eyebrows, the merest suspicion of a freckle, and clustered ringlets of every shade of gold.

'Dom it!' said Tog. 'Must see what we can do about it!' . . .

But nothing would have been 'done about it', had not Seven — hatted and cloaked for his all-night journey to Birmingham — chanced to encounter Penelope Lovell coming from her mistress's bedroom.

He had sat, for a short while, before the fire in Tog's study, after supper, grimly refusing every suggestion that he should help beauty in distress. He had lounged back — long legs stretched, crossed, toward the fire — in the shabby chair in which royalty in green pelerine had sat so bolt upright a little earlier.

'You are a sentimental old devil, Tog,' he had said, and negligently pushed a hot coal back within the bars of the grate with the toe of his shoe. 'Why am I to spend perfectly good money in helping a perfectly useless young woman to avoid something she thinks disagreeable? Money spent on her is economic waste. She is economic waste herself. What the hell use is she to the world? I'll guarantee her duchy — if she has one — would get on very well, indeed, without its duchess!'

'Come, come, Sep! Don't be too hard on the child,' remonstrated Tog, pushing his spectacles up on his forehead, and looking up from the canary yellow knitting on which he was engaged.

'She makes nothing,' continued Seven. 'She means nothing. She *is* nothing . . . except an unnecessary ornament on the machine of life. Why should she be a princess . . . a potential queen? Only because she was born into a cot with a crown, instead of an orange-box in Seven Dials. She knows no more about the life of the people she may rule, than I know about the duties of a midwife. Less.' Her whole purpose of existence has been to destroy wealth, and not to create it. The only thing she's capable of is child-bearing. And that she is jibbing against. Let her do her job. I'll not help her escape it! . . . Anyhow she'll probably change her mind to-morrow . . . or the day after.'

'She's very young, Sep!' protested Tog, blowing out a great cloud

121

of smoke, and letting a vast quantity of ash fall from the end of his cheroot onto his knitting. 'Very young!'

'Very young!' snarled Seven. ' "Very young" be damned.' I've been very young. You've been very young. But nobody came and handed me . . . or you . . . into a morocco-lined travelling-carriage so that we could gallop away from the disagreable . . . Hell!'

He uncrossed his legs, glanced at the black marble clock on the mantelpiece, and rose to his feet, looking down on his companion, who was sitting rather primly upright in an elbow-chair by the round red-covered table, a glass of rum and water by his side, and a perfect blanket of yellow knitting streaming over his knees.

Tog scratched his head thoughtfully with a very large knitting-needle.

'For all that she's a princess, and God knows what else,' said Seven regarding him affectionately, 'she's not a hundredth . . . not a thousandth of the use in the world that you are, Tog! I don't believe the little bitch could knit a solitary stitch to save her life. I'd like to open a school for the governing classes. Professor Tempest's Academy of Adversity . . . for Princesses and Peers: Low Life in Practice and Theory: Courses in Hunger: Special Treatment for Arrogant and Backward Pupils . . . Diplomas in Humility conferred!' . . . He pulled the long red bell-rope beside the fireplace . . . 'I must be off!' . . .

It was after this that he saw Lovell — a grave Lovell closing the door of her mistress's bedchamber with infinite care, her heart-shaped face illumined by the candle that she carried along the dark passage.

She came toward him while he watched, head a little downcast, ringlets shining in the faint illumination that moved with her through the twisting shadows.

When he spoke, she stopped suddenly and looked up — but looked up slowly, and with the widening eyes of a startled child.

He said in a low voice —

'How did you get *that*?' And nodded in a futile attempt to indicate to her the purple bruise (visible even in that dim light) which marred the delicate loveliness of her face.

She did not hear, or else she did not understand. And answered only in questioning him his meaning by the faintest further widening of her violet eyes.

'How did you come by that bruise?' he asked, slightly more loudly.

She made no answer, but lowered her regard to the little flame in the brass candlestick that she carried. Bowed as her head was now, the discoloration on her cheek-bone was more marked than ever.

'Did *they* do that?' he asked a trifle louder yet. 'Did those fellows manhandle you to-day?'

'No, sir,' she said. Her voice was very low.

He paused. A sudden idea caught him.

Regardless of the fact that her gaze was not upon him, he jerked his head explanatorily towards her mistress's door —

'Did . . . did *she* do it!'

Lovell did not hear the question, but looked up at him in an appeal against interrogation; whitened, and then flushed.

Seven misread that quick glance of alarm, that swift flush. He thought that they were the answer to his question.

'So she did, did she?' he said — but to himself; nodded, as though confirming that it was exactly what he had expected. . . .

He revolved the problem of Anne Louise for a considerable part of his journey; until, in fact, he fell into a deep sleep from which he only awakened as the carriage went swaying through the chilly dawn into the grimy outskirts of Birmingham — past drab processions of scarecrows trailing toward drab factories whose filthy windows were oblongs of greenish-yellow light, the smoke of whose tall chimneys delayed the oncoming day.

He continued the debate within himself.

A princess of a ruling house had fallen into his hands — a princess who might, furthermore, one day be in a position to exercise the profoundest influence for good or evil over the lives of a great and numerous people.

He reflected a little grimly on his own education for command.

The carriage swung sharply into a street of earth-coloured houses — two ribbons of brick punched with holes — under an earth-coloured sky. A shawled woman with a child waited to let them pass. Her grey face was barely a face at all: it was a skull lightly covered with some dusty tissue: her eyes might have been stones. . . .

Seven decided on the establishment of an Academy of Adversity. For the good of a Ruler-to-be — for the good of the Ruled-to-be. For the very necessary education of a future queen in consideration for her subordinates, by affording her practical experience of their way of life.

To prove his fitness for the governance of a few thousand men he had had six years of bitter schooling: to enable her to rule a nation she should be given — perhaps six weeks.

CHAPTER VIII

INTERLUDE IN AN INN

The snuggery of the Aleppo Merchant Inn was deserted, except by Captain Henry Pedder; was silent, except for the crackling of the fire, the ticking of the grandfather clock, and the beating of rain against the many-paned windows that looked down to harbour and bay — grey quays, grey sea, grey promontories, and grey sky.

The room was low, and square, and small. One side was entirely occupied by windows; that opposite, by a high-backed settle upon which Captain Henry Pedder had spread himself very widely; the third by a big fireplace eye-lidded by a blackened shelf crowded with pewter mugs; and the fourth by the door which was flanked by the grandfather clock and by a shiny horsehair-seated chair.

Dusty sea-porcupines, a turtle-shell, the long jagged blade of a sword-fish, and other marine curiosities hung from the ceiling. The floorspace was taken up by a gate-leg table on which were several empty glasses, a hand-bell, an ink-pot with pen projecting from it, and a large blue-jerseyed portion of Captain Pedder — arms akimbo — as he leaned forward studying intently a sheet of foolscap paper covered with crabbed laborious writing.

The captain had a vast square face, the colour of the rough side of pale leather, and a vast squarish sort of nose, so pitted by its pores that the observer would at once think of the surface of a strawberry. His head was entirely hairless, but the great dome of it — instead of being of the shining pink or the shining white usual to baldness — was of the same dull grey as his face. It was perhaps this baldness, as well as the pouches under his cold slate-coloured eyes, that gave him the appearance of being much older than he really was — much older than the mid-forties.

'*Five* sevens is thirty-five ... two shilluns and e-leven pence,' said Captain Pedder out loud, after counting the tumblers on the table. 'Therefore *six* glasses at sevenpence is percisely three shilluns and sixpence.'

He rang the little hand-bell.

'Seven penn'orth of brandy hot,' he commanded magnificently of the towzled female head that appeared round the door. 'Seven penn-orth, my little duck!'

124

'Yess, captain,' said the head, and forthwith vanished.

'That'll be the tenth time I said "little duck" to her,' meditated the captain. 'Six seven-penn'orths of brandy is forty-two pence . . . Divide by ten "little ducks" . . . that's fourpence farthing *per* "little duck" . . . fourpence farthing as near as kiss me!'

Refreshed by this abstruse calculation, he was giving his attention once more to the foolscap sheet before him, when the head of the 'little duck' reappeared in the crack of the door.

'Gentleman wants to see you,' she announced. Her shabby face took on a conspiratorial expression — 'Shall I say you're out, and not expected back till ever so? . . . In the four-ale bar, he iss!'

'Gentleman! . . . Four-ale bar!' echoed Captain Pedder, stiffening as he sat, so that he was quite motionless except for his slaty eyes. 'Gentleman! . . . What sort of gentleman?'

With a quick twist he reversed the sheet of paper, dipped quill into ink-pot, and began on the blank side in a very angular writing —

'My deare Mary,
'This wil inform you . . .'
Then —

'What sort of gentleman?' he repeated in a tone in which oil and vinegar were mixed.

The 'little duck' projected a bosom as well as a head through the door slit — the brown cotton dress that covered the amplitude was stained with sweat.

' 'Tisn't the Customs,' she reassured him with a sly smile. 'A tall gentleman. Dark. Sharp way of speech — he has. Yess, yess — fery, fery sharp!'

'Old Hen Pedder knows how to deal with the Customs Collector,' said he. 'But "fore-warned is fore-armed", my little duck! . . . It isn't the Collector or one of his men? . . . You are sure?'

She shook her head vigorously.

'Then don't you keep the gentleman a-waiting . . . If he isn't Customs, he may be customer!'

Captain Pedder gave a great guffaw at his joke, revealing a set of teeth that were very white and even, and singularly small. He was still rumbling with merriment when Seven Tempest was shown in.

'You , . . . Captain Pedder?' asked Seven, throwing off his shabby black cloak, and setting down a rather battered hat on the window-seat .

' "Fair exchange is no robbery",' said the captain. 'And who might *you* be?'

'Surname — Cash,' replied Seven, drawing the shiny chair up to the table, and sitting down. 'Christian name — Business!'

'Good enough names,' admitted the captain, eyeing him pretty closely, although the smile on his lips was still one of benevolent amusement. 'Pervided you live up to them! . . . Live up to your name — live up to your motto: that's *my* motto!'

Seven made no comment. He regarded Captain Pedder inscrutably — blue jersey stained almost to a green — black silk neckerchief knotted loosely about great throat — immense folded arms resting upon the table. He also noted the six glasses, the ink-pot, and the sheet of fool-scap.

'Captain Henry Pedder . . . master of the barque *Joan Dearlove*?'

'If your name's what you said,' returned the other in his rumbling slow tones, 'then that's me, mister!'

'Bound for New Orleans, Louisiana, with a cargo of slate!'

'And why not?'

'To say nothing of passengers!'

'Passengers?' repeated Captain Pedder: his cold eyes stared through the windows at the grey sea-scape, and the small black scrawls upon it that were ships tossing at anchor with naked masts. 'W-hoy, that's another pair of shoes . . . that's another pair of shoes!'

As he spoke he shot a swift glance at Seven from under lowered eyelids — a glance that was swift and bright, and unaccompanied by any visible movement of head or face muscle.

'I am not interested in shoes,' said Seven curtly. 'Neither do I care whether you are complying or not with the Passengers Act. All I want to know is: Have you got any room left?'

' "Any room left"?' echoed Pedder ruminatively. From his trouser pockets he produced a small brass box and a large horn-handled knife; he cut off a section from a dark bar of tobacco, on the palm of his hand; put it in his mouth and mumbled over it for some moments, until the yellow juice ran out of his mouth and down the runnels incised at the corners of his lips. ' "Any room left!" . . . And what might *you* know about it, mister?'

Said Seven —

'I know one of your passengers . . . Sarah Liddell. She . . .' he paused for an instant ' . . . is my . . . aunt!'

'Sarah Liddell!' said the captain after a moment's pause. 'Sarah Liddell! . . . Now that's downright curious. I ain't got a passage booked in that name, but I got freight. I got a consignment of furniture for New Orleans from a party so-called!'

He meditated on the coincidence, and continued — 'Not to tell you the word of a lie, in course she *might* be a passenger. And again she mightn't . . .' He had a burst of confidence — 'It's my soft heart that's done it! . . . Here am I with a cargo of Welsh slate! — Jesus knows what the Yanks want it for, but they do, just like they buy Caithness stone! Slate's heavy, so there's room and to spare in the hold. I got space. People wants it. I sell 'em so many square feet. They put their furniture — or anything else on board. And if they put themselves on top of their furniture, what's that to do with me? I got five foot six head-room in the hold. Everything *very* snug and conformable! . . . Nice little conveniences, too — if you take my meaning! Very nice, indeed! . . . And then, plenty of water, and firing in reason!'

Seven cut in —

'What's the fare?'

Captain Pedder removed the mangled remains of the quid of tobacco from his jaws. With a far-away expression he turned over the foolscap sheet in front of him — examined it.

'I got a nice little space,' rumbled Pedder, 'right aft. Up agin the bulkhead on the starboard side. Very snug! Eight foot by seven!'

'Eight by seven!' mused Seven. 'Eight by seven! . . .' And then, suddenly, 'How much is the freight?'

'Eight times seven is fifty-six . . . Multiply fifty-six by two shilluns . . . Is a hunderd and twelve shilluns — say — five pun' ten!'

'Five pounds,' snapped Seven.

Captain Pedder contemplated him. He drank a little of what once had been a brandy hot, and shook his head disapprovingly over its decline in temperature.

'Young man,' said he, 'do you know what's the lowest fare to Ameriky? . . . Well, I'll tell you. It's two pun' ten shilluns! Two pun' — ten — shilluns! . . . And two in a berth at that!'

'Five pounds!' reasserted Seven in his most uncompromising manner.

'Five pun',' said Pedder mournfully, 'is robbery! It's imposing on me! It's making me a laughing-stock! . . . Why, here am I offering you room and enough for four people *and* some bits of furniture — to say nothing of a New World, where money and land's to be had for the asking . . . And you say five pun'!'

He shook his head in an aggrieved manner: took a further sup of his tepid drink: regarded the grandfather clock by the door. In a semi-circle above the face was painted a very violent representation of a stormy sea; against this background there tossed — in accordance with the beat of the pendulum — a frigate under full sail.

'Five pun'! All the way to Ameriky, for as many as can crowd in, for five pun'! Why I couldn't even buy that clock for five pun'!'

'Why should you want to?' asked Seven. 'Five pounds!'

'Five pun'!' said Captain Pedder with a very heavy sigh, and examined his foolscap. 'Five pun' is one hunderd shillun'. One hunderd shillun' is' — he paused for some considerable while in deep calculation — 'is one hunderd and seventy-one glasses at sevenpence — as near as kiss me!'

He spat out a stream of yellow tobacco-juice on to the sawdust-strewn floor; sighed again.

'You've got the money?' — A cheerful chink of gold assured him — 'Cash, you said the name was?' — He took up the quill, squared his elbows, and wrote the word 'Cash' in one corner of the rough diagram at the bottom of the sheet. 'Lot B — Cash! ... Sailing day's Wednesday. All ornery freight to be aboard Tuesday mid-day.' He added meaningly, 'I shall anchor off Rhosmaen Cove after dark — if anyone wants to come aboard private-like.'

'I understand,' said Seven. 'Give me a receipt.'

'Receipt!' said the captain. 'Here it is! ... Five golden jimmy-o'-goblins! ... *Thank* you! ... Right as 'rithmetic!'

He took the five heavy coins in his left hand — shot them up a foot into the air — collected them in a huge grasp as they fell — and displayed them to Seven in his open palm, fat golden sovereigns, each miraculously arranged at the base of a thick thumb and four thick fingers.

'Right as 'rithmetic!' echoed Captain Pedder, not sharply as one who is certain of the axiom, but slowly, as one who meditates the conundrums that lie behind such a statement — slowly, as if a great intelligence were busied on other matters.

'Now, *in re* provender — I can find you a bargain! Two bargains! Real bargains — none o' your chandlers' muck! ... Real pork! Real flour! Freshly barrelled! Lovely and sweet!' — And Captain Pedder smacked his lips in ecstatic demonstration of the sweetness of his salted pork and his flour!

'Provide my own,' said Seven, rising to his feet, while Pedder shook his ponderous head in deprecation of the refusal of so handsome a bargain. 'All I want is the carpenter to knock up a bunk!'

'Bunk!' said the captain, as though astounded at such sybarite luxury.

'Bunk ... Shall I pay him or you?'

'Me,' said Captain Pedder in a flash of speech as swift as a swallow's swoop.

'How much?'

'Timber's dear,' calculated Pedder thoughtfully. 'I don't remember when it's been more so. Very dear! . . . Man's time — screws — nails — lashing! I don't know as it can be done for less'n ten shillun'!'

'Five!'

'Seven-and-a-kick!'

As Seven threw the money on the table, the door-latch clicked: both men looked quickly round.

A magnificent but seedy figure stood in the doorway — frogged purple surtout, shiny at the seams and buttoned up to the throat; yellow cane with red glass knob; shabby tall hat presiding at a jaunty angle over a palish face with a perky nose, twinkling eyes and an engaging smile. The hat was removed, to show a mane of fading yellow hair streaked with grey so that it looked like sand on which foam yet lingered.

'Ah, business! Business!' said the magnifico in a high cheerful voice. 'Ah, business! . . . I won't intrude, dear boys! Not for a moment . . . Come back whenever you're done . . . Pedder, my dear feller, my Small Lady would like a word with you. *When* you can find time . . . Now, sir, please don't discommode yourself for me. The Small Lady and I . . . '

The bright twinkling eyes had taken in the document on the table, the money in a little pile beside it. Their proprietor came farther into the room. He seized Seven's hand in his own — on which there glittered a large ring with a gold and ruby fire that was almost — but not quite — real.

'A fellow traveller, I do believe! Is it not so? A fellow traveller to the fabulous lands of enchantment! Excellent! Splendid! Permit me to shake you by the hand, my dear sir! . . . Vyvyan is the name — with two "Y's" — V-Y-V-Y-A-N. Horatio Vyvyan!'

'This 'ere's Mr. Cash,' said Captain Pedder after a pause, introducing the silent Seven with a jerk of his pen, and then scratching the nape of his neck with the nib in a nonchalant fashion.

'A *compagnon de voyage*?' demanded Mr. Vyvyan (pump-handling Seven's arm) with so British an accent that even Captain Pedder was able to understand and nod in assent, on Seven's behalf.

'Ah!' said Mr. Vyvyan enthusiastically. 'You, too, then are bound for Summer Seas — for the Garden of the Hesperides — for the Glory in the West! You, too, will linger watching the phosphorescent water lave the shining sides of our bark! . . . You remember the words of the poet? —

"Around the prow the waters bright,
    In circling rounds of broken light,
Are glist'ring, as if Ocean gave
    Her countless gems to deck the wave." '

'You have made the crossing before?' asked Seven, extracting his
hand from the other's clutch, and reflecting with some sardonic
amusement on his conception of the Atlantic in January.

'Not exactly,' admitted Mr. Vyvyan, whose eyes now ranged the
empty glasses on the table as if he were speculating on the possibility
of their replenishment. 'But I am by no means unacquainted with the
sea. By no means unacquainted!'

Seven folded his receipt and placed it in his pocket-book, and picked
up his hat without remark.

'*A reverdersi*,' said Mr. Vyvyan elegantly, making a sudden dash
at Seven's hand again. 'We shall look forward to your further
acquaintance, Mr. Cash . . . It will be a great comfort to my Small
Lady. Captain Pedder will forgive me, I know — but this is not our
usual style of travel. *Not* our usual! Luxury and exclusiveness has
been our keynote hitherto. Mixed company — very mixed, I believe.
Honest, splendid people — but, as my Small Lady was saying to me
this morning, *not* our class!'

'No?' said Seven.

CHAPTER IX

TOGARMAH FINDS HIMSELF FORSAKEN

It was a most domesticated scene that met Seven's eyes, when he entered Togarmah's room, on his return from interviewing the master of the barque *Joan Dearlove*. It was walled about with a glassy shimmer of fire-light and lamp-light and quivering shadow, reflected in the multitudinous pictures that were its background.

There was a tray on the red-covered table, with decanter, sugar-basin, lemon, and three glasses — one large and two small. A kettle sang gently on the hob to an accentuation of small spurts of steam.

On one side of the fire sat Tog, puffing clouds of smoke from a long cheroot, short tartan-clad legs crossed and stretched out, shabby slippers near the blaze, and a stream of yellow knitting proceeding from his busy needles. He was watching with deep interest — as well as listening to — Anne Louise.

Highness sat opposite Togarmah, tips of toes (only) showing at the hem of her strawberry-coloured dress, and shining head bent over the heavy book that lay open in her lap.

She was reading aloud the article on spontaneous combustion in the immortal work of the peerless Mr. Partington to an enthralled audience of two — for the boy Daniel squatted (open-mouthed) on the floor between them.

Seven stood unnoticed for a moment in the shadowy doorway.

The young voice went joyously on —

' "On the night of the sixteenth of March, 1802, in one of the towns of the State of Massachusetts, the body of an elderly woman disappeared from some internal cause in the duration of about one and a half hours" ... There! Mr. Togarmah, what did I tell you?'

Tog tore his gaze from the fairy-tale face opposite him, and looked wistfully at the bottle of rum on the table, as though to calculate how combustible its contents were. The homage to the princess expressed in his whole attitude — and in the manner of the small boy — irritated Seven beyond reason.

At that instant Anne Louise raised her eyes from the book, to receive due tribute to her knowledge; and was suddenly conscious of the arrival and of the hostile regard of her host.

'Good-evening, Mr. Tempest!' she said; and he found in her

greeting to him a subtle rebuke for failure to observe the common courtesies of life.

'I say, ma'am,' intervened Daniel with great interest, 'how much do you suppose would set a fellow on fire? . . . What would happen if one drank three bottles of rum straight off? . . . Wouldn't it be awful to see flames coming out of one's mouth?'

Tog had glanced up, nodded to Seven, and returned his attention to the subject under discussion —

'My poor old father drank a bottle of brandy a night for most of his life,' said he. 'I don't know that he was any the worse for it. Dom'd if I do! He got a red nose. One all over blobs. But he didn't explode.'

'They don't say anything about quantity,' said Anne Louise in her precise English, consulting the work of reference, and ignoring Seven. 'It must vary . . . Oh! — Mademoiselle de Thuars drank three bottles of wine and one of brandy on the day she died . . . Was that a lot? . . . There was nothing left of her but her right foot!'

'Ah-h-h,' sighed Daniel, ecstatically revelling in the horror.

Seven came to the far side of the table. He was still hatted and cloaked. He had left the door wide open, so that the inimical darkness of the passage behind him intruded upon the warm intimacy of the room. He stood, looking down, fingers pressed on the red tablecloth.

'Your Highness should arrange to start packing to-morrow,' he said. 'As little as possible.'

'Packing?' said Anne Louise, looking up quickly.

'You will have to leave for Rhosmaen early on Wednesday morning.'

She closed the book on her lap.

'Why? . . . Where's Rhosmaen?'

'You embark there. I've booked your passage in the barque *Joan Dearlove.* . . .'

She was on her feet. The book fell to the floor. She was very erect. She stood with her arms straight down beside her, so that her finger-tips touched the arms of the shabby chair from which she had risen — as though to assure herself of the reality of things.

'Mr. Tempest,' she said, and could not wholly control her voice. 'How *can* I thank you enough?'

' . . . In the *Joan Dearlove,*' repeated Seven, leaning a little farther toward her across the table. 'In the *Joan Dearlove* for' — he paused a moment — 'New Orleans!'

'New Orleans?'

He could see her searching within her recollection for knowledge of the port — for its nearness to that goal of her desire, the castle of

Lecques islanded amid the darker green sea of forest, in far-away Provence.

'New Orleans — Louisiana — America!' he explained.

She was utterly dumbfounded, and twice repeated the word after him, with differing inflexion. 'America! . . . America?'

He said very coldly, not looking at her, or at Tog — who had dropped his knitting and sat upright, regarding him over the top of his foggy spectacles with an air of suspicion —

'Yes! . . . America!' He hated it that he must give an explanation which was untrue although he knew it to be utterly sound. He went on, 'America!' Paused . . . 'Because — because you cannot possibly get to Lecques without being caught on the way . . . If you had gone direct at once — you stood a faint chance, a very faint one. But not now. I have thought it all out.'

'America!' said Anne Louise again, as one who spoke of some unimagined country upon the other side of the grave. 'But I don't want to go to America! Why should I go to America?'

He spoke slowly, as though to a stupid child; but would not meet her eyes —

'You've got too many royal relations.'

Then — because he knew, without seeing, that she looked at him uncomprehending, as at one who spoke in riddles — he elaborated:

'You can't go to Lecques now, and you know it, if you trouble to think at all. The moment you reach the Continent you'll have your Uncle Leopold — or his father-in-law, King Louis Philippe, or his nephew King-Consort Ferdinand, or one or other of your royal clan — on your tail. And if you hang about here much longer then your other dear relation, Victoria, will snap you up for uncle! Although she's young, she's very proper — judging from the newspapers — and wouldn't approve of adventurous females. You're not safe anywhere in Europe . . . That's one disadvantage of being so thoroughly royal, isn't it? So many important and blue-blooded relations ready to hound a young lady down!'

'Are you trying to be rude, Mr. Tempest?'

'Not a bit,' he returned. 'I am being sensible . . . If you don't want my help, you needn't have it. What happens to you doesn't matter in the least to me or my business — unless I invest in your escape. I'll help you on a cash basis — not from chivalry . . . You see I'm not a prince or a peer, but just an ordinary business man.'

'So it seems!'

' . . . And I want to see my money back. With interest! If you get caught I undoubtedly lose my money . . . Your only chance is to go to America — where nobody can touch you — and bargain with your wonderful royal relations across the breadth of the Atlantic. Your only chance!'

He now looked to see what effect he had had, and almost swerved from his intention before the tribulation expressed in her face. Her eyes did not leave him, and he could see that she endeavoured to read his purpose.

'But . . .'

'It's the only chance I'll give you. Because it is the only practicable one . . . This is a business proposition — your Highness!'

'Now, Sep!' said Tog, leaning forward to the kettle, 'be practical, of course. But, dom it! don't be just commercial!'

Two ladies argued with one another. The proud Duchess of Limburg fiercely rejected the proferred assistance — spurned the huckster who bargained about his miserable money. Anne Louise Elizabeth Caroline, a seventeen-year-old orphan, on the other hand, insisted on escape, no matter what the humiliation.

A third lady intervened. She was the pupil of Uncle Leopold, the scholar of Baron Stockmar, the student of Lady Augusta Wentworth. She coldly debated Mr. Tempest's theories; concurred in their accuracy; suppressed the duchess; soothed Anne Louise; said in a cold and business-like manner —

'If you will advance whatever is necessary, Mr. Tempest, I will undertake to pay any rate of interest you think fit . . . You would like me to sign something, I suppose?'

'Naturally,' said Seven evenly. 'I should expect it.'

Another thought occurred to her —

'But Lovell . . .! The doctor said to-day that she would have to stay in bed for another ten days at least!'

For the girl had developed influenza and a very high temperature within twenty-four hours of their arrival at Judgment.

'She can remain here until your return. If you let me know what her wages are I will see that is she paid regularly. Or, of course, you can dismiss her — and save money! . . . I should have to charge you for her keep.'

Tog paused in the midst of counting his stitches to snap —

'Don't be a dom'd lodging-house keeper, Sep!'

'But . . .' She hesitated.

'You mean,' said Seven, 'that you don't see your way to doing without a maid even on an incognito journey to America?'

Once again Togarmah came to the rescue.

'Don't be a plain fool, Sep! Do you expect any young lady to fancy a long voyage like that without having a woman companion? . . . Aren't I right, ma'am?'

Anne Louise nodded. Anger had made her almost speechless.

The explanation, however, appeared comparatively reasonable to Seven. He meditated for a moment, and when he spoke it was in a much less disagreeable tone.

'Old Sarah Liddell is sailing in the *Joan Dearlove*. That's how I got to hear of the ship. She was a servant here for many years. She is thoroughly reliable. You have already come across her. I could make some arrangement with her, if that suited you . . . There is no chance at all of the girl Lovell being well enough to go?'

'None at all,' said Tog who was undoing row after row of yellow knitting and cursing beneath his breath as he did so. 'Joe Morgan has been to see her twice to-day, and is coming again first thing to-morrow. There are,' he lowered his voice meaningly, 'complications!'

A door slammed somewhere in the darkness without: quick footsteps made an echoing approach on bare boards.

It was Wentworth. He paused in the doorway dramatically, a hand on the jamb. He did not, however, need to emphasize the fact that he was a messenger of ill tidings, for even in the lamp-light the pale locks showed dank with perspiration, and his pink-and-white face seemed more white than pink.

'They've found the trail!' he said in a hurried tone . . . 'Mr. Tempest, can I have a word or — '

'How do you know?' asked Seven half-turning, and leaning with one hand on the table, the other in a trouser pocket. He had taken off his hat and set it brim uppermost on the cloth: it gave an air of impermanency to the scene; it seemed to turn Tog's snuggery into the waiting-room at a coach-office.

'It was in Tregyb,' he answered. 'A fellow came into the yard at the Spenser Arms while I was there, and started nosing about.' He dabbed at his brow, and restored the handkerchief to the tail of his elegant riding-coat. 'Wanted to know if anyone had seen a yellow chariot. Described you!' — he nodded at the princess — 'Described me! Luckily it was dark! Everyone swore that they had never seen or heard of us . . . And came whining after me for cash when he had gone! . . . They cleaned me out!'

'That means there'll be a watch at every port in Wales, as well as England, by now,' said Tog. Took up his yellow knitting, and set furiously to work as though he hurried to make a cloak of invisibility for a distressed princess.

'There'll be no watch at Rhosmaen — because there's no port,' remarked Seven.

'Rhosmaen?' questioned Wentworth.

'Mr. Tempest proposes,' explained Anne Louise, 'to send us to America.'

Henry Wentworth had ridden back to Judgment in panic. The nearness of the pursuer had brought home to him the fact that not merely was the end of a gamble in adventure in sight, but that financial and social ruin were hard upon him. That the husky cockney voice, with its persistent questioning in the waggon-crowded courtyard of the Spenser Arms, was the first whisper of an inexorable doom.

'America?' said my Lord thinking rapidly ... It put him three thousand miles away from all his troubles: it gave him five — perhaps six — weeks in which to win the prize he aimed at ... 'Amewica!' said my Lord recovering his poise. 'Well, Mr. Tempest, you *are* a sportsman! A bully sportsman!' ...

Twilight was on its way when the carriage drew up at the entrance to Rhosmaen Cove — a rough track that wound quickly out of sight, downward between the wooded hills.

A little group had long been waiting, their horses held by a groom some distance up the road. The clatter and jingle of the arrival were still in the air when Tog flung his final words to Seven — flung his disapproval and his life of ease at the dark silent figure —

'You're a dirty blackguard, Sep,' he said. 'A dirty, dom'd, virulent bastard! And I'm dom'd if I'll stay with you. I'ld rather sweep a cesspool out in Hell! ... You think I'm your serf because you pay me? Well, I'm not. When we get back, I pack!'

Seven considered the square indignant figure — flat hat, flapping topcoat surmounted by shoulder-cape like a coachman's, square red face, and spectacles that looked as though they had been dipped in a London fog.

'Don't you ever clean your specs, Tog?' was his only reply.

It was Daniel who went leaping to the carriage door, and wrenched it open so that Highness (wrapped in a dark and hooded cloak) might descend.

His shrill voice came to the two men —

'I say, ma'am, old Tog is dressing Sep down! Like billy-oh! Not half ! ... And all because of you! ... Don't you really want to go to America? Why? ... Crikey, I wish *I* were going!'

Seven swung on his heel, and disappeared forthwith down the lane, closely pursued by Wentworth whose ideals in relation to finance had yet to be attained. Anne Louise followed at a distance, under the escort of Tog and Daniel, the latter talking hard.

Somewhere below them, amid the thin grey woods, a stream rushed. The cold sky was grown pale with the pallor that presages the darkness of night. Already a yellow light twinkled in one of the cottages that shrank back into the shelter of the gradually steepening hills.

As they descended the long slope of the narrow valley, the noise of the rivulet grew ever more vehement as though to assert itself against the increasing murmur of the sea.

They emerged at length upon a hill-side covered with gorse and bracken. Below them three or four cottages — with smoke drifting from their chimneys — fringed a pebbly ridge lapped by the tide, and faced a ruinous stone jetty that curved about a sort of backwater of smooth and leaden sea. The farther wall of the cove, barren and iron-grey, was scarred by an abandoned quarry; and a great slope of tumbled boulders appeared to threaten the dwellings below with avalanche.

A quarter of a mile out to sea lay a ship, her sails furled. Night came so quickly that, even as they descended toward the jetty, the vessel lost her sharp black outline against the grey of unshining water, and (when she swung a little) you could not say whether she had two masts or three; her geometrical rigging became a tangle — a blur.

Then a couple of pinpricks of light appeared on her decks. And — since she was bound for so far distant a destination, and already clear of shore — they served but to emphasize the ship's remoteness from the familiar things of the land — from hillside and woodland path and cottage, from Britain, from Europe. They gave her the remoteness of a star. . . .

It was quite dark when they came onto the jetty. The seaward wall had been breached in a couple of places, and a mass of broken masonry left strewn about the gaps. A clumsy derrick, long derelict, loomed in the night like an empty gallows.

'America!' said Daniel, straining his eyes toward the lights of the now invisible ship. 'I wish *I* could go to America, Sep! . . . I could easily work my passage. As cabin-boy!' He meditated on the joys of Atlantic and American travel — 'Rum! . . . Pirates! . . . Rattlesnakes! . . Red Indians! . . . Sep, couldn't I? . . .'

'No,' said Seven.

A boatman was awaiting them at the top of a steep flight of steps, at whose foot a boat swung gently.

'You for the *Joan*?' he asked. 'You'll be the last aboard.'

They stood for a moment, a dark group clustered at the head of the water-stairs, while baggage was stowed in the swaying craft below.

Anne Louise felt like a princess on her way to exile. She extended her hand to that loyal old courtier, Tog, in the subdued but dramatic manner in which she pictured Lady Jane Grey, Marie Antoinette, or Mary Queen of Scots proffering a farewell hand —

'Good-bye, Mr. Togarmah,' she said. 'You have been very, very kind . . . I shall never forget!'

'Good-bye, ma'am,' said Tog, baring his head and bowing low.

He could no longer distinguish Anne Louise's face: he would have liked to do so, that he might have a last glimpse of its youthfulness for his private memory, and a recollection of royalty in distress to impart to history. He held her hand: he fancied that, to be correct, he should have kissed it: he would have liked to do so: in fact he would have definitely kissed the small fingers, had it not been for Seven's cynical presence. As it was he cleared his throat, and added in the shamed manner of one who is unused to mentioning the Deity except in oath —

'God bless you! . . . *And* keep you . . . my dear!'

'Good-bye, Daniel!'

'Good-bye,' said Daniel, taking her other hand. 'I say, I *do* think you are — I mean . . .' Stopped embarrassed. 'I say, let me come out as far as the ship with you! Do! . . . I say, Sep, let me go out in the boat!'

He waited for no refusal, but was down the steps, over the gunwale, and sitting crouched in the bows on the instant.

Anne Louise bowed to Seven — a rather jerky small bow —

'I will see that you get your money back, Mr. Tempest. With interest! . . . With good interest! Don't fear!'

She turned away through the darkness. Wentworth handed her down the steps, and into the boat. With studied elegance my Lord did his performance, bending a little over the small figure in a manner that semed to imply courtesy and respect, and infinite capacity for protection.

Seven watched the ritual from the stair-head, hat pushed back, cloak flung back upon shoulders, hands in pockets of strapped trousers: watched with a faint twisted smile which Tog could sense though he could not see; as though watching the by-play of marionettes in a shadow-pantomime.

The boatman had brought out his oars; was already levering his craft away from the dripping water-stair, when Seven broke into sudden and violent action.

He sent his tall hat spinning before him down the steps — as though he had flung it into the ring; swung on Tog —

'Psha!' he exploded. 'I'll make certain we see the last of them!'

And was down the steps — cloak fluttering from his shoulders with the useless wing-beating of a fledgling bird — and leaping with a thud into the rocking boat. . . .

Tog, peering seaward from the jetty, could see nothing except two or three sharp points of light rocking slightly with the lift and fall of the sea: could hear nothing across the murmur of the water except, after a long while, the faint echo of a bellowing voice, followed by the creak of a windlass and the clank of a chain.

Many minutes elapsed. Then he caught the sound of oars in rowlocks — a whole progress of small noises: bump — creak — splash — grunt!

He went to the tip of the jetty. The wind pierced to the marrow through top-coat, yellow muffler, tartan shooting-jacket, flannel shirt; brought tears to his eyes and dewdrops to his nose. His hands, in red woollen gloves, were like so much ice. His senses were not so numbed, though, that he could not see that there was only one darker blur in the dark blur which moved so slowly across the blurred water below him.

'Hey!' he called . . . And his voice was echoed from either black headland — 'Hey!'

He saw the white smudge of an upturned face.

The boat veered from its course toward the rustling beach, and a moment later nosed against the landing-place. With immense deliberation the boatman made fast, shipped his oars, and stepped ashore, carrying a horn lantern which he proceeded to light.

'What the hell?' said Tog. 'Why? . . . Where? . . .'

'I'm sure I can't tell you nothin'. Inteet — nothin'! May pe thiss can!'

The man produced a crumpled paper from inside his hat, and tendered it to Tog, holding up the lantern with the other hand so that he might have light to read by.

'Going to see for myself how the experiment works' — the note ran, in an almost illegible scrawl, which Tog read half aloud, his lips shaping the syllables as he deciphered them. — 'I meant to all along. Have made arrangements for being away three months. I've given you power of attorney for anything to do with the house. The paper is with Brough. Have been getting soft, so have taken no baggage, not even a toothbrush. Write to me by fast packet to the Red Diamond agents at New Orleans: Garnier, Royal Street. You're a surly devil. — Sep.

'P.S. Look after Daniel.'

Tog took off his hat — scratched his grey stubbly head: took off his tortoiseshell-rimmed spectacles — re-read the letter again as if to make certain that the lenses had not misled him: then turned a slow gaze on the empty boat.

'Where's the boy?' he asked, as though he suspected the other of being a conjuror who had caused a passenger to vanish into thin air. 'Where's the boy?'

'Poy?'

'The boy you took out to the *Joan*, you dom'd fool!'

'Oh, him! . . . He gave me the writing. Yess, and told me not to wait. He said you'ld pay.'

The boatman omitted to explain that Daniel, having embarked for the shore after bidding farewell to the voyagers at the top of the accommodation ladder, had pressed the note and half-a-crown — all that was available — into his hand, and returned to the ship very privately (being aided by the darkness) via the fore chain-plate.

BOOK THREE

ATLANTIC SEMINARY

*

CHAPTER I

NIGHTMARE IN A FLOATING CELLAR

ANNE LOUISE ELIZABETH CAROLINE, Duchess of Limburg and Princess of Lecques, lay on a hard wooden shelf, and watched Daniel the Dom'd — that highly successful stowaway — peel potatoes by candle-light for to-morrow's dinner.

That ledge against the ship's side, in the fetid gloom of the hold of the barque *Joan Dearlove*, represented all her sovereignty — both duchy and principality. It was so narrow a dominion that she could only just lie flat in it. Beneath was a huddle of sacks of vegetables, amid which Daniel would burrow out a nest and curl himself to sleep of nights.

An old grey blanket was Highness's bed-curtain, as she lay there, wrapped in a crumpled cloak, head on hand, and bare elbow pillowed hard on a flounced petticoat that had once been white — a petticoat folded rather untidily over the volumes of Mr. Partington's invaluable Cyclopaedia.

The after bulkhead formed one wall of the cabin: the other partition was constituted by the high oaken back of a dismantled kitchen dresser belonging to their neighbours and by fragments of packing-case. They were screened from the passage-way by red and brown blankets, which were strung from dresser-back to bulkhead and swung to and fro with the rolling of the uneasy ship.

Daniel, tasselled Cossack cap much to one side of head, was perched whistling very cheerfully, by the foot of her bunk, on a case of preserved provisions — red tin pots of all sorts of shapes with the paint flaking off, and with grimy white labels announcing their contents as 'Prime', whether leg of pork, stewed breast of veal, giblet soup, or even round of beef. He was peeling potatoes with a clasp knife, immense vigour and great difficulty, by the light of a guttering candle in a glass-shaded candlestick on the top of a barrel of flour beside him.

Every now and again he would rise to his feet; balance himself to the roll of the vessel; drop a long peeling over his shoulder onto the uneven slabs of slate that floored their abode; and peer anxiously at it as though he were a wizard examining auguries of great import.

141

'It's an "A", Anne!' he declared triumphantly. 'That's the third time! An "A"! You can't get away from it!'

'Why do you want it to be an "A"?' asked Anne Louise.

He was suddenly overwhelmed with shyness; he temporized —

'What does "A" stand for?' he inquired in a low gruff voice.

' "A"!' said Anne Louise, leaning out a little from her bunk and studying the knot of brown peel, ' "A" stands for Animal — for Algebra — for Asterisk — for . . . '

Daniel reseated himself on his box. He took up another potato. His face became very red — very red indeed.

' "A",' said he — paused — took advantage of a moment's steadiness to slash away fully a third of the potato exactly as if he were sharpening a pencil; ' "A" stands . . . er . . . stands for Anne! . . .' paused again; and then said very fast — 'I wonder why potatoes haven't shells. Like nuts! . . . Bam! Hit a potato with a hammer; crack the shell, and there you are! No peel — no trouble! . . . I say! I bet Sep could invent a potato without peel! . . . I'll bet a thousand pounds he could! . . . A hundred thousand pounds! A million pounds!'

'You like the name "Anne"?' said Anne Louise, ignoring the wager.

Daniel, with the air of one who had already committed himself far enough, nodded in an embarrassed manner, and tackled the job on hand with such vigour that he narrowly missed losing the end of his left forefinger.

Anne Louise, in silence for a few moments, watched the earnest face bent to its task in the faint yellow radiance that quivered in the small cube of airless dusk.

'Daniel,' she said in a low voice, 'if I had some potato peel — and threw it over my shoulder — I know it would come out "D"! . . . Come and sit here and talk to me.'

Seven Tempest, squatting in the alley-way beyond their frontier of red and brown blanket, heard just the murmur of their talk, as he peered along the reeling, reeking, dimly-lit cellar that was the hold of the *Joan Dearlove* — a cellar full of confused wailing and tormented shadows cast by the flames of a score of candles; a cellar long and narrow, and so low that he could not stand upright in it.

It was a cellar that rolled; nosed gently downward; surged gently upward; and at the same time quivered gently, so that every component of its structure, and everything within it, vibrated individually as though to emphasize the impermanency of their association.

The alley-way was broken only by the steep ladder to a scuttle —

faintly-illuminated horn lantern hanging from topmost rung — and by the great shafts of the masts.

On either side of this lane was a jungle of furniture inhabited by the owners — dismantled dressers and tallboys, in the shelves and drawers of which small children slept uneasily at night; dower-chests that served, too, for sleeping places; chairs lashed together and piled as high as the deck above; curtained poster-beds — with abbreviated posts — that in themselves constituted private cabins; heavy tables which made two-storey apartments; and a whole medley of boxes and barrels and shapeless lumps of household goods.

It was not merely a floating cellar, but a cellar that might well have been the warehouse of a second-hand dealer.

None of the other three-and-forty passengers was visible. Old blankets, quilts, coverlets, curtains — in various stages of fading and raggedness — had been used in pitiful attempts at privacy. Everywhere, however, there was the sound, the smell of humanity.

Above the noises of the ship and the sea and the creaking struggle of furniture to escape its rope lashings, there rose a hive-like hum of talk — a hum diversified by the shrillness of a violent quarrel between two elderly women who shared a square of deck-space with three elbow chairs, a grandfather clock (on its side), a chest-of-drawers, a number of barrels of provisions and one mattress; a hum diversified by a low and continuous moaning from someone living in a curtained bed with a carved oak canopy on which were repeated fat cupid faces, the intertwined initials A.H.-E.H., and the date 1613; a hum diversified by the whimpers of a baby, and by the ceaseless retching of a child.

Seven rose to his feet, and stood listening, with head stooped to avoid the deck beams above. He was in his shirt-sleeves, and his strapped trousers were incredibly creased, for he had slept in them now for four days.

Without a by-your-leave he lifted a corner of the filthy patch-work quilt that served as screen to the neighbouring lair, and poked his head within.

In the narrow and shadowy cavern between the upper and lower halves of the dresser on one side, and an up-ended table and stack of corded boxes on the other; amid a huddle of untidy packages, were a couple of young women, two babies, and a child.

One of the girls lay curled up in sleep, face buried in arm, dark hair spread about her.

The other — a prettyish, dirtyish goblin with wide mouth and wide snub nose — sat, feet folded under her, on a blanket between the legs of the table. The bodice of a green-and-white striped dress was wide open, and two goblin babies sucked at her dingy breasts. Her weary head joggled to and fro against the underside of the table-top. Her eyes were half-closed, and she swayed with the rhythm of the ship as if she had been a stuffed doll.

A candle, down to its last inch, flickered in a saucer-wide morass of grease on the broad ledge of the dresser. One of the long drawers had been pulled out a little, and served as cot for a goblin child of two years old — a child with a wizened face that was yellow and blue; a child that retched, and whimpered weakly, and retched again more violently, and shuddered convulsively in the filthy shawl that wrapped it, and then started the horrible sequence afresh.

'Hey!' said Seven sharply. 'Hey!'

The goblin mother's eyes widened for a second: the heavy lids fell again.

'Hey!' repeated Seven.

'Yess, misster?' The response was almost automatic.

'D'you want that child to die?'

'T'issn't mine,' said Goblin, and shrugged her shoulders a little more snugly into the angle of the table. Her head nodded forward, and her arms dropped into her lap so that the goblin babies slid down from the nipples to which they had adhered, and set up a thin hungry wailing.

'Listen to me, you bitch!' He leaned still farther into her grotto of furniture; shot out a long arm, and suddenly tweaked her by the nose. She did not cry out or endeavour to beat him off; she just awoke and stared at him unblinking, as if such rough arousing were well within the normal range of her experience.

'Wake up!' said Seven violently. 'If you don't do something about it, that child's going to die! . . . It's been going on like this for four days.'

The goblin mother's eyes travelled from his face to the drawer — which might as easily have served for a baby's coffin as for a cot; thence to the sleeping girl stretched at her feet.

'T'issn't mine,' she reiterated. 'T'iss Megan's.'

'Wake *her* up, then,' commanded Seven. A lock of dark hair had fallen across his forehead and made even more saturnine the long dark face he bent toward her.

'T'wouldn't be no use,' she said, lifting the babies up to her breasts again, and eyeing him. 'Megan's tiddley. She's been tiddley all day.' — He noticed then that the sleeping girl held an uncorked black bottle clutched closely to her body; that she was breathing stertorously, with little catches of the breath and moans. — 'And Tom's tiddley, too!

Drunk as a duke! He's with Ira. The pair of 'em couldn't stand an hour ago. Drunk as two dukes!'

'Tom?'

'Tom — he's my man!' She paused; added in a voice that was wearily indifferent, '*And* her's — sometimes! When Ira takes a fancy to me. But I'm not going to look after her bastards for her — no, misster! *No*, misster!'

'You won't, won't you, you dirty little rump-faced whore?' said Seven. He thrust the curtain aside, and stood for a moment in the narrow opening brooding over the lair and its occupants, his head bowed so low to avoid the deck beams above that his long chin rested upon his chest.

'No!' repeated the rump-faced whore. She had become fully awake. She now regarded Seven with lustrous eyes. She shook her tangled red head in a gesture that implied not merely refusal but also regret at having to proffer such refusal to so compelling a personality. 'No, misster! I've enough trouble with my own bastards — yess, indeed! She can look after hers. *And* the one she's got coming!'

But Seven was not looking at her. He was looking at the drawer and at the dirty and ragged bundle within it — a bundle that writhed feebly, and moaned feebly, and retched feebly, and all the time was made to slide up and down its wooden crib (like a large shuttle in a small loom) by the sullen rolling of the ship.

'That brat'll die,' said Seven, and advanced one foot within, treading on the dark red skirt of the sleeping girl.

He pulled the protesting drawer farther out; leaned over — keeping his balance with a hand upon one of the projecting legs of the table, and extracted the child. . . .

Daniel was saying earnestly —

'You know, Anne, I *do* think you . . .' as Seven entered the sanctuary of Highness of Limburg and Lecques, unheralded and uninvited.

The small boy sat by Anne Louise, hat at feet, yellow hair all ruffled, hand on the edge of her bunk, gaze fixed ardently on her young kind face.

Seven lurched in; seated himself next the candle on the case of provisions whereon Daniel had been perched, paring potatoes, a few minutes before.

Anne Louise's eyes regarded him frostily for an instant — turned away to smile on Daniel — found her admirer gazing open-mouthed at that tall dark man who sat so quietly and carefully unpeeling the dirty bundle which lay upon his knees. Daniel's astonished interest was so great that she was compelled to watch, too.

Seven stripped off a sodden shawl that was grey with dirt, and dropped it in the passage-way between the cases, which, set against the walls of their home, served for settee, table, dressing-chest, and so forth.

He unwrapped another and still dirtier shawl.

A wizened filthy creature — that seemed to Anne Louise's horrified regard to be a fantastic travesty of childhood — lay on his lap. A wizened creature clad in one short garment whose filth was stained brown and green with excrement. A creature whose strength was so spent that its most violent paroxysms could only make it shudder.

He took off the garment.

Anne Louise could not look upon the hideous nakedness of that goblin body quivering between life and death. She turned her face away because she felt that even the terms Life and Death would be wrongfully used about such a Thing. That little huddle of skull and skeleton — from which it needed no imagination to believe that the flesh had already begun to shrink — could never be acquaint with Life and Death, only with Existence and Dissolution.

Seven noted the averted head. Some sixth sense told Anne Louise that he had done so, and of the flicker of scorn with which he made observation.

He enveloped the little body in a clean towel which Daniel got for him from a bundle under the bunk, and sat holding it to him in the crook of his left arm — clutched awkwardly perhaps, but still clutched so that it rode in harmony with the pitching of the vessel as if in a rocking-chair.

'Get the medicine-chest, Daniel! It's on the case next you,' he said in a quiet and matter-of-fact voice. 'Put it beside you ... That's right! ... Get out the measuring glass! ... Right! ... *Now* the first — no, the second bottle in the front row ... *Second* from the left! ... Second! ... Your other left, you fool!'

' "A.V." on the label, Sep?' inquired Daniel, holding a largish round bottle toward the light.

It was full of a golden brown liquid.

'Put in a finger's breadth! ... Right!'

Seven stared at the square mahogany case. The lead-foil lining had already begun to go green. The roughly finished glass stoppers of the phials in their rows looked like the acid-drops of his early childhood set on edge.

'Find me *Tinct. Op*.! Or *Op. Tinct*. ...! In the back row ... Show me! ... Now pour out one drop! ONE drop!'

'Same glass, Sep?'

'Yes, you fool ... Not a bucketful ... Not — Christ Almighty, it's not for an elephant! ... Pour it away! ... When I say one drop, I mean one drop!'

Anne Louise came to the rescue of Daniel. She leaned bare-armed out of her bunk —

'You hold the glass, Daniel. And give *me* the bottles — "A.V." first!'

She decanted the right amount of golden-brown elixir into the glass, and one drop — and one alone — of a sweet-smelling dark brown fluid which sank heavily into the gold, and was only dissolved in it after long stirring with a silver button-hook.

After that Highness remained — chin on hand — a spectator (and a patently interested spectator!) of proceedings.

One drop at a time, between the little creature's retchings and shudderings, Seven poured into the blue-lipped mouth. Half a drop! ... Some of it returned in a trickle that dribbled over chin onto scarecrow body, and onto the arm that enfolded it ... More and more it retained ... Its quivering died away.

Under his direction Daniel made a pap of powdered biscuit moistened with wine. He fed the child with the clammy mixture out of an old iron spoon. Presently it was eating almost greedily, so that its tiny lips made a smacking noise, and its stick-like arms reached out to the spoon as though to hasten progress.

And then it became tired; it drowsed; it dozed; it slept.

With soft rags wetted with spirit from a bottle in the medicine-chest, Seven proceeded to wash the grime from off it, a few inches at a time, very thoroughly and yet so gently that it did not stir.

Then he cropped the matted black hair with a pair of surgical scissors, dropping the congealed locks on to the dirty wrappings at his feet; cropped to the point of baldness.

'There's a woman asleep on the deck next door, Daniel,' he said very quietly as he cleansed the almost naked skull as best he could.

'Yes, Sep?'

'Take those stinking rags from the floor — don't spill the hair off them; *we* don't want lice! — and drop them on her face, Daniel! Put them on her face just where they are wettest and juiciest! ... Roll up your shirt-sleeves first ... Give the bitch back her own child's filth.'

'On her face, Sep?' said Daniel with fearful joy, eyeing the stained, damp, reeking rags.

'On her face.'

'My eye! I'll bet she'll be wild! I'll bet a hundred pounds she will! I'll bet a thousand pounds! Wouldn't you, Anne?'

He rolled up his sleeves. A grin of profound anticipation widened his mouth. . . .

Seven sat for a long while afterwards holding the child cradled in his arms, and whispering to it — with head bent very close — as though to make certain that Something very distant should hear and should obey.

Anne Louise strained to make out what it was that he murmured, while guardedly she watched the shadows and light of the candle flicker on his strange dark face. She noticed the spotlessness of his white shirt, open at the neck, and without collar. Since he had brought no baggage with him, she imagined that somehow he must wash it every day — Daniel's shirt, perhaps, as well.

He seemed as imperturbable and lacking in self-consciousness whilst he rocked and crooned to the sick child, as he had been four nights ago when a furious Wentworth — having viewed their accommodation in the *Joan Dearlove* — demanded explanation. Anne Louise was proud to think that then she had vied with him in calmness — had said no word where (she knew) he expected outburst; had betrayed no emotion or surprise by even the flicker of an eyelash. She knew, though, that she could not have sat there thus unconcerned nursing a sick child, willing it to sleep by whispered idiocies, before unfriendly eyes.

Heavy feet trampled overhead — clattered on the top rungs of the ladder.

A great voice bellowed —

'Lights out! . . . All lights out!'

Seven rose to his feet, the child in his arms.

'It can't lie out on the bare deck with me,' he said, not even looking at her. 'You'll have to give it house-room.'

Before Anne Louise could reply, he had placed the towel-wrapped bundle in the bunk beside her — touching her. She flinched involuntarily from the contact, and knew at the same instant that he had observed the movement with a cool contempt.

As he turned to go, hand on the curtain of blankets, he added —

'See that it keeps warm. If it wakes during the night, give it the remainder of the dose . . . Blow out the candle, Daniel, and come along.'

Words of furious protest rose to her lips, but were still un-uttered when the light was extinguished and she was left, propped on an elbow, staring through the darkness at the invisible bundle by her.

Seven shepherded Daniel out; it was a rule that the boy should withdraw for a quarter of an hour or so at bedtime, and return after he had ascertained that Anne Louise had settled for the night; just as he would disappear in the early morning, and Highness would awaken in the twilight of her domain — a twilight so little removed from darkness that nothing except vague shapes could be perceived in it — to hear freshly-drawn sea-water slopping to and fro in the brown leather bucket in the middle of the floor.

Anne Louise strained away from the changeling in her bed, but could not escape the touch of it against her, or escape the small panting breath that rose almost directly into her face. It was a filthy, sick, and verminous creature that lay under her blankets and her cloak — she was bedded with an Obscenity! When Daniel fell asleep she would slip out of her berth and try to doze on one of the packing cases.

And then — perhaps it was because of the faint gasp that it gave or because of some flutter of its miserable little limbs — she suddenly felt a wave of shame sweep over her — shame that something helpless and unhappy should cause her disgust.

Resolutely she drew the child to her; gently raised it a little so that its head — its shaven naked skull — was cradled on her bare arm; tucked her coverings more securely about it.

She lay awake long after Daniel had stolen in and curled himself up in his lair among the potatoes, meditating about the child — whether it had a name; which of the two sluts she had seen was its mother; what its past was; what its future would be. She meditated, too, upon the ship — not as a ship, a thing that swung gallantly on the long swells between the loneliness of the sea and the loneliness of the stars, but as a mad pantechnicon infested with strange creatures from worlds entirely other to her own.

The feeble light in the lantern hanging under the scuttle sent no glimmer into the darkness that beset the dominions of Limburg and Lecques. But the ruler thereof could visualize everything within the borders — the small carpet-bag at the foot of her berth, ornamented with a pattern of red cabbages on a green background; the knots in the wood of the chest that was full of red tin pots; and the rusting hoops of the tall flour-barrel next door to it, where the candle usually stood. Beyond the flour-barrel was an equally large cask of salt beef topped — roof-high — by a big sack of ship's biscuit resting on a case of wine. Amidst them all were wedged, somehow, a roll or two of spare blankets, a keg of butter, a jar of pickles, and various cooking utensils.

On the other side, backed by the rough bulkhead which cut off the after portion of the hold, was a similar rank of baggage and stores. By the head of her bunk was the battered wooden box, studded with brass-headed nails, with which she had been made to replace her own coroneted trunk. Her dressing-case stood on it; and, above, a small mirror hung from a nail. A side of bacon bruised its fatness by constant bumping against the bulkhead from which it was suspended over a couple of chests of provisions.

What provender, too! The supplying of it had fallen to Tog's department; had involved the most immense discussions and elaborate calculations. Anne Louise had not even known that ocean voyagers carried their own stores with them, but Tog said that he had heard that it was not unusual; and she had been drawn into the council that followed a solemn progress through kitchens, larder, still-room, store-rooms and cellars.

'Food for three people for six weeks! Sep did say three people! I suppose he means to find some woman for you, after all,' Tog had said, pulling up the chair in his boudoir-gallery and pushing his short legs a little nearer the fire. 'Now how does Sep know it will be six weeks? How does anybody? Wind and weather won't worry about Sep's theories, dom it! May be seven weeks — and then where would you be, my dear? Where *would* you be?'

Anne Louise had not known.

'Let's say seven weeks ... No, call it eight! Must have a margin, dash my wig! ... That'll be food for fifty-six days for three people. Same as finding a dinner, dom it, for — for a hundred and sixty-eight. Now we've got something to work from! Nothing like method, my dear young lady.'

And so proceeded to have packed a vast supply of everything — from oatmeal, rice and sugar, to two kinds of tea, ginger, and green tomato chutney. One of the household slates was even promoted to a temporary home on his mantelpiece, with the words 'Atlantic Voyage' inked on its frame, so that note might be instantly made of any new idea for the comfort of the travellers. Seven had displayed no interest in these preparations at all, except on the night after their goods had been sent away for shipping — the night before departure — and Tog had made the appalling discovery that they had been given no supply of cinnamon or carroway seed.

'Cinnamon!' Seven had suddenly flared up. 'What the hell do they want cinnamon for? Or carroway seed? ... They're not a posse of elderly maiden ladies travelling in the family chariot from Kensington to Harrogate with two lap-dogs, a parrot and a folding night-commode! . . . They can do without their carroway seed. They've enough of everything else to last them for a year. More!'

'Now, Sep!' replied Tog severely. 'You've got to allow for contingencies. Margins, my boy, margins!'

'Cinnamon . . . .!' reiterated Seven sarcastically, leaning back against the mantelpiece, and staring into the cloud of cigar smoke in which Tog surrounded himself. 'Cinn . . .'

'Ugh! You and your dom'd night-commodes, and your dom'd cinnamon,' broke out Togarmah in dudgeon. He seized a book from the shelves beside him; turned over the dog's-eared leaves with a wet forefinger; read out —

' "Bread and flour for an adult — Six pounds each per week." And that's precisely what I've allowed for.' Cast his eye over the pages —

' "Butcher's meat — three-quarters of a pound per diem!" '

'Cinnamon!' said Seven.

' "Cheese",' continued Tog, ignoring the interruption. ' "Half pound per week." Eight half-pounds is four pounds. Multiply for three people, and you have twelve pounds. And *that's* what they have got!'

'What's your authority?' asked Seven.

Tog, without deigning verbal answer, held up the book so that its title — 'A New System of Practical Domestic Economy' — was visible. He went on —

' "Butter — three-quarters of a pound a head." That's eighteen pounds all told. "Sugar — " '

'What about an eighty-pound chest of preserved stuff? — Big pots! Little pots! Round pots! Square pots! '

Tog paid no attention, beyond rubbing his bullet badger-grey head with his disengaged hand in an irritated manner —

' "Sugar — three-quarters of a pound each." Same total as of butter.'

'Cinnamon?' said Seven.

' "Candles . . ." '

'Cinnamon?'

'Rot your cinnamon!' ejaculated Togarmah in a passion, jerking himself up in his chair, his spectacles down his nose, and the book on to the floor. 'Cinnamon, me foot!' . . .

And now —

Dear Tog! Highness, lying in the hard bunk she shared with the scarecrow baby, thought of what she would do for Tog when she was free of Uncle Leopold and the smelly ship and Mr. Seven Tempest and Henry Wentworth. He should stay with her, for as long as he liked, and hunt boar in the forests of Lecques, or shoot wild duck in the marshes where the Lecques stream oozed into the sea.

She must do something, too, for that cheerful old mountain of a woman, Sarah Liddell, who had sat beside her administering comfort and brandy during those first two dreadful days of sea-sickness; who radiated good sense and protection, and still appeared to treat her capacious bosom as a store-cupboard.

The hive-like noise of humanity within the hold of the *Joan Dearlove* had died down to a low murmur — down to the sound of uneasy stirrings, an occasional half-strangled breath, a groan, whispers, and the creaking of the ship and of all its crazy contents as they wrestled with the lashings that kept them fast. Someone nearby fumbled about their makeshift cabin, and cursed in a low voice.

The ship's bell sounded: six strokes. Its muffled clangour reminded her of the chapel bell at La Cadière, that little village almost submerged in a golden glade near Lecques.

She closed her eyes tightly. She saw again the small whitewashed church, faded Virgin in blue robe over the west door; small whitewashed green-shuttered houses flanking it and the stone-rimmed well; leafy canopy of tossing trees roofing them all in, so that it seemed like a brightly lighted scene in a toy theatre. In only a moment the church door would swing slowly open, and the oft-seen procession would emerge — youngest Negrel in lace-fringed cotta, enormous boots peeping out from under red cassock, proudly holding aloft the brass processional cross studded with glass rubies; the still smaller (but equally proud) Fraissinet swinging the heavy censer; a dramatic pause — thin wisp of scented smoke mounting to the rustling leaves — then Father Pinaud, very red-faced, grave, fat, short, and bearing before him in his two hands, with intent reverence, something that shone. . . .

The child in Anne Louise's arms awoke; whimpered; retched; was sick.

CHAPTER II

A MATTER OF PECULIAR DELICACY

THE *Joan Dearlove* swam smoothly under a grey dawn sky, and through a yet greyer sea. Her hawse-holes, like eyes, stared down at the weary water that divided almost without foam before her cutwater. The great square sails spread from her yards were patched and stained, and grey, too — with the greyness of ditchwater. The broad streak along her dingy sides, painted with imitation gun-ports, was no longer white. The rigging — that complex network linking spars and canvas; the tenuous thoroughfares of rope which ran skyward, narrowing as they went — was wet with the fogs of night, and as colourless as the threads of a spider's web.

A few bedraggled hens picked their disconsolate way about the littered deck, amid coils of rope, spars, coops, and casks. A lean pig snuffled round the coaming of the hatch, studied Seven uncertainly, ambled forward again, collected greedily a yellowing cabbage-stalk outside a grimy sort of little cottage with a very smoky chimney just abaft the foremast, and poked an inquisitive snout in at the door. There was a loud crash within; the pig withdrew squealing; and a shirtless hairy little man, in a red night-cap, leaped out in chase with a frying pan.

Seven had washed in a bucket, shaved with a razor he had commandeered from Henry Wentworth; he now stood at the foot of the short ladder mounting to the poop, wrapped in his cloak, staring with a frown over the ship's side.

There was a voice at his elbow — a mellow voice, a rich voice, a throaty voice.

'Ha!' it said. 'Good morning, my dear sir! *Good* morning!'

Mr. Horatio Vyvyan had emerged from the scuttle in the hatch. He was still in his seedy befrogged surtout of dark purple cloth, but wore — as though it had a nautical smack — a sort of velvet smoking cap with a long tassel. His face was just a trifle less perky and more pale than was its wont. He joined Seven at the bulwark; thrust right hand into the bosom of his coat, and flung the other out vaguely toward monochrome of sea and sky; spouted —

> 'The dawn is overcast; the morning lowers,
> And heavily in clouds brings on the day!'

153

'Ah!' said Seven, courteously if vaguely.

'Addison's "Cato",' explained Mr. Vyvyan, looking at the Atlantic as if he were disappointed that it had not been suddenly illuminated by a celestial spotlight while he declaimed. ' "Cato" — Kemble's adaptation for Covent Garden. Wonderful language — organ-like, sonorous! What a tragedy — terrific! You have seen it, my dear sir, I suppose?'

Seven shook his head.

'Little demand for high tragedy now,' commented Mr. Vyvyan in his most tragic tones. '*Un*fashionable, unfortunately!'

'Never been inside a theatre in my life,' said Seven.

'Never — been — inside — a theatre!' echoed Mr. Vyvyan completely thunderstruck.

'Never had the time.'

The other eyed him as if he were some strange creature new to science.

'Religious scruples, perhaps?' he essayed, obviously incredulous.

'Got no religion,' said Seven.

'*What* you have missed!' said Vyvyan in shocked tones, referring, of course, to the drama and not to the Almighty. 'Glamour — enchantment — beauty — the music of words! Words! Like thunder — like the sighing of violins — like, er like waterfalls! One's public — how they hung on one's lips in the old days! How they shuddered!' He stared over the ship's side through the lattice-work of the shrouds at the greasy sea, as though he stared beyond the footlights into the depths of a crowded theatre: flung his arms out: distorted his face into a mask of woe and horror: shook back his fading mane —

' "O sight of woe!" ' (declaimed Mr. Vyvyan)

' "O Marcia, what we feared is come to pass! . . .

' "Cato is fallen upon his sword!" . . . My first big part, dear boy! Porcius, Cato's son. Appeared in Norwich, Cambridge, Yarmouth, King's Lynn, Colchester, Ipswich. Tremendous success . . . *Tre*mendous! Audience wiping their eyes with one hand, and clapping with the other. Old gentleman in a fit. *As*-tounding!'

Seven broke in on his meditation on that triumphal progress —

'You have an engagement in America, I suppose?'

Vyvyan hesitated a moment before replying: twisted the wonderful ruby ring on a not-too-clean finger.

'In a manner of speaking . . . yes. In a manner of speaking, yes!' And proceeded, 'I hear there is a great demand for theatrical, er, what I may call — talent in the States. A discriminating and thoughtful public!

A responsive public! One's art demands discrimination — and thought — and, er, response . . . I was a disciple of the great Kemble. I even trod the boards with him. At the age of five. I appeared as the child in that fine old drama, "The Stranger", with him. In the metropolis. *Not* a large part, but very moving. You know — clutching with tiny hands at father and mother as they are about to part for ever. Cries of "Dear father! Dear mother!" A communal embrace — fall of the curtain!'

'So you decided to enlarge the sphere of your activities?' said Seven, swinging round to look to the door of the dwarfish cottage, outside which two or three shawled women were now waiting with cooking-pots, their thin wide skirts pressed against their legs by the rising wind.

'My Small Lady and I decided to investigate . . . New fields to conquer! . . . New experience! Nothing like new experiences!'

'Even this?' questioned Seven, indicating all the ship with a sweep of the hand.

'I must say, dear boy,' replied Vyvyan after rather an awkward pause, 'that this is not at all what we have been used to. Not *quite* what we expected, anxious as we were to study life from — er — an unaccustomed angle.'

'Not luxurious enough?' asked Seven with the suspicion of a smile.

'My Small Lady does not ask for luxury,' said Mr. Vyvyan gravely, 'although brought up in considerable affluence. Very considerable affluence. Governess — gig — genteel establishment — sherry and brandy at eleven in the morning, with cheese — prayers at nine-thirty after supper. Her father was a most respected man, very well-to-do — until his misfortune. An apothecary. He had a fine shop in Tavern Street, Ipswich. A wonderful business! . . . What cold roast for Sunday supper! What beef — rosy red with creamy yellow fat! Pickled cabbage! Pickled walnuts! Pickled tomatoes! Horse-radish as curly as shavings from a carpenter's plane . . . What mutton too! Many's the baked shoulder I've had with onion sauce that the Royal Family might have sat down to at two o'clock dinner and smacked their lips over. What meat! . . . It was *too* good — that was his trouble!'

He shook his head a little sadly in a gesture that implied regret for vanished banquets and also present shortage.

'You were saying about your wife . . . ?' asked Seven, bringing him back to the subject.

'Yes,' said Mr. Vyvyan. 'Brought up in the lap of luxury — and now this!' From some recess about his person he produced a half-

smoked and rather shaggy cheroot with which he toyed elegantly.
'She is a woman of strong susceptibilities. Very, very delicate-minded.
Ship-board life is rough — but no matter! A picnic — an experience! . . .
But — there — are — *other* — things!'

'Other . . . ' began Seven, turning over possibilities in his mind.

'Things,' explained Mr. Vyvyan mysteriously, 'which mean little
or nothing to you and me, who are — er — what I might call men of
the world. But a great deal to a delicately-nurtured female. You
are married? . . . No! . . . You might not understand.'

And, having revealed so much of the inner feelings of his Small
Lady, Mr. Vyvyan appeared to change the subject.

'The young lady in your party,' said he, 'seems a most genteel young
person. She reminds me greatly of Miss Wallis who played Joanna
to my Cheveril in 'The Deserted Daughter'. Quite the lady!'

Seven nodded an assent to the encomium on Anne Louise.

'Your sister, may I ask?'

Seven hurriedly recalled to mind the alleged relationships of his
party.

'A cousin,' he replied. 'My mother's youngest step-sister's only
daughter. An orphan. She is travelling with her brother.'

Mr. Vyvyan had not encountered the brother.

This was not surprising. He had been seasick ever since the ship
sailed. He was accommodated with a mattress against the poster-bed
that the fat woman and her husband had erected almost under the
main hatch. Fair lad — very fair.

Five or six women and a couple of down-at-heel men were clustered
now outside the galley door. Seven picked up the frying pan at his feet
ready to join in the rush, and held it balanced on the rail.

Mr. Vyvyan examined the contents with a hungry interest that was
ill disguised.

'Ham rasher!' said he. 'Apple-rings! Eggs! . . . Fresh eggs, may
I ask?' He put the battered cheroot, unlighted, between his lips, and
took up one of the eggs out of the pan. It was large and smooth and
brown. He held it up to the light with the grave regard of a
connoisseur.

'Fresh,' agreed Seven. 'From my — my uncle's farm. Packed in
bran.'

'Ham — *and* eggs — *and* apple-rings! A breakfast for Lucullus! . . .
You are your own cook, sir?'

'Yes,' said Seven.

'Well, well! I fear I know nothing about the — er, culinary — er craft. The demands of my art have been too great to — er — permit me to impinge on the female domain. And my Small Lady, *of course*, never had to soil her hands with so much as a dish cloth. *Never!*' said Mr. Vyvyan with so much emphasis that Seven was assured that of recent years, at any rate, the Small Lady would have felt herself very lucky if she had had a dish-cloth wherewith to soil her lady-like hands. 'Waited on hand and foot — hand and foot! Very awkward now — very awkward, indeed.'

At this point Red Night-cap poked itself out of the cottage door; shouted something incomprehensible, to the accompaniment of a noise made obviously by the beating of iron spoon on kettle.

A muffled shout responded. One after another, like troglodyte apes appearing from their caves, half a dozen hairy creatures climbed out of a dark hole in the fo'c'sle, and lurched aft to the galley with their pannikins.

'Crew's breakfast ready,' commented Mr. Vyvyan, still staring with protruding grey eyes at ham, apple-rings, and the smooth contours of delicious-seeming eggs. 'You'll be able to get to the kitchen — galley, I should say — fire in a moment . . . Bless my soul, I must be going to — er — ascertain what my Small Lady fancies . . .'

He turned to go: paused as though suddenly struck by a thought — 'By the way, I suppose you couldn't possibly spare a couple of eggs, if — *just* if — my Small Lady should fancy them? Don't hesitate to say if you can't manage it.'

Seven was about to refuse, bluntly and point-blank, when Mr. Vyvyan added a rather jerky explanation in his throaty voice —

'We're travelling rather light. A little too light, perhaps . . . Lack of variety . . . Not used to catering.'

Generosity won. Seven took two eggs from the frying pan, and held them out to the gratified actor.

'I — we — are excessively obliged. Superbly so!' said Mr. Vyvyan. 'You must let me pay for them, of course . . . My purse is downstairs. No matter, though, I shall remember!' He established an egg in each of the deep side-pockets of his coat; added in a measured tone: '. . . And, as I was saying, I know my Small Lady would be glad to make the acquaintance of — er — your young relative . . . I am sure so.'

As he announced this high compliment, a bonnet, a face, a figure reluctantly emerged from the hatchway near them — a once-smart bonnet of champagne straw with a bunch of cherries under the brim; a prettyish long pale face; a figure in a chocolate-coloured dress (wasp waist — puffed shoulders — wide lace collar) that was at the same time lady-like, elegant and shabby.

There followed her from the depths below a fat voice which remarked loudly —

'Slops, indeed!'

'Oh, Mrs. Liddell! . . . Pray, Mrs. Liddell! . . . Hush, Mrs. Liddell!' said the young lady in a low flurried tone; turned as though to force a desperate way back; was driven under protest by someone ascending behind her, to step on deck over the high coaming of the hatch as genteelly as she might.

Mrs. Liddell surged up the ladder into view. Vast hat — secured by scarf about enormous red face — was succeeded by stupendous bosom, by massive body, and finally (as she navigated the sill of the hatch) by a brief revelation of elephantine legs.

'And slops I will not do. No, my girl, slops I will *not* do!' said she, making her landing.

'Please, Mrs. Liddell, let me go back!'

Mr. Vyvyan, who had started in a rather theatrical manner on first hearing the plaintive voice, cast a swift glance behind him; caught sight of the grouping of the two ladies twelve or thirteen feet away. The beginnings of a smile of greeting faded from his pale face; he hesitated; looked uneasily at Seven to see if he were paying any attention to the scene. But Seven seemed to be studying a sea that was monotonously grey except on the far horizon, where it was flecked with white as though the wings of a squall had shed snow upon its sombreness.

Mrs. Liddell seized the other by the arm —

'If you were sick, ducky,' she said, 'there's nothing that old Sarah Liddell wouldn't do. But if you can walk, then you can . . .' she lowered her voice to a mumble. . . 'So come along o' me.'

'I couldn't! . . . Really, I couldn't! I should die! . . . Let me go. Please to leave go!'

The plea was almost agonized. The prettyish, yellowish face had gone chalk-white. One or two of the women by the galley door had turned and were watching the scene curiously. Vyvyan seemed to shrink within himself: it appeared as if he were about to swing round and go to the assistance of the unhappy lady in the champagne bonnet, when Seven touched him on the arm —

'See, the gulls have come back. There — no, further to your right! None yesterday or the day before, and then they hail in sight when we're five days out! Curious, isn't it? I've often thought about their flight — the mechanics of it, I mean. . .' And so ambled on with a restraining finger on the other man's sleeve. . . .

Said Mrs. Liddell in an inexorable rumble —

'Once you've been once, you'll not mind it again. . . Hey, my girl! Ho, my girl! *You* come along!'

'I order you to let me go,' said Mrs. Vyvyan — and burst into tears.

But Mrs. Liddell had already set off along the narrow rope-littered sail-shadowed lane that ran between the bulwarks and the masts, windlass, pig-stye, hen-coops, long-boat housed above the main hatch, and goblin cottage with its smoking chimney. She drew the other after her by the hand, although the younger woman hung back like a child being taken to meet punishment.

The little knot outside the galley door divided to let them pass. There was that in Mrs. Liddell's face which forbade them snigger or comment or smile, or do ought but watch. . . .

'How something that is heavier than the air it displaces can be supported in the air, is a very interesting problem in dynamics,' remarked Seven, still watching the flight of the gulls, keeping one hand on Vyvyan's arm and supporting the frying-pan upon the bulwark with the other. 'Have you read Cavallo on aeronautics, sir?'

Mr. Vyvyan had *not* read Cavallo on aeronautics. He was trying unostentatiously to see what had happened to his wife, who was now hidden from his view somewhere behind the grubby white cottage with the smoking chimney, the ship's belfry — where a tarnished bell swung uneasily to the slow lifting of the seas — and the foremast.

While Seven apparently meditated upon Signor Cavallo's theories, the actor stared up the empty alleyway on the port side toward what looked like a very small sentry-box set against the ship's bulwarks. . . .

As a matter of fact there were two of these sentry boxes, facing one another by the break of the low fo'c'sle. They were tarred, so low that the most diminutive of sentries could not have stood upright in them, and had doors which rattled noisily upon the latches to the rhythmic surging of the ship. . . Forward — click: sideways — clatter-clatter.

The sentry-box toward which Mrs. Liddell towed her captive had the letter 'W' painted very roughly on its door.

Near it a short ladder led up to the fo'c'sle, and at the top sat a little man in canvas petticoat and a faded blue coat. So broad was his brow and so pointed his chin that his wrinkled brown face seemed to be perfectly triangular. The queer pattern of his skull was repeated, too, in his large triangular mouth, for the lower lip came down to a point in the middle exactly as if it had been split at some time and not properly repaired. He was mending a rent in a pair of canvas trousers with a sail-maker's needle and twine, and singing below his breath some old sea song whilst he did so, in a grumbling rumbling voice. The material he was repairing was so stiff that he had to push it against the needle which he held upright upon the planking of the deck.

'Here we are, ducky!' said Mrs. Liddell, coming to a halt, but still keeping hold of the young woman.

'Here we are!' echoed the goblin on the ladder.

'Here we are!' repeated Mrs. Liddell not noticing the intrusion, 'and nobody about! In you pop!'

'Pop!' echoed Goblin.

Sarah Liddell unlatched the door with her free hand. With a sudden vigorous thrust she pushed into the dark entry that shrinking creature in champagne bonnet and fashionable-shabby chocolate-coloured dress with smart puffed sleeves. Bonnet got battered: sleeves got battered in the violent ingress.

'Mrs. Liddell . . .' came a bleat.

'Clack!' went the latch.

'Nobody knows! All to yourself, my girl!' said Sarah composedly, and faced round against the world in front of the absurd hut as though a large dragon in faded red had taken up sentry-go before it.

Mr. Vyvyan, tasselled smoking-cap quivering with his agitation, had witnessed something of the little drama; had been in a pitiable state of uncertainty; had almost started off to the rescue of his Small Lady; had been restrained from so doing by an increased pressure on his arm from Seven and a new burst of confidences about the aeronautical theories of Sir George Cayley in 'Nicholson's Journal'; had come to the conclusion that no one had seen the business but himself.

'A stoppage, ma?' asked the little man with the triangular mouth — who was hidden from the actor's view, and much too far off to be heard. 'Your daughter got a stoppage?' inquired he in a most friendly manner, looking up from the gargantuan repair upon which he was engaged.

'Stoppage?' said Mrs. Liddell, becoming aware of him for the first time. 'Stoppage! And what's it got to do with you, I should like to know? *I'll* give you a stoppage you won't like!'

'I do believe you could, ma,' said the little man entirely unruffled.

'Stoppage!' repeated Mrs. Liddell in a great state of indignation. 'Can't a lady have a stoppage — or anything else she likes — without you interfering? Hey, my man! You look after your own bowels without nosing about after other people's!'

'Well, ma, I'm not interested in them that's stopped. I'm interested in stoppages. Suffered that way meself — something cruel.'

Mrs. Liddell was understood to express the wish that his next stoppage would be a permanency.

The little man ignored her hostility.

'My int'rest is scientific, ma!' he answered her. 'The beautifullest creature without a stoppage is no int'rest to me. A scholard of stoppages — that's what I am!'

'Yellow soap and water luke,' snorted Mrs. Liddell, 'is what I'ld give you!'

'Ma'am,' said the little man in a most earnest fashion. 'Soap's all right for coarse constitootions — for them what's tough like nelephants. Soap for nelephants with stoppages — yes! But for me Morison's Pills There's a dozen times I'ld have been laid in the silent tomb but for them. A dozen! . . . No, a hundred! I reckon I got a mile more bowel'n most. It takes some moving, ma! Indeed it does!'

'Morison's Pills!' said Sarah Liddell thoughtfully, propping herself against the door of the privy, and examining the wedge-faced man with a friendlier eye. 'Them's what I give Liddell when he's taken with his heavings.'

The wedge-faced man laid down his shirt on his knees. He wagged his head in an ecstacy of recommendation.

'*What* them pills will do! Two for ornery things! Eight for smallpox! Or appleplxy! *Or* hydrophoby! . . . Meself — I've taken twenty!'

'Twenty!' echoed Mrs. Liddell surveying the wedge-faced man with a new respect. 'Twenty!'

'Started on two,' said he modestly. 'Worked up by degrees. Did me a lot of good. Pills at night — rum in the morning. Took a dozen — felt bad! Went on with 'em. Took eighteen — worse! Took twenty, 'n something seemed to go "click". *That* beat my innards. That told them there wasn't to be no fooling. That made me master!'

'Ten's the most Liddell has had,' said Mrs. Liddell, ignoring in her interest faint raps on the door behind her. 'Ten's the most, Mr.—?'

'Reid's the name! Most of 'em call me "Snorker" . . . Ah, them *is* pills! The more the merrier! Smooth as milk, and strong as — as a steam-engine!'

A plaintive low voice from the sentry-box demanded Mrs. Liddell's attention. She turned round — put intimate questions in a stage-whisper, with her mouth close to the rattling door. The answers were apparently satisfactory, for she raised a hand to the latch while she gesticulated with the other to Mr. Reid that he should beat a retreat — which he obligingly did. Mr. Vyvyan had already discreetly withdrawn below, and all that could be seen of the distant figure of Seven was his back . . .

'Well, Sally, what's all this about?' asked Seven when the good lady, having shepherded her charge back to the hatch, came to anchorage beside him.

'That young woman and her airs!' said Mrs. Liddell explosively. 'Thinks she is the Duchess of La-Di-Da, I suppose. Wants ladies-in-waiting, maids-of-honour, mistress-of-the-robes, and a keeper-of-the-royal-night-stool!'

'She does, does she?' said Seven, looking down at her with a wry smile. He was propped negligently against the great water-cask which stood at the break of the poop, and gently rolled the eggs in his frying pan to and fro.

'When she was sea-sick and couldn't help herself, I didn't mind obliging.'

' "Obliging"?'

'Obliging,' asseverated Mrs. Liddell. 'Obliging with the slops! You take my meaning, Mr. Sep? . . . If she can walk, then she can walk to the privy — for all her airs! Like other people! . . . Four days now she's been going about like a ghost. Too genteel, too delicate-minded, too lady-like to be seen going in and out of the privy!'

'What's wrong with it?' asked Seven, looking along the deck to the little black sentry-box.

'I'm not saying it's nice for respectable women. I'm not . . . The crew hang about, passing remarks. There's one filthy little rat sits outside half the day, and l-e-e-e-rs!' She took a full second to pronounce that last syllable, thereby giving the word a most sinister sound.

'He sits outside and leers, does he?' said Seven thoughtfully. 'I'll deal with him next time he starts leering — and pretty quickly!'

'I was brought up nice as you know, Mr. Sep,' said Mrs. Liddell, adjusting some of the odds and ends in the store-cupboard she carried in and about her enormous bosom. 'But if I can go, and your little lady — who anybody can see with half an eye *is* a lady — can go, then the stuck-up wife of a tuppenny-ha'penny actor can go. As I say, What can't be borne must be endured! . . . And this ship is pretty horrible, Mr. Sep!'

'You're getting fussy, Sally-ally!' said Seven, poking her vast front with his frying-pan.

'That's the self-same word your father used to me years and years

162

ago!' said Mrs. Liddell, swaying her bulk to the increasing movement
of the ship with the yielding condescension of a very large tree in a very
small gale. She added enigmatically, after a moment's pause, 'It was
after he had asked me to oblige, one Sunday evening . . . I was clearing
the supper things.'

' "Oblige"?' asked Seven once more, feeling that the conversation
was starting all over again.

'He wanted me to give him a baby.'

'Another son for his collection!' commented Seven.

'He said I ought to have a fine child. I said I would be glad to oblige
him in any way he wanted — he was a fine looking man, Mr. Sep,
you know — so long as it didn't end in babies. He snapped out "Fussy
fool!" — his very words; told me to bring in the sherry and hot water;
lit a strong segar, and opened his paper. For all the world as if he had
just been complaining about me apron! . . . That would be a good many
years before you were born . . . Your poor mother . . .' For a minute
or so she seemed lost in retrospect, and then added inconsequently
enough, 'I wish you hadn't come on this ship, Mr. Sep!' . . .

More than once in the days that followed Seven found himself
wishing the same thing. While his pattern of life had not made him a
sociable man, it had given him an enormous appetite for activity of
mind and body; and life on board the *Joan Dearlove* was sheer stagna-
tion. He was civil — and even helpful — to such of the passengers who
approached him, but there were none to whom he cared to make any
advances, or from whom he invited them. His main interest lay in
watching, and guessing, and speculating on the reactions of Anne
Louise and Daniel to their new life.

Pedder had little to say; but, though he was generally affable,
Seven noted that his crew — mostly aliens — watched him warily.

The first-mate was a foul-spoken Irishman with a lop-sided mouth
and an always-open yellow shirt that showed a jungle of red hair upon
his chest.

With the Yankee second mate, however, Seven had some conversation. It was a reasonable little man — a little man with the longest
and most twisted nose in the State of Massachusetts, and green-
gooseberry eyes that were remarkably protruding. He would recite
'Marmion' or 'The Lady of the Lake' by the yard; argue the merits
of American cotton as against British flax for sail-cloth; discuss the
European balance of power, paddlewheel brigs, the adoption by the
French navy of shells instead of round-shot ammunition, or anything

else. He had ten children — the eight sons being named after the eight presidents of the United States.

'It's a strange co-in-ci-dence, yes-sir,' said he, 'but my last, my little Buren, were born on President Van Buren's inauguration day. Mother said, "That's the last little president you'll get from me, Seth, I guess!" but the election's on'y next year, and I cal-klate Mother'll do what she can!'

It was early in the morning that they talked, on a deserted deck. The galley fire had just been lighted, and black smoke suddenly poured out of the tall chimney and went streaming past grey sails between grey sky and grey sea.

'Why do you allow naked lights down below?' suddenly said Seven, voicing a question that had been in his mind ever since he came on board.

'They allus allow 'em in a slate ship,' answered the man with the twisted nose. 'Why, in the smaller craft — in the schooners out of Port Dinorwic — they let the passengers have cooking fires in the hold! Don't reckon it's the wisest thing, but it's the use. Slate don't burn, after all!'

'Ships do.'

'Aye-aye,' said the father of eight presidents : meditated, continued — 'especially when . . .'

Meditated afresh, and left the sentence in mid-air.

As the day aged the wind rose, and the old wagon of a vessel lumbered on, beneath full spread of sail, across a glass-green sea that was laced with swiftly-running lines of snowy foam, toward a horizon where the dark mountains and white peaks of a cloud continent were piled. A thin scatter of cold rain occasionally wetted the draggled decks.

Most of the passengers — drably coated or shawled — drifted up from the airlessness of their cellar home; trailed miserably about the litter of the deck; sat huddled on coils of rope and boxes in the shelter of the cook-house or of the long-boat; the children played listlessly together, or quarrelled in a high sing-song.

Right forward, a little knot of the crew squatted on their hunkers, gambling and arguing, in that narrow stage which was flanked by the dingy sentry-boxes and had as background the marine slum tenement that was the fo'c'sle — a shabby white-and-black-painted wooden wall with ladder in the middle, fogged port-hole to one side, and dark entry with hooked-back door to the other.

Anne Louise appeared, escorted by the faithful Daniel. She wore a plain grey dress, was wrapped in a dark green shawl, and was bonnet-less. Her ringlets — holding so many shades of gold — were ruffled by the Atlantic wind. She stood in silence by the shrouds of the main-mast, a few feet away from Seven, staring across a sea that darkened every instant, and as it darkened so heaved the more sullenly.

He wondered of what she thought as she stood there, under the singing cordage, aloof from all but the yellow-haired small boy at her side. When he had first watched her amid the squalor that was to be her home for weeks, he had only seen in her a princess, representative of old and bad dynasties who ruled peoples ignorantly and oppressively by virtue of inheritance and a right they termed 'divine'; a princess who was to learn realities by humiliation — even that she must not strike her maidservant.

Now he saw her as a proud child who, as she had accepted his word that his plan of escape for her was the only one feasible, so also had accepted, with a strange composure, the harsh life into which she had been flung — even accommodated herself to it. She recognized her obligation to him, while abominating it: it amused him, however, to question whether her scorn for Henry Wentworth and his wails at discomfort was not almost a stronger emotion than her dislike of himself. Indeed her whole attitude to the luckless young man had greatly intrigued Tempest. For she ignored him to the point of extreme discourtesy: she addressed no remark to him, and replied to him — when she must — in cold monosyllables. He had been driven for companionship to the Vyvyans, in a corner of whose sail-cloth cubicle he spent interminable hours listening to interminable recollections of the theatre, or interminable stories of genteel life in Ipswich 'when dear Papa was alive'. Seven wondered what was the nature of the barrier between the pair, and recollected that she had done her best to persuade him on the morning of their departure that Wentworth's escort was quite unnecessary to her well-being.

He regarded her from beneath lowered eyelids: told himself with cynical amusement that there stood her Highness the Duchess of Limburg. In gown and shawl plain enough for a maidservant, her escort a school-boy, and her Court a shipload of smelly emigrants — a Personage for whom England, France, Belgium, and Germany were, without doubt, being discreetly but thoroughly ransacked.

Anne Louise, suddenly looking round, surprised the half-smile on his face.

She turned her back on him and walked quickly off — forward — toward the fo'c'sle — toward the small tarred sentry-boxes. . . .

One of the four men who were playing cards, looked up as Anne Louise approached; said something to one of his companions — a small fellow with ruffled grey hair and wet grey face and snub nose. There was a snigger.

The door shut.

The man with the wet grey face rose to his feet. With a humorous gesture adjoining secrecy he tiptoed toward the sentry-box — knocked at the door, and bent as if to listen. Even as he did so, he was flung face downward on the deck with great violence — was picked up, and towed along the deck with dragging feet by the nape of his neck.

CHAPTER III

CAPTAIN PEDDER STRIKES FOUR BELLS

CAPTAIN HENRY PEDDER stood on the poop, leaning easily against a high flat skylight, which looked something like an old-fashioned table-tomb. He wore a tall and nearly conical top-hat of most foreign appearance — spoils of a wager with the master of a full-rigged French ship at Le Havre — a double-breasted blue pea-jacket, black neckerchief, and white calico trousers. His great splay feet were bare, big toes almost at right angles to the rest, and small toes contracted as though they were gripping the deck.

His square pale face and grey pale eyes were without expression. He seemed to brood over his ship, as though the bond between them was more than that of master and craft; as if their histories were linked and their destinies united; as if by his knowledge of her secrets, as well as by his will and hidden energy, he might at any moment impel her — old and weary as she was — to new and desperate enterprise.

Old she was; and weary she was. It was sixty years since she had first slid through the mists and greasy waters of the Mersey, outward bound for Africa to collect slaves from the barracoons of Whydah and Benin . . . Captain Pedder knew! . . . She had been battered by the guns of French and American privateers — reeled a dozen times over the precipices of sea off Cape Horn — carried every sort of cargo, from Indian silks to scurvy-ridden emigrants . . . Captain Pedder knew! . . . She had been stormed and looted by Ching-Yih's pirates off Macao — survived half a hundred disreputable adventures and the assaults of all the Sixteen Seas . . . Captain Pedder knew!

He not merely commanded the *Joan Dearlove*: he also blackmailed her.

It was with dispassionate interest that he observed Seven appear up the poop ladder trailing a small man behind him by the scruff of his neck, as negligently as if he were a child with a rag doll, and paying no heed whatever to the wretched creature's cries and struggles.

'Mornin', Cap'n!' said Seven, flinging down his captive like a wet sack.

'Mornin', Mr. Cash,' returned the captain. 'Wind's freshenin' a bit from the East. Barometer fallin' more'n I like. We shall have a nice little blow pretty soon.'

Said Seven easily — standing by the rail, and looking along the dancing vista of masts and sails and rigging —

'I suppose we're somewhere in the region of the mid-forties!'

'Right, Mr. Cash! Not far out, Mr. Cash! Neat piece of work, Mr. Cash! You can't have just guessed it. Seaman yourself, Mr. Cash?' responded Captain Pedder raising his eyelids. 'Latitude 45, Longitude 25 it is! Twenty-five times forty-five! Twenty-five times forty-five is . . .?'

'. . . Sixteen! . . . Sixteen days of gale to the month this time of year.'

'Sixteen! . . . Twenty-five times forty-five is — sixteen! . . . Right as 'rithmetic!' said Captain Pedder in high good humour and much merriment, regarding Seven very speculatively the while.

His laughter died away: he looked with disapproval at the man with the wet face, who was sitting on the deck with a rather dazed expression, dabbing at cuts on either eyebrow with a dirty rag.

'Very good, Mr. Cash! Ve-e-e-ry good, indeed! . . . But what's this you're messing my nice deck with? Hey, Mr. Cash?'

'Small matter for you to deal with, Cap'n,' explained Seven, contemplating the small man for a moment as if assessing the damage. 'Gentleman is a nuisance. Public nuisance. Lifts curtains when women passengers are undressing. Says dirty things to the children. Sits outside the women's convenience. Knocks at the door when they are within it. So I've brought him along for you to deal with.'

' "Brought him along for me to deal with," did you,' repeated Captain Pedder, also obviously assessing damage. '*Did* you now?' And his voice was so low and vibrant that it was as if he had growled.

'He got a little damaged coming here,' remarked Seven grudgingly. 'That's all. Perhaps I should have been more careful. Didn't seem worth while taking much trouble.'

'Ah,' commented Pedder thoughtfully. Then his voice brisked. He had obviously decided to accept this explanation as eminently reasonable. 'Quite right, Mr. Cash. Quite right . . . For a bit I fancied that you'd dealt with him yourself! . . . And then I should-a been angry. Ve-e-ry angry, Mr. Cash! No one deals with my crew but me — even if it is only old Johnny Gennaro. Or any other bloody Eyetalian . . . Get up, you bastard! . . . Get up, you whelp! . . . Get off my clean deck, you incestuous goat!'

The wet-faced man had just risen, words of protest bubbling from his lips, when Captain Pedder's bare foot caught him on the chest and shot him with a crash down the ladder on to the deck below.

That single act of violence had a peculiar effect on Pedder.

He stood motionless for a moment at the head of the ladder . . .
Quite motionless . . . His face, from being a vast square of pale grey
leather, slowly flushed to the dull red of a sunset reflection on snow.
His mouth was so tightly clamped shut that the lips almost vanished.
He leaned outward from the rail over the deck; regarded without any
shadow of expression the body lying there — watched it stir to life —
struggle to its feet — and then stagger away. His nostrils suddenly
dilated; his eyes widened; he beat a fist on the top of his absurd hat,
so hard that it echoed like a drum; he pounded down the ladder with
the speed of an angry cat baulked of its prey; leaped on bare feet along
the crowded deck, thrusting through the women clustered at the galley
door, and oversetting a child in his course.

Gennaro had reached the gallows from which hung the ship's bell —
a heavy mass of bronze looted from the carcass of some much larger
ship. The men with whom he had been playing cards clustered about
him. One of them was about to strike the hour. The immense figure
of the ship-master was among them before they were aware.

Anne Louise, joined that moment at the ship's side by Seven, watched
a scene that was quickly over.

It was like an incident in a theatre, she thought. The little group of
little men confronted by one as big as an ogre, in the centre of a
miniature stage bisected by the shaft of the foremast; ship's bell
fidgeting on the man-high gallows: tarred sentry-box with clacking
door in either wing: for background, the superstructure of the fo'c'sle
with a head or two peering out of a dark burrow in it, and 'Snorker'
Reid sitting on the top step of the ladder.

The two little sluts, their neighbours, pushed past to get a position
in the front row — Green-and-White-Stripes with one of her babies
nuzzling at the gap in her open bodice, and the other dark pretty
creature in a dirty red dress.

The ship was bowing and curtseying to the rising sea; at one moment
Anne Louise could see all the littered length of the fo'c'sle deck and
the bowsprit lifted up toward the grey dull sky; at another it was the
grey shining water that showed above the low rail.

Captain Pedder said nothing to his victims: he just loomed over
them, top-hat on the back of his big head, feet dancing with little
mincing steps — though his great trunk moved not at all — and his
huge hands hanging at his sides with the palms forward.

'Cap'n . . .' pleaded Gennaro.

'No jawbation!' said Pedder. He licked his lips. 'No jawbation,
you rats!'

Gennaro was staring horrified at the captain. Anne Louise fancied that his horror was not so much of what was immediately to happen, but of something else of which the coming outburst was the merest portent — something infinitely worse than an isolated act of punishment.

'A leetle joke, Cap'n . . .'

His voice rose to a scream, for on the instant Pedder was upon him — had struck him to the deck with two ferocious blows on the jaw — had leapt full weight on his stomach as he lay recumbent — had leaped off his body.

'Johnny Johns!' said Captain Pedder in a smooth voice as he stood over him. 'Poor, poor Johnny Johns! That's for Johnny Johns! Johnny Johns has been a bad boy!'

He turned on the others.

'Sounding four bells, weren't you, scum?' he remarked. 'Well that was one bell!'

With the speed of a tiger he dealt with the other three flinching men.

In one moment he had scooped them in a gorilla-like embrace to his enormous chest: in the next he had plucked them thence one by one, crashed them face foremost with hammer force into the tarnished curve of the great bell, and flung them bloody-visaged away.

Then he paused, as though meditating fresh violence. His hands clasped and unclasped as if eager to be at other throats. There was blood on them, and with it he smeared his face when he wiped his lips. He appeared to be utterly unconscious of the silent audience which had gathered at the head of either alley-way. His eyes were glazed as if he were very drunk; became at length cognisant of his surroundings; noted the women among the onlookers; and then brightened, so that with their lighting up, the whole expression of his face was changed.

'See, my little ducks!' he bellowed. 'Look-ee, little ducks! Here's how young Hen Pedder sees after his little ducks!'

He stooped, caught up a moaning bundle by an ankle, and raised it high in the air, as though displaying a skinned rabbit to a crowd on market day.

'There, my little ducks! Who'll say that young Hen Pedder doesn't look after ye?'

He advanced toward them, still demonstrating his victim: they broke rank and retreated — all except the dark-haired slut in a red dress, who gave him a wide-mouthed smile.

'Ha!' said Pedder, greatly delighted, marched toward her; flung his victim at her feet. 'That's a girl! . . . That's a little lady! . . . See how I pertect ye from insult! . . . See how I look after ye! . . . Worth a kiss, isn't it? . . . Four bells — one kiss! Wish it had been a hunderd bells!'

The girl gave a squeal as he came to a halt before her and towered over her — a squeal in which there was no fear! She made no attempt at escape.

He scooped her up — immense arm encircling waist; kissed her loudly on the mouth; lightly tossed her on to a shoulder, where she rode, clutching hat, ear, big head, wriggling and giggling; and thus proceeded to the poop.

As he strode he sang loudly —

'O when I was a little boy, and so my mother told me
    Way, haul away! Haul away, Joe!
That if I didn't kiss the girls, my lips would go all mouldy!
    Way, haul away! Haul away, Joe!'

At the foot of the poop ladder he paused —

'Four bells — one kiss! Not good 'rithmetic . . . Shall we go and argle-bargle about it, little duck? . . . Shall us? . . .'

With that he bounded up the ladder still carrying the girl, and vanished from sight with a burst of stentorian laughter.

Anne Louise thought he was like some great beast returning to a lair with its prey.

CHAPTER IV

SUDDEN TERMINATION OF A *SOIRÉE MUSICALE*

THE girl in the red gown did not reappear for more than a week. During all that time she remained invisible to her fellow passengers: no mention was made out loud of her: her paramours presumably contented themselves with the shared embraces of her sister: she might have vanished utterly from the ship.

A child died . . . and another . . . and two women . . . and then a man, from some infection that lurked in the evil-smelling darkness. Their bodies were thrust overboard at night in clumsy bundles of old sail-cloth, while a wild-eyed scarecrow of a preacher — from some remote Carmel or Bethel in the hills encircling the Amman valley — gabbled incomprehensible sentences in Welsh over the heaving black waste which swallowed them up.

The man — a friendless, feverish creature, who lay on a pile of blankets in the remotest corner of the hold, and had no other baggage than one large sack — took long a-dying. He groaned, and mumbled, and sometime screamed; but the burthen of his agony was always the same — 'I *told* her I should!' . . . Just that, and nothing else — 'I *told* her I should!'

The only cessation of his moaning came when Sarah Liddell sat down beside him, and read from a shabby brass-cornered Bible — book held close to a rush-light stuck into sawdust-covered floor; read the verses from Micah, beginning —

'Rejoice not against me, O mine enemy; when I fall, I shall arise; when I sit in darkness, the Lord shall be a light unto me!'

Nevertheless Anne Louise knew that about an hour after the lights had been extinguished the sick man would start tossing on his frowsy bed, and would call sharply into the darkness — 'I *told* her I should! . . . I *told* her I should!'

She even came to lie awake until he broke out again into his defiant explanation, wondering for what very hidden sin it besought condonation . . . And then he, too, at length, went his way into the dark sea.

It was on the following day that Megan, the black-haired slut, reappeared.

She came down the poop-ladder slowly; sullen anger in her bearing. Seven, seated on the hatch-cover, looked up from the crude wooden toy he was hacking for a sick child. He surveyed her openly and dispassionately: noted a cut about her mouth which bled a little; and that a purplish bruise almost closed her right eye.

'What . . .' she began, spitting at him like an angry kitten, when a loud bellow sounded from the deck above, and she scurried to the protection of her fellow-women gathered at the galley door.

Captain Henry Pedder so suddenly manifested himself at the foot of the ladder that he might have been materialized out of the misty Atlantic morning, which had left every rope and sail and plank wringing wet. Seven imagined that he had leaped from the poop-deck.

The big man stood still for a moment, swaying easily to the rhythmic movement of the ship: his heavy lidded eyes followed the actions of the men swinging on the foot-rope of the main-yard as they took in a reef of the great square of bulging canvas; stared at the cloaked figure of Anne Louise speculatively, for a long while, until he became aware of the close regard of Seven: then slowly he turned his head and attention to the shawled drab figures about the caboose. He stalked towards them, and stood among them not saying a word. The ship's boy, emerging carelessly with a pannikin, ran into the brooding figure without; spilled some of the hot soup on his captain's bare feet. Still without word, Pedder took him — almost lazily — by the throat, with one hand; with the other he struck him twice — with an inattentive violence — upon the face, so that the blood spurted from nose and mouth.

Sometime toward dusk Megan's red-headed sister disappeared. There was no need to search for her; and on the following morning her green-and-white striped gown was seen flaunting on the poop. A committee of women passengers fed the survivor of her twins with a pap of ship's biscuit, molasses and water. . . .

'They *do* say,' said Mr. 'Snorker' Reid very slowly, lifting his regard from the shirt which Anne Louise was constructing for Daniel out of an old petticoat, and surveying the deck to left and right before he continued: 'They *do* say as *he* — the cap'n — was one of Mrs. Ching's men when he was a lad . . . She was one of the gashliest pirates as ever was in China seas. Five 'undred ships, they say she had! And a fresh husband every week!'

'Was Captain Pedder one of her husbands?' asked Daniel, greatly interested. He was seated beside Anne Louise on the coaming of the hatch, and never moved his fascinated eyes from Mr. Reid's queer triangular mouth except to study the string belt which the little man's nimble fingers were plaiting for him.

There was no one within earshot. Mr. Reid settled himself more comfortably upon a hen-coop with a very fluttered occupant, and continued in a low voice to tell his young friends of the more lurid events in Captain Pedder's history, pausing ever and again — triangular mouth slightly ajar, wedge-shaped head tilted to one side — to appreciate the high-lights. With his sea-boots and black tarpaulin petticoat and faded blue short jacket, Anne Louise thought he would have looked like a pirate himself, had it not been that the bright blue eyes in his mahogany face were very mild, and that his scanty grey-brown hair was as fluffy as a baby's. Of murder, rape, and other incredible deeds of violence he told: and always emphasized how mild a man the cap'n was until something aroused his lust for blood — how much of a monk with women until. . . .

'I were in Tappanooly when they rescued the cap'n from the Battas . . .'

'Where's Tappanooly?' asked Daniel.

'Sumatra . . . Fust time I'd seen the *Joan Dearlove*. They only got him back just in time. Been interfering with the women. One of the rajahs caught him, and sentenced him to — *huhum*, they call it.'

'What's *huhum*?' inquired Daniel.

'Being eaten alive!' — 'Ah-h-h!' sighed Daniel in an ecstasy — 'Them natives'd got him tied up stark naked to a cross, and the head carver was a-sharpening his knife when our fellers came . . . Some say that they'd cut the fust slice!'

'Where?' asked Daniel.

'They *do* say,' began Mr. Reid; caught a glimpse of green-and-white gown on the poop; shook his head. ' . . . But it can't be.'

And was not to be enticed into anatomical revelations. He diverged from the disreputable history of her captain to the disreputable history of the ship.

'I mind my old dad tellin' me,' said Mr. Reid ' . . . but it's many years ago now! He was servin' in the *Norfolk*. It must-a been' . . . he calculated . . . 'in '02 — the year Wall and Crawley was hanged . . . No! The year arter — when Hatfield was put away.'

'Five days out of Kingston they sighted the *Joan*. That's what she was called then. There was a light breeze, my old dad said, and smooth water. But she'd got her main-tops'l close-reefed, and her fores'l reefed, like it was a heavy gale. She were yawin' about like a drunk just ashore arter a ten months' v'yge . . . She'd a hunderd and eighty-fower blacks

aboard from the Rio Pongo. Slaves! . . . And they'd all gone blind! . . .
And the crew'd all gone blind! Stone blind! All bar one man!'

Mr. Reid paused for some time to let them savour the terror of the
tale.

He added — 'My old dad said that their eyes were all gummed up —
like they was festering. Off- something: I fergit what they rightly call
the sickness! When it started the cap'n — a Scotsman from Aberdeen,
he were — threw twenty of the Samboes overboard what got it worst, so
it shouldn't spread . . . But it weren't no good . . . *He* was the next!'

He turned his head, and spat over the rail into the water with an air
of finality.

Anne Louise, hands and shirt-to-be on her grey lap, stared into a
shining bright cloud-scape segmented by the criss-cross of the shrouds —
at the shining press of sail that strained its curves out and away from
the yards and the spiring masts. Beneath just such a sky, and under —
perhaps — those very masts, this self-same ship had wavered blindly
amid the vastness of the Atlantic, manned by a sightless crew, and
freighted with sightless slaves.

She rose, while Reid meditated for an instant, and went to the side.
She looked onto a brilliantly green sea that was hummocked to the
horizon by a quick uncertain swell, as though it were a vast field hummocked with mole-hills. Every mole-hill was crested with foam that had
the bright whiteness of snow.

She had often thought, almost affectionately, of the *Joan Dearlove* as
of an old and crowded farmhouse set adrift on the Atlantic; which one
had to be sorry for because it was not rooted in a deep dale or clinging
to the sheltered side of a mountain, but — most unnaturally — made to
battle all the time up great hills of water, or to wallow in the depths of
ocean valleys. Now, however, the ship had lost any friendliness and
familiarity; had become something sinister, and was haunted, rather
than commanded, by her captain.

Mr. Reid, diverted by some secret train of thought, rambled into a
disquisition on the merits of Schmidt's 'Mineral Magnets', which had
apparently greatly toned up his system at a time when he had been even
more than usually concerned about his health.

'All blind?' interrupted Daniel.

'Stone blind! Bar one!' asserted Mr. Reid. 'Same thing happened a
few years back. In '19 or '20. French slaver, *Rodeur*! *And* a dago ship
the *Leon*! She was a slaver, too. Yes, young feller, *and* the *Leon*!'

'I *say*!' said Daniel enthralled. 'I *say*, Mr. Reid!' . . .

The evil-smelling darkness and the squalor of the hold; Henry Wentworth's ceaseless whine; a constant consciousness of scrutiny by Tempest; the oppressive sociability of Mr. Horatio Vyvyan's Small Lady; even Pedder's increasing brutality to his men — these things Anne Louise could bring herself to bear, although the strain was beginning to tell.

Mr. Reid's tales of the past, however, super-added spiritual horror to material discomfort. The ship grew to be a monstrous thing, and the darkness below deck became crowded with other than human passengers. The restless shadows, cast by stacked furniture and packing-cases and arras of fluttering blankets, surged and battled in the candle-lit hold with every movement of the quivering ship — even as the blinded slaves had surged and battled; as though they were the very ghosts of those captives rather than the shadows of material things. Or were perhaps both.

When Anne Louise lay in her berth at night she kept the grey curtain tight drawn before it, so that she should not see, in the darkness beyond a darker figure fumbling with outstretched arms across the cabin floor....

The days wore into weeks ... The *Joan Dearlove* trundled on across the contemptuous Atlantic; down the lonely ocean lane that skirts the Azores and goes westward and southward into the golden-brown seaweed swamps of the Sargasso Sea ... The reign of Green-and-White Stripes on the poop came to an end with a suddenness which precipitated her down the ladder, clothing torn in shreds and face swollen from blows and tears.

That night Anne Louise awakened suddenly, knowing well that one of the fumbling ghosts had touched her with its groping fingers. She was glad to be awake.

And then heard Daniel whisper —

'Anne! ... I say, Anne!'

He had emerged from his lair, and was standing by her side, hidden by the curtain, and steadying himself against the motion of the ship with a hand upon the edge of her bunk.

She had to remain silent for an instant until she was certain that she had her voice under command.

' ... What is it, Daniel?'

'Did you ... Did — did anything? ... Did you feel anything? ... Just now?'

'No!'

'Something touched *me*. I thought at first it was you ... Then it touched me again.' He spoke in a very low voice.

176

'It must have been a rat.'

'A rat?' This was a new idea. He meditated upon it uncertainly. 'A rat!' Accepted the notion. His whisper became brisk and assured — 'Of course that's what it was ... I'll catch it if it comes again! By the tail! That'll teach it! Bet you I do! Bet you a hundred pounds!'

He paused; sought to remove any possible misapprehension under which she might be labouring. Anne Louise pictured the small form standing there in the dark, in a singularly baggy night-garment that she had constructed from her own underwear, ruffled head a little to one side as if speculating on the degree of credence he would receive.

'Really,' said Daniel, 'I thought at first it was you. Pretending to be a ghost — or something!'

'I'm not surprised,' asserted Anne Louise.

'But you see, I — don't believe in ghosts ... *Of course*!'

'Of course, Daniel.'

'Some people,' remarked Daniel thus encouraged, and lifting the edge of the blanket and poking his head through the gap, the better to carry on conversation, 'some people *are* afraid of ghosts ... I'm not! ... Are you?'

'Not a bit.'

'Most ladies are — and rats — and mice — and ...'

'I'm not,' lied Anne Louise.

'Not even of *your* ghost — the ghost at Lecques — the one you told me about — the beautiful lady with the skeleton hands?'

Recollection of that story obviously momentarily shook his self-confidence.

'Oh, *that*!' said Anne Louise, assuming the sleepiest voice possible. 'That was just a tale. I think my grandfather invented it.'

'Ah!' said Daniel, satisfied again, and speaking with some severity. 'People shouldn't invent ghost stories. They might frighten some people. And it's lying, isn't it?'

Anne Louise assented, with a counterfeited yawn.

'If I saw a ghost,' grumbled Daniel, retiring again to bed, 'I'ld — I'ld laugh at it! Like anything! ... Bet you I would!'

But Seven did not laugh when he heard of the mysterious rat. He, too, had awakened during the night. He had thought to see a big figure fumbling and peering amid the shadows of the hold ... He moved his blankets so that he should lie across the entry to the domain of her Highness the Duchess of Limburg and Princess of Lecques.

During the morning the wind rose, and repeated squalls of rain drove like hail upon the deserted decks. The ship rode on her way jerkily, with the up-and-down movement of a rocking-horse, her masts almost bare of sail. By the afternoon she was staggering up grey-green mountains of sea which were suddenly transformed into grey-green valleys, down to whose deeps she plunged with such violence that every timber in her groaned and shook separately and in unison, while an avalanche of water streamed over her and ran boiling back into the boiling flood. She leaned over so that the very tips of her lower yard-arms almost dipped themselves into the curved sea ; reared up like a horse that would fall upon its back, and (instead) crashed forward as though she would penetrate, suicidally, the vast depths of the Atlantic.

Long before, all the loose gear had been lashed fast : the poultry and the pigs had been housed under tarpaulins in the long-boat which was stowed amid-ships : the passengers had been sent below decks, with a barrel of drinking water, and the hatch battened down over them.

For six days they remained helpless in the darkness, and squalor, and stench of a floating sepulchre that writhed and leaped in the torment of the storm.

For a great part of the time that darkness was utter, for the lanthorn under the scuttle eventually flickered out, and there was nothing else that could be lighted with safety. The noise was horrific : the wailing of the children, the retching of the sick, the frightened crying of women, were all lost in the uproar of the storm without, in the thunder of the great waters that beat on the deck above, in the inferno of creaking, and squeaking, and bumping which never ceased. Some of the household furnishings broke loose from their lashings, and crashed to and fro in the dark : a heavy chest became unmoored, lumbered uneasily about the hold, and then was hurled upon a sleeping child, crushing both its legs.

There was no means of cooking food. Anne Louise and Daniel did well enough from the store of preserved provisions that the forethought of Togarmah had laid in, but the other emigrants lived on salt beef and green bacon, with raw potatoes and handfuls of uncooked oatmeal or flour.

Anne Louise lay in her berth practically all the time, with Daniel retired into his den below. In the pitch-blackness they played Alphabet games : they loved their love with an A because she was ardent, or amorous or artful; with an M because she was mute; and so to a Z because she was zealous, or Zelanian — Anne Louise's contribution, which was hotly contested by Daniel, and soundlessly queried by Seven who lay listening without. They competed for rivers and cities whose names began with P or L. They also played interminable games of

'Animal, Vegetable or Mineral?' and told one another interminable stories.

It was Seven who took charge of the drinking water and doled out a small ration to every passenger each morning — there was none to spare for washing. He also evolved an extremely primitive sanitary arrangement which served its purpose sufficiently, although those lodged near it complained very bitterly on various grounds.

The stench was intolerable, and the atmosphere they breathed was rather a noxious gas than air; it not merely smelled, but also tasted. It was as if they lived and ate and slept in a dense fog. Anne Louise felt that even should the most brilliant light burst through the walls of the *Joan Dearlove's* hold, it would illumine nothing but a swirling mass of greasy vapour that it could not penetrate.

The injured child died: lay curled for three days on its blankets, until Seven emptied into a sack the contents of a barrel of flour; and crammed the little body into the cask with a packing of sawdust off the floor; and made Joe Liddell carpenter a tight lid — a very tight lid . . . As if to counterbalance the loss, a child was born in that reeking cellar; whimpered a little, but survived. . . .

The storm subsided. Seven awoke one morning early to see a faint grey light filtering into the hold: the scuttle in the hatchway covering had been opened. The fumes, the miasma of the dreadful place rose up to the narrow vent, and twisted through it in a wreathing steam.

He went up to a deck which had been swept clear of litter. The long-boat had gone from its station over the main-hatch: the goblin cottage with the tall chimney had vanished utterly, together with all its pots and pans: evidence of their passing was to be seen in the splintered bulwarks on the port side of the ship.

The *Joan Dearlove* rode easily on the long swell of the Atlantic. The sunrise overtook her. The leaden meadows of the sea became silver — became faintly gold.

At the head of the poop-ladder stood Captain Pedder; stood top-hatted and splay-footed in the opening, with a hand on the rail on either side. He stared along the length of his battered ship. In his huge face was no weariness . . . and no triumph. Seven felt that his expression was that of a god who appreciated no offering but that of violence — that the battle of his ship with the Atlantic was but one paltry item in the list of sacrifices he required; and that the prospect of renewed violence alone would awaken him from immobility.

A little later he appeared in the twilit alleyways of the hold, followed by the first mate. Stooped beneath the low deck-beams, he passed with silent tread along the narrow lane between hugger-mugger of furniture and packing-cases, and swinging screens of blankets. He peered, without word, into all the various lairs as the occupants began to bestir themselves with the filtering in of daylight and the dissipation of human-made fog by clean ocean winds . . . Peered into all but that of Highness of Limburg and Lecques. Seven Tempest stood lazily, and yawning, on guard before the Duchy; did not stir from the frontier of red and brown blankets as Pedder approached.

'There's a young woman dressing in here,' said Seven with finality.

Pedder halted: eyed him. Although no muscle of the sailor's face stirred, it was obvious that he was assessing afresh the tall man before him, who also could not stand erect beneath the low deck. He said nothing. He turned. He went away.

As the day wore on, however, the captain evinced further interest in the welfare of his passengers. He prowled again through the hold: inspected the distribution of water from the great cask at the break of the poop: supervised the construction of a temporary fire-place with sheet-iron and some rails against the lee bulwarks; read (with his hat on and without any shadow of emotion) the burial service over the flour-barrel that contained the battered relics of the dead child; ordered the production of a small cask of rum and watched his mulatto steward deliver a ration to all on board.

During all these proceedings he did not speak a single unnecessary word. With careless unconcern he pulled Henry Wentworth back by an aristocratic ear when he pressed forward out of his turn in the rush for water; without comment and without oath he had clouted to the deck the cabin boy whom he found idly regarding the distant black hummock of a whale on the bottle-green sea.

In the late afternoon one of the older girl-children — the daughter of the wild-eyed preacher — appeared on the poop. Where Pedder had found her, or when, nobody knew; but her cheek was bulged with sweet-meat, and she and the captain played a violent game of catch-as-catch-can around the skylight and round the helmsman with screams of laughter. Then there fell silence. The mother sat waiting on the lower step of the ladder. Dusk came: then night. And with the coming of night the captain's steward brought back the child so utterly drunken that she had no conception or memory of what had befallen her — or not befallen her — despite the most intimate questionings.

The next morning found Captain Pedder deep in conversation with the Vyvyans, leaning over the rail between them.

Mr. Horatio was deeply impressed: his Small Lady was deeply

impressed. They hastened to convey their sentiments to Seven, Anne Louise, and even the unresponsive Wentworth who had grown more and more sullen over his ostracism by Highness — an ostracism which he (quite rightly) ascribed to breach of confidence by Lovell.

One had — burbled the Vyvyans — to be broad-minded. One's profession taught one the shallowness of social convention. One saw through shams. One realized that genius was not bound by ordinary limitations — and was it not genius that could conduct a craft across the pathless, limitless sea, for over three thousand miles to so distant a shore?

Mrs. Vyvyan, too, was greatly interested in this man whose origin was wrapped in the densest mystery — who was deprived of all relationships, and had found no friends in his lonely course across the oceans of the world. She could not entirely condone, but she could forgive, his occasional lapses from the standards of gentility and moral behaviour set by the social circle in which she had been brought up. '*Such* an interesting man! . . . Misunderstood!' was the burthen of her explanation.

They supped with Captain Pedder that night.

At noon the next day they dined with him, and afterwards promenaded on the poop-deck — Mr. Horatio declaiming choice selections from his favourite parts to the glassy sea, to a glassier Pedder, to an embarrassed helmsman. . . .

The mulatto steward soon appeared with a tray of brimming rummers full of brown liquor. Mrs. Vyvyan sipped at hers in the most genteel manner possible, but Mr. Vyvyan, following Pedder's example, drained his glass at a draught, held it out to be refilled, and burst into an impassioned declamation from 'Titus Andronicus'. After the second glass his enunciation lacked the precision that should be expected from a disciple of Thespis. Mrs. Vyvyan ignored him: she and Captain Pedder were pacing the deck, making the round of the table-tomb of a sky-light and the companion-hatch, in the genteelest promenade possible to a lady wearing a dashed brown satin dress and a gentleman with a top hat but no shoes to his feet.

At 5.30 precisely the Vyvyans supped with the captain again. At least the steward rang a bell very fiercely, and all three disappeared from view.

Deep blue night slid over the ocean. A strong wind roared out of the cloudless darkness toward a rising moon, and a silvering horizon, and died down again.

A faint yellow light showed in the dusk of the fo'c'sle: there were lemon-coloured slits beneath the table-top of the flat tomb on the poop. Sounds of polite revelry were wafted to the main deck, for there was no other noise except the slapping of the long swell against the ship's side, the subdued creaking of cordage, and the drowsy hum — as of a sleepy hive — which came up from the hold.

Faintly into this idyllic peace — muffled by wine and by distance — came the lady-like pipe of Mrs. Vyvyan's voice raised in an elegantly nautical song:

> 'Roll on, O deep and billowy tide,
> And bear me swiftly to my bride!
> Blow winds! Blow storms! Away with calms!
> I hasten to my lov'd one's arms!'

Boisterous applause from Captain Pedder followed. A little later a strange medley of sound broke out from the cabin; as if Pedder were singing, and Horatio declaiming, and Mrs. Vyvyan applauding, all at one and the same time.

Still later, Mr. Vyvyan appeared at the companion-head, flung a dramatic arm to the stars, hiccupped a denunciation of someone or something, reeled, and crashed straight to the bottom where he lay completely unconscious and smelling of rum.

Anne Louise, who had come on deck to fill her lungs with clean air before retiring to the night fetor below, gasped as he fell; but Seven — he had become a second and inescapable shadow in the last few days — stirred not a finger. He turned his head and regarded the prostrate man for an instant, and then looked away again, without comment.

Mrs. Vyvyan's tinkling parlour voice began afresh.

> 'Thy loving heart, with jasmine twined,
> Permit me to my bosom bind! —'

sang she, a trifle out of tune. . . .

At that moment — presuming that the heart referred to was Mr. Vyvyan's — 'Loving Heart' turned over on its face, was very sick, and endeavoured to climb the steep descent to the hold on all fours, and head first.

Anne Louise pulled at the sleeve of the silent man beside her —
'He'll break his neck,' she said.

'Does it matter?' asked Seven, just sufficiently turning his head to make certain that the downward journey would be accomplished without any serious disaster. 'Does it really matter?'

> '. . . And, with such whispered love caressed,
> That naught shall tear it from my breast!'

continued Mrs. Vyvyan.

Having thus asked permission to bind a jasmine-twined heart very firmly to her bosom, Mrs. Vyvyan suddenly ceased her song, and began to scream.

Anne Louise had never heard a woman scream from sheer terror before.

She found, however, that the silence which followed immediately upon the screams was more appalling still. She peered up through the dusk at Seven's face, but it was turned resolutely seaward. He showed no sign of having heard anything unusual.

'Didn't you hear?' she asked.

'No!' replied Seven.

At that instant Mrs. Vyvyan began to scream again. It was not the lady-like squeak of her girlhood; nor the heart-stirring scream with which any one of a dozen young actresses she knew would fling herself passionately across the stage. It was a thin weak cry — something between the wail of a newly-born baby and the half-sigh half-whistle of the wind through a key-hole. It ended suddenly. Very suddenly.

'Why don't you go . . . ?' said Anne Louise fiercely.

'Where?' replied Seven still looking out to sea.

' "Where?" ' repeated Anne Louise, so furious that she shivered from her anger. 'Where? . . . Go up! . . . Stop it! . . .'

'Your Highness,' answered Seven, addressing her formally for the first time since they had sailed, 'may now realize *one*, only one, of the reasons why I refused to change your accommodation to the after-cabin.' He continued his study of the sleek and shining waters.

'That woman . . .' began Anne Louise in a choked voice.

'. . . knew quite well what to expect!'

'No!'

'Yes!'

The hood of her cloak had fallen back from her head. Even in the moonlight he saw how pale and tense had become her face. With a sudden desperate gesture she turned, fled to the poop-ladder, and was flying up it. Swifter still than she, he turned too; was at the foot of the ladder in a single stride; had stretched out and torn her backward by the hem of her gown so that she fell violently into his arms.

She was not in his clasp for a second; for he had swung her round, and shaken her as if she were a naughty child — a furiously naughty child.

'You fool!' he said. 'A captain is God in his ship! . . . Are you trying to stage a mutiny?'

'You *must* help her,' stammered Anne Louise in overpowering anger. He still shook her.

'You *must*!' — It was a command.

And 'You *must*!' — It was a statement of social obligation.

And 'You *must*!' — It was a plea.

And then her resources gave out: she tore herself from his grip; and burst into tears; and bowed her head in her arms on the ship's rail, and sobbed as might any child . . . Never before had she permitted herself to break down utterly in public.

Seven looked at her for an instant, with a twisted smile that — strangely enough, and for the first time — held sympathy with her in distress, and also some sardonic amusement at the cause of it. He could not bring himself to believe that Vyvyan's Small Lady had been entirely unaware of the risks she ran, or that her outcry did not represent a polite protest against too rapid ardour rather than genuine consternation. It was no sense of knight errantry, but Anne Louise's despair that sent him, with a half-laugh, to investigate. . . .

The cabin was narrow for its length, and panelled with a dark wood in which shone the reflections of two bracket-lamps on the forward bulkhead.

Captain Pedder, with his back to the door, lounged on the far end of a table still covered with a once-white cloth and littered with glasses and bottles. His hat was beside him, his arms were folded easily, a bare foot swung nonchalantly to and fro, and his great bald head nodded with the emphasis of his remarks.

Opposite him, under the lamps, on a red-upholstered locker that ran the width of the cabin, was crouched Mr. Horatio Vyvyan's Small Lady, staring, as one hypnotized, at the indecently naked head and feet of the big man. Her pretty bonnet (with the cherries under the brim) was on the floor; her dark ringlets framed a long pale face with large and darkened eyes; one hand was pressed hard on the shabby velvet cushions to keep her body upright, and the other endeavoured to hold together a long rent in the bosom of the once-fashionable chocolate-coloured gown. The wide lace collar to the dress had utterly vanished.

'And *now* my little duck,' said Captain Pedder, with an air of finality, '*will* be a little duck to poor old Hen Pedder! Won't she?'

He was about to slide off the table end, when Seven, standing unobserved in the narrow doorway, said —

'Good evening, Mrs. Vyvyan! . . . Good evening, Cap'n!'

In one swift movement the sailor had swung to his feet, turned, slammed his extraordinary hat over the baldness of his head, and leaned as if about to spring across the length of the narrow table at the newcomer. His huge body hid Mrs. Vyvyan from view, but Seven knew that she had immediately risen, and was adjusting her ruin of a gown and her distorted face to a more public view.

Said Seven, very easily —

'Forgive the intrusion . . .' And paused for a moment as if waiting for the glowering man opposite to proffer forgiveness. His face was actually without expression, but a dark lock of hair had fallen across his forehead and, in its faint suggestion of a question-mark, hinted a quizzical amusement at the situation.

Seven continued — and his ease and confidence seemed to hold the other man with their spell —

'Mr. Vyvyan has had an accident! . . . Oh, very slight! . . . A fall . . . Don't worry, Mrs. Vyvyan! . . . There's no need . . . But he thought . . .'

Pedder said nothing. He just swayed a little to and fro, his great hands resting on the table. He did not move his eyes from Seven, as if he were making sure that his memory should always carry the correct image of the tall man confronting him — of the broad shoulders, cleft chin, veiled eyes, long grave nose with the faintest twist to it, and the insulting lock of dark hair.

Mrs. Vyvyan had fluttered into some concealment of her disorders.

She fluttered also into gasping speech: Was he badly hurt? . . . How kind of Mr. Cash . . . She must go . . . Must go at once . . . Must!

She came down the cabin to Seven's side. She was shuddering. She drew in her wide skirts as she shrank past Pedder so that they should not touch him. With the other hand she held together the wreckage of her bodice. She did not speak another word, or join Seven in his courteous 'Good-night!' . . .

Seven had to hand her up the companion-way, for she trembled so greatly that she could barely walk: and when at last she set foot upon the serenity of the main deck — a chiaroscuro of moonlight and sail-shadows — she tottered as if she would fall.

'Hold up!' said Seven, and set strong hands upon her shoulders and propelled her toward the hatch.

But across the Small Lady's bemused mind had surged all the recollections of the code of parlour gentility in old Ipswich days — of procedure in familiar circumstances in the romantic drama. She suddenly flung back her head; reposed herself on Seven's broad chest; gasped 'My preserver!' and burst into floods of tears.

'Hell!' said Seven, and was aware that Anne Louise had emerged from somewhere out of the darkness.

185

CHAPTER V

THE SHIP THAT REACHED NO HAVEN

CAPTAIN PEDDER went below decks shortly before 'Lights Out!' on the following day to inspect his passengers' quarters again. He had fortified himself for the task with seven large tots of neat rum, and he moved, peering, through the candle-lit dusk of the hold as if he were an intoxicated sorcerer about to select a victim from the dungeons for his next repast.

Not far from the foot of the companion-ladder a sort of cavern, about two yards square, had been screened off with sail-cloth by the Vyvyans amid the jungle of furniture. Captain Pedder lifted a corner of the curtain and stared in, chewing a quid of tobacco with a slow and sideways movement of his jaws.

He was unobserved for a few moments. Mr. Vyvyan's Small Lady seated on an untidy bundle of blankets, was engaged in repairing the damage done to her dress at the *soirée musicale*, by the light of a candle stuck on a provision box. Blankets, box, kettle, and a large and bulging carpet-bag were the only equipment of the apartment.

Captain Pedder permitted himself to belch; and then to chuckle when she looked up startled, and shrank back, and went pale.

'Well, my little duck!' said he in a blurred low voice. 'Forgiven old Hen yet? Forgiven poor old Henny, hey?'

At that someone tapped him sharply on the shoulder.

He swung about; and as he did so, Mr. Vyvyan leaped back, and assumed a posture of the most dignified and theatrical defiance.

'You are a cur, sir!' said Vyvyan throatily. '*Aboard* you may be captain of the ship! *Ashore*, sir, God-dam-me, I shall know how to deal with you — as a private individual! . . . And deal with you I shall! Horse-whipping is too good for you!'

Mr. Vyvyan thrust a hand into the bosom of his seedy purplish frogged surtout, and struck an attitude intended to convey to any witnesses that he had at that moment thrown down the gage of battle to the captain.

Captain Pedder said not a word. He did not even look as if he had heard a word. He kicked out — and high — a long white-trousered leg. His yellow naked foot struck Mr. Vyvyan in the face, and struck so hard that the actor went reeling across the alleyway and into the lair opposite.

Then the ship rolled slightly . . . gently. And with that movement Pedder staggered, lost his balance, and crashed over sideways.

Forward from the bottom of the companion-ladder, the passage through the hold widened into a sort of clearing which was the focal-point of the underworld life, the common playground of the children, the conference place of the adults. At this moment it was deserted, except at the far end. There Ira and Tom, the Welsh miners who shared their concubines in common, were squatted on their hunkers playing cards, by the light of a guttering candle stuck in its own grease to the top of a cask.

The two little men had paused in their game at the approach of Pedder: they had watched him as small beasts might watch uncertainly a larger: they had risen with his downfall: they had stood crouching to the spring like dogs waiting the order to attack.

The order came.

For the screen of red blankets about the mouth of the den into which Vyvyan had been projected, was suddenly torn aside. The gaunt figure of the preacher from the mountains, clad only in a shirt, stood in the opening. He flung both arms up toward the deck above as though summoning the fury of Jehovah to pierce into that godless place: he mouthed tremendous invective from Isaiah against the desecrator of childhood: he hurled himself upon the prostrate man with the ferocity of a wild beast.

His action unleashed the other men. They, too, leaped snarling to the attack . . . Pedder half rose: was on his knees, with his enemies clinging to him like dogs tearing at a wild boar: fought one arm free, just as Vyvyan, who had been whimpering on the outskirts of the battle, threw himself atop: went down again under the weight of numbers.

The struggling mass heaved itself about insanely in the obscurity between the thickets of piled-up goods in whose depths faint lights fought the restless shadows, and whence peered the dimly-seen faces of a growing army of watchers. The noise of conflict was drowned in the creaking of the ship and the rising hum of excited comment.

By a stupendous effort Pedder rose again to one knee: his mouth was open — round as an O — to bellow for help . . . A woman, swaying to the movement of the ship, struck him full in the face with a frying-pan, and screamed objurgations as she did. He went down yet again into the snarling pack.

For about a minute Seven, seated on a lower rung of the companion-ladder, watched the progress of battle. To his surprise Sarah Liddell squeezed past from the darkness behind and fell — literally — upon the tangle of heaving bodies. The woman who had struck Pedder tore savagely at her thin gown.

Seven rose; retreated up the narrow gangway to the Duchy of Limburg; and thrust his head between the red and brown blankets that were its frontier. Anne Louise was already in bed. Daniel the Dom'd, in an astonishing night attire of cream flannel was about to say his prayers, kneeling against the brass-nailed trunk which held the royal treasure and served as the royal dressing-table. Anne Louise, leaning on an elbow, was presiding at the ceremony with an expression of almost maternal encouragement.

Said Seven —

'Get up! . . . Get out! . . . On deck. Now!'

'Why?' asked Anne Louise, resenting this intrusion upon a religious exercise.

Seven crossed the frontier without apology. He entered the royal domain unbidden. He took up the cloak and shawl that lay on one of the cases.

'Find your stockings! Find your shoes! Put these on! At once! . . . Daniel, find your trousers! And your coat!'

His urgency was such that Anne Louise had swung her long legs out of the bunk before she realized that Highness was obeying an order — had been wrapped in a shawl, and was pulling on stockings like an obedient schoolgirl, whilst Daniel tucked the terrific tails of his nightshirt into the limited storage space of peg-top check trousers.

'Come on!' Seven urged. 'Quickly! *Very* quickly. There's going to be trouble. You are better out of it.'

Anne Louise was aware of a huddle of bodies threshing about at the foot of the companion-way — a sort of dark octopus of flying limbs and a babble of inhuman sounds. She found herself impelled upward on to a deserted deck that stirred ever so faintly over a moonlit ocean.

'Keep in the dark!' said Seven. 'Keep in the shadow of the poop! Keep out of sight!'

The uproar below was inaudible on deck. Not a soul was visible except the dark figure of one of the watch right forward on the fo'c'sle. Someone, however, leaned whistling on the rail above their heads.

'Hey!' said the someone, 'why ain't you folks berthed down?'

It was the second mate — the father of eight presidents.

'Cap'n's having an argument,' said Seven in a low voice. 'It seems best for quiet folk to be out of the way.'

'Ah-h!' commented Long-Nose in a meditative sigh, and spat juicily into the sea.

At that very second a heaving jelly of a creature squeezed through the opening in the hatch, and rapidly travelled — breathless and ungainly — toward them.

It was Sarah Liddell.

'Mr. Sep!' she said, and gasped and heaved as she spoke. 'Mr. Sep, come quickly! They'll murder him!'

'Why not?' said Seven.

'They'll murder him!' And plucked at him — tore at him, with urgent hands.

Long-Nose, whistling more loudly, to show that he had not heard, ambled diplomatically out of ear-shot.

'Again — Why not, Sally-ally?' asked Seven.

She shook him, big man as he was —

'Mr. Sep! He's . . .' she began.

And then all hell seemed to have been let loose. Cries — screams — shouts — poured up in a medley to the night through that one narrow entrance to the warren below. A tongue of yellow fire flicked straight upward out of the scuttle; vanished; was succeeded by a stream of smoke as white and dense as a river fog under a full moon.

There came a fresh burst of flame through the narrow opening: its reds and yellows filled the space; it was fringed with a blur of hot and quivering gases, that were almost — but not quite — invisible. A few fat and sooty-black ashes spiralled up swiftly and then fluttered to the deck.

The tragedy was swifter than any telling. One minute the curved expanse of the great sail on the lower yard-arm had been a graduation of shadows fringed on the starboard side with a broad band of ghostly moonshine; the next it reflected the glare of fire spouting, with ever increasing intensity, from the hatch as from an open furnace-door.

From forward came the frantic shrilling of the bo'sun's whistle: the long-nosed second mate landed on the main deck beside Seven with a thud.

'Up with you! Up with you!' said Seven fiercely; and Anne Louise found herself being impelled with Daniel up the ladder to the poop — that poop where Green-and-White-Stripes had flaunted herself bravely so short a time before; where Mr. Vyvyan's Small Lady had promenaded in a genteel manner but a day or two back.

Green-and-White-Stripes! . . . The Small Lady!

Anne Louise hesitated at the head of the ladder, and looked back.

In the confusion below she saw Seven and Long-Nose struggling with the pump, and Sarah Liddell by the scuttle-butt shielding her face from the heat, which even on the poop was almost unbearable.

As she looked something black appeared in the yellow square — crumpled itself over the coaming of the hatch — dragged itself on to the deck, not on hands and knees, but by the body writhings of a singed insect.

It was Pedder; and no one followed him, for the blaze, through which by some miracle of body and will he had come, rose on the instant into a great column of solid flame which shot up, enveloping the main-mast and seizing on main-sail and top-sail so that they both caught light and stirred in a furious agony. Fragments of burning canvas were torn off by the rising wind, and flew uncertainly into the night, white in the moonshine like tattered paper.

In the space of a few moments the *Joan Dearlove* had become a torch amidships, casting lurid reflections on the smooth heaving water.

Green-and-White-Stripes! . . . The Small Lady!

Anne Louise suddenly felt herself clammy with a spasm of awful sickness. They were below, somewhere utterly beyond escape or rescue, in a trap to which the entrance — and the exit — had been sealed by fire.

The great mainyard sagged at one side, fell amid a shower of sparks, and lay across the width of the ship, with shreds of sail still burning upon it — a flaming barrier, beyond which she could see small black figures capering aimlessly (it seemed) to and fro. The tarred shrouds were burning, and loose ends of rigging hung down, dark stalactites gold-tipped with fire.

Seven dashed toward the furnace door — was driven back — leaped forward again — was once more repulsed. And then the small breeze strengthened, and the fiery wall slanted away for an instant, in which he hauled the captain's body out of range, hoisted it upon a shoulder, and made for the temporary safety of the poop-deck.

Then came an explosion which seemed to lift the old ship out of the water. A solid mass of whitish flame heaved itself up into the night, enveloping the mainmast and the foremast. The deck, somewhere about the main-hatch, burst asunder, and opened into a crater showing a hold that glowed red-hot.

Green-and-White-Stripes! . . . Mr. Vyvyan's Small Lady! . . . The child that had been born three nights before . . . Lord Henry Wentworth, whose black stockinette pantaloons she had attempted to steal so many, many years ago! . . .

Anne Louise was never able to recover a clear idea of the swift sequence of events that followed — of those last few strange minutes aboard the *Joan Dearlove*.

Burning fragments fell on the cabin sky-light, and on the deck beside them; and she was aware of a Daniel who leaped, shouting like one possessed, from flaming ember to ember, to stamp on them, to beat them out.

She was aware, too, of Seven and the long-nosed mate staring together for an instant over the forward rail, at the barrier of fire which was now mast-high and frothed at its summit into a spume of black smoke that was driven forward and upward, veiling the mounting moon.

She remembered hearing Seven say — 'Not a hope! . . . Not one!' and the little man respond, 'Aye, aye, sir!' and add — 'I told him there'ld be trouble if he kept that stuff below: that them bar'ls 'ld go up like volcaners. . . . He couldn't be bothered. He always took risks!' She wondered why the long-nosed mate called Seven 'sir'.

She was aware of Sarah Liddell crouched mountainously over the thing which Seven had heaved into the scuppers, and comforting it, and crooning to it while it writhed in agony . . . On the flat top of the cabin skylight was a wide deep box. She remembered peering into it on tiptoe, and seeing in the glare that its high sides sheltered a well-grown crop of mustard and cress. A big hour-glass stood beside it: the sand had all run out. Some superstition stirred within her: she reversed it, and the sand began to pour down again in a thin thread. By that she found herself comforted, as if she had herself given more time, and — with more time — more life to the old ship.

Mr. 'Snorker' Reid — his queer triangular face yellowed by the reflection of the fire; his queer triangular mouth agape — stood clutching uselessly the spokes of the useless wheel,

She knew, too, that presently he also said 'Aye, aye, sir!' and let go the helm, and busied himself in the most unflurried manner, with the mate, at a tangle of rope . . . There was a gap full of distant shouting, of swift movement, of great heat, of crackling and of hissing, and of alternating spurts of shadow and of flame. She distinctly heard Mr. Reid say, 'Everything decently, and in good order — as the hangman said!' as he lifted her into the boat which hung quivering from its falls over the stern. . . There was no wake to the ship, she noted: the *Joan Dearlove* had ceased to move. . .

A little later she found herself rocking on the Atlantic swell in a small and crowded boat, seated in a puddle, with her head upon Mr.

Reid's knee. Mr. Reid appeared to be making disparaging comparisons between the present disaster and his most recent previous experience. . . '*Amphitrite*. . . In '32. . . One 'underd and thirty young wimmin convicts aboard . . . And every one of them drownded — drown-*dead*. I saw them in the morning all washed up on Boulogne beach. In cotton gowns. Like dead jelly-fish.'

Anne Louise, dimly aware of an enormous glare accompanied by a roar, acutely aware of the boniness of Mr. Reid's knee, reclined with closed eyelids, wondering whether the sea delivered up dead ladies with due regard to decency.

The *Joan Dearlove* was a mass of fire from end to end. In places her sides had burst away from the ribs of the hull so that she resembled a roasting skeleton. She was no longer a ship, but a bonfire. Steam rose from the hissing water in which she still floated. The dark sea was made bright by the reflection of her flames, and the roar and crackling of her conflagration were loud above the murmur of un-numbered leagues of ocean.

BOOK FOUR

TWO KINDS OF ROMANCE

*

CHAPTER I

INTERLUDE IN A PALACE

AT precisely fourteen minutes past nine by the buhl clock on the colossal mantelpiece of grey marble, the King of Hanover stalked into his study from the adjoining dressing-room. Unusually for him at that time of day, his toilette had not yet been completed; and he wore a long dressing-gown of dark red silk and a black silk scarf wound many times round his throat.

He lowered his great form stiffly into a gilded elbow chair, back to the open fire, facing — across a malachite table supported by sphinxes — three tall windows that revealed a grey sky and a vista of wet gravel bounded by a balustrade set with damp urns and dripping statuary. There was another tall window at either end of the lofty room, which was papered in red; and over the fireplace hung a full-length portrait of the Elector George Louis, afterwards George the First of England.

Before the King many documents were arranged in piles with military precision and neatness, under paper-weights of little bronze cannon mounted on bases of reddish marble, the muzzles all loyally pointing away from Majesty. For an instant he examined the alignment of this artillery; then — fierce old head thrown up, and jutting chin forced to the arrogant angle at which he had carried it for eight-and-sixty years — he slowly turned the glare of his one eye about the room as if inspecting a parade. For all that his regard was as the peering of the nearly blind, there was about him the suggestion of immense and violent power. The great hand that rested upon the table had the fingers bent so that it resembled a talon. The slow swing of the bald shining head, with its great beak of a nose, and the hooded gaze from under the fierce brows, were those of a bird of prey.

The clock on the mantelpiece chimed the quarter.

The talon seized a small gold bell, and sounded it once, harshly, imperatively.

The business of the day had begun — fifteen minutes earlier than usual. . . .

TWO KINDS OF ROMANCE

It was not until nearly the half-hour that General von Düring, Majesty's secretary, emerged from his apartments and started at a quick shuffle to the royal suite.

He was old, lean, tall, and astonishingly dusty. His shabby blue uniform — with the tarnished gold embroidery about the high collar — was dusty; his thin grey hair was dusty; his anxious long-nosed face was dusty; and the light in his faded eyes was so quenched that they seemed dusty, too.

In one hand he carried a battered leather portfolio; with the other he supported an extremely long pipe from whose capacious china bowl trickled a thin stream of tobacco smoke, poisoning all his wake.

He had lighted it when he got out of bed. Since then the amber mouthpiece had but rarely been removed from his mouth during the processes of washing, shaving, and breakfasting on biscuits dipped in coffee. All these operations were, in fact, performed almost simultaneously; and during them he even further busied himself in annotating in red ink the King's English correspondence (which had arrived by courier very late on the previous night) with the aid of a small dictionary propped against the mirror on his toilet-table.

He clambered, with queer broken-kneed action, down an enormous chilly staircase hung with enormous chilly pictures of dead-and-gone Kings and Electors of Hanover: crossed an enormous chilly hall; and turned into a lofty corridor with a floor of black and white marble. Two hussars in blue tunics, with drawn swords, stood before the folding doors of mahogany at the far end. Nearer — under one of the long windows that showed a cheerless sky and tossing black branches — four attendants, in liveries of crimson and gold, awaited his coming, stiffly at attention. One of them held out gingerly before him a long-handled shovel that appeared to be red-hot: a second bore a salver with a glass of water and a saucer full of brownish crystals on it; and a third had an old-fashioned military cloak folded over his arm.

General von Düring's amble became a sort of gallop; and as he galloped so he blew out a perfect fog of tobacco smoke.

He came to a halt — standing with his shaky old legs as wide apart as if he were straddling a ditch — and surrendered himself to their services.

Deferentially and swiftly the pale-faced men swarmed about him. As one removed his pipe, so another enfolded him in the long dark horseman's cloak (which he had worn twenty years and more ago at Waterloo) and buckled the strap tightly about the throat; so yet another poured the brown crystals on to the angry red of the shovel —

from which arose forthwith grey smoke and the piercing sweet smell of incense — and thrust it under the cloak, and held it between the general's legs.

The solemn morning ritual of the fumigation of Excellency was in progress. A necessary ritual, indeed, since Majesty abhorred the smell of tobacco.

Von Düring stood there for full two minutes, his mild old horse-face lifted blankly to the vaulted ceiling while thin streams of incense trickled out of the collar of the cloak and up to his large nose. He snuffed loudly at the purifying element; seized the glass of water, rinsed his mouth still more loudly; spat the water out on the floor.

An instant later the great doors had swung open, and General von Düring, reeking like a newly-censed cathedral, shambled into the presence of his master.

But someone was already in attendance — someone who had accompanied the royal courier back from England. For sitting very much at his ease, facing the King across the shining width of the malachite table and the regimented documents, was a very small, very exquisite gentleman in a violet-coloured coat and pale green trousers. He had the sparkling dark eyes, flushed olive complexion and smooth features of an Italian shepherd lad. He looked like a schoolboy masquerading in a man's clothes — at a distance. There was, too, something uncommonly youthful in his enunciation and high light voice. He paid no attention to the arrival of von Düring, beyond flashing him a quick glance and nod of recognition, but continued what he was saying —

' . . . So I said, "I don't care a damn what you think. It is a true story" . . . '

'Was it?' interrupted the King.

The little man's answer was a snigger. He proceeded —

'So they printed it in full, sir. All the other papers copied it. It went round Town like wild fire. And now they shout "Mrs. Melbourne!" after the Queen when she's out driving. They do really! I've heard them myself!'

He giggled, and the King of Hanover permitted himself a grim smile.

'It's a good angle to the campaign,' continued the little man pressing the tips of his small fingers together in a judicial manner, and gently swinging a highly varnished boot. 'It's got the merit, too, of having some foundation . . . Here's my Lord Melbourne, twice accused in the courts of adultery — last time only three years ago — become the bosom friend and confidant of the maiden Queen of England! He may be Premier, but that doesn't mean he's always got to be at the Palace! As he is. Lolls about on sofas — goes to sleep after dinner — throws his "Damns" about — criticizes her dresses. Just as if he were at home. Perhaps he *is*!' — So strange an expression suddenly extinguished the youthfulness of the little creature's face, that even the unimaginative general found himself wondering whether he were really Humphrey Cobbold, once the King's chaplain and now his secret and very private agent, or some malignant sprite from the depths of a German forest. — 'He's always liked his lady friends young. The older he gets the younger he'll like 'em. He must be sixty — and she's eighteen. *He* adores her. *She* thinks there's nobody in the world like him. You should see them together, sir! See 'em together!' He rolled in an ecstasy of merriment on his chair.

The King was leaning forward, his arms upon the table. One big hand, with strong shining nails, fidgeted with a cannon paper-weight.

Mr. Cobbold put on his knees a small purple leather portfolio that had been on the floor beside him; opened it; produced a thick wad of newspaper clippings — sought through them — found what he wanted — donned an enormous pair of horn-rimmed spectacles which made him look more than ever a malevolent elf.

'My little budget!' said he with a satisfied air. 'It'll prove to you, sir, that I haven't been idle. That your money has been well spent. Have a look at 'em, sir, when you've a minute to spare. Words! — Words! Words that'll do more damage than bombs! Words *do*! Words are lovely, dangerous, poisonous, deadly things! . . . I may be prejudiced in favour of my methods,' he continued thoughtfully, 'but I think I can obtain results which mere brute force cannot. *I* can ruin a reputation; break old friendships, and' — here he paused for an appreciable space of time — '*and* undermine a throne.'

The King made no comment. He swung round the muzzle of his miniature piece of artillery, gauged the range of the dank Apollo on the balustrade of the terrace, adjusted the angle of fire, corrected it again; and then, having presumably demolished the statue, turned his attention to the matter in hand.

'Well?' he asked curtly.

' "Out of his mouth went a sharp two-edged word." That's from the Book of Revelation,' said Mr. Cobbold. 'Out of *my* mouth come sharp two-edged swords, too. Lots of them. Very sharp! All very, very sharp! . . . Here's one of them . . .'

He took up a cutting from the bunch which he had placed on the table, and read a few lines from it in a delicate little voice —

' "If Lord Melbourne sees the virtuous of the land avoiding the Palace balls and Court receptions as they would a pestilence — if he sees even common respect withheld from one whom, but for his despicable policy, we should reverence and love — if he discovers that cold loyalty towards the wearer of the Crown in these days puts the Crown itself in jeopardy . . . "

'That's the *Morning Post*. Crown in jeopardy! . . . Palace compared with a pestilence! Isn't that a pretty dish to set before a — young Queen?' Mr. Cobbold giggled again and looked to the King for approval.

But Ernest made no comment. His heavy grey eyebrows were contracted over eyes that were unquenchably fierce even though one was sightless. His lips were parted in a snarl that showed big glittering teeth the colour of old ivory — as if the mere mention of the Crown of England called up before his gaze the figure of his niece, the young girl who had deprived him of it. He seized the little golden bell and sounded it with a single jerk.

'Here's another "sharp sword" — from an open letter to Melbourne in *The Age*,' continued M. Cobbold, perceiving that the King made no comment. 'Listen to it — it's good —

"My Lord, you are exposing the highest personage in the land to be the jest of the vicious and a source of pity to the well-disposed. . . If you affect not to know it I tell you plainly that ever since the Coronation, the enthusiasm of the people for their young Queen has been sensibly decreasing."

'A pretty comment about any young lady! A very pretty comment about a young Queen! — "Jest of the vicious"! Isn't it prime?'

In answer to the bell a little man in black had glided into the room. Over one arm he carried a pile of clothing surmounted by what appeared to be a mass of broad bandage material. At a gesture from the King he set down the heap upon a chair and waited deferentially, sallow face turned toward the floor.

Ernest pushed back his chair; rose to his feet; took up his stand close to the fire. He said suddenly: —

'I read in some Paris paper that Melbourne has decided that it is impossible for him to marry Victoria himself, and so . . .' He interrupted himself to break out violently, 'What an honour! Linking up *my* house with the spawn of a rascally attorney! God blast it!' Lost the thread of his discourses — recovered it: 'So now they say he's doing his damnedest to keep Victoria single! Afraid of losing his influence! . . . Think that's true?'

He had thrown off the dressing-gown as he fired the question, and now stood confronting the room in white shirt, under-drawers that came to the knee, and black silk stockings. Even clad in such guise he was too big, too dangerous-seeming a man to look ridiculous.

For the first time since he had entered the room, General von Düring spoke from his seat at the far end of the long table, in precise guttural English. He had trouble in his pronunciation only with the sound of the letter 'W'.

'Lady Jersey mentions the matter in a letter to your Majesty arriving last night.' He put the missive uppermost on the pile before him, and glanced at it. 'She says she knows for a certainty that Lord Melbourne raised the qvestion vith the Qveen last month. They vent through the list of princes. The Qveen vas qvite firm. She said she had no intention of marrying — at any rate yet.'

'Who was on the list?' asked Cobbold who had listened attentively.

Von Düring took up a sheet of the letter and read out a string of royal names, while the King delivered himelf to the ministrations of the man in black.

'The Duc de Nemours!'

'Bloody Papist!' commented Ernest. 'She can't marry him, if she would. Under the Constitution.'

The man in black was binding yards of fine muslin about the middle of the old body. Yard upon yard. Very tightly. Constricting the old belly — restoring to the old waist the gallant outline of youth. Mr. Cobbold, watching the operation, thought that in such wise must the embalmers of ancient Egypt have swathed the rigidity of a mummified corpse.

'Prince Villiam of the Netherlands,' continued von Düring.

'Bigger dam fool than his father! And that's saying a good deal. . . Tighter still, Karl!'

'Prince George of Denmark.'

'Dissolute bastard! . . . I said "tighter", blockhead!'

'The Grand Duke Michael.'

'Bloody Cossack! The people wouldn't stand for a savage from the steppes.' The King barked with sardonic laughter. 'God, what a pretty list of pretty lovers for a pretty lady! What a list of gutless scallywags!'

The man in black had completed his task; was securing this muslin casing of a king with small gold brooches down the side.

'And . . . ' interposed Mr. Cobbold, 'And . . . ?'

General von Düring raised his eyebrows.

'Surely there's another name on Lady Jersey's list?'

The older man ran his eye over the sheet before him.

'I beg your pardon — Prince Albert of Saxe-Coburg-Gotha. He has a separate paragraph to himself.'

The Elf took off his spectacles; became once again Beautiful Youth: pensively wiped the lenses; relapsed into profound meditation. His expression was that of a thoughtful seraph painted by one of the Italian Old Masters.

'Albert is our only real danger,' he said at length. 'He's *too* good-looking! He's a perfect Greek god! He'ld make a lady abbess's heart beat faster! And his uncle has been intriguing on his behalf ever since he was born ... An astute man, the King of the Belgians, sir!'

'Leopold is an infernal slippery rogue,' said the King with a snarl, as he was eased into close-fitting trousers of dark green.

'It's Albert I am particularly campaigning against,' remarked Cobbold.

He produced another budget of newspaper cuttings and rapidly skimmed the cream of them for the King. The excerpts which he read ranged from sarcastic and contemptuous criticism of the prince to virulent and poisonous abuse. He wound up with a quotation from *The Age —*

' "We think Prince Albert of Saxe-Coburg intellectually and morally most unfit to be trusted with the happiness of our young Queen, who is in such a state of vassalage, induced by the cunning influence of the Baroness Lehzen, her former governess, as to be publicly talked of. in the salons of Paris as the mere puppet of her uncle, Leopold. . ."

'Remarkable what these political writers will do if only they are given a lead across country. A little dinner at White's — an introduction to a marquis or to D'Orsay — a box at the Opera — an occasional party with plenty of "bubbly" and a few little dancers — a political tip hot from the House — *and* an occasional "loan" — wonderful what effect they can have, sir! I reckon, they'll help to spoil that young man's chance of a double bed in Buckingham Palace.'

'The Whigs campaigned against me,' said the King with fierce relish, 'and now, by God, they are beginning to see how I can campaign against them!'

He seated himself again in his shirt sleeves, and the man in black undid the scarf and began to wind round his throat the nine folds of muslin bandage that should keep his head up and his chin out, no matter what the fatigues of the day.

'A great deal of Lady Jersey's letter is devoted to the position of Her Majesty,' said von Düring from his end of the table.

The King turned his regard to the general — a matter of some difficulty now.

'Read what's germane,' he commanded.

The old man fluttered the pages; read slowly the paragraphs which follow.

'The Queen's position is far from enviable. Mr. Greville himself said to me the other day, "Her popularity has sunk to zero, and loyalty is a dead letter." From my own observation I can endorse that.

'Her extraordinary — liaison, I can only term it — with the disreputable Melbourne has alienated many people who would otherwise be inclined to support her.

'The whole Tory party is in a state of fury at her blind political partisanship, and even a number of the Whigs are ratting because they are afraid of what the future may hold.

'Stories of her coldness to her mother have done her an incredible amount of harm, especially with the middle classes.

'On the other hand her ill-treatment of Lady Flora Hastings and its tragic sequel — you know, of course, that the unfortunate woman is dead? — has set against her all the Hastings family and its immense ramifications and connections as well as the mob. They had to have the Guards under arms all night before the funeral, and an *enormous* force of police accompanied the coffin.

'Meanwhile the feeling against the foreign *camarilla* at the Palace grows. They say — and believe — that she does nothing without the advice of a foreigner — King Leopold, or Lehzen, or Stockmar. What position the latter holds in the royal household I do not really know — a sort of peripatetic political tutor to the entire Coburg family, I suppose! At any rate the mob has become very hostile to foreign influence. They hissed her at Ascot, and shout "No more foreigners!" after her. I don't believe Melbourne will let her marry an alien if he can help it. I don't believe the country would stand it!

'I am most strongly convinced that now is an overwhelmingly favourable opportunity for your Majesty to put forward your own son, Prince George of Cumberland. . .'

'Ah!' sighed Mr. Cobbold, when von Düring had reached this point.

The King said nothing. He sat with his elbows on the table, twisting a great signet ring — set with a blood-red cornelian — on the third finger of his left hand, while the valet adjusted a black stock that rose to his ears.

'He is excessively good-looking in a most romantic style. He would, one day bring back the Crown of Hanover to England. Above all he is an Englishman with an English education. His blindness is neither observable nor complete, and certainly does not detract from his appearance.'

'Ah, good! Very, very good!' commented Mr. Cobbold in a highly approving manner. 'Nothing like having a second string to your bow, sir!'

The King's thoughts flowed furiously along a dozen channels. Strange about that blindness — that *he* should have lost an eye in battle; his son been rendered blind by an idly-swinging bunch of keys; his *father* become sightless in his old age! . . . If George were to marry Vic then *his* descendants would occupy the throne of England, even if he himself did not! What a sell for those dam-fool brothers of his, Sussex and Cambridge! Kent would turn in his grave! . . . He had always been able to manage George easily: would he be able to manage Victoria through George? . . .

Still, one didn't like to drop the idea of being King of England, oneself, one day. By God, one would show them how a country should be ruled — no truckling to the mob — no dithering before demagogues like a startled old lady in front of a burglar! One had abrogated the Constitution of Hanover as soon as one had become King: one had expelled from his post anyone who had objected to that proceeding. One had handled democracy very firmly. One had handled aristocracy equally firmly. One had abolished precedence from title and estate, and given rank at one's will in military degree. Some of the old countesses and baronesses hadn't liked being given the status of lieutenants when the chaplain's wife was a major — but who cared? One could do the same thing again — in England. A strong man could! . . .

There was, however, no certainty that his campaign would succeed despite Cobbold's optimism: Victoria might grow wise — or prove unexpectedly tough; the mob difficult to stir to action. It took so much time, and one did not grow any younger. One didn't wish her personally any harm, but . . . ! He visualized a dozen enchanting calamities that might occur to the young Queen. It might be as well to have that 'second string' to one's bow with George as suitor. Even if she married him, *things* still might happen. In child-bed, for instance. She was a weakly creature.

But this was day-dreaming! . . . George was already booked! . . . He mentioned the fact with regret whilst automatically allowing himself to be invested in a dark green uniform coat with silver frogs and an extraordinarily high collar of grey astrakhan.

'Can't be done! . . . George is booked — to Anne of Limburg!'

Von Düring looked up sharply. The name had been on the tip of his tongue ever since he had finished reading, and the King had fallen into reverie.

Mr. Cobbold raised inquiring eyebrows.

'I beg your pardon, sir?' he said uncomprehending.

The King explained curtly —

'Been thinking of marrying George to the Duchess of Limburg. Everything very private at the moment. Negotiations well in hand — practically complete, in fact.'

Mr. Cobbold's childish features assumed the expression of a sulky schoolboy. He seemed almost to pout at his employer.

'Now I *do* think your Majesty might have kept me informed on your plans. I really do!' he complained.

'And what the Hell have these plans got to do with you, my friend?' asked the King; and very slowly turned his head within its immense stockade of muslin and silk and fur, so that he brought the baleful glare of his one good eye to bear fully upon the small man.

'Everything, sir,' answered Mr. Cobbold in a malcontent tone, not one whit discomposed. 'Here am I working for you — planning for you — campaigning for you — and you make a most important move without telling me a word about it. Lucky it is that I know now! Very lucky!'

'It is, is it?'

The King kept his fierce regard fixed on Cobbold, who met it boldly for a moment, and then nonchalantly moved his chair a little so that he sat sideways to the table presenting his delicate profile to Ernest. Then he crossed his legs; bent his eyes on the idly swinging toe of a beautifully varnished boot, and continued, a hint of malicious pleasure in his voice —

'In the ordinary way the match would ha' been excellent. Very good move for you in England, indeed.' He ticked off the advantages of the alliance on the fingers of a hand as white and delicate as a girl's as he recited — 'One: she's got English blood in her. Grandmother on her father's side was the heiress of the Bannerdales. Two: she's Protestant. Three: the richest bride any British prince would have had for more than a century. Four: she's as pretty as paint, and her father was drowned trying to rescue the crew from an English wreck. Five: she's a member of one of the oldest royal families in Europe, with French and Flemish blood going back to the Deluge. You've got the five "R's" all there — Race, Religion, Riches, Romance, and Royalty. But . . .'

'But?' echoed the King, who had listened to the recital with every sign of impatience.

Mr. Cobbold grinned from the pure felicity of being able to impart an ugly and disconcerting story — grinned till he showed a row of decayed and yellow teeth —

'Her Highness has mizzled — vanished — eloped!'

'What's this story, you miserable little rat?' said Ernest fiercely. He rose from his seat, and leaned over the table toward the little man, as though he were a great carnivorous beast about to spring on his prey. His big white hands were splayed upon the shining green surface of the table. His face was darkened with passion — a darkness the more sinister because of the contrasting whiteness of the snowy foam of whisker and moustache and of beetling eyebrows.

Mr. Cobbold paid no attention to the insult; his eyes still were on a glistering foot, which swung, perhaps, a shade faster.

'She bolted over three months ago. With Henry Wentworth, the Duke of Suffolk's second son . . . They've kept it a dead secret. There's not half a dozen people in all Europe know . . . They've not found them yet!'

'Is that true?'

With a violent gesture the King swept papers and little bronze cannon from before him to the floor.

'Ab-so-lu-tely!' asseverated Mr. Cobbold, shifting his glance from toe to emerald and scarlet pattern of the Persian carpet. 'Ab-so-lu-tely!'

The King mouthed colossal oaths. He raged up and down the room, watched discreetly by the two men who were now upon their feet. Christ Almighty blast that bastard Leopold! Did the bloody Coburger think to plant damaged goods on *him*? It was not the collapse of his plans that angered him — for already he saw great merits in the new scheme — but the insult to his House. Leopold had undoubtedly meant to hush the matter up so completely that this fornicatress, this trollop, should still have been welcome to the Court of Hanover as a fitting person one day to share the throne!

'It simplifies matters a good deal, sir,' suggested Mr. Cobbold when the King had at last fallen silent, standing with back to the fire under the portrait of his ancestor who stared down at him with august mien and fleshy nose from out of the dark thicket of an immense peruke — that ancestor who, too, had had trouble with his womenkind and had immured an erring wife for thirty years. 'King Leopold can hardly complain when your Majesty breaks off negotiations.'

'Complain!' said the King. He turned to von Düring. 'Hey, Stink-pot, I will write to the Coburger after luncheon. See that a special courier leaves for Brussels with the letter to-day. I'll let him know what I think of him and his strumpets! I'll put the Sodomite in his place! I'll give him something to think about!'

'That'll clear the ground, sir,' said Mr. Cobbold approvingly. 'I'ld suggest that the Prince pays an immediate visit to England... The Queen is highly sentimental. Slim figure, romantic profile, flaxen hair — apart from anything else — should favourably affect a very impressionable young woman. He's never mixed in politics, so that she won't be suspicious of his interference — or the Whigs either.'

'Where is the Crown Prince?'

'At the Welfen Castle, sir,' von Düring answered.

'Send immediately and tell him to come to Herrenhausen at once! Arrange that now!'

Von Düring went gladly. Outside the great double doors the fumigators would be awaiting him: only on this occasion they would be awaiting him with pipe, small leaden jar of tobacco, and a tinder-box. He hurried.

The little man joined the big man before the fire. He stood beside him on his blind side, and talked earnestly and at length in a low voice, miniature hands deep in the pockets of pale green trousers, chin sunk in fine frill of shirt, eyes directed on the floor. In so low a voice as if he would not even wish the portrait of the florid be-wigged gentleman over the fireplace to catch a single word.

...'In the way she is going on, time is on our side unless she marries someone else, *and* has children.'

The big man made no comment but a grunt. He twisted his neck within its high rampart so that his sighted eye could look down on the top of a sleek and shiny head.

'Our only risk in this connection is Albert of Saxe-Coburg — absolutely our only risk. And I can think of a number of quite pretty ways of dealing with that young man.'

Once again the voice sank almost to a whisper, as though Mr. Cobbold were only reciting to himself the list of methods. The big man's expression did not change. He continued to look down on the small dark head. It seemed as if he did not listen — were pretending to himself that he did not listen — or, at least, were hearing (without attention) the ramblings of a child.

'And then . . .' said Mr. Cobbold; and his voice sank till it was just a breathing. When he concluded, he suddenly looked up for the first time — a quick roguish glance into the orgulous face bent over him. He smiled — and an exquisite smile it would have been but for the yellow teeth that the parting of the rosy lips revealed.

The King of Hanover straightened himself; threw back giant shoulders; was shaken by dangerous and silent laughter.

'By God,' he declared, 'I must know nothing about this. I *do* know nothing about it . . . I believe you are the spawn of the devil himself! At any rate George shall leave for England in a week or so. . . .'

'All this has cost money. It may cost a great deal more,' said Mr. Cobbold a little later, facing round to his employer, and speaking briskly as became the complete — if miniature — man of business 'I put up £500 for the Young England Association alone.'

'That's the devil of a lot of money!' grumbled Majesty. 'What's it all about?'

Mr. Cobbold chose his words with care —

'It's an association of young men who don't approve of the present regime, sir. Youngsters who don't like the modern craze for democracy — or mobocracy — or whatever you care to call it. Run on military lines. Passwords. Secret meetings of masked members armed with swords and daggers. Pistol practice. More'll be heard of it one of these days!'

The doors swung open.

General von Düring entered, revived, refreshed, reeking of incense anew. . . .

CHAPTER II

THE HOUSE OF GERTRUDE ENGLISHWOMAN

A GREAT ship slid through the glass-grey waters of the Sound. In the distance, where the opposing Danish and Swedish coasts were but smudges in the morning mists, she might almost have been an iceberg, its summit crowned with snow. Her topsails were white and cloudlike, and the mainsails were a shadow darkening smokily to the smooth sea. As she drew nearer her sails — stained and shadowed with the grey of the rime at a road-edge — piled themselves up into a semblance of solidity. Seen half-beam she loomed like a truncated stone pyramid on a black rock.

The watcher, in the octagonal look-out tower on the roof of Mr. Peel's dwelling and warehouse in Elsinore, closed his telescope. He had recognized the vessel as the *Kriger* of Copenhagen, and had no further interest in her. There was no business for his employer in a home-coming West Indiaman. He went downstairs and made report to one of the clerks in the counting-house overlooking the cobbled courtyard. . . .

Two hours later Seven Tempest stood on the steps outside Mr. Peel's street door. He wore a patched pair of white calico trousers and a short jacket that had once been blue. A black cotton handkerchief was knotted loosely round his throat, and he carried a seaman's knitted cap. He was browner, leaner, more saturnine; and after he had pulled the brass bell handle with great violence, he beat a fierce tattoo with the knocker.

The door swung open. A man-servant in morning undress, obviously English, regarded him sourly, hand still on the knob.

'And what might you want,' he demanded, 'a-knockin' at the door as if you was the Pope?'

'Mr. Peel in?' asked Seven curtly.

'He is in — and yet he ain't in,' said the servant beginning to close the door. 'You go up the yard to the h'office instead of coming raging at the door of a gentleman's private 'ouse.'

In another instant the door would have been shut. Seven set his foot against it — charged it with his shoulder — sent it swinging back, and the servant staggering with it. He entered the hall in a furious temper.

'Tell Mr. Peel that Mr. Tempest — Mr. Seven Tempest — wishes to speak to him! At once!'

Before the man could reply he had turned through a wide open door on his right, into what appeared to be a dining-room.

It was a dusky room with dim seascapes and naval pictures in gilded frames along the panelled walls, and Chippendale chairs set about a mahogany table. Windows on one side looked on to the street, and on the other on to a big courtyard where men were rolling barrels from a wagon into the opening to a cellar. On the mantelpiece over the open fireplace was a cannon-ball from a sixteen-pounder, mounted on an ebony stand with a brass plate recording the fact that it had crashed into the roof when the British fleet, under Nelson, had forced the Sound on its way to bombard Copenhagen in 1801.

A three-weeks-old copy of *The Times* lay open on the table, and, overhead, someone was singing 'The Last Rose of Summer' to the tinkling accompaniment of a pianoforte. Altogether it was a very English interior — one typical of a dozen such in Elsinore in the days when the King of Denmark still levied toll on every vessel that passed in and out of the Baltic, and all the great British shipping firms were represented there.

There was the sound of footsteps outside. Seven's quick ears heard someone say in what was intended to be a whisper — 'Very well, Pritchard! I'll see the feller! . . . Send for two of the warehousemen!'

Then there bustled in a little round-about sort of man with red face, well-filled red waistcoat, very high collar, and white hair brushed up into a peak in front.

'What's all this about, hey? What's all this about?' he demanded in the fussiest manner possible, and became no calmer after he had taken stock of the shabby caller. 'My servant tells me you forced your way into the house! Leave it at once or I shall call the Town Guard!'

'Are you the agent here of the Red Diamond Packet Line?' asked Tempest coolly, ignoring Mr. Peel's threats.

'If you don't go *at once* I shall have you arrested.'

'Are you agent for the Red Diamond Line?' repeated Seven, and emphasized the first three words of his sentence by rapping with his knuckles on the table.

'What the hell . . .?' said Mr. Peel. 'If you've got any business, go round to my office!'

Out of the corner of an eye, Seven could see two large men coming across the courtyard toward the house, under the leadership of the lackey. He still insisted —

'Are you the Red Diamond agent?'

'And if I am, what then?'

'I am Mr. Tempest.'

But Mr. Peel had had overlong experience of impersonators, of glib gentlemen with suspicious letters of credit, of 'ship-wrecked' mariners. He merely said, 'Well?' and cleared his throat and cascaded the money in a pocket.

'I tell you that I am Tempest!'

'What of it?'

'You know my position in regard to the Red Diamond!'

'I know Mr. Tempest's position.'

Seven flushed an angry red. His temper was rising, but he restrained any outward manifestation. He could hear heavy breathing outside the door, presumably betokening the arrival of Mr. Peel's reinforcing column.

'*I* am Tempest,' he re-asserted.

'You choose a very odd rig — demned odd rig — for your Continental travels in that case!' said Mr. Peel, putting his thumbs in his waistcoat pockets, and examining Seven's attire with a critical eye.

'Ship-wrecked!' was Seven's terse explanation.

'Ah!' said Mr. Peel, in a tone which showed that he knew all about shipwrecks in which the survivors lost all their proofs of identity. 'Ah!' said Mr. Peel. It was exactly as if he had said 'Aha!'

'Barque *Joan Dearlove*. Burned out a hundred miles East of Great Abaco ... Two months ago ... Lost everything ... Picked up after five days in an open boat by the Danish West Indiaman *Kriger*, on her way home from New Orleans.'

Peel registered the information.

'Where was she bound?'

'New Orleans. Cargo of Welsh slate.'

'Odd thing, God-demn-me, for the head of the Red Diamond Line to travel to America in a Welsh slate ship!' meditated Mr. Peel. 'Any other survivors? I suppose not. There never are.'

'My — niece,' said Tempest. 'My — nephew. Another passenger.' — 'Passengers! In a slate ship!' interjected Peel, with lifted eyebrows, resting his shoulders against the high mantelpiece — 'The cap'n, mate, and a seaman ... Cap'n lost both his legs.'

'Cap'n and mate!' said Peel. His manner suddenly changed. There might prove to be something after all in this story, odd as it seemed, if the captain and mate could identify him. Of course, there was no doubt that the man was out of the ordinary. But what in the name of all that was merciful should Mr. Tempest of the Red Diamond Line and a dozen other great concerns be doing in a lumbering Noah's ark ship on the Atlantic? His tone was suave and conciliatory as he commented, 'In that case you can have no difficulty in proving your identity, sir.'

Seven stared at him for a moment without replying. The wreck — legless and scorched — that once had been Captain Pedder, the long-nosed mate, knew him only as Mr. Cash — the mysterious Mr. Cash who had wanted to get quietly out of the country. From very long ago there flashed into his mind the nursery rhyme about an old lady who also had lost her identity, even to herself. The jingle ran — he recalled —

> She began to shake, and she began to cry,
> 'Lawk-a-mussy on me, this be none of I!'

He suddenly smiled — a twisted, humorous smile, as of one thoroughly appreciating an enormous joke against himself. He looked almost benevolently at the inquiring face which confronted him; he picked up his knitted cap from the sleek mahogany table; he quoted —

' "Lawk-a-mussy on me, this be none of I!" . . . I *shall* have difficulty in proving my identity, sir. So I won't try. Good-day to you!'

And was gone. . . .

Seven was still smiling to himself a little later as — a pace in front of them — he led Anne Louise and Daniel along Strandgade, that street wherein basked in sunlight and mellow prosperity the dignified establishments of Mr. Peel and the other great English shipping agents.

A capacious blue shawl — very much faded — hid the deficiencies of Her Highness's shore-going toilette; she wore no bonnet, and her ringlets danced in the sunshine more flecked with gold than ever. Her face was tanned: it had, too, become a grave face, with a gravity far remote from that with which once she had been used to masquerade. . . For seven weeks she had helped Sarah Liddell nurse back to some sort of life the tattered body and mind of Henry Pedder. A small white scar showed above one of the eyebrows, of whose faintly inquiring twist Uncle Leopold had so heartily disapproved.

Daniel by some miracle had preserved his blue tasselled Cossack cap: otherwise he was habited in a pink cotton shirt much too large for him and a remarkable pair of trousers apparently constructed from sail-cloth.

Behind them marched an immense porter in blue-and-white striped shirt and blue-and-white striped trousers, carrying a wooden chest full of clothes provided by the generosity of the crew and passengers of the *Kriger*.

Seven came to a halt at a corner where an apothecary's shop displayed a low window with an array of glass jars full of herbs and, in the centre, a case containing some small and hideous sea-creature having a remote resemblance to a mermaid. On the opposite side of the lane was a tavern bearing the name and sign of 'The Leaping Dolphin'.

'This is Skottestrædet — Scots' Street,' he said. 'There's an inn here, which one of the passengers recommended. It's cheap, so it'll have to do until I can get money from somewhere.'

'How long will it take?' asked Anne Louise, who had been under the impression that Seven had only to show himself to obtain unlimited funds, and had been extremely astonished at his failure.

'Month — with luck. Unless I find someone here who knows me . . . or a Red Diamond ship calls before.'

They started to walk up a narrow street of low whitewashed houses with steep roofs.

Yet another month! As she trod the uneven cobbles she tried to visualize Lecques, and could not. The immediate past had blurred her recollection of things that were more remote: she could not conjure up the grey towers amid the pines, or the slope of the dark red roofs, or the face of Aunt Sophia nid-nodding in her big chair over her interminable embroidery, or the golden foam of mimosa at one end of the flagged terrace, or the precise colour of the triangle of sea that showed in the distant gap in the woodland . . . She stopped to close her eyes for just a moment to see if those scenes would not come back — but Daniel bumped into her from behind, and Seven halted for her in front . . . Another month! But when she was back in Lecques, neither the King of the Belgians nor the King of Hanover should ever force her or persuade her to leave the safety of its walls.

Seven paused again to ask directions from the porter. The man smiled and pointed to a house but a few steps from where they stood — a long house whose eaves came down low over small latticed windows in which were set red geraniums. An archway showed an untidy courtyard where a few hens scratched about an empty cart. The street door, a couple of steps up, revealed a glimpse of a table spread with a white cloth and many dishes.

'They call this the House of Gertrude Englishwoman,' remarked Seven. 'English travellers have stayed here since the Flood.'

He mounted the steps; knocked with his knuckles on the door.

A plump blonde serving girl, with flaxen plaits and a swelling white bodice constricted by black velvet stays, appeared at once and invited them to enter.

It was a low room with bare whitewashed walls. Chairs were scattered in some disorder against the long table which was littered with the remains of the midday meal. Only one guest remained — an old man bent over his plate at the far end, near a great stove covered with blue and white tiles. There was a barricade of dishes about him. He had a thin woolly white moustache which shot out rhythmically as he ate, until the curving hairs rubbed the tip of his hooked nose.

Daniel dropped with a sigh of relief into one of the rush-seated chairs, eyeing greedily a platter full of radishes, which lay within his reach.

'I say, Anne,' he said in a low voice, 'do you know that that's the first radish we've seen for' — he calculated — 'for a million years! ... Keep *cave* for me!'

He stretched out a hand.

Anne Louise shot a glance at the old man, but his head — so bald and so yellow and so covered with bumps and knobs that it resembled a white raspberry — was bowed over the food. Seven, sitting on the edge of the table, was staring with a whimsical expression out into the street.

She took a single radish and held it between finger and thumb, examining it as if her interest was purely aesthetic, as if it had been some ornament that had aroused her curiosity. She hesitated — raised it to her lips — and then bit it in half.

At that precise moment the door at the far end of the room opened, and a woman entered. (Anne Louise popped in the other half.) She was slim and lovely, with the aloof bearing of an immortal: her black hair was coiled about her ears: her wide eyes under the straight dark eyebrows were curiously green. To pride in carriage was added disdain in a short and curving upper lip.

She came down the room — ignoring Anne Louise and Daniel — so silently that Seven was unaware of her presence until she spoke to his back.

'I am Margarethe Thirkelsen ... What do you require?' Her voice was very low, and rather deep; her English without accent.

Seven rose to his feet, and turned toward her, his head almost touching the beam that crossed the ceiling. Some instinct told him that she immediately made swift observation of his shabby sailor dress, and dismissed it as a factor of no importance; and that, after the first glance, her steady regard was not one of assessment by an inn-keeper, but for some other purpose which he could not divine.

'Want lodgings. Cheap,' he said.

'For the three?'

'Yes.'

She looked at Daniel for a brief moment, and then, for a longer space of time, at Anne Louise.

'This is a respectable house,' she said — and her voice was entirely without expression. She indicated a question by the faintest movement of her head in the direction of Anne Louise, who flushed under her tan at the implication.

'My niece,' affirmed Seven without batting an eyelid.

She looked from Seven to Daniel in quick judgment —

' ... And your son?'

Anne Louise saw something that was not embarrassment or amuse-ment — but rather, appreciation — twist Seven's lips into the shadow of a smile. Covertly she examined the faces of man and child.

' ... Nephew,' Seven corrected.

'Very well. I will arrange it,' said Margarethe Thirkelsen.

'What are your terms?' he asked. 'I have very little money. We have been ship-wrecked. I have eight pounds — English gold — until my credentials arrive, or I find someone who knows me.'

'That can be arranged,' she answered as if it were a matter of indifference. 'Come, I will show you. Then you will like to eat, is it not?'

She led the way into the recesses of the house, through a maze of half-dark passages with doors set deep in the thick walls, with sudden steps up and down, unexpected turnings with mysterious entries at their end, and staircases that wound as abruptly out of sight as if they would hasten to hide themselves from view. Up one such staircase they came to a square whitewashed attic with a great gable window overlooking the courtyard. In it were a hummock of a bed in each corner, a wardrobe, a wash-stand and a couple of chairs. The floor was bare but very clean.

'It will be best for the child to sleep here with your — niece,' said Margarethe. 'They will be company one for another. I will have a curtain put across the room ... Come!'

She shut the door on Anne Louise and Daniel, dismissing them — so to speak — from the parade, and shepherded Seven down the stairs.

He found himself eventually in a little whitewashed room, whose lattice window opened on to a very small enclosed garden of close-cut grass, half in sunlight, half in shadow. The opposite wall was masked by ivy of darkest green which formed the background for a bank of oriental poppies of a luminous and brilliant red. The noises of the street and house were very faint, and somewhere on the roof above a couple of doves were cooing.

Margarethe Thirkelsen stood with one hand on the door jamb, watching him as he examined the room. She wore a plain gown of as dark a green as the ivy; and, where it was cut to a point low on the bosom, there was a large brooch in which was set a fire opal that held among the many colours in its changeful depths a flame as scarlet as the flowers.

Seven was aware of her scrutiny: it did not disconcert him — it puzzled him; for it was neither a regard that was meant to invite a reciprocal attention, nor was it the stare of idle curiosity. He raised his eyes to hers —

'I am afraid that this room is better than I can afford — at the present,' he said, and looked again at the flowered hangings of the bed that was recessed into an alcove, the dark oak press against the bare white wall, the shining brass wash-basin on a small chest in the window, and the red and black woollen rug (with the inscription 'S.T. 1831' in yellow in one corner) on the brick floor.

'It can be arranged,' she replied, and turned to go. 'I will send Kristine to show you the way back in a few minutes.'

After a hurried dinner, Seven vanished. He did not reappear until supper-time, when he squeezed in between crowded table and wall and dropped into a chair which had been kept for him between Anne Louise and Daniel — who sat next the old man with a white moustache, and watched his every mouthful with a hypnotized attention.

Seven gave no explanation of his disappearance — not even later on when they walked for a little up and down the darkening street where the dim windows one by one burst into yellow life with candle and lamp. At the inn door, however, he suddenly halted; from his trousers pocket produced a leather purse; tilted into the palm of his left hand a couple of coins which shone golden in the light that streamed out; presented them to Anne Louise.

'You and Daniel need a few things,' he said. 'Buy them to-morrow, only be economical. This is all you'll get!'

'How can you spare it?' she asked in surprise, making no effort to take the money. 'You said you'd only got eight pounds. If you give me two to spend what are we going to live on?'

'God may possibly provide,' answered Seven putting the sovereigns into her hand. I also shall have to do my best about it! . . .'

In the days that followed they saw little of him. He was gone at some early hour, and did not return until supper, weary and silent. He would exchange but few words with them, glance at the shipping lists in the *Helsingørs Efterretninger* (which he borrowed from the old man with the white moustache) and then depart to bed.

Anne Louise and Daniel were thus left to their own devices. No one in the house displayed any interest in them, except Kristine and Astrid, the plump Swedish maids, and the old man—generally known as Onkel Olav—whose overtures were confined to recommending some particular dish, with much gesticulation of knife or fork and a mowing of his toothless jaws.

The other guests — there were perhaps twenty of them — were strange silent people who sat together in small exclusive groups, spoke but little — and softly — at table and grudged their laughter, and watched one another under lowered lids. The moment a meal was finished they all departed — vanished into the dim recesses of the house, which seemed to swallow them up into its silence.

Traversing the long mysterious passages Anne Louise often felt that someone had just preceded her on tiptoe, and that someone else was following soundlessly after. On several occasions she had looked back sharply over her shoulder; once even she had summoned up courage to lie in ambush in a recessed doorway; but there was no reward to all this vigilance.

Margarethe Thirkelsen appeared to ignore their very existence. She was never to be seen about the house; although at dinner and at supper she would come into the dining-room, and stand for a minute at the head of the table, looking down its length. She gave no greeting, said not a word, and made not a gesture; but in her presence whatever conversation there was seemed to die away, and her guests bent more closely over their plates as if they were afraid to meet her gaze.

She was always dressed in a gown of dark green with pointed waist and wide skirt. One night she appeared with a pair of drop-earrings whose opals shone — with equal fire to that of the great brooch — against the whiteness of her neck; and wore them ever afterward. . . .

Anne Louise and Daniel spent most mornings sitting under an ancient ivy-beset oak-tree, on a small hill about a mile outside the town. White goats with long beards and oblong eyes were tethered along the grassy lane, and a little farther on was a windmill with creaking sails. From their vantage-point they could look across a shallow dell (in which was a clump of farm buildings and fir trees) to peaked roof and gable window of the city; to the green copper-sheathed spires of the great castle of Kronborg; to the wooded Swedish shore across the narrow blue waters of the Sound; to the throng of shipping at anchor in the roadstead — barque and brig and schooner, and even an occasional paddle-steamboat with funnel almost as high as its masts.

The long afternoons they passed on the beach beyond Marienlyst, where Anne Louise conscientiously continued the education of Daniel, which she had begun on shipboard. They studied French; they studied German; they studied mathematics — using the sand as a convenient blackboard for the demonstration and the working out of problems; they studied general knowledge — the much-regretted Cyclopaedia of Mr. Partington had made Anne Louise singularly conversant with all subjects in alphabetical order up to (and including) those beginning with the syllable 'hum'. Sometimes she would busy herself with her sewing; but she was no needlewoman, and the results of much thought and irksome labour were often very peculiar.

Once they had gone to see Sarah Liddell, who had installed herself as nurse-attendant on Captain Pedder in lodgings near the customs house quay. The old woman seemed to have a sufficiency of funds — Anne Louise presumed that somewhere in the vast bosom of her gown was treasury as well as storehouse. But there had been a restraint about the interview in the small room whose window looked over the dockyard wall on to a tangle of masts and rigging: for beyond the inner door Pedder was fitfully dozing, and the nearness of that furious and outraged spirit seemed to oppress them.

The very next morning Sarah came to the house in Skottestrædet to say that an old ship-mate of Pedder's had just learned of his disaster and offered to take the pair of them back to England. So they were sailing in the steamboat *Nymph*, bound from St. Petersburg for London, on the following day.

It was a Sunday, and Seven saw her alone, in the deserted dining-room.

'And what then, Sally-ally?' he asked.

She did not know.

'Got any money?'

Enough to last for a short while yet.

He sat on the edge of the long table regarding her thoughtfully. She was the only link between Seven-the-man and Seven-the-child. He could vaguely recall her twice-yearly visits to Minerva House — always associated with the housekeeper's room, which was soaked in a green gloom from the laurel shrubbery that darkened the barred window; with an inevitable gift of brandy-balls in a sticky paper packet; and with the smack of noisy farewell kisses . . . Then, long after, he had found her at Judgment; and there she had remained, large, efficient, red-faced, until her surprising autumnal marriage five years ago.

'Did my father know that you used to come and see me at Minerva House, Sally-ally, when I was a child?' he asked.

'No, Mr. Sep.'

'How . . . ' he began; changed his mind. 'Do you know, Sally-ally, that no one ever kissed me when I was a child excepting you?'

Her great red face crumpled, and for a moment he thought that she was going to weep.

'I was there when you were born, Mr. Sep!' she said. 'And a bitter time your poor mamma had! . . . And I was your nurse until Mr. Fielding sent you away. You'd have been three then.'

'I owe you for those kisses, Sally — and for the brandy-balls — and for a lot of things, then *and* now. I'm going to give you a letter to take to Judgment when you get back to England. You'll have nothing to worry about!'

At that, weep she did — silently, the great tears rolling down her cheeks, and dripping on to her cotton gown, and making dark splash-marks on the capacious shelf of her bosom.

To give her time to recover, he talked at random . . . She would probably find 'Snorker' Reid already at Judgment when she got there. The little man had only signed on in the *Halcyon* for the voyage home. He had promised him a shore job, and given him a letter to Togarmah Smith . . . He himself might not be back for a little. It would take anything up to the best part of three weeks to get where he was going in France . . . What was Pedder going to do when the stumps of his legs had entirely healed?

As she was departing, full of grateful thanks, he mentioned Pedder again —

'Mind you turn the fellow over to his friends, Sally-ally. You've done your duty by him — and more. He'ld have never survived those five days in the boat but for you. He's a bad and dangerous man — and none of your responsibility!'

She shook her head as if unconvinced that she could disburthen herself thus easily.

CHAPTER III

CHAPTER III

INTRUSION OF A SENTIMENTALIST

ANNE LOUISE and Daniel first came under the approving notice of
Mr. Washington Hallett, a wealthy young gentleman of Hallett,
Virginia — known by his intimates as 'Washy' — as he emerged from
R. T. Datow's Perfumery and Tobacco Warehouse (Wholesale and
Retail) which stands in a narrow cobbled street opening on to the
market-place in Elsinore. It was a shop with so inordinate an amount
of steep brown red roof that the small building seemed to be pressed
into the ground by it, and the very entry forced a step below the
pavement level.

He had been making his usual daily purchase of scents, soaps and
cigars — not that he could use a tithe of what he bought; but that the
protracted commercial transaction enabled him to gaze with reverent
delight upon the charming little face of the young lady who attended
to his requirements.

As Mr. Hallett spoke no Danish, and the young lady no English,
and as he was conscious all the time of close scrutiny by someone
through the glass panel of the door dividing small shop from living-
room, the courtship had not proceeded far. But then none of his
courtships proceeded far: Mr. Hallett's very innocence steered him
clear of ladies likely to speed the pace, and the others, alas! soon
developed or revealed sad imperfections and flaws. One day, however,
he would undoubtedly find the ideal: if he sought earnestly and long
enough!

He shut the street door regretfully; had paused on the step while
his grizzled negro servant relieved him of the numerous packages,
when he heard a clear treble voice exclaim —

'Look, Anne! Why, there's a black man!'

At the welcome sound of English speech he looked round. The pair
were approaching on the other side of the street; and his gaze shifted
quickly from Daniel — a civilized and Christian Daniel once more, in
blue peg-top trousers and blue check blouse — to Anne Louise.

One glimpse of grey eyes in tanned face — of lips curved in hint
of a smile — of lights in dancing ringlets beneath Quakerish bonnet —
of slim form in Quakerish gown — of enchanting small nose: one

217

glimpse was more than enough to drive from his mind all the thoughts of Ingeborg which had filled it but a moment before!

'I say, Anne, do you think that black men . . .'

He was aware of the merest flash of apology in the eyes that met his own for so short a fraction of time . . . They were gone by . . . His gaze followed them; and then — after thrusting the pile of parcels into Samuel's arms — he followed them, himself . . . At a discreet distance.

A little later the romantic Mr. Hallett might have been seen visiting in rapid succession a milliner's, a haberdasher's, a linen-draper's. He emerged from the last with an expression on his honest freckled face in which triumph, embarrassment, expectation were all nicely blended. He had been combining the imagination of a poet with the strategy of a general. . . .

It was Daniel who first saw and recognized him the next afternoon as Mr. Hallett kept watch on the inn from a vantage point at the end of the street.

'There's the man with the black footman,' he announced to Anne Louise, as they came out of the door.

As a matter of fact it was Mr. Hallett's second spell of duty, for he had paced Skottestrædet for most of the morning — timing his arrival, unfortunately, long after Anne Louise and Daniel had set out on their after-breakfast walk.

At first Mr. Hallett had marched rapidly up the street as if he had an urgent appointment at the other end. Then he had turned and gone back just as speedily — as though remembering that he had left important papers behind him. After that he had ambled up the street — had cruised up the street — had drifted up the street — had crawled up the street: he had done the course in three minutes, and he had done it in twenty minutes; for he had timed himself by the small gold watch which lived in a pocket in his elegant yellow waistcoat at the end of the thin gold chain encircling his neck. He had studied the windows of the few shops until he knew every article in them — from the dried mermaid in the apothecary's, to the pink silk bonnet with white tulle ruching on the under-edge and a trimming of moss-roses, which the little milliner had copied from a two-year-old model by Petko of Vienna. He hurried past the inn — dawdled past the inn — averted his gaze from the inn — stared at it as if it were a shrine.

Refreshed by a hurried lunch he had returned, to meet with immediate reward.

The moment he recognized Anne Louise's grey gown he sought

refuge from observation in the nearest doorway — a manœuvre watched with the intensest interest and understanding by Onkel Olav from one of the geranium-decorated windows of the inn. . . .

They were walking along the dusty road under the high grey wall of stone and the high green rampart of lime-trees that shielded the Palace of Marienlyst from view, when rapid footsteps approached from behind.

A rather breathless voice exclaimed in English —

'Excuse me!'

Daniel looked over his shoulder. Anne Louise halted and half-turned.

The slim young gentleman — the enviable possessor of a black servant in pea-green uniform and gold-laced hat — was hastening up to them. In his hand he held a white handkerchief.

The elegance of his appearance — of admirable russet-coloured coat, primrose-coloured waistcoat, tightly-strapped fawn trousers — was offset by the embarrassed boyishness of his ingenuous countenance. He swept off a sleek pale yellow hat from his sandy locks, and bowed very low, and blushed very deep.

Anne Louise sketched him a little bow — it was so long since she had had to bow that she felt as if her neck were unaccustomed to the operation.

'Forgive the intrusion!' said Youthful Elegance — and he had recited the formula a hundred times to himself, if once — 'But I opine — I believe — that you have — er — had the misfortune to lose your handkerchief.'

He proffered for examination an article that the Duchess of Limburg might have been proud to carry on occasions of the greatest state; of the finest lawn with two inches depth of lace around its hem.

'Yours, I believe, madam,' said Mr. Hallett.

Anne Louise inspected it cursorily.

'I don't think so, sir!'

'But, madam,' lied he in tones of protest, 'I actually saw you drop it!'

This astounding assertion overwhelmed Anne Louise, who had had but little dealing in the course of her career with the habits of the young male. She looked again at the handkerchief as though some conjuror had produced it from the empty air.

'It cannot be mine,' she declared. 'It really cannot be. I have none like it. None at all!'

'But . . .' he protested again, as if unable to deny the evidence of his eyes, although unwilling to give the lie to so charming a lady.

'But . . . ! Won't you look and see if you have not lost it . . . This might be the one you had forgotten about and taken without knowing it . . . I found myself out walking the other day' — said he with much simplicity — 'in a pair of almond-green trousers! Do you know I was flabbergasted. I thought I must have taken someone else's in a fit of absent-mindedness. And they were mine all the time. I had just forgotten . . . Just forgotten! Very absent-minded — at times. Perhaps you are, too, madam, if I dare suggest it? . . . My old aunt, for instance . . .'

'You forget your own trousers!' interrupted Daniel, highly interested. 'You *must* have been tiddley!'

Mr. Hallett ignored the aspersion except by a polite though worried smile.

Anne Louise, to avoid further discussion or revelations, produced from some secret recess a very small, very plain handkerchief. As the owner demonstrated it to him, Mr. Hallett's quick eyes caught the initials 'A.L.' embroidered in a corner — and very badly embroidered too, being Anne Louise's maiden effort.

'You see,' said Anne Louise, thinking what a pleasant-faced young man it was, 'here's mine . . . You must have made a mistake!'

Even if Mr. Hallett were to have made no mistake previously, he immediately proceeded to make one.

'Of course, *you* know!' he declared in a manner that betokened deferential dissatisfaction. 'But it is a coincidence, isn't it, that this handkerchief has got your name on it? . . . "Anne" — you observe!'

Anne's grey eyes widened. She looked directly at him. — What a darling she is! thought the infatuated Mr. Hallett. Isn't she adorable? His imagination carried him on whirlwind flight across three thousand miles of sea and some hundreds of miles of land, and he saw her coming in her dress of Quakerish grey out of the great white portico of his house at Hallett, and stepping over the green lawns to greet him. He saw . . .

'But how did you know that my name was Anne?' asked Anne Louise; and even as she spoke realized the truth. She was amused. She was angry: and then more amused than angry, as a hot flush surged over his guileless countenance. She took pity on him.

'I am much obliged to you, sir,' she said. 'Thank you very much . . . Come Daniel, we must not detain this gentleman any longer! Good afternoon, sir!'

And she gave him a grave little smile, and a grave little bow as she turned away.

He stood for a moment looking after her, the rejected handkerchief still outstretched in his hand.

The affair had not gone quite according to plan. But what a stride forward on yesterday! — he told himself.

Yesterday he had never spoken to her: indeed, during a great part of the wasted yesterday he had even been unaware of her existence — had never dreamed that speech could be so musical, or eyes so grey, or ringlets so retentive of all the lights and shadows that play on a field of swaying wheat. Yesterday he had seen *her*: to-day he had spoken to *her*: to-morrow? . . . What of to-morrow? Suddenly he knew what he would do on the morrow. He stalked back to the town, his lips moving as he shaped neat speeches, quick replies; occasionally he chuckled. He increased his speed: once more he visited the linen-draper.

And as soon as he was out of sight and hearing, Anne Louise had started to laugh. She laughed till she was forced to stop and find that cheap handkerchief with the initials 'A.L.' amateurishly embroidered on it.

'What are you laughing about?' demanded Daniel, anxious to share the jest. 'Oh! That fellow and his trousers — the green trousers! He *must* have been tiddley. Did you believe it, Anne? Bet you a hundred pounds it wasn't true! . . . But what's he want to say it for! . . . I wonder what his aunt forgot! . . . Perhaps —' He relapsed into profound speculation of a nature that would undoubtedly have embarrassed Mr. Hallett's aged aunt. . . .

Mr. Hallett began an elaborate and circumspect toilet at an early hour the next morning in the large dark bedroom at his inn, with its large dark bed, and even larger and darker mahogany wardrobe.

There was a long cheval glass conveniently placed between the two windows, but Mr. Hallett found its habits extremely uncertain: at one moment the chill depths would reflect his upper half minus the legs, and at the next, of its own volition, the mirror would swing slowly forward on its stand and reveal only his lower half as far up as the bottom waistcoat button. No amount of wedging with paper would correct this fault for longer than a minute. On so important a day it was essential that his attire should be flawless: he summoned the pea-green liveried negro Samuel to keep the mirror steady.

Mr. Hallett had devoted much thought to the need for harmony between his own costume and a Quakerish little dress of grey which was accompanied by a Quakerish little bonnet of the same shade.

His wardrobe provided him with the perfection of coats in smooth dark grey, with dove-coloured trousers that fitted like a glove, pale blue velvet waistcoat with silver buttons, and dark blue neckcloth — the arranging of which took fully ten minutes.

He admired the sartorial effect in the glass; deprecated sandy hair, freckles, wide mouth, indeterminate nose, lack of stature; found handkerchief, gloves, and hat to harmonize with the general scheme of things; demanded a favourable verdict from the grinning Samuel; bounded downstairs out into the sunny morning like a schoolboy leaving his class-room for a half-holiday.

Good Fortune was his escort; for even as he turned into Skotte-strædet, he saw his quarry ahead of him.

Like a Sioux Indian or a sleuth hound he trailed them through the streets of Elsinore, figuratively on tip-toes, and at so curious a gait — now hurrying, now darting for shelter into a doorway, now walking at the rate of a funeral cortège, now coming to as abrupt a halt as if he had collided with an inevitable barrier — that passers-by were for ever bumping into him, or being bumped into.

Thus is explained the fact that Anne Louise, turning a corner, narrowly escaped walking full-tilt into the gentleman of the previous day's adventure. So gently was he strolling, cane in hand, regard lost in space, that only a most observant person would have deduced from his crimson face and the perspiration on his open brow that he had run like a hare for a quarter of a mile so that he might meet instead of overtake.

Mr. Hallett suddenly became aware of the identity of the person he was encountering. Very suddenly. In fact he started. Started as dramatically as ever had the late Mr. Horatio Vyvyan in his most histrionic moments.

'Ah!' said Mr. Hallett, having come to a halt so immediately in front of Anne Louise and Daniel that they had to halt too, or else walk round him as if he were some obstruction left by the road-mender.

'Ah!' repeated Mr. Hallett, trying to remember what his next lines were, becoming redder than ever, and compromising with — 'Good - good morning, madam!'

And he swept his hat off most magnificently.

The sudden apparition of the hero of the handkerchief episode considerably surprised Anne Louise — casual encounters such as that stage-managed by him, were without the range of her social experience. His re-appearance did not, however, alarm her. He was such a young — such a very young — gentleman, not more than two or three years older than herself by the calendar, but two or three decades younger in knowledge of life. Neither was he a very large gentleman, being only

little taller than herself. Also the very high collar on which his chin
rested looked too tight for comfort on so warm a day, and she felt
that he needed instruction in the choice of his cravats. Altogether it
appeared to Anne Louise that, if they had been properly acquainted,
he would have made an excellent companion for Daniel in his wilder
romps.

All this flashed through her mind in the infinitesimal space of time
in which she decided on her treatment of the situation.

So she sketched her little bow, and she responded to his greeting
demurely —

'Good morning, sir!'

'This is very lucky,' said Mr. Hallett, talking at great speed lest
he should become panicked and stammer. 'Very lucky! . . . Quite a
coincidence! . . . *Very* lucky coincidence! . . . I blame myself very
much . . . So absent-minded, you know! All Americans absent-
minded . . . Something to do with the climate . . . And it *was* your
property, you know! . . . I can't apologize too much. Been absent-
minded from a boy. Noted for it. In the family, I think. Now my
dear old aunt, she used . . .'

'*My* property, did you say, sir?' asked Anne Louise, interrupting of
design what promised to become a monologue on the subject of absent-
mindedness in the family of her unknown interlocutor.

'Oh, didn't I say?' said Mr. Hallett, carefully resuming his hat. 'Now
there's another instance. Of absent-mindedness. I might have gone
away again and quite forgotten to say that it *was* your handkerchief
after all!'

'Mine, after all!' echoed Anne Louise, trying to adjust herself to this
revelation. 'But . . .'

The crucial moment had come: everything must be put to the test.
That romantic plotter, Mr. Washington Hallett, of Hallett, Virginia,
in the United States of America, must take his desperate leap. He took
it —

'Yours indeed,' he assured her. 'How I came to be so forgetful I
can't imagine . . . Absent-mindedness . . .' Here he nearly rambled
away from the chasm before him; steading himself; took a breath.
'Let me explain! . . . But — Ah! you were taking your morning
walk? You must not let me interrupt it. If you will permit me to
accompany you. Just a part of the way . . . Long enough to explain . . .
We *were* going in the same direction, I believe!'

So saying he turned round in the opposite way to that in which he
had been going, and remained poised on one foot with the other

varnished toe pointed forward, a little off the ground, as though to urge Anne Louise to an immediate start.

Whether it was the force of suggestion, or curiosity about the mystery of the handkerchief, or some appeal that peeped out of his honest eyes, or a mixture of all three — Anne Louise did not know. The fact remains that she moved forward, in (it is true) rather a guarded manner, as though disclaiming all responsibility, and preserving every right to break off negotiations.

Mr. Hallett's senses reeled.

He had succeeded past belief! That divinity with the grave eyes and the dancing ringlets and the Quaker grey gown and bonnet was walking with him — Washy Hallett — in the flesh, and not as a fairy princess in one of his waking dreams!

The song of birds in the blossoming trees that lined the road; the jewel-green of the fantastic copper roofs of the great castle below them; the flashing whiteness of buildings on the wooded Swedish coast across the Sound; the under-breath of the little wind that was just strong enough to flutter a leaf in the hedgerow, but too weak to raise even a ripple on the shining blue waters of the Baltic — these things had suddenly become a magic to Mr. Hallett.

'A beautiful day, madam!' said he approvingly. 'Fairylike, one might call it! Fairylike — definitely fairylike!'

Anne Louise brought him back to the matter under discussion.

'You said, I think, that you had a handkerchief of mine! I can't understand how it is possible. The one you showed me yesterday certainly was not mine.'

Mr. Hallett — thus brought back to earth, and advised that his position was not yet secure — put hand to breast-pocket, produced a minute package tied up in tissue paper with a grey silk ribbon.

'Yours, I believe, madam!' he said triumphantly.

Anne Louise came to a halt. She undid the little parcel under his anxious inspection. It contained a handkerchief not unlike her own — but of immeasurably superior material — with the initials 'A.L.' embroidered on it by a master-hand, in much the same sort of character as she herself had attempted.

'But . . .' she began.

'I took the liberty of having it laundered,' he said. 'It had — er — become soiled in my pocket.'

To any woman — even to Anne Louise — it would have been obvious that that handkerchief was brand new. She found laughter trembling on her lips, and restrained it only by an effort.

'But this is not the handkerchief you showed me yesterday,' she managed to say.

Once again Mr. Hallett braced himself to lie.

'That? . . . Oh, that was my aunt's,' he said with simple trusting faith to her credulity. 'My fault entirely! Getting more and more — er — absent-minded! Picked up her's — put it in my pocket. Picked up yours, put it in my pocket . . . Tried to give you her's. Tried to give her yours . . . Now I've put it right. Very stupid of me! . . . Such a coincidence! Her name being Anne, I mean! . . . Do you think it wise to stop here, madam? It is a little cool for you out of the sun. Should we not move on?'

But, Anne Louise, conscious of anxious freckled face turned toward her, of ridiculous handkerchief, of a Daniel who was obviously about to say something devastating — Anne Louise suddenly smiled; suddenly made the delicious gurgling sound of a baby; suddenly burst into a peal of laughter, which the enraptured Mr. Hallett at once described to himself as 'silvery'. He listened, enchanted, even if puzzled.

Mr. Hallett in sympathy started to laugh, too; he had no objection to laughing at himself in such company.

It was when they were continuing on their way — none gainsaying Mr. Hallett's presence — that Daniel reverted to a subject that had been weighing on his mind —

'What *was* it that your aunt forgot, sir?' he inquired.

'What did my aunt forget?' repeated Mr. Hallett at a loss. 'When?'

'Yesterday you said that your aunt was so absent-minded that she *even* . . . and you didn't say any more. I wondered what it was she forgot.'

Mr. Hallett had obviously put his aunt and her absent-mindedness entirely out of his thoughts. He pulled himself together; played desperately for time —

'Ah yes! My old aunt — er — my old aunt Anne! Er — very absent-minded! . . . Anne! Most curious coincidence! Two Annes! You an Anne — her an Anne! . . . Yes, very absent-minded! . . . Yes — yes! I remember. Well, one night — she had a reticule, you know. She used to keep her keys in it. *And* a handkerchief. *And* scissors. *And* a little box with green and red comfits. All sorts of things, don't you know! Well, one night she put the reticule . . .'

In two days' time Mr. Washington Hallett, in constant attendance both morning and afternoon, was being accosted as 'Washy' to his face by a greatly admiring Daniel. Within three days Anne Louise was referring to him — behind his back — by the nickname. On the fourth day he very tentatively addressed her Highness the Princess Anne Louise Elizabeth Caroline, Duchess of Limburg, and Princess of Lecques — not that he knew anything of all these ranks and titles — as 'Anne', and watched her reactions to this incredible daring with great anxiety. But Anne Louise did not appear to have remarked on the boldness, and merely continued to reprove him for attempting to harmonize a blue and red spotted neckerchief with a bright green shooting coat and white hat.

He was so far emboldened by this that, later in the afternoon, he implored her to call him 'Washy'; and over-rode all objections: simultaneously issued an invitation to a carriage excursion on the morrow; and again over-rode all objections.

'I say,' said Daniel, after they had parted at the inn door, 'I say, Anne, Washy is awfully sweet on you! Isn't he?'

'Nonsense!' said Anne Louise, although she knew in her heart that it was not nonsense.

Her feelings toward Washy — if she had come to analyse them — were those of a mother, a maiden aunt, an elder sister; were the feelings she bore toward Daniel, with only slight and unimportant modifications. She would have slept, for instance, with Washy on the other side of the curtain that divided her attic bedroom, with as little concern as she did in the case of Daniel.

'Bet you Washy's sweet on you! Bet you anything you like!' insisted Daniel. 'Wouldn't it be a lark if he knew who you really were?'

Washy spent an extremely busy evening.

The finest landau in Elsinore had to be hired for the occasion, with a guaranteed impeccable coachman and guaranteed impeccable horses. Fruit and sweetmeats had to be chosen for the purpose of light refreshment on the journey: a courier had to be sent to the seashore hotel which was the object of the excursion, to order the finest and most elaborate luncheon that Denmark could produce. A toilette had to be selected worthy of the occasion — eventually a symphony in blue, topped by a broad-brimmed hat such as he wore sometimes at home, a little exotic (perhaps) but, he flattered himself, intriguing.

Anne Louise, too, lived up to the occasion. She appeared in an enchanting outfit — as good as new — which had been given her in the *Kriger* by one of the first-cabin passengers, a charming little actress (whose heart was so large that it left no room for conventional morals) returning from New Orleans. There was a tight little bodice of dark green that came to a long point in front, with sleeves which were close-fitting except where they were puffed at the elbow; a very full skirt of heavy grey silk having faint green lines running down it and a pattern of delicate mauve flowers; and a little mauve bonnet trimmed with lilies-of-the-valley.

The general turn-out even impressed the critical Daniel: and as they bowled along the road — pea-green Samuel next the coachman on the box — between little villas bowered in roses and a sea that sparkled as if it had been powdered with gold dust, Washy felt that here was Paradise on earth.

Lunch, too, was ambrosial, from the soup with which it began — soup so hot that raw eggs, dropped into it when it was served, appeared to cook themselves on the spot — to the hot-house strawberries with cream-cheese and sugar that provided the conclusion. The lemonade was nectar, and so were the little glasses of crême-de-menthe which they drank with their coffee.

Afterward they sat, in placid content, on the veranda of the hotel and speculated on the occupants of the bathing-machines, which had immense canvas over the seaward doors, so that genteel females might take their dip under a sort of tent free from the observation of the impolite.

'How much longer shall you be in Denmark, did you say?' asked Washy at length, turning a little so that he might steal an occasional peep at the miracle of Anne Louise's profile as she sat on the rustic seat between him and a fidgety Daniel. He had asked the same question several times before; but it was needed this time to pave the way, so to speak, for a demand for further information.

Anne explained — as she had explained before — that it might be a fortnight or three weeks before Seven's business was completed.

'And then . . . ?'

'Then? . . . Why, I shall go home — to Lecques.'

Washy inquired where was Lecques; learned it was in France.

'France? Ah, France!' said Washy, in a tone that showed that he was acquainted with such a geographical area. 'That *is* a coincidence! Would you believe it, *I* am going to France, too!'

Anne was conscious of a gentle nudge from Daniel.

Yes, Washy was going to France, too. Quite definitely! It might be any time. He couldn't tell at the moment. His old aunt — his old Aunt Anne, you know! Yes, it depended on her very largely . . . France, of course, was a big country. And where might Lecques be? Near Marseilles! Ah! . . . His old aunt — you couldn't say where she would land!'

'But . . . ' began Daniel, and fell silent at a warning glance from

Anne Louise. She knew that Washy was watching her to see if any sign of scepticism as to Aunt Anne's existence should show in her expression.

To bolster up his creation, Washy then swung into a remarkable narrative of the old lady's proceedings on various occasions: all being intended to prove that if she landed at Lecques in a pair-oar boat from a Black Ball liner which ordinarily only called at Liverpool, it would be nothing out of the way. On the contrary, quite to be expected.

And so they passed that pleasant afternoon, in Paradise — thought Washy; though Daniel felt that the entertainment did not come up to the level of lunch.

But then Mr. Hallett asked no more of God than that he might be permitted humbly to sit beside Anne Louise, humbly to admire her, humbly to adore her. His hand just touched a fold of her wide dress — remained touching it: in his most vivid dreams his imaginings never carried him farther than that. He was utterly content.

He told very simply of his life in Virginia — of the great colonnaded house at Hallett set about by lawns and trees in the midst of wide plantations — of his orphan-hood — of the visit he had just been paying to his mother's father, an old Swedish baron living near Stockholm — how he had come to Elsinore to see Hamlet's grave, and had stayed on because — er — of the sunshine. It was, indeed, so artless a tale that Anne Louise, in reciprocating confidences regretted that she could not tell the truth. Her home was in France — True! She had been staying with Daniel's guardian in Wales — Quite true! They had decided to go on a visit to America. Very true, indeed! They had been shipwrecked — too true! They had lost everything: women passengers in the *Kriger* had had to fit her out with clothes — also true!

Only one mischance marked the day. Anne Louise lost her hand-kerchief.

Said Daniel as they climbed the stairs to their garrett —

'You know Washy pinched your wipe, Anne! I saw him do it! I *said* he was sweet on you!' And added: and blushed: 'And I'm not surprised . . . But you wouldn't be allowed to marry him, would you?'

And Washy — having paid a moonlight visit to Skottestrædet, and watched Onkel Olav's attic window until the light was extinguished, in the fond delusion that it was Anne Louise's — went home as one returning from a vision of the Grail.

In the privacy of his room he drew from the breast-pocket of his coat a crumpled handkerchief. He pressed it to his lips — gently, as though it were of gossamer that might dissipate into filmy fragments at any touch more rough than the beating of butterfly wings.

He pressed that crumpled handkerchief to his lips: and he kept it at his lips for a long, long time. He did not even feel ridiculous to himself — the acid test of the genuineness of such actions.

His eyes were shut. The so gentle pressure of that scrap of linen upon his lips was the spell that summoned the magic in the mirror of his mind. A tatter of dreams fluttered across the mirror, like the reflection of a torn and faintly-coloured tapestry: he was at Anne Louise's feet, the hem of her skirt put to his lips; her hand lay lightly on his as they went through some stately dance; but never was he other than the humble squire of a high-born lady.

And because it was unfitting that so sacred a thing should witness the sordid rites of the toilet, he wrapped it in a silk scarf and put it in a drawer while he made ready for bed.

He went to sleep with the handkerchief under his pillow, one hand just touching it, so that he should be certain that it was still there.

Anne Louise dreamed of Lecques — of Aunt Sophia — of the forest that surged about the dark red roofs of her home.

CHAPTER IV

A QUESTION OF FATHERHOOD

WASHY had to go to Copenhagen about his passport: he did not explain
that it was, in fact, to get the French visa, which, his inquiries had
informed him, would be necessary were he to visit — Lecques, for
instance.

It was surprising how blank Anne Louise and Daniel found the day
without him. In a short fortnight they had come to look for his dapper
figure awaiting them by the milliner's shop, or in the doorway of the
mermaid-owning apothecary; had come to expect new and wonderful
plans for morning or afternoon expedition or entertainment — plans
which Anne Louise would at first reject and finally be compelled to
accept by his unquenchable volubility and his insistence.

Washy's existence was kept no secret from Seven, although the
manner of their first acquaintance was glossed over. Seven, however,
appeared to evince no interest. Once only — when Daniel had dis-
coursed at length on the day's doings — did he comment to Anne
Louise —

'Well, you are old enough now to look after yourself!'

'Quite!' she had responded curtly.

So, carefree therefore, they went rowing, sailing, carriage-riding: they
picnicked most luxuriously — Samuel in attendance — on the sand-
hills and in the pine woods: they drank coffee, and ate exciting pastries
at a table under a striped awning in the street before a smart café.
Anne Louise's attitude, however, never altered: instead of having to
act as aunt to one small boy, now she had two young charges. She was
an elderly and battered woman of the world — that was what her
manner implied — and Washy was just a slightly older version of
Daniel.

They were a little dull, therefore, that afternoon without Washy, as
they lay on a sandy hillock tufted with spear-grass, near the sea;
Daniel upon his back plaiting what he said was to be a sun-hat, Anne
Louise face downward and drowsy. They were conducting their conversation in French — somewhat erratically on Daniel's part. It was a
heavy windless afternoon, grey with heat.

Anne Louise lifted her head and stared out across the waters. In

230

the foreground stiff grasses made dark scratches — like the up-and-down strokes in an Italian-hand copybook — against the skyline where dark glassy sea met bright glassy sky. The grass scratches were more definite, bolder, than the queer square cobweb drawn by the filaments of rigging and the masts of an incoming ship upon the horizon.

Said Daniel in English without any sort of prelude —

'I say, Anne, do you think La Thirkelsen was right?'

'Qu'est ce-que tu me dis?' reproved Anne Louise.

'J'entends . . .' he gave it up. 'I mean when she said to Sep the day we came — looking at me — "Your son?" Do *you* think I am Sep's son? . . . It would be rather a lark if I were, wouldn't it?'

She leaned upon her elbows and regarded him, chin supported in cupped hands. He, too, turned and met her gaze with a smile of innocent satisfaction.

'But how can I tell, Daniel?'

'Aren't I like him at all?' said Daniel a little damped. 'Isn't my nose like his — or somethin'? P'raps we've both got the same secret mark. There are bits of my back that I've never seen in all my life . . . You tell me to-night when I undress.'

'But surely you know who your father was?'

'I never thought about it — much,' said Daniel shaking his head. 'And, you know, Sep never knew who *his* father was until he was nineteen . . . Should I go on saying "Sep" to Sep, if he's my father; or should I have to say "Sir" or "Daddy" . . . I say! Can't you see Sep's face if I suddenly said "Yes, Daddy!" or "No, Daddy!" to him. Oh, wouldn't it be prime?'

He was convulsed by delighted laughter.

Togarmah had revealed Sep's origin and history to Anne Louise, not from the mere pleasure of gossip, but in order to explain and excuse the man he idolized. He had told the story very bluntly, and now the girl found herself wondering at Daniel's knowledge of its sinister details, even though he did not understand their full implication. It seemed a strange story for a child to know.

'Sep's father had seven sons,' meditated Daniel. 'And he named them by numbers. That's why Sep's called Seven. Sep's never seen any of the others — he told me so . . . I wonder if he's got any more, besides me!'

'Nonsense!' said Anne Louise briskly, and then foolishly added: 'Why, Seven's not even married!'

Daniel, chewing a grass thoughtfully, was prepared for that.

'Sep's father wasn't married, either. And *he* had seven boys.'

'But you're not called after a number, anyhow!'

Even that did not gravel the indomitable Daniel. He considered awhile; spat out a piece of grass; broke out again —

'P'raps he called us after the alphabet! Arthur — That's A . . . And — and, Bertram for B . . . And Charles . . . And Daniel for D . . . *And Daniel for D*! Bet you ten thousand pounds I'm right! Bet you five million billion pounds I'm right!'

He rolled over and confronted her triumphantly.

In that moment Anne Louise knew that Margarethe Thirkelsen had divined correctly. In that bright face she suddenly saw Seven as he must have been long, long ago, before ever he had embarked upon the course of education laid down for him by his strange begetter . . . before ever the bitter years of test had set their stamp on him. In grey eyes, in brow, in cleft chin, and even in the way in which a lock of hair fell on the boy's forehead — albeit a yellow lock and not a black: in all these she saw Seven Tempest.

She found that she wanted to weep — for the child that had been, as well as for the child beside her. Could it be that Seven had caused him to be born so that Daniel should undergo the horror which he himself had experienced? Would Seven carry out his father's experiment upon his own son?

Something of what was passing through her mind had undoubtedly occurred to Daniel, too. He turned over onto his back again, and remained for a little staring up into the vaporous sky.

'I don't think I shall like going down a mine,' he said, and gave a little sigh.

They were both rather silent after that, until Daniel raised another matter which had obviously been demanding his profound attention —

'Do you know what I think, Anne? . . . I think La Thirk is sweet on Sep!'

'Why on earth should you think that?' asked she, recovering from a day-dream in which she rescued Daniel from his fate by whisking him secretly away to Lecques.

'Haven't you noticed how she looks at him — almost as if she could eat him? When she comes in at supper time she just stands and stares at him. She never looks at anyone else. I think he knows it, too, although he pretends to pay no attention. Bet he does! And he *always* gets more to eat then anybody — *and* the best helpings!'

Anne Louise had not noticed these phenomena. She said so. But, meditating while Daniel babbled on, she realized that on several occasions she had seen Margarethe Thirkelsen in talk with Seven, but never with any other person except members of her staff. She could not imagine anyone falling in love with Seven — still less Seven as a lover . . . Presumably, however, it had happened at some time or other. Whence Daniel.

Could Seven be preparing to continue an alphabetical list of offspring? What Christian name began with an 'E'? — Edward — Edgar — Evelyn!

She pulled herself together.

'You're talking rubbish, Daniel!'

But Daniel had a strong streak of obstinacy: he refused to believe his theory to be rubbish. He elaborated it. He put into words the vague ideas that had passed through Anne Louise's mind.

'After all, Sep's father had seven sons,' he asserted in support of his proposition. 'And La Thirkelsen's awfully good-looking!' . . . He paused for consideration whilst he nibbled the soft stalk of a piece of grass . . . 'I don't think I should like her to be *my* mother . . . Now, *you* . . .!'

Anne Louise acknowledged the compliment suitably.

He regarded her with a kindling eye —

'You know, I think you'd make an awfully good mother, Anne! . . . If this had been a book, Sep would have fallen in love with you. But of course you couldn't marry him. And I don't suppose you'd care to have a baby without marrying him, like Ellen?' — Ellen was a housemaid at Judgment who had incurred the responsibility of maternity without that of wifehood — 'Would you?'

Anne Louise would not. Furthermore if Seven were the last man in the world, Daniel might rest assured that she would not encourage his attentions by so much as the flicker of an eyelid.

Daniel considered that she was unnecessarily severe.

They debated the matter as they walked back to the inn — at least until they were suddenly and surprisingly confronted with the solution of the mystery of Seven's daily disappearances.

In a narrow alley of tall houses with overhanging gables, a wagon was drawn up beside the entry of a warehouse with a hoist projecting from its upper story. Porters were going to and fro loading the clumsy vehicle, which blocked most of the fairway. A tangle of rope and barrels were strewn around. A chain and hook jingled over the tailboard.

As they skirted the obstruction, Daniel clutched at Anne Louise's dress.

'Look!' he exclaimed in a low voice.

But Anne Louise had already seen.

Seven had just emerged from the dark archway. He had on a leather apron, and was carrying upon his right shoulder a case which was tilted a little against his head so that his face was inclined toward them. Even so his expression gave no indication of the fact that he had noticed them, as, indeed, he could not fail to have done.

'It's Sep!' said Daniel in the utmost astonishment; and cried out 'Sep! Sep!' very loudly.

But Seven merely dropped the case with a resounding bump on the tail of the wagon, swung round on his heel, and disappeared within the warehouse without word or sign.

Anne Louise's meditations while they finished their walk were chaotic, and rendered the more so by a buzz of comment and question from a greatly intrigued Daniel.

The resentment she had felt against Seven from the time of their first meeting had been kept alive during the voyage in the ill-fated *Joan Dearlove* by his attitude, which had been a nice mixture of domination, watchfulness, dislike, and indifference.

The nightmare five days in an open boat after the destruction of the ship had, however, shown him in a different light: he had become the leader of a desperate expedition, for Mate 'Long-Nose' and 'Snorker' Reid had accepted his captaincy without question; he had proved himself gentle and considerate to Daniel and herself — very gentle and considerate: he had helped Sarah Liddell with what rough doctoring was possible for the wretched thing that lay in the bottom of the boat and moaned and writhed: his energy and his optimism had never failed. After that she had admired him without liking, even although once aboard the *Kriger* he appeared to relapse into a pose of cynical unconcern toward her.

Now, however, she knew that she would never be able entirely to dissociate him from the child of long ago who had looked at her out of Daniel's eyes — that whatever he might do or say, she would be conscious that behind the mask of Seven-the-Cynic there lurked the spirit of Seven-the-Daniel. She found, too, something almost noble in the spectacle of the proud master of Judgment voluntarily working as a common labourer, so that she and the boy might live at their ease.

Seven was more taciturn than ever when she encountered him at supper that evening. She had meant to express the hope that he was not tired, and to have shown in her manner something of the admiration and appreciation she felt for him; but he had proffered a very curt greeting as he seated himself at table, and devoted all his attention ostentatiously to his broth.

Anne Louise, her new sentiments thus chilled, ate her meal in silence. Daniel was not, however, to be quenched.

'I say, Sep,' he asked with a mouth full of veal, 'what were you doing when we saw you?'

'Working,' said Seven without looking up.

'Why?'

'Money.'

'Haven't we got any?'

'No.'

Seven did not offer to elaborate upon the situation, so presently Daniel started on a fresh tack.

'What was in that box you were carrying?'

Seven looked sideways at the boy for a moment before replying — 'Onions and overcoats.'

Daniel digested this information.

'Where was it going to?'

'Brazil — by way of Berlin and the Bahamas.'

'Where's Bahamas?'

'Eat your supper instead of asking dam-fool questions!' said Seven.

At this juncture he became aware that Margarethe Thirkelsen had entered the room and stood before the stove facing the length of the crowded table. Amid the litter of dishes and tankards was set a number of pewter candlesticks with candles which had burned so low that the shadows of the guests shifted on the walls behind them like attentive servants. She gave no greeting, as usual, and Anne Louise noted that — although they must have been conscious of her presence — none of those at the table, excepting Seven and Daniel, raised their eyes. She saw that Margarethe was looking toward the street door, her dark head up, her brows a trifle knitted; the great opals in brooch and ear-rings flamed against her whiteness. She was so beautiful and proud, so expectant and so still, that she seemed more than woman — to have the blood of fatal enchantresses in her, of Circe or Morgan-le-Fay.

The street door opened without warning.

An officer of the Town Guard appeared in the opening. He wore a magenta uniform with vast lapels of dark blue, and a large shako. In the candle-light his face showed lean, brown, and sardonic, with a grey moustache and a small tuft of beard — a face such as was that of Henri of Navarre.

The draught rushed in through the open door: the candles flickered: everyone looked round, and then swiftly back to their plates: next to Anne Louise a German woman — with iron-grey corkscrew ringlets —

gasped. There was absolute silence except for the tapping of knife and fork and spoon.

The officer said nothing at all. He displayed no interest in the occupants of the room. He just nodded his head very slightly as if in answer to some question that had been set him by Margarethe Thirkelsten; helped himself to a thimbleful of *akavat* from a bottle near-by, and went in silence as he had come.

Seven had returned to the contemplation of his meal, and it was Anne Louise who saw the faintest shadow of a smile curve Margarethe's lips in response to the officer's gesture; who noted the quick scrutiny by those green eyes of Seven, Daniel, and herself before departure: remarked too, with amusement, that the small boy was staring at the young woman with unmistakable hostility, spoon in air.

She wondered whether Daniel's instincts were correct, and that something in the lean dark man on her right was in process of evoking the passionate spirit dwelling in that still body, behind that lovely mask which displayed no emotion but pride. She could not decide whether dislike or distrust of Margarethe Thirkelsen was her predominant feeling.

The German woman, her ugly intelligent face glistening with perspiration, turned to her companion — a white-haired man whose eyebrows and lashes were practically invisible, whose lined forehead and wrinkled cheeks were criss-crossed with the white scars of sword-cuts.

'Herr Je!' she said in a harsh, low voice. 'What do the police want? He did not even look to see who is here . . . Something has happened . . . Poland — Hungary? . . . Yet she should have let us know if it were no longer safe.'

Seven, having arrived very late, was left to finish his supper in company with Onkel Olav. The old man produced a long pipe with a china bowl — on which was depicted the late King Frederick the Great of Prussia in three-cornered hat and blue coat — assumed a tasselled velvet cap and pair of steel-rimmed spectacles, pulled his chair up alongside the window, and settled down to his newspaper. Only when Seven rose to go did he lower the sheet on to his knees, and look carefully round the room.

'My friend,' he said in English — and his voice was very high and old — 'It is time that you left this place. More than time!'

Seven had never heard Onkel Olav speak before, except to demand food: had no notion that he knew English. Between surprise and annoyance he halted, scowling, hand on back of chair.

'And why so?' he snapped.

'My friend,' said Onkel Olav, peering up at Seven with his head a trifle on one side, to see what effect he should have, 'you have two so young persons on you dependent. Very excellent young persons! It would be well for their sakes that you should go away!'

His earnestness was such that Seven bit back a caustic comment, and contented himself with —

'I should like to hear your reasons for that statement, sir.'

'An officer of the Town Guard does not this house for nothing visit.'

'Well, he didn't visit it on my account.'

The old man nursed a bony leg — contemplated a green-and-red carpet slipper and the shiny patches on his threadbare pantaloons. He said nothing.

'Don't the police usually visit inns in Denmark?'

'Not this — unless *she* asks.' He rubbed his long thin pink nose. 'They do not mind what here happens. For here all are foreigners. Political exiles — refugees . . . They plot against Austria; against Russia; against Hanover; against Prussia. There is much plotting. Against everything except Denmark. So long as there is no plotting against Denmark, never will the police interfere. They find it convenient. Strange things happen here! Very strange things . . . There are no Danish guests here. There never are. So long as nothing to a Dane happens no one cares . . . You know why there are no Danish guests? . . . They are afraid! . . . You know the other name of the House of Gertrude Englishwoman?'

Onkel Olav drew a large red handkerchief from the tail of his velvet collared coat, which was green with age. He blew his nose vigorously and looked up at Seven for reply. His spectacles caught the light of the two near-by candles, and the lenses shone like pools of yellow flame.

Seven shook his head.

'I will tell you,' said Onkel Olav, lowering his voice. 'I will tell you because I think those young persons you have with you are truly excellent young persons . . . The Danes have always called this house, Heksenhuset — the House of Witches . . . The House of Witches! . . . They still do!'

Seven had not thought of witches since the days when he had lain in bed, a small boy at Minerva House, reading by surreptitious candle-light, a horrific book entitled *Gallowgrim, or the Nottinghamshire Witches*. The word bridged a gap of more than twenty-five years — recalled that night when he had been surprised at his illicit pleasure by Miss Wivern, herself witchlike as she stood hook-nosed and nightcapped in the black oblong of the open door. He smiled, as much at the memory as at Onkel Olav's disclosure of superstition.

Said the old man, as if explaining everything —

'Often are witches young — and very beautiful!'

Witches — young and beautiful!

For an instant his imagination toyed with the idea of the witch-hood of Margarethe Thirkelsen. It seemed not unfitting that a witch should be mistress of that house of silent people and long and shadowy passages and winding stairs — that her spell should lie on it and on them ... *And* on him! For he admitted to himself in that moment of clarity that some strange force drew him to the dim house and — almost against himself — to its dark proud owner. Long ago he had promised himself that he would have no more to do with women, but now he was conscious that every day he was being brought — by no spoken word, no gesture, no look — into the orbit of her sorcery.

He harked back —

'I still don't understand about the police visit.'

'They will for her have checked the truth of everything you have told her ... For her they will do many things! ... Now she knows that what you have told is true, you should go. So it will be better.'

'Why?' said Seven, and found himself resenting the warning.

'It will be better for the young persons that you should go, before ...' He broke off; continued: 'It will be better — for the girl much better. There may be much unhappiness for her. Go! I know Margarethe Thirkelsen. In this house have I seen very strange things happen!'

One of the candles flickered out.

Seven, standing in silence, thought that strange things might well happen in the house. Saw Margarethe Thirkelsen, in some shadowy room, anointing her naked body (but faintly to be perceived) with the compelling unguents of witchcraft.

He would have put further questions, but Onkel Olav suddenly raised the newspaper as a wall between them — as a barrier against further questioning. ...

When Seven opened his bedroom door, he found Anne Louise, in her grey dress, sitting bolt upright on a wooden chair against the wall, her sewing lying tumbled on her lap. There was a candle on the little table beside her, and, with her brown-golden head thrown back against the white wall, she stared with unseeing eyes at the darkness which pressed against the uncurtained window.

CHAPTER V

INTERLUDE IN A BEDROOM

ANNE LOUISE had not heard the door open, and did not realize Seven's presence until he had taken a step into the room. Then she rose, flushing, to her feet.

There had been rain about nightfall, and the smell of a wet garden came in through the open casement with a little whispering breeze which caused the candle flame to flicker, and quivered the folds of rose-patterned bed-hangings.

'I came here,' she said — and, in her nervousness, smoothed the folds of her grey dress — 'because there is nowhere to talk in this house. And we never see you at all, except for a short while at supper.'

'Yes,' Seven said non-committally; and the monosyllable might either have been question or assent. He was not anxious for conversation: he was only conscious of extraordinary weariness. He seated himself on the bed within its snug alcove, and stared at his cracked shoes.

Anne Louise would not be discouraged. She kept to the path which she had mapped out. She spoke, still standing, a grey girl with shining hair against the shadowy white wall:

'I am afraid I have been rather ungrateful . . . I have never thanked you for all you have done . . . Thank you very much! *Very* much!'

Her voice was low; and she looked at Seven, willing him to raise his head and meet her eyes — so that he might realize how genuine was her gratitude, and that she knew all about the Seven-Daniel whom he tried to hide.

Although he would not look up to see all this, yet deep within him Seven-Daniel stirred and spoke with the great Mr. Tempest.

'She is a very young princess,' said Seven-Daniel. 'Yet she did not complain when you sent her to sea in a slum — when she slept, one of some fifty, in a space smaller than that of the state bedroom in a gimcrack palace. She endured horrible things on shipboard without murmuring. She nursed, in her own arms and bed, a filthy lousy baby with dysentery; not just for one night, but for half a dozen. She neither fainted nor screamed when the ship went down, a furiously flaming coffin. She showed no fear during those days and nights when an open boat swung up and down the long swell of the empty plains of the

TWO KINDS OF ROMANCE

Atlantic. She helped to wash and clean and feed through seven long weeks the hideously maimed body of a very loathsome man. 'She is very young' — said Seven-Daniel — 'but she is indubitably a princess. Render her homage, Mr. Tempest, because she has come bravely through!'

But all Mr. Tempest would say aloud, was —

'I do not think I have done more than was in our bargain.'

Said Anne Louise —

'Much, much more than the bargain! . . . You have been a sort of guardian angel! . . . But for you, my uncle Leopold . . .' She paused. 'All sorts of things might have happened, too, during the voyage . . . but you were always there when you were needed . . . That night I went to sleep in the boat and it rained — it was *your* coat! . . . And now you . . .'

Seven-Daniel continued —

'Your pupil has come most creditably through her course of instruction at the Academy of Adversity, my dear Professor Tempest . . . Perhaps — *just* perhaps! — she didn't need the schooling! . . . Congratulate her, anyhow, on passing with honours!'

But Mr. Tempest, still regarding his long legs and broken shoes, could only bring himself to say very quietly —

'I have kept a note of all your expenses, as agreed . . . For any personal assistance there is no need to thank me. My presence on board was entirely accidental. I needed a holiday. I took one, on the spur of the moment.'

Even as he spoke he knew that he had said this ungracious thing, almost against his will, only so that he might preserve the outward showing which he had worn so long.

In some strange manner of divination she realized what lay behind his reply, and wholly discounted the rebuff.

It was with half a smile that she said: 'I didn't flatter myself that you came as my courier! . . . But that doesn't alter the fact that I'm very grateful to you, Mr. Tempest. And have good reason to be!'

He crossed his legs, muttered something unintelligible, and shot a swift glance up at her.

She was still standing, and the flickering candle on the table between them made her shadow mount almost to the ceiling. Her regard met and held his. He did not remember ever having looked into her eyes before. He grudgingly admitted to himself their beauty and their honesty.

She went on —

'I suppose your money will be here soon . . . Couldn't we talk over plans — now? It would make — home seem so much nearer.'

'Home' was a fatal word.

Said Mr. Tempest to the small wraith of Seven-Daniel, 'Home! . . . *You* had no home to look forward to while you underwent your test. All these weeks she had been saying to herself, "Only a little while longer now, and then I shall be home!" Home was always just round the corner — for her. *You* had to go on and on and on, the present being a purgatory, and the future offering you no hope and no prospect even, of relief. What reality can there be to an experience when the end is known?'

He said out loud, and looked into the darkness that masked the garden as he spoke —

'You still think of going to Lecques?'

'Of course!' — And he knew (without seeing) that she had knitted her brows in puzzlement — 'Why should I alter my ideas?'

'There's such a thing as duty!'

'Duty!' she echoed. 'I don't understand.'

'Haven't you sometimes thought — on our travels — that your duty might perhaps lie — not at Lecques?'

Still she did not understand.

'In — Hanover, for instance.'

'You are talking in riddles, Mr. Tempest.' Her voice had now become a little impatient. 'Won't you say plainly what you mean, please.'

'Haven't you wondered, after all your experiences,' said Tempest repressing the admonitions of Seven-Daniel, 'whether you ought not now to behave as a woman instead of a frightened child? Whether you ought not to do the duty set before you, instead of running away from it?'

She stared at him, as at one who had suddenly taken leave of his senses.

'Do you mean: Marry the Crown Prince of Hanover?'

He answered her bluntly, 'Yes!' and renewed his examination of the darkness.

'But why now?'

He thought to see for an instant a faint blur against the blackness without, as of a face turned momentarily toward the window. He rose to his feet, closed the casement, and drew the sprigged curtains with great deliberation, before turning to face her and reply —

'Because now you have more experience and knowledge of the

world: because you should have learned the meaning of the word "Duty".'

'So that I should have been through all this . . .' She could not find a word for a moment — 'this horror, for nothing? That I should go back to where I started from? That I should run away — just to run back again?'

'Not "for nothing"! Not "for nothing"!'

She confronted him, head thrown back, shoulders against the wall, her hands loosely clasped before her — yet not so loosely clasped but that she could feel the roughness of her fingers from weeks of unaccustomed needlework.

'If you now think it is my duty to marry a blind man whom I have never seen, why didn't you think so long ago, when you helped me to escape "my duty"?' Her voice was very low: she hoped that it was not uncertain.

'The operative word is "think",' said Seven. He was standing with folded arms, feet well apart. His shabby cotton trousers were too short for him by several inches, and Anne Louise noted that he had rent one of his dark red socks toward the top — probably in putting it on: subconsciously she wondered if she would be able to find any matching wool. 'The operative word is "think",' repeated Seven. 'How do you know what I thought "long ago"?'

'Well you appear to have reached a different conclusion . . . Why have you changed your mind?'

Seven started to pace up and down the room, hands behind back. Anne Louise felt that this was unfair: she had meant to do it herself: the movement seemed to give an advantage, for one's opponent was forced to watch one all the time as if awaiting physical attack.

She had to repeat her question. When Seven answered it, his manner was entirely different — impersonal — without emphasis — the manner of an unworldly tutor elucidating to a rather dense class a particularly gory passage dealing with murder or incest in a Greek Tragedy.

'Have you ever thought,' — he answered her question by another — 'that perhaps I helped you, not to escape *from* a duty, but *to* it?'

'I don't understand,' she said with a puzzled expression, following his pacing with her eyes.

He explained, using violent terms in a quiet voice, as though translating into speech the mental processes of someone remote, and not himself —

'Well, can you see any reason at all why I should have concerned myself with your affairs? Why I should involve myself in your folly?

242

'For money? — I am one of the richest men in England. For social prestige? — I don't care a tuppenny damn for all the dukes, princes, queens, popes in the wide world. For the sake of a pretty girl? — I could find plenty prettier than you if I wanted to; which I don't. Out of old-gentlemanly benevolence, or chivalry, or general meddlesomeness? — Certainly not!'

'You have given me a lot of reasons why you should not have helped me. Suppose you tell me, at last, why you did!'

The Duchess of Limburg had forgotten Seven-Daniel, and the man who earned their keep carrying heavy cases from warehouse to wagon: she had also forgotten Anne Louise. Her voice showed the forgetting.

'I don't believe in the idiot sons of rich men inheriting the father's riches — or the imbecile spawn of lords becoming great peers in their turn, just because they are spawn. I don't believe in frippery princesses becoming queens, because they are princesses. I don't believe that vast wealth and power should be at the mercy of the accident of birth.'

'When you have *quite* finished expounding your social gospel . . . !' interjected the Duchess of Limburg.

'You know what my father did to me — to all his sons? . . . Tog told me he had told you . . . You know the seven years I was put through — six of them sheer hell! *Years* of test — not weeks! *Years* of bitter learning — not weeks!'

Some inkling of what was to come dawned on Anne Louise. She suddenly found that she was trembling from an emotion that was between anger and fear. Her hands tightened their clasp of one another.

Seven paced slowly up and down the room, into the little island of light about the candle, and out of it — eight short reflective paces up; eight short reflective paces down. His ridiculous white cotton trousers flapped against his ridiculous red socks. The long black lock of his hair continually fell forward upon his forehead and had to be swept back.

He spoke to Anne Louise, not harshly — but explanatorily. He spoke so low that the eavesdropper who stood without the window could not catch a single word.

'*You*,' he said, 'are a princess. By the sheer accident of birth you are supposed to be of some finer clay than the rest of us. People abase themselves before you. They call you 'Your Transparency' or 'Your Magnificence'. They render you devoted service which you repay with a medal and a bit of ribbon. They proffer you the powers of a god for good or evil . . . You accept them as a right! . . . Because you are Royal!'

He paused as if he expected Anne Louise to make some comment.

She said nothing. He continued his tutorial monologue in a most matter-of-fact tone, for he intended no offence.

'One day you were to be Queen of Hanover — even possibly Queen of England! You were to be given a position of unbounded influence over millions of people! You were to be allowed to make men or break men — to foment wars, to undermine governments, to hinder great reforms! . . . And for why? Because you were better, wiser, more prudent than any other woman? No! . . . Just because you were the daughter of your mother and father — and for no other reason at all.

'When you came to Judgment — Was it a century ago? — you were a raw schoolgirl. Probably more ignorant in all the essentials of life than any schoolgirl of your age. Yet you were to help rule a small people — they had no say in the matter — perhaps even to help rule a great nation. You knew nothing of the world except by hearsay. You knew no more of the life of the masses of those you'ld one day rule than I know of the habits of the orang-outang — probably less.

'People backed out of your royal presence so that you should think the human frame was unprovided with behinds . . . You hadn't sat in a privy with men shouting rude jests at you through the door, *then*! You hadn't known *then* what it was to go hungry — to go thirsty — to live in darkness as one of an unconsidered herd amid stink and filth — to see lice crawling on a child's body — to watch drunks fighting for the embrace of a strumpet — to know of brutality, disease and sudden death — to cook bacon — to make clothes and darn socks — to bandage a scorched eyelidless face — to hear fifty people roasting without possibility of escape! . . . Your Highness has learned a lot about human nature! And about the condition of the poor! Your Highness's future subjects should benefit!'

He halted in his pacing and swung round before Anne Louise.

'There will never be a Queen with such knowledge as you have!'

She challenged him —

'Then you tricked me onto that hateful ship?'

He nodded.

'Quite true. I sent a man to make enquiries about you at the Spenser Arms when Wentworth was there, so that you should be panicked into taking the first chance of escape that offered . . . One of my own ships sailed two days afterwards from Liverpool. As a matter of fact you could have quite safely gone in her . . . In a cabin painted French grey with rose-coloured silk curtains and silver-plated lamps on the bulkheads — cost me thirty-five shillings did each of those sconces!'

She was about to flare at him — two months ago she would have done so — when suddenly she realized that her fate was still in his hands; that he alone could bring her to her haven; that it was he who should send her posting along the winding dusty roads across half Europe to that fairy-tale castle of refuge amid a southern pine forest. A dreadful panic seized her: supposing he should decide to continue her 'education', what could she do?

'You — you — will let me go — now?' she stammered; and despised herself for the tremor in her voice.

'Now?'

'I mean as soon as the money comes? . . . Straight back to Lecques . . . Straight back!'

'Don't you think that your duty lies — not in a toy castle and remote estate, but in a wider field? In Hanover. In England, perhaps.'

It was realization of his stupidity that served as spark to her anger.

'You fool!' she flamed. 'Do you think really that the King of Hanover will want me for a daughter-in-law? After I have wandered about the world with a man and a small boy as chaperones, and no one else. Are you really such a fool as that?'

Seven was palpably taken aback. The question of the nice observance of conventions had not seriously occurred to him. He was silent for a moment, pulling at his chin and lower lip.

'I am a rich man,' he said at last —

'You have said that on several occasions.'

He ignored the interruption.

'I am a rich man,' he repeated. 'I think I can arrange everything so that in the eyes of the world your reputation is absolutely unspotted. I can arrange for your honour to go to the wash! . . . I can provide you with aliases, and alibis, and discreet chaperones. I can silence those who know too much.' He glanced at her with a whimsical gleam in his eye. 'A purely-business arrangement between us. At a reasonable profit to myself, of course!'

'I will not live a lie,' said Anne Louise. Panic was gone now. Intense rage had taken its place. She wanted to scream, and to throw at him the heavy candlestick on the table beside her — anything to efface the mockery of his expression . . . But she restrained her anger. 'I ran away to escape marriage with George of Hanover. He *must* know it all by now. Do you think his own pride would let him go on with the business — even if I were willing? Which I'm not.'

He propped himself against the oak chest with the brass wash-basin atop. A distant church clock chimed a jangle of thin bell-music into the night, and then struck the hour across the sleeping town. He counted the strokes — eleven. Time to draw the discussion to a close.

'We can finish this talk to-morrow,' he suggested.

'No,' she said violently. 'I want you to understand that I would rather walk across Europe — rather crawl on my hands and knees, than marry that man. I am going nowhere else than Lecques, whether you help me or not.'

For to her mind there suddenly had come the thought of Washy — that humble-minded cavalier, Washy, who would leap at an opportunity to be of service, if only she could bring herself to ask him! Washy who would do anything, and demand nothing!

'It is a pity . . . ' Seven began.

'A pity that your course of education has been wasted? All your tuition wasted on a miserable little duchess! Instead of inspiring a queen-to-be!'

He found himself admiring her in her anger. Across the years there came back to him the memory of how he had passionately confronted his father in that long candle-lit room with the crowded tables and the pictured ships along the walls. How would the old man have dealt with her? — he wondered. The memory of his own rage made him sympathetic to hers, although he did not show it. But it was rather gently that he said . . .

'I think that the time will come when you will thank me for that education — and the people you come to rule, even more so. You are angry now, but you will not always be. One day when the heralds proclaim you, and the trumpets sound, and the chamberlain with his white staff precedes you, walking backwards — even on that day you will remember the queue at the galley-door waiting to cook their few poor scraps, or lining up to fill their pannikins with smelly water; you will remember a ragged woman doctoring a dying baby in her arms as best she might; you will remember 'Snorker' Reid, braver in his tatters than any soldier in scarlet and gold lace, singing loud songs in a water-logged boat so that you might not realize how near was death; you . . . '

'Don't!' said Anne Louise, 'I can't bear it.'

'When you recall all that, you will know more of your people than any of your ministers of state! . . . And *I* shall have been your tutor!'

She made a little gesture, suddenly tired, as if she saw no possible escape from all those memories, whatever of happiness the future might hold.

'You will help me go to Lecques?' she asked. It was a question and not a plea; for she had convinced herself now that she could appeal, and not in vain, to Washy.

'As soon as my credits come,' he answered.

'There — there — will be no more — experiments?'

He went to the door. With his hand upon the latch, he said —

'There shall be no more — experiments — upon the Duchess of Limburg . . . No more!'

As he stood there, head slightly bent, faint smile creasing the corners of his mouth, something irresistibly reminded her of Daniel. Almost before she knew what she was saying she had spoken —

' . . . Or on Daniel!'

And knew by his start that her suspicions were true. She heard Daniel say again — 'Daniel for D! . . . Bet you ten thousand pounds I'm right. Bet you five million billion pounds I'm right.'

' . . . Or on Daniel!'

Surprise still flickered on his face as he answered —

'So you'ld like to cut short my career as an experimenter! We will talk about it later!' . . . He was holding the door ajar. Neither of them could hear the faint rustling in the dark passage without — as if the draught had caused a curtain to flutter; or someone had taken refuge in the yet darker entry to a winding stairway . . . 'So far as the Duchess of Limburg is concerned, your Highness can be assured that you shall be treated as a Highness from the moment the journey starts — if you wish. I will even provide a brass band and scarlet outriders on cream-coloured horses, and twenty ladies-in-waiting — all guaranteed virgins . . .'

He pulled the door wide open — then closed it; for she had taken up her sewing from the table, and then paused on her way out, barely a pace from him.

'When did you first think of this — experiment — you tried on me?' she asked in a low voice; and did not mind if he heard its coldness, for all the time she was saying to herself 'Why didn't I think of Washy before?'

'Almost as soon as you asked me to help you play truant,' he answered. 'I thought about it a good deal. At first it was just a germ of an idea. Then later . . . '

He paused. She urged him on — and in her mind something repeated continuously, 'Washy! Washy! Washy will help!'

'Later? . . . Well?'

'Later it seemed to me to be a theory that should be put into practice. That you needed — instruction!'

'And what finally persuaded you?'

'No one thing,' he said, meeting her gaze steadily. 'But, to be perfectly frank, one small factor was your treatment of your maid — I forget her name!'

'Lovell!' exclaimed Anne Louise in the utmost astonishment. 'My treatment of Lovell! . . . Are you quite mad?'

'I suppose,' he said sarcastically, 'that it was so usual a thing for you to strike your servants that you would not recollect such a trifle!'

'Strike my servants!' she echoed. 'I have never struck a servant in my life.'

'There were bruises on the girl's face to prove it!'

'They prove nothing . . . Did she say I struck her? If she did, she lied.'

'She implied it.'

But Anne Louise had need to say no more, for the puzzlement on her face was a sufficient warranty of her innocence.

'Why should she imply it? . . . It was Henry Wentworth who hit her. It was a cowardly thing to do. She told me so herself. She's going to have a baby, and he's the father. She told me when she heard that she wasn't to go with me to America. She was afraid for me — with him . . . I promised I would keep it secret. But I also promised myself that when I came back to Europe I'ld see he married her!'

' "See he married her!" '

It was Seven-Daniel then that smiled a little on the princess who would right wrongs so easily, who would be the fairy-tale princess, who would wed duke's son to maidservant, and so make a happy ending to the story!

'I see I was wrong,' he said. 'I'm sorry . . . But I don't think I regret what I have done. I don't. In fact I'ld do it again . . . Good-night madam!' . . .

It was past midnight when Captain Hansen, of the Town Guard, was aroused by knocking on the street-door. After a short interval he came downstairs in a striped flannel bed-gown, loose slippers, and tasselled cotton night-cap pulled over his beaked nose. He unbolted, unchained, and unlocked the door with much rattling and banging, and let his visitor into the house.

In a crowded little parlour, reeking of stale tobacco, and lighted by a solitary candle, he listened carefully to what Margarethe Thirkelsen had to say: swallowed a glass of *akavat*, and made her repeat it afresh: took a vast pinch of snuff from a large brass snuff-box, and went over the main facts out loud.

What it came to, then, was that she had overheard part of a conversation between two people registered at her inn in the English name of Cash.

In parenthesis, the man was he about whom the police had made inquiries for her; and his story of a journey to America interrupted by ship-wreck had proved perfectly true. That he was working for Andersen Brothers was also correct. She had understood this from his visit that night?

To continue. Such snatches of their talk as she had caught had been too broken to convey the purport. What she could swear to, however, was that this man Cash had referred to the girl as the Duchess of Limburg, and had addressed her as Highness.

There had been no indication of jesting? . . . No! . . . No uncertainty about the title and rank? . . . No! . . .

Limburg was a small duchy lying between Germany and Belgium — he remembered marching through it when he served with Alten's Hanoverian division at Waterloo . . . It had lost its independence, and most of it was seized by Belgium after the Belgian revolution of 1830. . . .

Now let us be thoroughly methodical. Let us survey the position. One: Was this girl the Duchess of Limburg? Two: If so, in the name of all that was wonderful why was she masquerading in Elsinore? Three: How could he find out the answer to these questions without causing offence if she proved to be so great a lady? And, four: What business of the police was it, anyway, if she were the duchess?

'Deep waters — dangerous waters!' said Captain Hansen. 'Possibly very hot waters! And I don't want to get scalded! . . . Even for you!'

He took another pinch of snuff, another glass of *akavat*, to aid in clear thinking.

Margarethe had not troubled to throw back the hood of the dark cloak she wore. Her face in the dim light was hidden from him, with all its pride and contempt.

She said, 'If Limburg is as you say, then it has become part of Belgium, and the Belgian envoys will look after its affairs abroad. Why do you not send at once to the Minister in Copenhagen? If it should prove a mare's nest, then all you will have done is to make routine inquiries of him. You can't be blamed for that! If, however, there should be something in the business, then you will get the credit, and the Minister will have to take the responsibility for any unpleasantness that may follow.'

'The same idea had occurred to me,' said Captain Hansen. 'I will write a letter to the Minister.'

He found quill pen, paper, and a chipped china inkstand. He pulled a chair up to the table, and squared himself to write.

'Now Frøken Thirkelsen, how would you word it?' . . .

Dawn had not yet broken, but the blackness of night was becoming grey, when a man in uniform clanked out of the Guard post, swung himself onto the back of a big bay horse, and set off at a brisk trot through the fine rain along the road to Copenhagen.

CHAPTER VI

FURTHER INTRUSION ON A PRINCESS

THE travelling carriage had stood at the inn door since the early after-noon, to the great interest of Onkel Olav. The old man sat in the geran-ium-decked window of the eating-room mumbling at his pipe, and staring at the shining maroon-coloured panels, the silver-plated lamps, the four sleek horses who fretted and stamped under the care of a diminutive postilion in maroon livery, as if the spectacle had induced a trance.

The white-haired German with the scarred face, coming out of the courtyard archway into the sunny street, pulled up dead at the sight of the equipage; noted coronet and elaborate coat-of-arms upon its door, and spat viciously in its direction; looked down the street, and saw in the distance a high shako such as worn by the Town Guard; looked up the street, saw another tall figure looking into space with elaborate unconcern; slid back out of sight.

The two gentlemen waiting inside the carriage, with windows pulled up, had become almost as impatient as their horses. The conversation, which they carried on spasmodically, was in French.

The elder, a small neat man in black, fidgeted perpetually — with rings, watch, hat, cravat.

'If this should prove all moonshine! . . .' he complained for the fifth time, and tapped white fingers irritably on a neat black knee.

For the fifth time his companion soothed him.

'Well, Monsieur le Ministre, at any rate the particulars appear to tally with such information as his Majesty has circulated!'

'Psha!' said the Minister.

He felt that there was no need at the moment for diplomatic urbanity. He had lunched, on the road, most abominably. There was a mass of very private information about the Czar's attitude to the new Belgian state which he had just received, and was anxious to digest and transmit to his royal master. There was, too, a pleasant little dinner party that was rapidly slipping into the realm of might-have-been.

'Psha!' said he, and added, 'You've only seen the girl once, two years ago, D'Albertine! You probably won't recognize her!'

'Just two years ago, sir,' said D'Albertine. 'His Majesty did me the honour to present me to her Highness when she was in Brussels. She was a very striking young lady in my opinion! Not easily forgotten!' and he stroked a fair moustache in a manner that seemed to imply that he, too, might have created a very favourable impression.

At that moment the door opened, and the brown sardonic face of Captain Hansen appeared in the aperture. He brought up two fingers to the shiny blackness of his shako in salute.

'My man signals that the young — er — lady is approaching now, your Excellency,' he said.

There were few pedestrians about, and the two men, looking through the front windows of the carriage up the cobbled slope of the street, could see that a young girl in grey, accompanied by a small boy and a young man in a somewhat exotic costume, had just turned the corner into Skottesrædet.

'Well, is it she?' demand Excellency, clasping and unclasping his fingers.

'It's too far off to see yet, sir,' responded D'Albertine, leaning forward and watching the trio as they came nearer. 'It looks like her Highness at a distance!... Very like!... It *is* her Highness!'

'You are certain — *absolutely* certain?'

'Yes.'

'And why in the name of the Virgin does she want to travel about Denmark with a retinue of school-children?' fretted the minister preparing to descend. ...

Anne Louise, abreast of the carriage, was suddenly confronted by a neat urbane little man in black — a little man whose neat face was neatly creased in a neat smile, who carried an immensely tall hat with practically no brim in one hand, while he placed the other vaguely in the direction of his heart as he made the neatest and most deferential of bows from the waist.

'I wonder — er — madam, if I might have the honour of a few words with you? *In private*,' said the neat little man in French, underlining the last two words.

An appalling fear welled up in Anne Louise's heart. She clenched the nosegay of wild flowers she was carrying. She looked blankly into the neat little face —

'I do not know you, sir!' she answered in English.

'What,' interjected Washy, flushing scarlet, 'er — what is the meaning of this? ... Shall I — er — knock him down, Anne?'

And he clenched his fists.

The neat gentleman ignored him. Still standing before Anne Louise in the most obsequious attitude, he said —

'I must implore you to let me speak to you privately — very privately. Captain D'Albertine — whom you may remember — will present me.'

Captain D'Albertine, bare-headed, bowed very low. Washy disliked him and his beautiful blue uniform with heavy gold epaulettes, even more than the neat gentleman : disliked him because he very much doubted his ability to knock down so big and splendid a young man.

'Your High — You may remember me, madam. In Brussels. Two years ago. Captain D'Albertine. I had the honour of being presented to your — you . . . May I now present Monsieur le Comte de Charlemont, his Belgian Majesty's envoy in Copenhagen?'

Anne Louise saw the two faces — neat little face with neat little grey whiskers, and big blond face with golden moustache — as vague blurs against the sheen of the maroon panels of the carriage. She heard, as if at a great distance, the jingle of harness, and Washy snort and clear his throat preparatory to some outburst : a linnet in a wicker cage outside a gable window across the street broke into song : Daniel shuffled uneasily : she let drop her hedgerow posy, and the white and blue flowers lay unheeded at her feet.

'In Brussels' . . . 'His Belgian Majesty'! Uncle Leopold had found her at last! The journey, which had begun with the raid upon Henry Wentworth's dressing-room at Severall a generation — or two generations? — ago, and had lain across all England and Wales and the wide Atlantic, had come to a bitter finish. Standing there, silent, in the quiet street she found that she could no longer picture the happy place that was to have been journey's end ; its towers and forests were blotted out by the vague blur of two faces — one neat and grey, the other blond — against the panels of the carriage.

She made one desperate effort.

She drew herself up, and surveyed the small bowing figure. She spoke in English —

'I do not understand!'

And Washy said violently —

'Now look here! In the States we'ld . . . '

If Seven had been there — she knew — he would have whisked her away from these bowing, dangerous men : would somehow have found an unexpected avenue of escape. For it never occurred to her for one moment to think that the treason might have been his.

Captain Hansen was standing, just out of earshot, by the inn archway. He took a great pinch of snuff, and flicked the dust of it from off the dark blue lapels of his coat. His eyes never left the group by the carriage.

Anne Louise realized that there was nothing that she could do. She spoke again, and this time in French.

'May I ask what you require?'

'A few private words!' M. de Charlemont besought her with anxious intensity, and rubbed his neat little hands together as though he would rinse them from any responsibility for this unpleasantness.

'Well?'

He waved a hand in a despairing gesture. Its sweep indicated Washy and Daniel, the intent face of Onkel Olav staring through a miniature hedge of scarlet geraniums, a maidservant watching from a window across the way, Captain Hansen, and an approaching foot-passenger.

He coughed in a deprecatory manner — a neat crisp double cough, like a double knock, a cough without any slurring, beginning sharply and ending tidily. To cough and gesture, M. de Charlemont added —

'In private — I beg you.'

'There is nowhere in the house.'

'You will deign, perhaps, to come to the consulate?'

'Why?'

M. de Charlemont looked as near distraction as his neat little face would permit. Again he gesticulated. He shrugged his shoulders; he threw out his hands.

There was no one within hearing of their low voices.

Said Anne Louise, speaking very steadily —

'You are aware that I am not a Belgian subject — that I decline to recognize the annexation of Limburg?'

'His Majesty is your legal guardian. Was appointed by the late duke.'

'My father could not guess that within five years of his death his duchy would have been stolen by his brother-in-law!'

Again he washed his hand in deprecation.

'I have His Majesty's instructions. I have also authority from the Danish Foreign Office ... Madam, I *do* ask you ... '

She knew that it could be of no avail to play for time: that the moments of her liberty had run out, just like the sand in the fire-illumined hour-glass on the poop of the flaming *Joan Dearlove*.

'*Anne*! What are they talking about? Isn't there anything I can do?' asked Washy desperately. He would have liked to trample to the earth the neat little gentleman in black — to have called out to mortal duel the blond officer whom he suspected, furthermore, of regarding with supercilious amusement that broad-brimmed low-crowned hat which was his especial pride.

'My things?' said Anne Louise to M. de Charlemont.

He seemed to assess discreetly, from her attire, the likely quality and quantity of her baggage.

'That shall be arranged immediately — *for* you.'

Relief was evident in his face at her surrender.

She said, indicating Washy —

'I should like to speak in private with this gentleman. He knows nothing of my history, and is in no way concerned with it.'

De Charlemont, noting the nearness of Captain Hansen and the shakoes at either end of the street, bowed a neat assent, and withdrew with D'Albertine a pace or two away.

'Washy!' said Anne Louise in a low urgent voice. 'Will you please do something for me?'

'Anne,' he answered, 'what is all this mystery about? I couldn't understand a word of their jabber.'

'I think that Daniel has guessed. Haven't you, Daniel?'

But Daniel was past reply. He stood with averted head, crimson-faced, biting his lips so that they should not quiver, eyes fixed on the ground.

She took the child's small warm hand in hers.

'Daniel will tell you a lot by-and-by! All sorts of things of which you have never guessed ... But I want you to do something for me, Washy! Will you, please?'

He would do anything for her. Anything in the wide, wide world.

And, indeed, he would have gone forth to any hopeless battle on her behalf — would have stood up in the chill morning to the sword or pistol of the big blond Captain D'Albertine gladly, if she had so required.

'I have to go away now, Washy,' and she paused. 'I may not see you and Daniel again for a time. But I *shall* see you again! ... Will you go away from Elsinore *now*? And take Daniel with you? And hide him so that Seven shall never find him? And be very, very kind to him for my sake — until I can have him?'

Of course he would! He would have adopted a whole family of orphans for her sake — an entire orphanage!

'You'll go with Washy, won't you Daniel, *now*?'

Daniel nodded his head. The big tears were running down his face, and trickling onto his nose; and his lips could no longer be restrained from trembling.

'And if you should be caught, Washy,' — 'I shan't. Indeed, Anne, I shan't!' — 'just say that you did it for me because I thought there had been enough experimenting. Remember that! . . . Because I thought there had been *enough experimenting*!'

'Because you thought there had been enough experimenting,' he repeated. 'But, Anne, can't I . . . '

'Washy, my dear, there is nothing you can do at all — except that! . . . Where can I write to you?'

'Write to me at my grandfather's near Stockholm.' He wrote down the address on a leaf of paper from his pocket-book. 'They shall always know where to find me.'

He prided himself on the quick decision, and his heart sang when she smiled on him.

By a glance she told M. de Charlemont that she was ready to go.

D'Albertine leaped to the carriage door, and held it open to usher her into the maroon depths.

'Good-bye, Daniel!' she said, and stooped down and kissed the wet face that had been turned away. 'You'll be happy with Washy, won't you? . . . Bye-and-bye — quite soon — you shall come and live with me — always. Good-bye, dear Daniel!'

She put out her hand to Washy: he took it in both his, as if it were some holy relic — remembered his hat, snatched it off, dropped it; seized her hand again, and put it to his lips.

— How could he ever set those lips to food or drink again after they had touched that hand? —

It was he, who — elbowing aside the big blond officer in his glory of blue and gold — handed Anne Louise into the carriage.

She looked back through the little window above the seat as they drove away; to see Washy and Daniel staring after her. Then Washy stooped and began to pick up the scattered flowers of her posy. . . .

Onkel Olav broke the news to Seven when he returned late that evening — so late that the old man was alone at his place at the head of the table. Although without doors was still the clear pallor of summer evening, candles had already been lighted and emphasized the dusk of the long room which had but two small windows — and they obscured with pots of geraniums. Onkel Olav was dipping gobbets of sweet cake into his coffee, and eating them noisily and with much movement of white moustache, head down-bent until his nose nearly touched the rim of the large blue cup before him.

'So they have gone!' he said without looking up, as Seven dropped into a chair and helped himself from a dish of cold sliced meat.

'Who've gone?' asked Seven indifferently.

'I told you there would for the girl be unhappiness,' said Onkel Olav, speaking with a very full mouth. He raised his head and gave Seven a quick sidelong look out of blue watery eyes. The quality of that glance, apart from this words, would have warned Seven that much was amiss.

'What do you mean?' asked Seven, suddenly become very still.

Onkel Olav wiped his lips on a red cotton handkerchief. He cleaned a surviving tooth in his upper jaw with his tongue — its broad bluish underside showed in his open mouth like something raw and dying.

'The miss — she went three — four — hours ago. In a red carriage. With two gentlemen. Ve-e-ery fine gentlemens! . . . And the boy have gone, too. I know how not.'

Seven was utterly taken back by the news. He sat staring at the old man in silence.

'The carriage for her nearly three hours waited,' said Onkel Olav, thoroughly enjoying himself. 'There was on the door the tokens of — how you say *Adel*? — of . . . nobility. A crown — a little crown . . . The gentlemen spoke with her for a few minutes. What they say I could not hear. I think they talk together in French . . . And then, ph-ph! they are all very quickly gone!'

'She will have left a message for me,' said Seven, and rose from his seat to ring the hand-bell which lived on top of the stove — a brass bell having for handle a horned devil.

'You need not to ask,' remarked Onkel Olav, evincing even greater enjoyment of the situation.

'Why?'

'The gentlemen speak with her as she come back from a walk with the boy and the young man who always accompany them. They speak. She goes. She comes not into the house at all.' He renewed his attentions to cake and coffee.

Seven remained on his feet, hand still on chair-back, looking down on the old man's bald and yellow cranium.

He found himself surprisingly overwhelmed; not sentimentally, he told himself, but from a business point of view. He had made a contract with Anne Louise, and had failed to carry it out! His pride was hurt by the fact!

Still regarding Onkel Olav's white raspberry-like pate, he analysed the position.

How was it possible — he asked himself — that the emissaries of King Leopold should have discovered Anne Louise in so remote a place as Elsinore?

Or was it that she had suspected him, and, fearing there would be further 'experiments', had surrendered herself, as being the lesser evil? But then, had he ever given her reason to doubt his pledged word — such a promise as he had made the previous night? . . . And why should she thus resign the adventure at its last stage, of her free will? At the last stage — for in a week, or little more, his credits would have arrived, and the journey, begun so long before, could have been completed with the minimum of risk.

Of course she might have accidentally encountered friends who had come to her aid . . . But in that event why had she left no message for him, and why, too, should Daniel have disappeared?

On the whole, however, he was inclined to think that the third possibility was the most likely.

He took a candle from the table, and went through the shadowy house to Anne Louise's garret.

The curtain dividing the room into two had been drawn back : the cord that supported it was serving as a washing-line on which hung a small blue shirt, some socks, a white petticoat, and a pair of white stockings. The square window was open to the paling sky, and the room was as full of cold light as a sculptor's studio.

He thought, rather grimly, that there would have been little purpose in her returning to the house to collect her possessions : there was nothing worth the taking — a battered hair-brush, which presumably she shared with Daniel — a broken comb — a tooth brush — a pair of worn blue shoes.

He opened the wardrobe. There were a couple of undergarments of some sort on a shelf; from a peg hung the green-and-grey dress that served for best, and, next to it, her little mauve bonnet trimmed with lilies-of-the-valley.

For some reason the empty dress brought home to him the personal aspect of her departure — that the girl, whose fate had been bound up with his for so long, had gone from his life as suddenly as she had entered it. He had always thought of her in much the way that a doctor regards a patient, or a school-master views one of his class — as a 'case' for study, as a 'subject' for instruction : he had never thought of her as a girl, as a pretty girl.

Now, looking at the folds and pathetic shapelessness of the dress, he found himself remembering Anne Louise, as he had seen her two or three days before, coming down the narrow street with something almost dancing in her step, wide faintly-patterned skirt dancing to her gait, gold-brown ringlets dancing under the charming little bonnet. For the first time he wondered what her innermost reactions to him had been; and knew at once that the answer lay in her message-less departure; knew, too, in a moment of great clarity, that the answer lay in her abduction of Daniel. He saw it all now. When help came she had not forgotten Daniel: last night she had pleaded that there should be no 'experiments' on him: to-day, having the opportunity, she had endeavoured a rescue. It was all in keeping with the spirit which had planned to right the wrong committed upon Lovell, by marrying her to a duke's son!

He stood, thus, lost in meditation before the open wardrobe in the fading light, the extinguished candle in his hand.

There was a faint rustle. He looked up, half-thinking to see Anne Louise suddenly returned. But it was Margarethe Thirkelsen who stood in the doorway, regarding him.

CHAPTER VII

THE EDUCATION OF A SUPERIOR PERSON

SHE had watched him for some little while before he had become aware of her: watched — reading in his attitude before the wardrobe the dejection of an abandoned lover, and finding in that dejection the justification for her betrayal of the girl. No sign of what she thought or hoped was shown, however, in her eyes. Nor did her expression change when he looked up, realized her presence, and asked an entirely unexpected question —

'Where is the boy?'

She, too, had asked herself that question. She answered him with the inquiry —

'Is he not with the girl, Miss — Miss . . .?'

'You know that she has gone?'

'I have been told so. I saw a carriage before the house. I heard that she went away in it. I know nothing about it myself — and nothing about the boy.'

Suddenly he closed the wardrobe door upon the delicate pattern of the dress, upon the ghostly lilies-of-the-valley on the little bonnet, with — she thought — the gesture of one shutting the covers of a book after the last chapter has been read: and in turning toward her he gave the door a gentle push, just — she thought — as the reader might thrust the volume away in dismissal, a gesture of finality.

'He can come to no harm with her,' he said, and felt quite genuinely that the matter could rest there for the moment. In any case there was nothing that he could do until credentials and credits arrived for him.

'You have been so long away,' said Margarethe, 'that they have cleared the table. Only now have I learned that you have not yet had your supper. Come! I will see that you have something to eat!'

He expressed his indifference to food; but she was insistent.

'You are a little distressed — but naturally! Still you must eat. And then you shall go to the police — to Captain Hansen. He is a good friend of mine. It will doubtless be explained satisfactorily.'

She watched him whilst she spoke, eyebrows slightly lifted as though to ask whether her suggestion was not a good one.

'I will consider the matter,' he answered non-committally.

She did not attempt to continue the subject, but half-turned and then paused in the doorway as if waiting for him to follow her.

'You are so late now that you will have to sup with me,' she said.

He knew that in some way she had made a change in their relationship, although her words held no invitation but only a statement of fact, and although her expression said not a little more than her speech.

He followed her downstairs, and through dark passages to a door opposite his own, set deep in the thickness of the wall: came from shadowy dusk into a room which glowed with warm light and colour as though all the dim attics and obscure corridors and sombre chambers existed but to encase its glamour.

It was very long and very low, with whitewashed walls along which stood heavily carved presses of dark and shining wood. At the far end was a tall Spanish cabinet of ebony and yellowing ivory, against curtains of a scarlet which had faded to a lovely ghost of bygone brilliance. Subdued and shadowed, too, was the colour of the ancient Persian rugs upon the floor — of the fantastic twisted decoration painted long ago on the great chiselled beams across the ceiling. There were books and curious ornaments and candelabra scattered everywhere, and over a massive oak table in the centre of the room hung a great silver ball, in whose bright surface were reflected and distorted the many quivering candle-flames.

On a chest by the door Seven noticed, as he entered, a crystal death's-head as big as his fist bearing a clock-dial in gold and black enamel in its brain-pan.

It was a strange room to find at the heart of so colourless a house, and in an inn.

Margarethe read his thought, for she said — and it was an assertion and not a question —

'You are surprised to find *this* in the midst of *that*!'

And conveyed what she meant by the word '*that*' in the merest movement of her hand, which in its gesture comprised all the rambling building with grass-sprouting courtyard, bare garret and loft, shadowy passages, furtive guests, Onkel Olav, the flitting figures of plump perspiring servant-girls, and the silence which followed the visit of Captain Hansen.

'Not surprised — interested,' answered Seven; and dropped into a chair, and took up in his hand an ancient cumbrous model of something made in brass and silver, floridly engraved, whose purpose he could not divine.

Margarethe remained standing.

'And, indeed, not very interested!' she said.

He looked up at her for a moment from the puzzle of rod, and ratchet, and toothed wheel.

'What makes you say that?'

'I do not think you are interested in things merely because they are beautiful or strange. You are a rich man — a very rich man, I should fancy, and a very powerful man! . . .' She was watching him as she spoke and, although his head was down-bent over the toy in his hands, she knew that she had taken suddenly all his surprised attention, and, thereby that her assumption was correct. 'But however rich you may be, I am certain that there are no graces or adornments about your home — or, if there are, only because they have been overlooked.'

He had satisfied himself about the toy. He set it down in its place on the chest at his side. He forgot it. Through his mind passed memories of the bare rooms, the derelict splendours of his house of Judgment.

He looked up again at Margarethe.

'And then . . . ?'

'You are not interested in things of that sort . . . The things in which you *are* interested are those that mean power, or speed, or economy of effort. And if they are not strong enough or fast enough, then you let them pass out of your mind as if they had never been. I wonder if you treat people in the same way?'

She was leaning a little forward, finger-tips pressed against the shining surface of the broad table, across whose length she regarded him, with much the same expression as that with which he had examined the brass and silver model. The jewel upon the bosom of her dark green dress barely stirred to her quiet breathing: it held as great a depth of light as if it burned within itself.

'You seem,' said Seven, 'to have made some study of me!'

'I study all those who come to this house,' she replied. 'And those who do not repay the study I also forget — as utterly as though they had never existed. I forget *people* just as you forget *things*!'

'People do not interest me,' declared Seven, leaning back and clasping his hands behind his head, 'except in their relation to things. A man means nothing to me personally, except in so far as he is capable of producing something — or administering its production.'

'And women . . . ?'

'Have had very little to do with them. Want less.'

' . . . But you have been in love?'

He thought for a little so that he should be honest in his reply: remembered the rose-petal face of the girl whom he had chosen to give him a son, and the regret for her anguish which had led him to abandon any effort to follow further in his father's foot-steps. He had been sorry for her, but never in love.

'No,' he said finally; and his tone was utterly decisive.

'But the boy ... ?'

At that he looked at her again, only more narrowly. But there was no flicker of expression on her face, beyond the same impersonal interest with which he had scrutinized the manner wherein pinion and wheel and ratchet engaged with one another in the toy at his side.

He saw no purpose in lying about the relationship between Daniel and himself, now, and to her.

'The boy? ... He was in the nature of an experiment ... Long ago. And not to be repeated!'

'And the girl? ... Another experiment?'

He found himself resenting the implication, not so far as it concerned him, but on behalf of Anne Louise: was faintly amused by that resentment. He replied —

'A theory of education. And a business contract. The first may have succeeded — time will show! The second a failure.'

She could not as yet penetrate the secret of that long dark face, or read what was written in the shrouded eyes: knew somehow that the untidy lock of hair fallen across his forehead like a question-mark, and the faint twist in the long grave nose, symbolized his ironic amusement at her failure. She was entirely satisfied, now, that his relation to Anne Louise was not that of lover — whatever else it was. Which was satisfactory; made things much easier; obviated delay ... She did not, however, think to regret the betrayal of one who might have proved a hindrance or obstacle to her plans in some unguessed other way. ...

After a meal, served on beautiful china and silver ware by a swift-moving and silent old woman, Seven found himself still facing Margarethe Thirkelsen across a table illumined by two many-branched candle-sticks. The other lights had been extinguished. The silver ball hung like a full moon above them as they sat opposite one another in that island of golden radiance amid the shadows; and a heavy decanter full of dark red wine threw a reflection on the polished wood as of the jewel in her bodice.

He fell to studying her again, as she sat thus with folded arms upon the table — studying the smooth dark hair, parted in the middle and looped about her ears; the level brows, the pale clear skin, the pointed chin, the long dark lashes of the downcast eyes, the wide mouth with lips which were too narrow rather than too full, the straight nose with delicately winged nostrils, the whiteness of her throat curving down to the hidden whiteness of her breasts.

It was Seven-Daniel who said suddenly to Mr. Tempest —

'This is a witch! She is putting her enchantments upon us! She is young and very beautiful, and full of a strange wisdom that I would like to learn. She is full of a strange strength with which she will wrestle and defeat the strongest man . . . I would wish to be defeated by this sorceress!'

And Margarethe looked up, as Mr. Tempest was about to chide Seven-Daniel.

The magic of her green eyes was the magic of a northern sea on a sunny winter day. In the instant in which he looked into them, he could see no emotion, no story in their depths, that denied the composure of her pale face. But spell there was! So potent an enchantment, indeed, that for the moment once again he fancied to see her anointing a shimmering body with witch's unguents, half-hidden by a mist of witchcraft — to see her leaning toward him and willing some wizardry upon him through the vapours rising from an invisible cauldron.

'I am desirable,' she said without prelude : and he never knew whether it was a question, a statement of fact, or an instruction.

It was Mr. Tempest who answered, calmly and judicially.

'Very, I should fancy!' And paused. And added, 'To those subject to desire!'

Her composure was not altered one whit; but he had the sudden fancy that perhaps the great opal upon her breast expressed for her, in its fire, emotions and desires which she never otherwise revealed. Or had she no passions, and did the waxing or the waning of its flame serve instead?

She rose; poured him out a brimming glass of wine, and less for herself.

'It is still early,' she said. 'While you drink your wine I will tell you something about this house, if you care. It has a curious history. And there are very few, indeed, who know it . . . I will return in a moment.'

She was gone from the radiance about the table, into the shadows that curtained the long room, and thence into the outer darkness; and only the faint rustle of her dress (like the rustle of grass in the wind) told of her going.

Seven rose from his chair and prowled round the room, investigating objects on chest and press and cabinet, that had been but half-visible in the dusk. There was a small pile of books on a narrow table standing between two curtained windows : he brought them to the light, and sat down again to study them.

They were all either in English or French, and — from their titles — appeared to relate to one subject only — hypnotism. They ranged from a shabby calf-bound copy of Mesmer's 'Précis historique des Faits relatifs au Magnétisme animal', dated 1781, and Bell's 'General Principles of Magnetism', to a manuscript translation of the Abbé Faria's work on trance states.

'Here are the books of magic!' said Mr. Tempest to Seven-Daniel, and fluttered the leaves almost contemptuously.

The discovery made him feel as though he had found some staid Nonconformist housewife playing in secret with the dolls of her childhood; or an associate in great undertakings pinning all his faith to a fetish made of blood-stained feathers and brightly coloured rags ... Margarethe was transformed from witch to child.

He swept the books on one side, and raised his glass to the light, and looked through the sparkle of cut crystal into the clear warmth of the wine, before he drank. It was sweetish, yet mellow and very strong.

He was still leaning on the table — elbow against scattered volumes — staring into the dark red depths, when Margarethe Thirkelsen returned.

She bore over her arm a bundle wrapped in a linen cloth, which she placed on the table between the two silver candelabra. A ruby reflection from the decanter stained the covering, and from it came the sweet scent of sandalwood.

She remained standing by the wall, looking down upon Seven, and upon the flat package on the table. She said no word.

Still cynically amused by the revelation of the character of her researches, he addressed her — without looking up — much as an adult might speak to a child busied in childish occupation —

'And what is this? More magic of the House of Witches?'

'You have heard the name, then? ... You find no magic — *and* no witch?'

He was about to answer 'No magic! No witch!' when his intrinsic honesty made him pause. He knew that despite the books of Doctor Mesmer and the Abbé Faria, there was indeed a witch, and indeed a magic. But he sensed again the challenge and the invitation that she had thrown out before, and avoided direct reply.

'*Some* people, I daresay,' he remarked as though doubtfully, 'might find your house full of witchcraft.'

He was sitting sideways to the table as he spoke, long legs negligently crossed, and had to turn his head but little in order to regard her almost secretly from under lowered lids. She stood as motionless, in her wide green dress against the shadowed white background of the wall as a figure in a canvas. Her hands were lightly clasped before her; and on the left forefinger he noted, for the first time, a ring with a great pointed gem, as bright as the jewel on her dress.

'You, of course, are immune to magic — uninfluenced by witches?' she said, with light satiric emphasis on the personal pronoun.

'I am a little too old to be subject to them,' he told her. 'I do not even know that I ever would have been . . . Certainly not to this sort of nonsense . . . !' He indicated the offending books by the merest movement of a hand: then added, with belated effort at courtesy — 'But you were going to tell me something about this house of yours . . . It is, I suppose, very old?'

'It has belonged to my family for over three hundred years . . . Shakespeare stayed here. And the courtiers of King James the First of England when he came to woo Anne of Denmark.'

The name 'Shakespeare' left him unimpressed: he had had no dealing with that poet — or any other poet, for that matter — since the days of Minerva House, and the Reverend Dr. Wivern, and Excalibur, the Sword-Umbrella. The long continuity of possession, however, struck him as remarkable.

He said as much, and added —

'I suppose the family was English in origin?'

'The name should tell you that,' she answered. 'This has been known as the House of Gertrude Englishwoman from those days.'

'You speak the language extraordinarily well.'

'My grandfather was English — and my father! . . . We have always preferred English — mates!'

He had somehow never thought of her as a daughter, or tied by any human affinities.

'Is your father alive?' he asked.

And realized, even whilst he spoke, that she would answer — as she did — indifferently: 'I do not know!'

In a quiet level voice, then, she told the story of the inn, and of the travellers who for three centuries had come and gone through its doors; of the strange gifts that they had brought — of the strange secrets that they had whispered — of the strange deeds that they had done — of the strange love that they had made.

Seven noted that the house seemed to have brought riches to those who possessed it, and that always it appeared to be women who directed its fortunes. He remarked on the fact.

'It is always women who have owned it,' said Margarethe. 'For all these hundreds of years it has passed from mother to daughter. It is ours. Why should we let it slip from our hands?

'We have given no man hold over us. We have chosen our mates from foreigners on their way North, or South, or East, or West. We have not held them from their journeyings; nor have we acknowledged them if they passed this way again . . . We have had wide choice. We have given them a little passion for a little while — and have sent them on their way — and forgotten them. What more should they want, or should they expect? I do not think that my mother ever asked my father his name. He was strong, and beautiful, and intelligent: he gave her a daughter to inherit her knowledge and her power. That was all she asked of him!'

So Margarethe's mother — and Margarethe — required only that of men which his father — and he — had exacted of women! It was a strange parallel.

'And supposing you had been a boy? Or ugly? Or unintelligent?'

'My mother had two other children . . . I suppose she sent them away. I never saw them during her life time, and have not heard of them since she died.'

And where were those six brothers of his?

She went on —

'She only spoke about them once — when I was very young, and the father of one of them came and made claim on her.'

'What happened?' asked Seven.

He remembered how someone had come and made claim on *him*, and caught his hands, and wept, and appealed to the love he had never borne her; and how he had given her the shelter of his name before she died in child-birth.

'He died,' said Margarethe. 'He was found the next day in the courtyard with a broken neck. He had fallen from his window during the night. While he was drunk, they said. But no one pries very deeply into what happens here . . . It is not well to ask more of *us* than we will give!'

Once again he looked sideways at her as she stood, in the golden radiance of the candles, against the silver shimmer of the wall — pale, lovely face; dark shining hair; white long throat curving to the yet more beautiful curves of the hidden breasts. It might indeed be that the recipients of her favours would often ask more of her than she would give.

Once again she appeared to have read his thoughts, and to answer them . . . without words.

She came to the table, and leaned over it, unwrapping whatever was enfolded in the linen cloth.

She was so near to him that her wide skirt brushed against his foot; and, when he bent a little closer to see what lay within, the warm perfume of her body was mingled with the faint recollection of sandalwood.

A doublet was revealed — of primrose-coloured silk, much faded, and embroidered with tarnished silver thread; the sleeves puffed and slashed with grey.

In the stiff formalism of its outline it bore no relation to the anatomy of humanity; but on the left side it was stained a rusty brown, and there was a small tear in the material. In that stain and in that rent its history was well written.

Margarethe lifted the garment to one side. Another doublet of the Elizabethan age lay beneath: it was of some brown material slashed with gold, and of so deep a shade that at first Seven did not notice the yet darker tinge which marked the track of blood pouring from a wounded throat.

'Pretty relics!' he said. 'And the moral?'

'He who wore the yellow jacket asked too much . . . Brown jacket would not ask at all!'

She paused. She stood erect, looking down on the tragic fripperies that should have been dust long ago. A fold of her skirt was still against his foot. He knew full well that yet again she extended an invitation to him — although she indicated it by neither word nor gesture: knew that she intended him to devour her with his eyes, to rise slowly to his feet, to turn her toward him without a word, to place his hands under her armpits so that his palms should rest against her breasts . . . and then to stoop his head as she raised her face — each stage of desire melting into the next in a rhythmic pattern.

Deep in his consciousness Seven-Daniel was reiterating his urgent desire — 'She is a witch! She is strong, and beautiful, and dangerous! Let me battle with her strength, and her beauty, and her danger — and be defeated!'

But Mr. Tempest — the builder of ships and engines, the owner of coal-mines and manufactories, the educator of princesses — was in no mind to furnish material for experiments by strange women.

'And so . . .?' said this Mr. Tempest.

'And so,' continued Margarethe, as if the pause had not lasted half a life-time of swift question and slow denial. '. . . And so my ancestress became wearied of the one, and angered with the other . . . She killed them.'

'*She* killed them!'

'She caused them to fight in this room, one night after supper. In a trance. They drew their swords on one another — in a trance. They fought — in a trance. They gave one another mortal wounds — in a trance. They died, for all I know, while still — in that trance!'

'Trance!' repeated Seven (as one who would say 'Nonsense!') 'You really believe that?'

She turned toward him very slowly. Yet again he was aware of the fire-glow of the opal at the opening of her dress, a little above the level of his eyes. She said —

'I know nothing about the power that drives the steam-engine. But I don't therefore deny its existence . . . You know nothing about the powers that are hidden in the human mind. Equally you have no right to deny their existence.'

'Trances and mesmerism! Charlatanism that only affects half-wits.'

'Curiously enough the better educated are more susceptible to the influence of hypnotism than the unintelligent.'

He looked at her again, with the tolerant expression of a kindly grown-up bearing with the prattle of a child. She showed no annoyance at his attitude, but said calmly —

'I will show you a small experiment, if you will spare the time.'

She took his assent for granted, and pulled a long bell-cord hanging against the wall.

'You noticed my servant, Anna, who waited on us? . . . She is English . . . You shall speak to her for a moment or two, and you will find that she is intelligent . . . Speak to her about England when she comes in. She has been away a long, long time, and is glad to talk to anyone English.'

The old woman answered the summons almost immediately: she entered quietly, and stood awaiting orders, decorous in stiff dress of black-and-grey check with small black silk apron. Her face — the colour of old parchment — was lined and wrinkled, and was beautiful in its serenity: her eyes were bright and of a faded blue: her hair — drawn back smoothly from her forehead — was silver rather than grey: her bony hands, a little distorted by rheumatism, were folded before her. Seven saw that she wore an immensely wide wedding ring of gold.

She replied to his questions about her origins and history respectfully and intelligently, and without servility. Her face lightened when she spoke of Suffolk, her native county, and of the spring-time sea of cherry-blossom that had lapped the hamlet from which she came. But it was very, very long since she had last seen the fairy sea of white

TWO KINDS OF ROMANCE

shiver in a little wind, and send spindrift of petals to powder orchard
and meadow and lane. She had married a Danish seaman, and come
to this land to live: he had been killed when Nelson bombarded
Copenhagen. And that, too, was very, very long ago.

Her old voice and slow speech, in which the broad Suffolk accent
yet lingered, brought back to him a sense of the reality of the strange
room and the strange house.

Said Margarethe —

'Anna! This gentleman will not believe that I can — give you — sleep;
can make you unaware of all that goes on around you; can make you
say and do things of which you know nothing when awake! . . . We
will show him, you and I!'

The old woman, one twisted and roughened hand resting upon the
table, had turned a little so that she might watch her mistress as she
spoke.

And when Margarethe had finished she gave a small confident nod of
her silver-grey head; and then flashed a quick glance at Seven, and
gave him a quick small confident nod, too.

An elbow-chair with a high back, upholstered in faded yellow damask,
was set against the wall. Margarethe pulled it round sideways. She
said in a low and even voice —

'Sit here, Anna . . . You will go to sleep . . . We will show this
gentleman what we can do — you and I!'

Anna seated herself obediently in the wide chair. She smoothed the
folds of black-and-grey check dress. She rested her hands upon the
carved arms, and looked intently up at her mistress.

Margarethe bent down to the woman. Her white slim hands she
placed over the swollen-jointed fingers, hiding them from view. She
swayed a little to and fro as she spoke — smoothly, easily, persuasively —
and was bowed so low over the erect figure in the high chair that the
barest whisper of speech served. Such a whisper it was that Seven
could hardly catch the words.

'Look at my eyes,' she said: and although Seven could not see Anna's
face, yet he could tell from the angle at which her head was pressed
against the chair-back that the old woman was gazing without falter
into the strange and beautiful green eyes.

'Look at my eyes!' said Margarethe, and spoke between long pauses.
'Your lids are getting heavy . . . Look at my eyes! . . . Your lids are
getting still heavier . . . You cannot keep them open . . . They are
beginning to close . . . They are closing now . . . They are fast shut —
fast shut! . . . You are asleep, Anna! Asleep! . . . Asleep!'

270

Margarethe drew herself erect: she turned about toward Seven, still covering one of the worn hands on the chair-arm with her own. The ghost of a smile — of a triumphant smile — haunted her lips.

Anna was leaning back, relaxed, with closed eyes, the reposeful profile of her ivory-tinted face outlined against the whiteness of the wall. Her breathing was the deep slow breathing of profound sleep.

'Is that all?' asked Seven, who had been sitting forward during the induction of the trance, watching intently, quizzical lock strayed across his forehead. 'It is not impossible to counterfeit sleep!'

'. . . This sort of sleep?'

She beckoned him to rise, and stand by Anna's chair, and to watch afresh. She bent over the woman: so close to him she was that he found himself looking down into the shining blackness of her hair, on to the white long neck, and the delicacy of white shoulders where they sloped into the dark green dress.

As though she was aware — without looking up — that he was regarding her rather than Anna, she warned him —

'Watch!'

With thumb and forefinger she grasped the wrinkled brown eyelid that was farthest from him . . . Very gently she raised it.

'Look!'

He stooped until his head nearly touched Margarethe's cheek, so that he might look as bidden into the eye of faded blue which her fingers revealed to him. He felt it to be almost an indecency thus to peer into the window of a woman's soul. But he intruded on no secret and on no privacy, for no sparkle of expression or of life shone from within. A little light was reflected: that was all. And the pupil had shrunk nigh to vanishing — to a pin-point, to a mere dark pricking in the iris which had once been of a forget-me-not blue.

For an instant or so after Margarethe had released the lid a tiny pucker of skin showed where she had pinched it up between her fingers.

He straightened himself at the same moment as Margarethe. They confronted one another across the sleeping woman. Again he saw the ghost of a triumphant smile touch her lips for the space of half a second.

'Did you ever before see an eye like that,' she asked, 'except in an opium-eater?'

He was honest: he shook his head.

She took the right hand of the sleeper in her own, and raised it so that the arm was extended fully, straight upward above the grey head. She released her clasp, but the raised arm remained in the position to which she had drawn it. The hand, dropping palm downwards from the wrist, with the fingers slightly spread, was almost on a level with his eyes as he stood at the side of the chair.

'You are asleep, Anna,' said Margarethe Thirkelsen. 'You are deep asleep . . . You know nothing . . . You feel nothing . . . You will do nothing but what I bid you!'

Seven took the work-roughened fingers in his hand: he endeavoured to force the stretched arm back to its place along the side of the chair, but in vain. He was aware of no conscious battling with him, but simply of the resistance of a thing that was rigid and inanimate. He feared to hurt her if he exerted all his strength, and so desisted.

'Do you still think her condition is a counterfeit?' asked Margarethe. She had watched his essay with an open smile, head and shoulders pressed back against the wall, hands lightly clasped before her.

'I suppose not,' he answered grudgingly. 'But . . . '

'Still another test? . . . You are difficult to persuade!'

'There is a good deal of difference between throwing an old woman into a trance in which she develops a rigid arm, and making two men fight a duel to the death.'

While her eyes held his, her hands were busied with her corsage.

'Can you bear pain?' she demanded: did not pause for his answer, but went on — 'There is a doctor in India — his name is Esdaile; he is an Englishman — who not merely heals by what you call mesmerism, but operates on patients while they are in a trance — painlessly!'

She answered the dubious lift of his eyebrows —

'Serious operations — painless operations — trance operations! He has cut out great tumours and amputated limbs while the patient has slept . . . There are others, too . . . It is extremely difficult to avoid showing pain if you are conscious of it — you will admit that?'

He admitted it.

'Well, then, watch again!'

With swiftly moving hands she had undone the button at the right wrist of the old woman's dress, and rolled the full sleeve back to the elbow, disclosing a shrunken fore-arm in which the sinews stood out like taut cords. It had been shapely, smooth and white in the days when the eyes were brightly blue, and the sunken cheeks without a wrinkle: now it was a pathetic thing — like a limb disclosed upon an anatomist's table.

Seven saw that Margarethe held the great opal brooch in her right hand: she straightened back the pin by which it had been fastened to her dress — a pin of gold, an inch and a half long, perhaps.

Then suddenly she drew the point, with swift precision, down the thin arm, from wrist to elbow, so deeply that a thread of crimson marked the track. There was no flinching — no flutter of a quick breath — no quiver of an eyelid; nothing to show that there had been any consciousness of pain.

But that was not enough.

Margarethe stood immobile for an instant, the brooch in her hand as though it were a dwarf dagger. She looked down at the entranced woman in the golden glow of the candle-light: looked away and into the shadows, as though to summon to her aid strange powers brooding in the darkness: looked closely at Seven, and gathered his gaze with her own green gaze and directed it back to the lean arm and the swollen jointed hand that was so close to his eyes.

She pressed the pin into the fleshier part of the arm a little above the elbow. Seven saw the skin dent as it resisted the entrance of the point, and then the golden sliver slid deep in — very deep in — so deep, in fact, that it could go no farther and the brooch hung against the yellow flesh as though it were an enormous gout of phosphorescent blood.

Anna had not stirred. Her breathing had become no faster. The position of her arm was unchanged.

Without a word Margarethe withdrew the brooch. A drop of blood welled up to the tiny mouth of the wound.

'Do you believe now?'

'Up to a point.'

'How shall I then persuade you?' she asked in the mockery of a tone of despair. 'There are limits to my powers. Even in regard to Anna. For strangely enough, in a deep trance, when pain is no longer felt, the moral consciousness is still awake. No effort of mine would, for instance, ever persuade Anna to undress before you. And if it was in the nature of a girl to be virtuous, no mesmerist on earth could ever make her surrender herself to love. But there are other curious things that I can do!'

She poured a little more wine into his glass, and made him sit down again. As she did so the thin sweet music of distant chimes sounded across the night like a tune on a musical box, and one of the town-clocks struck the hour. He counted the strokes — eleven. At this hour only the day before had he been confronted by Anne Louise ... Where was she now, he wondered.

Margarethe adjusted Anna's dress; set back her arm along the edge of the chair.

'This is difficult,' she said. 'You must watch with great attention. With concentrated attention . . . Anna! . . . You are still asleep — but your eyes are about to open . . . Your eyes are open . . . You are still asleep — with open eyes!'

The woman's eyes opened; but there was no consciousness in them, and they were fixed, unseeing, on the shadows without the circle of light in which she sat.

'Rise to your feet!'

She rose to her feet — rose straight, without assisting rheumaticky knees with the leverage of her hands upon the carved arms of the chair.

'Now go to the Spanish cabinet. Open the lower doors, and bring out my silver mirror.'

Anna walked across the room into the dusk where loomed the cabinet. Her pace was far different from the brisk tread with which she had waited at the table. She walked slowly, almost uncertainly; as though she were a sleep-walker; as though she were blindfolded and groping her way about amid unfamiliar surroundings. Her list-slippered feet were noiseless.

Seven had the fancy that in all the silent house there was no place so utterly without sound as that room: that in all the house, too, there was no light except where he and Margarethe stood by the high-backed chair, with the almond-shaped flames of candles illumining those stained silken relics of a three-hundred-year-old tragedy which lay between the candelabra on the great table.

Melted into the shadows at the far end of the room, Anna herself seemed but a shadow as she fumbled with the doors of the cabinet. He heard the squeak of the hinges, and the soft click as the cabinet shut. He watched attentively to see what next enchantment there would be.

'Raise the mirror above your head, and bring it slowly here,' said Margarethe.

He saw then that Anna held between her hands a large round mirror in a wide silver frame. It shone in the darkness like the reflection of the moon in dark waters. The woman came across the room more slowly than a priest bearing a holy pyx.

'Watch the mirror!' said Margarethe. 'Watch it closely! . . . Watch it very closely! . . . You will see very strange things!'

Was she about to try to persuade him that he saw pictures of the past in the silvery surface — or a forth-shadowing of the future? He felt almost a sense of disappointment at the puerility of her enchantments.

Anna halted on the verge of the circle of light, a few feet away from where he sat, holding the silver mirror so high above her that Seven had to throw his head back in order to watch it.

'Watch the mirror,' repeated Margarethe insistently. 'Watch it very closely! . . . You will presently see very strange things!'

He realized a feeling of strain in keeping his regard fixed on the shining thing held so much above the normal level of his eyes . . . The mirror seemed to increase in size — to be luminous in itself — to be veiled by a shimmering veil that scintillated as summer rain may scintillate in the sunshine.

Margarethe continued to speak in a soft low even voice, but Seven was hardly conscious of the meaning of her slow murmurous words. He was weary from a long day's work, and his eyes were tired by the glitter of the mirror.

He blinked. . . .

Even as he relieved himself from the fatigue of that fixed gaze, he knew the truth. It was not Anna who was to be the subject of experiment, but himself.

At the sudden apprehension he rose to his feet, and turned to Margarethe with a sarcastic smile. As he did so Anna lowered the mirror and receded into the shadows.

'I am afraid that I am not to be so easily spell-bound by any magic,' he said. 'It will be only wasting your time to try.'

'Do you think so?'

'I am sure of it. You will have to find someone much younger and more susceptible if you want to mould a man to your wishes . . . You are not likely to make me fight a duel to the death in a trance — or commit any other kind of lunatic extravagance!'

She made answer only by a slight smile and the faintest shaking of her proud dark head.

'I am very tired,' he said, 'and if you will forgive me I will be off to bed . . . Thank you for your entertainment . . . Good-night!'

She gave him her hand in English fashion, and regarded him directly with an expression which he could not read, but which seemed to be symbolized by the slightest possible upward lift of an eyebrow.

'You have amused me. Very much! . . . When you go to bed you will dream. And what you see in your dreams will be true. Remember that! I shan't say "Good-night!"; I shall say, "Sleep well!" '

As he went into the darkness of the shuttered passage, and she closed the door after him, he thought to hear a sudden burst of low laughter through the panels. Almost the laughter of gentle mockery. . . .

He entered his room.

The window was open; the curtains drawn wide. Brilliant sunshine streamed in: the walled garden was golden with the light of full day; the poppies against the dark green of the ivy were scarlet as tatters from a witch's cloak.

Utterly thunderstruck he sat down upon his bed . . . Only ten minutes ago — he would swear — had he heard the chimes of a town clock and counted the strokes that told the hour of eleven of night. Yet now it could not be earlier than six o'clock in the morning, if not, indeed, seven. He cast his mind back, but could recollect no break in the continuity of his consciousness . . . For one moment — one moment only — had he closed his eyes.

Had she, indeed, defeated him who had never yet been defeated by any man? Had she used him for her own purposes; as he had once purposed using women — as his father *had* used women? Had she arrogated to herself the right to enter, against his conscious will, into the pattern of the destiny of him who was used to pattern the destiny of others — even of a royal princess?

Against his will! And yet he recalled the phrase in one of the books he had picked up on her table — 'It is impossible to hypnotize a subject against his will.'

For long he remained chin in hands, elbows on knees, pondering the problem, in a mood that held both humiliation and furious anger with Margarethe and himself.

And so fell asleep.

In his sleep he dreamed. He dreamed that he was in a bed which was panelled on roof and wall, excepting as to one side only. A small silver lamp on a ledge at the foot filled its stage with a golden glow that did not seem to spread beyond its limits, for he could see nothing of the room that lay beyond, except a chaotic pattern of grey and jetty shadows.

Beside him, her black hair spread about her on the pillow, lay Margarethe Thirkelsen asleep. It seemed to him that there was almost a silver radiance from the lovely face; that there was some warm magic in the breath that fluttered at her nostrils; that the parted lips quivered to the utterance of a spell. He remembered women who had looked like children in their sleep; others who had become pinched and old when freed from the restraint of consciousness. Like none of these was Margarethe. She lay there — he felt — a sleeping witch, caught unawares while wearied of making enchantments.

From the vividness of this dream he was awakened by an insistent tapping on the door.

He rolled off the bed, and opened.

Margarethe stood without. She gave him no greeting, but her lips were curved in a smile which told him the answer to all his speculation.

'You slept well?' she asked, regarding his towzled head with an almost malicious show of benevolence. 'You look as if you had been wakened in the middle of a pleasant dream. I am sure it was a pleasant dream. You must tell me all about it one day. Dreams are often true! Here is a letter. It was brought early this morning, but I told Astrid not to give it to you then. I thought you would like to lie a-bed a little longer than usual as you said you were very tired last night. You went to bed late, too. Later than you thought, perhaps?'

There was no trace of any emotion — or of any remembrance of emotion — in her voice; only the lightest mockery. Her attitude — thought Seven in fury — was that of one who had gained a victory so easily as to think it barely worth the winning. His self-pride had been sent crashing — not in the splendour of magnificent disaster, but with casual indifference. It was as if an emperor had tripped over a toy and gone rolling in the mud. His inward humiliation was complete. He had sufficient poise, however, to thank her for her consideration.

'The porter who brought the letter has now come back for an answer. He is waiting in the courtyard.'

After she had gone he examined the missive. Undoubtedly news of Anne Louise! But the superscription on the cover — 'S. Cash, Esqre.' — was in a spidery hand that he did not know, and the impression on the red sealing-wax was just of a business-like monogram — 'R.P.'

The letter ran:

Strandgade 107
Helsingør.

Saturday,
June 8th, 1839.
'My dear Sir,

'I was in receipt at an extremely early hour this morning of a communication from her Highness the Duchess of Limburg, conveying certain information regarding your identity. This she has done in such a way that you are not implicated in her affairs. I cannot sufficiently express my regret that I should have treated your assertions with such incredulity on the occasion of your visit to me last month. You will understand, I am sure, that my position in the circumstances was one of considerable difficulty, and that I might easily involve myself in very awkward situations as well as financial loss were I unhesitatingly to accept all the statements of all my visitors without demanding proof.

'I hasten now to place the services of my establishment — such as they are — at your disposal, and, should you need to stay a little longer in this town before returning to England, Mrs. Peel joins with me in expressing the hope that you will treat our house as your own.

'Her Highness the Duchess of Limburg adds in her communication that she trusts that you will send an account of her indebtedness to her aunt, the Princess Sophia of Limburg, at the Château des Lecques, when it will be instantly discharged. She asks if you will continue to look after her maid, Lovell, until other arrangements can be made. She also sends this message — "Please say that the boy is in safe hands and will be happy. He will be returned when I receive a guarantee that there will be *no* experiments on *him*."

'I received the communication through the Belgian Consulate-General, who could — or would — give me no information relating to the present whereabouts of her Highness. I am inclined to believe, subject to correction, that her Highness is not altogether a free agent.

'I am, Sir, Yours to command,

'Richard Peel'.

So Anne Louise had met with great disaster . . . and even in that hour had spared thought for him, whom — in her view doubtless — she had good reason to loathe; as well as thought for Daniel whom she loved, and for an erring maidservant. Yet he had tried to play the part of Destiny to this bright self-less creature even as his father had played Destiny to him. He might have hardened and warped her, as he himself had been hardened and warped . . . he that was yet so poor a Destiny-maker that he could be made to serve the pleasure or the purpose of a woman innkeeper.

He wondered if Anne Louise regarded him with the same intensity of anger and hatred as that with which he had confronted his father after those seven years of trial.

BOOK FIVE

ANDROMEDA

*

CHAPTER I

THE GRAND DUCHESS DOTS HER 'I'S

THE Grand Duchess of Ehrenberg was awake and sober. It was her unvarying habit so to be at ten o'clock in the morning, and at four of an afternoon.

Propped by her pillows, she sat up in bed — a vast old woman in an old vast bed. She wore a close-fitting nightcap, with a frill so wide that it looked like a bonnet, and grey bed-jacket trimmed coquettishly with pink ribbon. The canopy of the bed — lined with rose-coloured silk — was supported by gilded pillars carved to represent extremely naked ladies standing on tiptoe with upstretched arms. Time had tarnished and darkened what gilding had not been worn away from sumptuous haunch and torso by the dusters of five or six generations; time had faded, too, the tapestry at the bed-head, whereon pink cupids disported themselves amid a maze of clouds and blue ribbons. It equally had subdued the brilliance of the wall-hangings which portrayed the amours of nymph and satyr with eighteenth-century elegance.

Convenient to her Highness's hand was a table on which stood a brandy decanter and glass, a large cedar-wood box of cigars, and half-a-dozen books with indecorous titles and still less decorous contents. The gold-foil tops of a couple of champagne bottles peeped over the rim of a wine-cooler on a tripod stand, which was placed in such a position that she could keep it satisfactorily under observation.

Through the great windows, which flooded the room with light, she could have viewed — though she had not consciously done so for twenty years — the misted grey and purple-blue of the distant mountains.

At the nearer window sat a bony young lady most unsuitably dressed in bright yellow; with a narrow face, large nose, long upper lip — on which there was the faintest suggestion of flaxen down — and a habitually pained expression. She was engaged on some fine needle-work in an abrupt and worried way, when not casting surreptitious glances at Highness, or reassuring herself as to the good conduct of a multitude of fat lap-dogs.

'Ottilie!' said the Grand Duchess in a weak voice — it was always weak from four o'clock in the afternoon until six.

'Highness?' said Ottilie, gathering together her work with a resigned air.

'Ottilie!' said the Grand Duchess in a still weaker voice — a voice that demanded sympathy for a frail old lady! 'When is the Duchess of Limburg visiting me?'

'Her Highness is expected to have changed from her travelling dress and to be ready to visit your Highness at a quarter-past five,' replied Ottilie with a sniff that meant that this was not the first occasion on which the frail old lady had been given the fullest particulars.

'I feel *very* poorly this afternoon,' said Highness plucking languidly at the sheets. 'I really think, Ottilie . . .'

And finished the sentence with a sidelong glance at the decanter with its seductive golden-brown cargo.

Ottilie wilfully misunderstood.

'I will fetch your Highness's tablets and draught.'

Highness never cared bluntly to demand liquid refreshment during the phases of sobriety that began — after alcoholic dozes — at ten a.m. and four p.m., and ended a couple of hours later.

Ottilie was always difficult — was always obtuse! One day she would get rid of Ottilie! In any case Ottilie must be punished!

'Ottilie!' said the Grand Duchess in her weakest voice, after a pause. 'Come here, child! . . . I feel very restless, and worried, and ill to-day. Which is quite absurd. You must put up with the foibles of an old, old woman, my dear! Be soothing! Be restful!'

The Baroness Dedel approached the royal bedside. A royal hand — fat and white — indicated a chair beside the table. It was a stiff high-backed chair which she abominated; a chair which offered no comfort or ease to an angular lady-in-waiting.

Part of the punishment!

'Sit down, child,' commanded the sadly feeble voice. 'Sit down, and be soothing! Talk to me — No! Conversation is *too* exhausting! . . . You shall read to me! That's it, Ottilie, you shall read to me!'

A bright red flush stained Ottilie's sallow cheeks. She sat down on the penitential chair, facing the light, and stared resentfully out of the window, without a word.

'What shall we read?' asked the Grand Duchess, noting these signs of disturbance with malicious amusement. 'Now, what would you like to read, dear Ottilie? . . . Something soothing! . . . I know — we will read *Klara* . . . There it is! . . . *That* — not that! The one with a blue book-mark!'

Highness lay back a little more among the lace-fringed pillows. She closed her almost lashless eyelids, and composed her white enormous face as if in anticipation of soothing enjoyment.

Ottilie dragged a bony hand from her silk lap, and grudgingly took the book from the bottom of the little pile, handling it as if it were red-hot or impregnated with a Borgia poison.

'Why don't you begin, Ottilie?' said the Grand Duchess in a small voice. 'Or are you reading it to yourself — and enjoying it by yourself? Selfish One!'

Ottilie had certainly for a moment been reading *Klara* to herself — but she had been far from enjoying it. She had opened that work at the appointed place. Her horror-filled eyes had gathered the general tenour of the narrative: the bright flush had spread from high cheek-bone to tawny neck with increasing brilliance. She looked from blurred page to the purple mountains and the blue heavens, as if seeking Divine aid or intervention.

'Come, child!' urged Highness, pleasurably aware of all this by-play without giving herself the fatigue of watching it; permitting the faintest hint of steel to sound in her subdued tones.

Ottilie had wedded Baron Dedel, Court Taster to the Grand Dukes of Ehrenberg, from a Lutheran parsonage of such robust purity that the good father had pinned together those leaves of Holy Writ which contained passages unfit for female eyes. The marriage merely meant an exchange from one poverty to another. Like most of the minor nobility of a minor German state, the Dedels had but the minutest private income: they were utterly dependent on Court favour not merely for their position in Society, but for everything above and beyond a roof, and the very barest necessities of life. Whatever the tyranny, Ottilie must perforce submit. She uttered now a silent prayer to the Supreme Being who — unless He had used His All-Seeing power! — had never viewed more of her body in her fortnightly bath than was revealed by a decent nightdress.

She read aloud the opening of a new chapter, in a hurried, flurried manner:

'"Hermann took Klara in his arms in a transport of passion that communicated itself to the young girl. Feverishly their lips sought — met — clung. Their warm breaths mingled in an intoxicating incense of love. Their bodies bruised each other with the intensity of the mutual embrace."'

After such a preamble it was hardly surprising that the love-making of Hermann increased in vigour with remarkable rapidity. His kisses became fiercer and yet fiercer —

'Highness!' moaned Ottilie, at length, in feeble protest. 'Highness!' There were tears in her voice.

'Don't stop, girl! Go on!' said Highness. 'Isn't it good?'

Thus adjured Ottilie continued miserably to read in a low shamed voice of the abominable conduct of Hermann and of the immodesty of Klara. Restrained by no considerations of morality the author revelled in every lascivious detail —

'Highness!' said Ottilie, 'I . . . '

'Go on! . . . Delicious! . . . I thought *that* would stir you . . . Have you ever had a lover, Ottilie? . . . Did he ever tear your dress? . . . Never mind! Go on!'

Ottilie went on. She felt that she was being dirtied in body and soul: she wanted to go away and pray that no pollution should remain in her mind; and bathe the eyes that had been soiled in the reading; and wash the hands that had been stained by the touch of the pages. She wanted to burn the book — to throw it at the head of the old sinner in the bed. But there were three little Dedels to be thought of.

The bolder Hermann grew, the bolder grew the author. The story from being immodest, became indecent; became obscene; became filthy beyond description. It was published by a Leipzig firm, and the title-page announced it as a translation from the French; but its grossness was peculiarly and particularly German.

'Ah!' sighed the Grand Duchess at intervals. 'Ah!'

Ottilie once again came to a halt. There were words ahead which her tongue resolutely refused to utter — words whose meaning were clear enough from the context, although she had never heard them spoken or seen them in print before. Every fibre of her tingled with their beastliness. Perspiration dampened her pink-and-white complexion and the soft down on her upper lip.

'Go on, Ottilie! You don't need to stop at every other sentence, even if you are thrilled to the marrow . . . It *does* waken the old Eve, doesn't it? . . . You, like me, I see . . .' said the Grand Duchess with the air of one conceding the right to an agreeable human failing '. . . are still interested in what we are not supposed to be. Frankly I often suffer from what the dear French call — so very cleverly — *nostalgie de boue* . . . Tell me now, between ourselves, does the Baron ever . . . ? Eh? Does he?'

She broke off to give a sideways malicious look at her unfortunate lady-in-waiting. What she saw told her that she had been sufficiently revenged. Furthermore she very badly needed a drink. Very badly indeed!

'I think after all that excitement perhaps, I shall require a little brandy. Pour it out for me, my dear! . . . Oh, no! More than that! Now fill the glass up with champagne. One of the bottles has been opened. It will do very well!'

The old lady was in full enjoyment of the first drink of the evening session when the castle clock solemnly clanged the quarter-hour.

. A fat young lady in lilac with round face, round black eyes, shiny nose, and shiny black hair — that looked as if it had been painted on her scalp — slid in through one of the less important portals of the great room. A moment later a discreet knock sounded against the panels of the imposing folding doors that were the principal entrance.

The Baroness Dedel and the newcomer cast agonized glances at the appurtenances of the bedside.

The Grand Duchess intercepted the look. With the impishness that invariably followed the opening of the second session, she said —

'We will begin as we mean to continue, my dear Ottilie! Fill up my glass before you answer, and give me a cigar!' . . .

Thus it was that Anne Louise first saw the Grand Duchess and virtual ruler of Ehrenberg — a mountainous old woman puffing a thin cheroot in the midst of a baroque bed as large as a cottage, her ladies-in-waiting posted on either side.

The State Bed-Chamber smelled as if its high windows — so full of purple mountains and clear sky — had never once been opened. Despite its vastness its atmosphere seemed compounded in equal parts of stale cigar smoke, the aroma of brandy, and the kennel. Dogs, indeed, were everywhere : they occupied every available chair ; they rambled masterfully about the room ; or toyed with delicacies set for them in porcelain dishes on the floor ; on red silk cushions in a child's mahogany cot near the door, a small mother gave suck to a litter of fat squirming puppies.

With that outward composure which she had shown ever since she surrendered to Uncle Leopold's emissary a fortnight earlier, Anne Louise advanced up the room followed by her two ladies. She held her chin very high.

At some little distance from the bed she made a profound curtsey — her scarlet satin dress rustling as she sank and rose ; and behind her, like automata, her ladies curtseyed and rustled.

The Grand Duchess — cheroot held carefully in fat white hand — graciously inclined enormous nightcap. Her ladies curtseyed and rustled, too.

'Your Highness,' said she unctuously, 'must forgive my seeming discourtesy . . . I am an old woman . . . My health — ! Almost bed-ridden . . . I should have welcomed your Highness in person if it had been humanly possible . . . But you see . . . !'

And she indicated by a wave of the cheroot-bearing hand that she was a poor weak old woman who might quite possibly never have the use of her legs again.

Anne Louise quite saw! . . .

So after that, each Highness presented her ladies to the other Highness; and there was more curtseying and rustling. And then, to complete requirements, the ladies were presented to one another, which occasioned yet another bout of curtseys and rustles.

After polite inquiries about the journey from Copenhagen, the ladies were sent to entertain themselves by a distant window, and Anne Louise was invited to seat herself on the penitential chair at the royal bedside.

The Grand Duchess regarded her speculatively for an instant or so, rubbing her colossal beak of a nose. She really did not know what to say to the girl: she supposed she must do the polite thing: but it was time for another drink: and have another drink she would.

'Forgive me, my dear, a moment!' she said, and raised her voice: 'Ottilie! . . . Ottilie, my love!'

Ottilie turned a long-nosed disapproving face in her direction. She approached her mistress as if approaching the scaffold.

'My medicine, child! My medicine!'

And the old lady gasped, and spread fat fingers vaguely over her vast bosom as if to claw out pain from its depths.

'Your draught, Highness? Yes, Highness!' said the dense Ottilie, preparing to back from the Presence.

Highness indicated the decanter with her eyes; but Ottilie paid no heed to the unspoken message: she began to move away.

Highness indicated the decanter with the shadow of a gesture of the hand; but still Ottilie continued on her way.

Curse Ottilie! She should be made to pay for her obstinacy.

'On the table, child! On the table! . . . More than that! That is not a full dose at all! . . . That will do! . . . You may as well fill the glass up with wine . . . It is . . .' said the Grand Duchess, addressing Anne Louise, as she took the brimming tumbler in her hand '. . . the only way in which I can bring myself to drink the stuff. Otherwise it tastes to me like sheer poison . . . Sheer poison!' she added, taking most of the potion at a single draught.

Anne Louise expressed sorrow at the distressful state of Highness's health.

'You know, my dear,' said the Grand Duchess, 'I thought from dear Leopold's letter that you were a mere child. A mere child! . . . You are much older than I was led to believe.'

'I am eighteen,' said Anne Louise, and saw that some new train of thought had arisen in the mind of the old lady whom Uncle Leopold had chosen to be her Jailer-in-Chief.

'You know, of course, that your little stay here is the climax of an incognito tour of Europe in the company of the excellent Baroness Holfender and Miss Talfourd?' continued the Grand Duchess after a while, and glanced to the distant window where those worthy ladies were making uphill conversation with her own attendants.

Anne Louise knew. Knew very well. Had listened unmoved to the messages, threats, arguments, delivered to her by Uncle Leopold's plenipotentiary, the Marquis de Chasteler, sent hot-foot from Brussels. Had only obeyed because she had no alternative, had no one to appeal to, and no means of sending such appeal if there had been anyone.

'Such a pleasant little tour!' continued the Grand Duchess in a voice full of fat chuckles. 'Rome — Venice — Vienna — Paris! . . . *So* respectably carried out with ladies, and couriers, and retinue! *So* incognito! So *very* incognito!'

The old lady chuckled and wheezed until she gasped and fell into a paroxysm of coughing and laughter, that was only cured by further application to the potion which she held. The mixture, indeed, had narrowly escaped being overturned on to the rather dirty white satin coverlet upon which were embroidered medallions of all the orders of chivalry bestowed on the Grand Dukes of Ehrenberg during the last half century.

'We shall be great friends, you and I,' declared the invalid. 'I fancy that you are just such as I was when I was your age. Though, of course, I was — what shall we say? — a little more cautious. Who knows, though, what I should have done if I had had your opportunity.'

Anne Louise fancied that there was perhaps some misapprehension with regard to the nature of her escapade. She coloured, but remained silent.

'Eighteen — you said, I think? . . . Well, well! . . . You can't begin too young. Old age comes on soon enough . . . I had my first lover when I was fifteen. He was my father's groom-of-the-chambers. We used to meet at night in a large loft that ran over the main building. There was a trap-door in my bedroom ceiling . . . Why nothing ever happened, I can't think. I was not the careful girl then that I became!'

The old lady's mind swam back through the golden haze of brandy and champagne to the golden days of hearty lust and robust indelicacies.

'One of these days, Naughty One, you shall tell me all about it! *All!*'

'There is very little to tell. I . . .'

The Grand Duchess heaved her great bulk round a little, the better to regard the girl at her bedside. She inspected her narrowly.

'The Coburgs were always a handsome lot. And you have more than your fair share of looks, although there's but little family likeness.'

'Thank God!' said Anne Louise out loud, determined that, at any rate, there should be no misapprehensions about her sentiments in that respect.

The old lady quivered with mirth: she shook the ash off her cheroot on to the coverlet, and lay back on her pillows, puffing vigorously.

'Good-looking and sly! That's the Coburgs! . . . And that's Leopold! In fact Leopold more than any of them! . . . It amuses me — really amuses me — to think of Leopold playing the part of Horrified Propriety. When you remember that he tried to seduce his brother's mistress in his salad days — that he hired himself out to Queen Hortense to secure her influence with her brother, the Bonaparte — that he carried on a liaison with a cookmaid at his London lodgings while he was courting his first wife — that he got that creature of his, Stockmar, to provide his own cousin to be his concubine — and yet to see him act, and hear him talk, you would think that butter wouldn't melt in his mouth, or that he barely knew one end of a woman from the other!'

'The King appears to permit himself a greater degree of freedom than he is prepared to allow to others!' said Anne Louise, contemplating the ringless tanned hands that lay on her shining scarlet lap.

'If you were to see the letter I received from him, you would realize that he is not prepared to allow *others any* freedom!' said the Grand Duchess with much meaning, and underscoring the word 'others' so that it quite obviously meant 'you'.

She paused so that the full import of her remark should sink in; and then began afresh a long and rambling narrative, which linked up in dark and illicit passion nearly every reigning house of any importance in Germany.

She told, with cynical amusement and much relish, of the betrayal of virtue — of the corruption of innocence — of medieval prerogatives in lust still exercised by princes — of adultery, bastardy, and nameless sins.

Anne Louise listened in silence. Occasionally she glanced at the jutting chin, jutting nose, and jutting cheroot of the narrator; occasionally she stared at the splendours of mountain and sky revealed through the none too clean windows. She was unembarrassed by the indecencies, unimpressed by the horrors, unamused by the follies. There was little to choose — she realized — between life at the court of some pinchbeck German sovereign and life as it had been revealed to her in the hold of the *Joan Dearlove*. The essential bestiality was still there, although it went clothed in brilliant uniform or silk through marble galleries or tapestry-hung boudoirs. She wondered, however, whether the dreariness of palaces was ever redeemed by such courage and endurance as she had seen amid the squalor of the ship. She doubted it, somehow. She wondered whether the sinister love-making in dark corners — titterings behind arras — whisperings and rustlings on backstairs — were, perhaps, not even worse than the affront of Captain Pedder's lusts.

The old sinner on the bed, between gasps and wheezes, had completed the tale of Uncle Leopold's elder brother, Duke Ernest of Saxe-Coburg. Had told how that pernicious prince had seduced a mere child — brought her to his duchy disguised as a boy — grown tired of her — attempted her murder in a carriage 'accident'; and, when that attempt had failed, had tried his hand at assassination by poisoned wine.

She returned once again to Uncle Leopold and his multifarious amours — amours with the frost on them — medicinal amours with a love temperature well below zero.

Even these revelations of Uncle Leopold's remarkable hypocrisy did not check Anne Louise's growing wonderment at his choice of a custodian for her. Unless the hypocrisy of Marie Theresa, Grand Duchess of Ehrenberg, were still greater than that of the Belgian King — great enough, indeed, to impose on an arch-professor of that quality, the old lady seemed little suitable as hostess or wardress.

Certain preliminary heaves disturbed the billowy sea of the immense bed — a sort of submarine disturbance. The Grand Duchess raised herself a little higher against the great wave of pillows. There was a click: from the high canopy there suddenly descended to either side of her a thick band of rose-and-gold brocade like a bell-pull. The Grand Duchess grasped one in each hand. For a fantastic minute Anne Louise thought that she was about to ascend into the roof of her bed like an orang-outang: but Highness's gymnastics were confined to a grunt and a heave which brought her bolt-upright, an ancient and enormous Aphrodite rising from a foam of sheet and pillow and coverlet. Highness, in fact, felt that the time had come for farewells, and for the commencement of the serious business of the day.

'My dear,' she said, when she had recovered her breath, 'I hope you will have a pleasant stay with us at Ehrenberg. We are dull old fogies — all of us. But we'll do our best to keep you as happy as we can — in the circumstances!'

Anne Louise was quite sure of that.

'In the circumstances!' repeated the old lady. 'Which means that we must be as discreet as we can. We must lull suspicions. We must recover (in deep retirement) from the fatigues of our long tour under the sheltering wing of old Cousin Theresa. We shall find sympathy from old Cousin Theresa, deep sympathy — but . . .!'

She paused. Her tone had been one of warning, but not unkindly. Anne Louise fully understood the implications of the word 'but'. She did not say so aloud, but bowed in token of comprehension.

On second thoughts, however, the old lady felt that she had perhaps better be a trifle more specific. Obedience to the whole Decalogue might be expressed in the single word 'but'. Again it might not.

'In the circumstances,' said she with renewed stress on the three words, 'I think I would not venture outside the castle without your ladies — or outside the grounds without an escort! . . . *Wiser* not! . . . *Better* not! . . . Now, as to letters! — You know, don't you, that your poor dear Uncle Leopold has already had to complain to Victoria that his letters to her were being opened in the post, and inspected by the English Foreign Office? . . . Now I am not saying that the post service here does that sort of thing — I am *not* saying that!' — Which meant, of course, precisely the opposite — 'But I cannot say what happens outside the Grand Duchy. I should be very guarded in your letters. Very guarded, indeed! I should be most careful to write letters — that your worst enemy could see!'

Anne Louise realized that the word 'but' equalled the word 'imprisonment', and that now generally 'i's were being dotted and 't's being crossed.

She had been prepared for it. There had been that about the journey from Copenhagen across Germany which had made it all perfectly clear.

Lying wakeful in inn bedrooms at night, listening to the heavy breathing of the baroness, she had found a parallel between her own travel and that of other ill-fated royal ladies making stately progresses to perpetual imprisonment or the scaffold . . . Had wondered whether a fresh headsman's block was made ready on each occasion for a royal or important client, or whether an old one was scrubbed and sand-papered into newness; whether a Prisoner of State could have her apartments redecorated twice a year for the sake of change; whether the study of Chinese and higher mathematics (with chess and the compilation of one's memoirs for relaxation) might not fully occupy a lifetime of confinement; how long it took to train spiders to come at call; whether after ten years or so of seclusion one took any interest in bonnets.

'Beyond little restrictions — and very wise little ones in the circum-stances — you will be free as air!'

Anne Louise preserved a meditative silence.

The repeated phrase 'in the circumstances' apparently brought a new train of thought to the old lady —

'There will be no *future* circumstances, I suppose?' she inquired delicately, disposing of her cheroot butt by tossing it on to the chill black and white marble floor. 'It is as well to know, so that we can make adequate plans and precautions.'

'I am afraid that I don't understand.'

'No little consequences? . . . Ehrenberg has its disadvantages. It is as dull as ditchwater, and as remote from civilization as Timbuctoo. But little consequences can be managed accordingly with the minimum of fuss, and without anyone who matters being a groschen the wiser!'

Anne Louise, without even flushing, signified that there would be no 'little consequences'.

'You can safely tell old Cousin Theresa,' pressed old Cousin Theresa. 'She's as silent as the grave!'

'I can assure you.'

'Perhaps it's as well! . . . Wise girl! Clever girl! I was just such another. But then I had, of course, none of these modern conveniences! . . . I thought at first that Leopold had hit on this spot just because of that! . . . Now, give me a kiss, my dear! I can see, indeed, that we are going to be great, great friends . . . I must rest now. I am an absolute slave to the doctors, and they insist on me resting in the early evening . . . Owing to poor Francis's — illness, I have all the State business to see to. Ve-ery tiring, for an old woman! . . . You will be fatigued after your journey, I am sure. You will prefer to dine in your apartments!'

Anne Louise bestowed a brief kiss on the large white floury cheek presented to her. To do so she had to lean a long way over the bed, and into an atmosphere most peculiarly impregnated with the smell of brandy, cheroots, and the violet-scented face powder with which old Cousin Theresa was liberally coated.

She and her ladies curtseyed and rustled, and dipped and rose, and departed through the great folding doors which swung open before them under the guidance of two impish little pages in shabby crimson liveries, who had been warned of their impending departure by the ringing of a very cracked bell in the ante-chamber.

Old Cousin Theresa straightened her frilled cap, adjusted one of the pink bows on the grey flannel bed-jacket; became once more the sadly afflicted Grand Duchess of Ehrenberg; turned to the business on hand.

But first of all — Ottilie! . . . A disobedient, obtuse, unsympathetic, wilful girl!

Ottilie must be punished!

Said Highness in a weak voice of great urgency:

'Ottilie! . . . The bed-pan! . . . Quickly! . . . Very quickly! . . . No, there is no time to ring! . . . Bring it yourself, girl! Quickly please!'

Ottilie brought the bed-pan with a flush on her high cheek-bones; adjusted it with averted face.

Ottilie should be made to wait! Ottilie must learn her lesson!

CHAPTER II

TRIBULATIONS OF TWO LADIES

A RATHER tarnished, rather dusty splendour generally marked the vast and ugly pile known as the Castle of Ehrenberg.

It lay at the end of a mile-long stretch of dusty avenue carved through a pine wood: two little dusty black-and-white striped sentry-boxes were dwarfed to dimensions only suitable (it would seem) for toy soldiers by the enormous wrought-iron entrance gates which once had been gilded, and by the ornamental palisade whose bars were high enough and massy enough to have served for the cages of dragons and dinosaurs.

The castle itself had the attributes of every kind of building imaginable, save that of a castle. It might have been a museum — an art gallery — a college — in the classical style: it almost might have been all of them at once. A queer cupola presided over the acreage of its roof just as though it had donned a peculiarly small skull-cap: the huge portico might have been transported from some Doric temple: the tiers of windows looked as if they were but rarely cleaned: the capitals of the pillars were fouled with the droppings of many generations of pigeons, and the yellow-painted stucco front was discoloured by damp and cracked in many places.

There was an immense cobbled forecourt, in which, even in spring-time, dead leaves and dust and scraps of paper eddied to and fro, and where a little grey water trickled out of a colossal fountain that was a tangle of water-nymphs, sea-horses, and conch-shells.

Within doors it was the same.

Dusty old ladies and dusty old gentlemen, dusty servants (legions of them) in all sorts of shabby liveries, moved about corridors as wide as streets or were lost in the immensity of apartments as lofty as churches. It would have strained the resources of an emperor adequately to have garnished and furnished and lighted and kept in order the enormous pile. Accordingly it was neither adequately garnished and furnished, nor adequately lighted and kept in order; and the result generally was a dusty and dusky emptiness that emphasized its huge dimensions.

The suite allotted to Anne Louise was at the back of the palace, on the first floor. It looked — across a terrace that was wide enough for the exercises of a battalion of infantry — to lawns that might have served as a parade-ground for a couple of divisions. Distant vistas of lake and Palladian summer-house showed at the end of broad avenues that converged through stately woodland.

Thither Anne Louise returned after her interview with the Grand Duchess: and there she took her dinner with her ladies — already, to herself, she called them her wardresses — in a dark red room from out of whose dusk she was watched by full-length portraits of peculiarly hideous grand dukes wearing full-bottomed wigs.

After the meal, which was both plain and badly cooked, they retired to the sitting-room of the suite — an enormous apartment known officially as the Chinese Withdrawing-room; although there was precious little that was Chinese about its spacious bareness, excepting a grey silk tapestry over the fireplace, on which sprawled a cluster of many-clawed dragons breathing pale gold fire from pale silver nostrils. The embroidery was flanked by two great porcelain jars ornamented with a delicate design in apple-green and rose.

For the rest, the plain white walls, the chess-board floor of black and white marble, the severity of the few ancient straight-backed chairs, the nudity of the shining oaken table round which a conference might have gathered, and the inornate shabby curtains of blue serge before the lofty window embrasures — all gave the room the air of being the chapter-house of a strict religious order, or an archbishop's boudoir. Anne Louise felt that there should have been a *prie-dieu* with crucifix and little red kneeling mat in one corner.

One concession to human comfort there was, however, although half-hearted: an angular seventeenth-century day-bed, with a solitary cushion, set on a Persian rug, was drawn up to one side of the chill marble fireplace which yawned like the mouth of a tomb. A small fire burned despondingly on the hearth.

On the day-bed, by royal prerogative, Anne Louise ensconced herself; and from its vantage watched with malicious amusement the efforts of her ladies to adapt themselves to the angles and general boniness of the monastic-seeming chairs.

She did not know which she disliked most: Baroness Holfender, tall and thin, with an iron-grey face, iron-grey corkscrew ringlets, iron-grey dress, and iron-grey manner; or Miss Talfourd, with her square red face, pinched red nose and grey moustache, enormous bust covered with cabbage-green satin, and fraudulently jovial air.

Within a week of her arrival at the legation in Copenhagen the Baroness had been produced out of thin air, apparently, by Leopold the Magician — just as he had produced the necessary outfit and the necessary jail, all at a moment's notice; just too as he had whisked a thoroughly disapproving Miss Talfourd out of a distant England and distant past to meet them at Cologne. How well Anne Louise recollected the cabbage-green dresses and assumed heartiness in the days at Severall. For twenty-four hours Miss Talfourd had thought to drop back into her old rôle of governess and general mentor. For twenty-four hours only! At the end of that period she realized that she had met her match in an utterly new Anne Louise.

Highness endured an hour of desultory conversation in English. It amused her to insist on talking in English, because the Baroness abominated the language, though she spoke and understood it well; just as it amused her to hurry through her meals because Miss Talfourd was a particularly hearty trencherwoman.

'I think I shall go to bed now,' she said at length. 'I shall be glad of a real bed after six nights in inns!'

'What a luxury — a real bed!' gushed Miss Talfourd. 'And to think that there will be no pererration on the morrow! . . . Those horses — those wheels — that dust — how wearisome they became!'

Anne Louise yawned without disguising the fact. She knew that the breach of manners irritated both of them — and rejoiced in it.

'I have hardly had any sleep since we started,' conceded the iron-grey lady. 'I always sleep badly when I am travelling.'

'Make up for it to-night,' said Anne Louise, speaking in the tone of one who cared little whether the iron-grey lady did or not.

She got to her feet — her ladies dutifully rising too — and set her hand to the blue bell-rope which hung from the wall.

'You need not attend on me to-night,' she said. 'Nicholson will do all that I require!'

There was a second's silence.

'It is not fitting, Highness, that you . . .' began the baroness.

'I do *not* want anyone,' said Anne Louise. 'I want to be by myself for a change . . . Nicholson shall bring me my hot water. That's all the help I need!'

'Perhaps then you will send word by her when you are ready!'

'Ready for what?'

'When your Highness is in bed.'

'I am not a small child that I need tucking up, or having someone to hear my prayers!'

'No,' said the baroness in her iron-grey tones — and Anne Louise thought to hear the insolence of a faint note of interrogation in her voice. 'Your Highness misunderstands me. I meant that I would not come to your room until your Highness was in bed.'

'For what purpose?' asked Anne Louise in her chilliest manner.

'I myself should like to retire *sometime*, if your Highness has no objection!'

'And what has that to do with me?'

'I supposed that your Highness wished to undress before I did!'

Light dawned on Anne Louise —

'You mean that you propose to sleep in my room?'

The iron-grey lady gave an iron-grey bow.

'We are no longer at the mercy of inn accommodation. There is no necessity.'

The iron-grey lady made no answer except in the tightening of the muscles of her jaw, and the deepening of the lines from nose to chin.

'I — propose — to — sleep — by — myself,' said Anne Louise, unmoved by these signs of disagreement. She set hand to the bell-rope again.

'My instructions . . .' said the baroness.

'Mine are: that I will have no one sleeping in my room!'

'His Majesty gave me very definite orders on the point.'

'I countermand them!'

'With all deference, your Highness, I cannot accept that order.'

'Do you think that I shall escape by a rope ladder during the night? Or that I have made an assignation with one of the sentries?'

The iron-grey lady sketched a shrug of the shoulders as though that gesture were the only suitable reply to angry childishness.

Miss Talfourd trotted into the combat —

'I am sure no one would ever suspect your Highness of noctivagation. But in the circumstances . . .'

'The circumstances! . . .' Cousin Theresa's little circumstances — little circumstances that hinted at little consequences! Anne Louise became extremely angry, but outwardly she preserved her temper.

'Please understand that I mean what I say. I — will — not — have — you, or anyone — sleeping — in — my — room! That is definite!'

And, if her voice was definite, so too was the Baroness Holfender's when she answered —

'I cannot disobey his Majesty's most strict instructions!'

Anne Louise pulled the bell-rope, and sat down once again on the least comfortless piece of furniture. She set the one available cushion at her back, put up her feet, arranged the folds of scarlet dress, and reclined at ease.

Nicholson — a smiling middle-aged Englishwoman, also conjured up by Magician Leopold — made her appearance. Anne Louise and she had taken to one another at once. Highness, indeed, knew the names, ages, and professions of all her brothers; and full particulars of all the various ailments she had suffered from since earliest childhood; and could have adequately filled in the burial certificates for those of her family who had passed to Other Spheres.

'Can you find me a pack of cards somewhere, and a pot of tea — real English tea — just for myself?' asked Anne Louise.

Nicholson could — did — made up the fire — set a lamp on a small table by the settee — was dismissed to bed.

Anne Louise, thus ensconced, sipped her tea, shuffled the pack, and proceeded to lay out the foundation cards for a game of patience.

As she dealt from the *talon*, and built up her sequences — knave upon ten; queen upon knave; and king upon queen: red card upon black, and black upon red — she was pleasantly aware of the resentful glare of Miss Talfourd, and the frozen anger of Baroness Holfender as they sat stiffly in their stiff-backed chairs on the other side of the wide hearth. The two women had been taken unaware by their mistress's recalcitrance; were unprepared with plans against such a situation; were too fatigued by the rigours of a long journey to cope intelligently with it. Added to the difficulty of dealing with a young lady, who was not merely a princess, but cousin of the Queen of England and related to kings, was the fact that there was a growing mutual hostility between them, based in its origin on the Holfender's hatred of the English and the Talfourd's scorn of the German.

Anne Louise gathered up the pack; shuffled and cut it with a business-like precision that both women considered almost unladylike; set out the cards afresh. She did not raise her eyes from the table.

Miss Talfourd sighed — loudly.

Long — very long — ago, Anne Louise had played patience of an evening against Tog in his snug little picture gallery at Judgment; and joked with Daniel; and eaten madeira cake and sipped hot pineapple rum punch. And long ago she had played interminable games with Daniel by the light of a single candle on top of a packing-case in the creaking, lurching lumber-room that was the hold of the *Joan Dearlove*. Now she sat — far lonelier and more lost than then — playing patience by herself in this icy chapter-house under the icy eyes of her ladies-in-waiting. What were Daniel, and Tog, and Washy doing now? . . . What was Seven doing?

A severe clock on a severe chest — that ought to have held the monastic chartulary — struck the hour of eleven. The heavy clangour of the castle clock repeated it . . . Anne Louise forsook the Original Whist Patience: she commenced operations on the Sultan.

At midnight she laid out the cards for Demon Patience.

Miss Talfourd sighed again rather gustily. She sketched the prefatory movement to rising and making her excuses. The rustle of her dress drew Anne Louise's chilly regard to her . . . 'How far am I to be constrained by Court etiquette in the case of a royal duchess who is also a royal prisoner?' Miss Talfourd asked herself . . . She saw a glint of supercilious superiority in the iron-grey eyes of the Holfender . . . 'Am I a weaker vessel than that German creature?' she demanded of her soul — and subsided, pretending but to have shaken out the folds of the cabbage-green dress.

Had Mary Queen of Scots, Marie Antoinette, Caroline Matilda of Denmark, Dorothea of Celle, or any other captive and royal lady before her, thought to weary her jailers by playing patience? — wondered Anne Louise.

At two o'clock in the morning she stacked her cards and laid the pack face down on the table. She looked up with a bright, malicious smile.

'We *are* having a late session,' she said cheerfully. 'It is still a long time to breakfast. Perhaps it would be more amusing for you if we played a few games of three-handed whist?'

By no word or gesture would the iron-grey woman deviate from the accepted standards of correctness to be observed in a Royal Presence. She bowed and drew her chair up to the table.

Miss Talfourd stifled all but the very beginnings of a groan. Her tired mind lingered for an instant rather lovingly on the details of the physical treatment that she had meted out to refractory young ladies in the past. But anything was better than sitting upright with folded hands staring into vacancy.

The game began. Went on. Interminably.

It was five in the morning when Miss Talfourd cracked and broke.

'I am not generally lip . . .' she said in a sudden last stagger of speech, as the last log on the hearth collapsed and spurted for a brief instant into its last jet of flame. 'Not lip . . .!'

'Not lip . . . ?' said Anne Louise helpfully, watching the substantial green bosom surge forward, like a billow of savoy cabbages, toward the table.

'Not lip — lipothymous,' finished Miss Talfourd in a sort of lexicographical daze. 'But I must either sleep or swoon!'

With that she trumped her partner's best trick.

Then her fiery face drooped into her bosom; her eyes closed; a noise that was between a gurgle and a snort came bubbling out of lips or nostrils — or both; her slack fingers showered upon the floor the cards which she was in the process of garnering. She sagged forward, and was only sustained against the edge of the table by the whalebone rigidity of the savoy cabbages . . . She was asleep. . . .

At eight o'clock a plump slatternly housemaid, arms full of brooms, brushes and dusters, came bumping through the door to be awe-stricken by the sight of the indomitable Duchess of Limburg playing bézique with the indomitable baroness, regardless of her other attendant who slept at a corner of the table, ungracefully, noisily, greying ringlets almost sweeping the green baize cloth.

'Ah, child!' said the great lady, 'draw back the curtains, and then tell my maid that I would like some tea and my bath made ready . . . You do not desire to be present at the ceremony, Baroness, do you?'

Daylight and sunshine came flooding in.

Anne Louise rose to her feet. She surveyed with grim amusement the haggard faces of her ladies. She walked with springing step and dancing ringlets to the chapter-house window, and surveyed the morning.

'What we need now, is a nice brisk walk!' said the Duchess of Limburg gaily.

CHAPTER III

CURIOUS USE OF A CORK

No hint or rumour of Anne Louise's vendetta against her ladies seeped through keyhole or door-crack of her apartments, although her proclivity towards card-playing until morning was a general topic of conversation throughout the castle before many hours were out.

Attended by baroness and former governess, the Duchess of Limburg rustled decorously on her lawful occasions about the great thoroughfares of the palace . . . She lunched informally with the Grand Duchess's ladies at twelve o'clock . . . She drove out during the afternoon, heralded by a scarlet outrider; escorted by an elderly equerry with a dark bitter face, on horseback; followed by another carriage in which half-a-dozen of the royal lap-dogs were given their daily airing . . . Conducted with faded elegance by the ancient Court Chamberlain with long white wand of office, she led the little procession of dusty old ladies and dusty old gentlemen to a somewhat meagre dinner in the gallery which overhung a banqueting-hall wherein the majority of the citizens of the Grand Duchy could have feasted. Afterwards she graced with her presence the Mirror Gallery — a cavern of glass which might have been the heart of an iceberg — where the dusty old ladies and the dusty old gentlemen played whist and chess, examined dusty albums at a large dusty round table, or manufactured strange dusty articles in Berlin woolwork and indulged in dusty small-talk.

A little before ten o'clock her Highness retired, amid a rustling of dusty curtseys and a bowing of dusty heads. Preceded by pages bearing candles, conducted once more by the Court Chamberlain, followed by the Holfender and the Talfourd, Highness made stately journey through an immensity of gloom to her battlefield. . . .

Arrived at the tomb-like fireplace in the Chinese Withdrawing-room, with only the writhing dragons for witnesses of the conflict, Miss Talfourd opened the real proceedings of the evening.

She rustled a small curtsey — definitely a minor curtsey.

She said —

'And now I must ask your Highness to excuse my further attendance for tonight. I have been indisposed all day. My health demands a full night's sleep.'

If Miss Talfourd's curtsey had been that of a thorough-going English woman who would stand no nonsense, the tone of her speech was even more so. If Holfender chose to sit up all night with this tiresome young woman, then she could. Miss Talfourd did not. If Holfender chose to observe the minuteness of rigid etiquette, then she could. Miss Talfourd did not. She did not beg to be excused: she demanded.

Anne Louise was wearing a dress of cream-coloured silk with trimmings of pale yellow — chosen and worn because she thought it emphasized the tan of her complexion, and so became an offensive gesture of defiance to Uncle Leopold, and to the delicate gentility of his deputies. Satisfied by that challenge, it was merely in a tone of tender reproach that she said —

'Oh, Miss Talfourd, confess the truth! You were just bored last night by our game. I wasn't playing well, I know. And I remember what an expert you are ... Suppose we do something else to-night! ... Bring your sewing, or — No! the baroness shall read to us. That would be delightful! I have found an English book.'

Miss Talfourd regretted —

'We shall miss your company during the watches of the night,' said Anne Louise, acknowledging defeat. She sank down gracefully onto the day-bed, and tucked her toes up on its brocade. . . .

By four o'clock on the following morning the iron-grey woman was practically speechless. She had read aloud from half-past ten without a break, buoyed by her determination to crush mutiny unaided and without deviating by a hair's-breadth from her conception of the correct conduct of a lady-in-waiting. The two main instincts of the German race were nicely balanced in her — the instincts of serfdom and of tyranny. If Anne Louise was in a sense her prisoner, she was also a Royal Personage. It was a battle in which the baroness fought, so to speak, with one of her hands tied behind her back.

The book was entitled *An Account of the New Zealanders*; was published in the Library of Entertaining Knowledge in 1830; and was apparently the only volume in the English language in the castle. It contained four hundred and twenty-four pages. At four o'clock, proceeding at an even pace, although with a voice that grew progressively hoarser, the iron-grey woman had read two hundred and eighteen of them. A remarkable enough feat, even taking into account the fact that from page eighty onward neither she nor her auditor could have had the remotest notion of the subject-matter.

At half-hourly intervals, approximately, the baroness raised her eyes from the book, only to meet the wakeful bright regard of Highness. Every now and then Anne Louise produced from her corsage a diminutive gold watch — the gift of an entirely sympathetic Countess de Charlemont — and timed Iron-Grey's pace; but the rate never varied from one of a minute and a half to the page by more than a second or so.

At four o'clock Highness decided that the time had come for a statement of her position, less from consideration for herself than out of mercy for the iron-grey baroness. And very iron-grey was that lady, sitting bolt-upright in her comfortless high-backed chair; her face greyer, and the lines bitten deep on it looking more iron-coloured than ever: even the eyelids which occasionally blinked shut, despite the iron will, looked of iron, too — rusty iron, so browned were they with fatigue!

Anne Louise set her long slim hands before her on the table, almost in an attitude of prayer; and, as she spoke, she gently rubbed the finger-tips together, feeling in imagination the roughnesses that had come from those long hours of needlework — hours of darning, of patching, of manufacture, for Daniel, for Seven, for herself.

'I think it would be as well if you realized the position,' she said without preface ... The baroness set the book down upon the table ... 'And that is that I don't propose to go bed at all! In the existing circumstances!'

The baroness bowed her acknowledgment of the confidence.

'This involves a certain amount of discomfort for yourself. But I do not see how it can be avoided — or why it should be avoided, indeed! There is no reason that I can see why I should have any consideration for you.'

'I have only been endeavouring to fulfil my duty, your Highness,' said the baroness.

'I am a great deal younger than you are,' continued Anne Louise remorselessly. 'I am a great deal stronger, and I am equally — if not more — determined. You will probably end by killing yourself!'

The baroness thought it highly likely, although she did not say so.

'I shall have regretfully to appeal to the Grand Duchess!'

'My good woman,' said Anne Louise insolently, 'you can appeal to King Leopold, the Shah of Persia, or the Pope of Rome! But all three of them won't get me to bed, if I don't want to go, short of stripping me and strapping me onto the mattress with their own royal and holy hands! ... I may be a prisoner ...'

The baroness protested with a slight shake of iron-grey head.

'I said "Prisoner", and Prisoner you know it is! I am a disreputable female vagrant sent to a House of Correction under your charge. You know that I can no more get out of this damned place than I can fly!

You know that I have been brought here, not only to be whitewashed, but to be punished! . . . You thought you'ld enjoy acting as jailer to a princess! You revelled in the prospect of seeing my humiliation! You know you did!'

There were patches of white on the iron-grey cheek-bones, and dents of white on the iron-grey nose: it was only by the summoning of her last resources that the baroness kept her voice from trembling with anger —

'This is mere childishness, your Highness, much as I dislike saying so!'

'It is far from childishness,' said Anne Louise; and there was that in her voice which would have warned anyone whose faculties were fully on the alert . . . Was it only six months or so since she had cringed before the rebukes of Lady Augusta or Miss Talfourd — she who now gave battle to one more redoubtable even than they? She went on in her young clear voice —

'Let us come to a clear understanding . . . I fully realize my position here. That amid all the beautiful deference, the Highnessing, saluting sentries, and generally idiotic ceremonial, I am as much a prisoner in fact as if I were chained in one of the dungeons below the moat. I accept that situation — because I can't do anything else. I accept the position that you and Miss Talfourd are wardresses as well as spies — because I can hardly ignore the fact.'

'If your Highness chooses to take that attitude . . .'

'I do . . . But if I put up with this infamous treatment, there is no reason why I should meekly accept the crowning humiliation of the presence of my uncle's spies even at my bedside . . . Or are you actually supposed to share my bed with me?'

'Your Highness cannot possibly suppose that Miss Talfourd and I care for our task?'

'You do not care for it particularly at present! But then it is not turning out quite as you fancied it would!'

'His Majesty gave definite orders . . .'

'You are aware that there is a drop of at least forty feet from the windows of my bedroom? . . . Yes! . . . You know that there is only one door to the room? . . . Yes! . . . And that it opens into the ante-room where the lady-in-waiting on duty is supposed to sleep? . . . Yes! . . . And you still insist? — You do!'

Anne Louise rose from the settee. The baroness indomitably rose, too. Anne Louise went to the fire-place, pulled the bell, and remained on her feet, regarding the room and the other woman speculatively.

A faint line of grey between the folds of the faded blue curtains told of approaching day; the lamp on the chartulary chest between the windows was flickering desperately, but those on the black marble pillarstands (which might have come from a grave-yard) on either side of the hearth still shed their mellow light on green-topped card-table, on the woman who swayed a little even as she stood in a mockery of deference, on the pale writhing dragons, on the chill chess board of the tiled floor.

An imperturbable Nicholson, in black silk, made her appearance in a surprisingly short space of time.

'We are a little late— the baroness and I,' said Anne Louise, as though it were the most normal thing in the world to find her maid fully dressed at such an hour in the morning. 'Very late, in fact! I should like some tea — as soon as you can make it . . . Would you like some too, Baroness?'

The baroness, who had anticipated no such mercy, wiped her dry lips with a harsh-looking handkerchief as she acknowledged the favour.

Nicholson vanished; returned — again in a surprisingly short space of time — bearing a tea-tray; poured out two cups. As she presented one to her mistress she gave the smallest perceptible nod.

Anne Louise sat down upon the settee — the baroness sinking thankfully back on her chair — and vigorously stirred her tea. She made affably royal small-talk while she sipped. What were the baroness's views on Chamisso — Hauff — Walter Scott — Charles Dickens — Victor Hugo — Balzac? From literature Highness turned to music. What were the baroness's views on Bach — Mendelssohn — Beethoven — Haydn — Mozart? And then art. What were the baroness's views —

But the baroness had no views. No views on anything.

The tide of interrogation had surged over her: submerged her: drowned her. Almost with the first sip of tea she had begun to nod. Her head had drooped forward over table and cup — been resolutely jerked back: had drooped again immediately — been jerked back once more, only less resolutely this time. Then, too, the lids had started to close of their own volition over glazing eyes. She fixed an unseeing stare upon her tormentor: took another sip of tea in order to keep herself awake — sipped herself into a sleep which was as much due to exhaustion as to drug. Her body sagged in its chair, a little to one side, the arms hanging down — palms backward — in peculiarly helpless fashion.

For a few moments Anne Louise still babbled on. Then she fell silent, and narrowly observed her victim. She leaned across the table and gently tweaked the iron-grey nose; but there was no response to the insult of that gesture save in waggling head. She rose, rustled round the table, repeated the delicious operation — repeated it with gratifying impunity.

With malicious triumph in her eyes, in her carriage, in her walk, Anne Louise proceeded to the window. She flung back the curtains to the morning.

Across the wide lawns and terraces the mists rose from the sea of trees that girdled the castle. At the distant end of a wide avenue there was the pale sheen of dawn upon the waters of a lake. Two small moving specks on the road between the walls of woodland were the only tokens of life. The colourless sky awaited sunrise — in so brief a time would shine like mother-of-pearl. The enchanted hush of the great house was lapped about by the early song of birds.

Anne Louise faced back to the room, and the indecorously sagging figure, made rather pitiful by the harsh severity of day-light.

She stretched luxuriously. She yawned enormously. Like a triumphant cat. Nicholson, making an almost furtive reappearance, found her still standing — hands set on hips of that wide elegant Uncle-Leopold-challenging cream-coloured dress — addressing her sleeping jailer, from the window-place, in such fluent and unusual language as evoked both consternation and admiration in the waiting-woman's breast.

'What was *it*?' asked Highness in a low voice.

Nicholson approached very closely —

'Stuff they give to babies to make them sleep, your Highness, when they're restive!'

They regarded their handiwork in a gratified silence for a moment.

'I'm going to bed now,' said Highness. 'To bed! And since there's no key and no bolt, I'm going to block the door with chairs and water-jugs! And I'm not going to open the door even if the Queen of England asked me to, on all fours ! And I'm going to sleep until I choose to get up. Not one minute less.'

The baroness had let her handkerchief drop on the floor beside her. Anne Louise picked it up thoughtfully. It seemed to awaken a new train of ideas. After a moment she placed it in the drawer of the card-table ; locked it and removed the key.

'Bring me a cork, Nicholson!'

'Cork, your Highness?'

'Cork ! . . . Only a cork!'

A few minutes later her Highness the Duchess of Limburg was busily engaged in ornamenting the face of her senior lady-in-waiting with an immense moustache and imperial in burned cork under the thrilled, scandilized, hysterical regard of her maid.

'There's no mirror in the room, and now she has no handkerchief to wipe it off with,' said Highness, and bubbled into fresh gay laughter. 'If this bell rings see that one of the men-servants answers it first!'

A trifle of gravity overclouded her for less than a moment. She wondered whether Mary Queen of Scots, Queen Caroline Matilda, Dorothea of Celle, that uncrowned Queen of England, or any other Royal captive, would have stooped to burnt-corking an attendant's face. Perhaps they had lacked the opportunity! . . . Well, no matter!

With a pleasing sense of duty well performed, Anne Louise withdrew to her bedroom, where the bed was shaped like a pagoda of red lacquer with golden dragons crawling about its steep roof and its columns.

She pulled back the curtains at the window, and once again looked out onto the morning, whilst Nicholson dealt with hooks and eyes. The sun had risen; the sky was flushed with all the hues of a fire opal; the dew which silvered the grass of the lawns below sparkled with the colours of the rainbow. The two specks had reached the top of the avenue, and had halted close under the protection of the spreading trees. Distant though they were, yet Anne Louise could clearly see that one figure was considerably smaller than the other — that one figure was probably a child, and that the other appeared to be wearing a wide white hat.

As she watched they turned, and were swallowed up in the woodlands.

Her heart almost missed a beat. Could it be that Washy and Daniel had succeeded in tracing her, despite the fact that she was morally certain that no letter of hers — with the exception perhaps of that sent to Mr. Peel in Elsinore — had ever been allowed to proceed to its destination? And, having traced her, were they now out reconnoitring the country? . . . Her dress slid rustling to her feet: she made no effort to step out of it, or away from the prospect and the enchanting hope revealed from her window. . . .

At eight o'clock in the morning Baroness Holfender — conscious of defeat, but unaware of whiskers — emerged from the portals of the princess's apartments into a morning-bright gallery. She proceeded to her own room in her stateliest fashion.

Two frowzy maids, engaged in floor-polishing on hands and knees, looked up as she passed, and their frozen and incredulous amazement gave place to hysterical mirth before she was even fully out of ear-shot; but she did not associate their ill-conditioned laughter with herself. She was, however, a trifle puzzled by the conduct of a sallow decorous lackey whom she next encountered, for the man's jaw suddenly fell and he clapped hand to mouth, turned tail, and fled with frantic splutterings through the nearest service door. She even deigned to look over her shoulder to see if any explanation should offer. . . .

Miss Talfourd's room adjoined her own. She went in to inform her colleague of developments, and to upbraid her for desertion.

That lady — much refreshed and restored — was sitting up in bed, wrapped in a fleecy white shawl, hair in curl-papers, enjoying her morning chocolate. Her astonished gaze took in burned-cork moustache and burned-cork imperial. She controlled herself for an instant sufficiently to ask, in a choked voice —

'My *dear* baroness, what a successful masquerade! Is it Cardinal Richelieu, or Charles the First?'

With that she positively rolled in the bed in an anguish of mirth which ended in the chocolate being spilled all over the sheets.

She described the incident a few days later in her weekly letter to her sister, who kept house for a nonagenarian father in a prim red-brick Nottinghamshire rectory:

'The woman positively fell into a phrenzy, my dear Sophy. She gave just one glance at herself in my mirror — not a very good one, by the way: but then there is a Shabbiness *everywhere* here except in the State apartments! — and seemed for the moment to have been turned to stone. Then — well, I think it *kindest* to imagine that she became temporarily dementate! She raved and raged until I imagined that she would do herself, or me, some hurt; and she actually and literally foamed at the mouth !!! These Foreigners, of course, have no *real* mental balance.

'Of course, after *that* she could not *possibly* stay! The old Grand Duchess knew all about the business within half an hour and sent for me immediately. A *most* extraordinary old woman, but *most* intelligent. We *quite* decided that it was best that Holfender should leave at once, and that Her Highness should write and explain things to King Leopold. H. H. said that it was quite unnecessary that the Duchess's ladies should act as Gaolers, and that *she* had arranged for every necessary and reasonable *precaution*: all that was asked of us was a general Supervision. One of H. H.'s own ladies, Baroness Dedel, a nice person and a *Protestant*, is to take the Holfender's place for the time being.

'Altho' H. H. rules Ehrenberg from her bed — it is *so* sad about the poor Grand Duke, her son, of course: he lives quite retired and is never seen, and signs just what he is told to — she knows *everything* that goes on. One feels that she must have Spies *everywhere*. I should not be so frank, indeed, if Mr. Podmore had not passed through the town on his way back to England and *very kindly* promised to take this letter with him.

'Well, I saw the Duchess and explained the position. "Live and let live — is my motto," I said in my *jolliest* manner, and I think she understood. So now I sleep in a sort of ante-chamber to her bedroom — which is *far* more comfortable than my old room — and we are both satisfied. She is *almost* English in her ways, and can be not unamiable. But then there is nothing German about her, for, of course, the Dukes of Limburg were French and Flemish by descent.

'I am afraid we have been very idle up to now, but we shall soon have to start serious reading. I have already prepared a time-table and a *very* carefully planned Schema of Study.

'We walk most mornings, and drive out of an afternoon. We usually have a cup of *real tea* (what a Treat!) at a pastry-cook's in the town where they make cream tarts and buns of *superlative excellence....*'

CHAPTER IV

THE $500 TART OF MONSIEUR PERPONCHER

MONSIEUR PERPONCHER had left France many years ago. It had been advisable. He had been too successful, both as pastry-cook and as lover. In his first capacity the Marseilles police strongly suspected him of having poisoned his neighbour — with the connivance of that neighbour's wife — through the medium of his celebrated cream tarts: in his second capacity he ran away with the lady, thus making suspicion a certainty.

The fugitive pair reached the remoteness of Ehrenberg, capital of the grand duchy of the same name. There they opened a shop which prospered exceedingly, and produced a daughter, who was a romantic rosebud of a girl when Monsieur Perponcher was fat and grey and Madame Perponcher was yet fatter — though her hair remained as raven as ever.

Perponcher's became an institution.

In the elegant saloon behind the shop, overlooking a minute cherry-orchard, the élite drank coffee, ate pastries — an inordinate number — and gossiped, of an afternoon. Upstairs, and in front, was another room sacred to the Really Important who could not, or would not, mingle with the commonalty: it had an enchanting view, across the low parapet of the town-wall, of wide meadows traversed by winding river, and wooded hills.

All sorts of little conspiracies were hatched at Perponcher's; all sorts of social storms, too, ruffled its tea-cups — for Perponcher's provided tea, thereby securing the patronage of the British Minister's wife and of the many English travellers who came to explore the romantic peaks and valleys of the Ehrengebirge. And gossip, conspiracies, and storms were all duly noted by Monsieur or Madame; for there were inquisitive friends in Munich and Dresden and Hanover who were sometimes interested in such things, and paid to hear about them — though not much.

Perponcher's was the lode star of Miss Talfourd's day. Rare indeed was the afternoon when the grand-ducal landau with four grey horses could not be seen halted under the lime trees that sentinelled the ramparts opposite its door — scarlet outrider walking his own and the bitter-faced equerry's steeds up and down — bitter-faced equerry sitting rigidly over a beer-mug at a green-painted table under the awning of the adjacent 'Swan-with-Three-Necks.'

'Tea,' said Miss Talfourd, 'is the most salutiferous of beverages!' To obtain the full benefit, accordingly, she never had fewer than four cups: but the healthful effect was probably neutralized by the surprising quantity of cream tarts which she devoured.

Anne Louise drank tea: she did not eat cream tarts, until one day. . . .

Monsieur Perponcher valued the royal patronage very highly — so highly that, at the outset, he flatly refused to have anything to do with a curious but profitable proposal made to him by an elegant stranger one evening as he was shutting up. That is to say — after he came to understand what the proposal was; for he spoke no English, and Mr. Washington Hallett knew little German and less French. Madame, called into consultation, was of no assistance.

Washy cast a desperate eye round the shop with its stacks of shrouded trays. Once more he penned Monsieur and Madame in a corner against their counter, and endeavoured to explain. Once more he set forefinger to lips and hissed 'S-sh!' to indicate the need for great secrecy.

'*Dollars*!' said he very slowly and emphatically, and looked anxiously from one fat sallow face to the other to see if there was comprehension of that all-important word. 'D-o-l-l-a-r-s!'

'Ah! . . . Dol-lars!'

Yes! It was a word they knew.

'*Five hundred* . . . five hun-dred!' continued Washy, thus encouraged. 'Fi-ve hun-dred!'

But drew a blank.

'Dollars,' he repeated, and held his hands up, fingers spread wide. 'Five hundred dollars!'

And proceeded to indicate the amount by opening and shutting his hands — a wearisome business when he had finally repeated the operation fifty times.

'Five hundred dollars!'

Monsieur Perponcher had kept tally.

'Cinq cent dollars!' explained he to his wife.

It was an astronomical sum, since the pair of them thought, not in terms of the American dollar, but of the Ehrenberg rix-dollar which was worth in English currency at the time precisely four pounds one shilling and a penny.

Both Perponchers nodded vigorously.

So far, so good! Washy proceeded.

'*For you*! . . . Five hundred dollars for you!' He touched Monsieur Perponcher lightly on the chest, and indicated delicately Madame Perponcher's capacious black-satin-covered bosom.

That fact, too, appeared to be grasped. The Perponchers grew interested. An assistant who appeared in the doorway leading to the garden-room was sent scuttling away.

' — *If I . . . me . . .*'

He pointed to himself. It was clear that the distributor of this fabulous sum was to be the slim, freckled young foreigner in a blue full-skirted coat, yellow satin stock, and yellow tall hat. Both nodded vigorously again.

He recapitulated —

'Five hundred dollars for you if I — ' and drew near the crux of his tale — '*can speak* to — Speak . . . Speak!'

In dumb-show he depicted what he fondly imagined to be the progress of a vigorous conversation, but what the Perponchers took to be a study of a singularly ravenous gentleman engaged in devouring something.

Monsieur looked at Madame with raised eyebrows.

'It is that he wishes something to eat?' asked he in French. 'A dinner? A banquet?'

'Wait, my old! It will probably explain itself in a moment.'

They assumed their most intelligent expressions, and Washy, thoroughly satisfied went on —

' — If I can speak to . . . the Duchess of Limburg — Duchess of Limburg!'

'La Duchesse de Limbourg! Bien!' chorused the Perponchers.

But the story had now become complex! It ran: — 'Five hundred rix-dollars for us, from him — eating — the Duchess of Limburg.' Which was odd, to say the least of it! . . . Better let him go on!

He proceeded:

' — To the Duchess of Limburg . . . *privately* — very privately!'

But 'privately' was a word that did not lend itself to demonstration. Desperately he thought of ways to convey his meaning.

He hurried into a corner where tiers of shelves rose to the ceiling. He buried his head in it, whispering sibilantly . . . He looked round. The Perponchers were staring at him blankly . . . He crept along the wall, as if avoiding recognition, whispering, with a hand held to his mouth . . . Still utter perplexity . . . He gathered himself for a fresh effort.

'Five hundred dollars for you if I can speak — ' here he munched very vigorously — 'with the Duchess of Limburg privately!'

And on the word 'privately' he suddenly ducked from Monsieur Perponcher's astounded gaze and hid behind the broad black satin back of Madame.

Perponcher may have been poisoner and pastry-cook, but he also had a sense of humour. He burst into a roar of gargantuan laughter — laughed until the oily tears ran down his face.

His wife was, however, of far sterner stuff. She smiled, it is true; but five hundred dollars were five hundred dollars — a serious matter. The young gentleman was a foreigner — therefore wealthy: his bright blue coat was superb as to material and style — again wealthy: he was eccentric — again wealthy! Twenty years of experience had told her that all well-dressed eccentric foreigners were wealthy. The dumb-show had been too astonishing to interrupt; but there was money behind it. And money was a serious matter — to be dealt with seriously —

She went to the door at the side of the shop and called upstairs.

A charming high voice answered her. A moment later the most entrancing young creature met Washy's eyes — a girl whose glossy black hair was smooth to her pretty head — a girl with a rosebud face in which gravity struggled with laughter; in a little yellow lutestring dress ornamented with roses, with little yellow sandals bound with broad yellow ribbons.

To her a slightly hysterical Madame Perponcher proceeded to explain the eccentricities of Mr. Hallett. Half way through she said very weakly, 'Mon dieu! Mon dieu!' and collapsed in uncontrollable mirth.

After a while, in slow very careful English —

'My parents would have you explain to me what you would of them, sir. They do not understand. Please speak very slowly. I have had an English governess and will translate for them, sir!'

'It is private . . . *very* private!' began the appreciative Washy.

Mademoiselle Perponcher comprehended that fact.

'One moment, sir!'

The street door was fast shut. She bolted it. The door opening on the staircase she closed. She drew apart the curtains which screened the glass doors leading to the saloon at the back, to make sure there was no eavesdropper.

Then she confronted Washy demurely, attentively, head a little bent, and hands folded before her.

'I say!' said he with a rush. 'What I wanted to say was this: I wanted your parents to give me an opportunity to . . .'

'Please not to speak so fast, sir!'

'I wanted your parents to give me an opportunity to talk to the Duchess of Limburg privately . . . by herself . . . without anyone knowing, you know! I said I would give them five hundred dollars if they would do it.'

'Five . . . hundred . . . dollars! It is rix-dollars you mean? But that is absurd!'

'Rix . . .?'

'It will be American dollars, is it not? . . . Our double-florins! . . . That would be more reasonable. But I do not think they would permit it . . . for any money!'

'Why?'

'If it were known, it would ruin my father's business.'

'If it did, I would compensate him,' said Washy earnestly, conscious of the broad acres and the huge bank balance at his back.

'I will see. I will ask them.'

A torrent of French followed — question and answer; gesticulation, expostulation; then silence: and Washy grew red under the combined regard of the Perponcher family.

Said Mademoiselle, looking up at him from under her long lashes —

'My father wishes to know why you cannot speak to her Highness in the ordinary way. Or write to her . . . It is only curiosity makes him ask. You should not answer if you do not wish! I do not think he will help you, sir, in any case.'

Washy suddenly was conscious that in her he had a potential ally.

'Can't you persuade him,' he asked, and looked at her in pleading fashion, head a little on one side. 'It is very, very important! Really important!'

'No one else may use the room when her Highness is there. She is always attended by a lady. An old lady with a red face. And Major von Prutz is within calling. He is a bear . . . No, sir, it is impossible that you shall speak with her!'

And she shook her shining head.

'But . . .'

A new idea came to her.

'You know her Highness?'

'Very well,' said Washy.

The innate forthright inquisitiveness of the French *bourgeoisie* came to the surface. She spoke very slowly —

'You . . . are . . . her . . . lover?'

And looked up very quickly and sidelong as she spoke, so that she might surprise the truth in his face whatever his answer might be. But

Washy was already so red from embarrassment that there was no tell-tale evidence.

'No,' said Washy, deeply shocked, for the word 'lover' seemed to him to have a peculiarly French meaning.

'A so great friend, perhaps?'

He nodded a vigorous affirmative.

'You could write to her. I could give her the letter secretly myself . . . I will ask my father.'

That was definitely a good idea!

But Father, anxious as he was to assist Monsieur in any way possible, desirous as he was to earn an easy five hundred dollars — even though they were American — would not be persuaded. If someone should see that note passing from hand to hand where would Establishment Perponcher be? No, Nanette; and again, No!

Nanette, however, thought Mr. Hallett (of Hallett, Virginia) a very charming boy. She liked his freckles, his flush, his ruffled sandy hair; she sympathized with his despondency; she adored his romance.

She entered the lists again.

The campaign obviously started on a new phase. The elder Perponchers listened; they argued; at long last they were reluctantly convinced.

Monsieur Perponcher then addresssed Washy for some considerable time as if he had been a public meeting. His peroration concluded with a dramatic gesture in which he swept the cover off a tray upon the counter. Beneath the cloth was revealed a serried mass of the famous tarts — small round golden things capped with small scarlet strawberries asleep in foamy nests of whipped cream.

'My father says,' announced Nanette in triumph, 'that he will sell you a cream tart for five hundred dollars!' . . .

The cream tart that Washy bought for five hundred dollars appeared before her Highness the Duchess of Limburg the very next afternoon, as she sat at the round table in the window of Monsieur Perponcher's State Apartment, watching the green kid-gloved hands of Miss Talfourd busied with urn and tea-pot and sugar-basin and the delicious operations of an almost sacred rite.

She had not wanted a cream tart. She had not asked for a cream tart. In fact she had definitely refused the suggestion that she should partake of a cream tart, when it was put forward by the great Perponcher himself as he supervised the organization of the royal entertainment.

The cream tart was there all the same. It had been taken in silver tongs from a great dishful and placed on her plate by the pretty daughter of the house. She was about to protest when she realized that the proprietor of the establishment was making the most extraordinary faces at her from behind Miss Talfourd's back. A wide smile creased his face and almost hid his eyes beneath rolls of yellow fat: he nodded reassuringly at her, like a Chinese mandarin: his eyes were obviously fixed on her plate.

Perhaps this was something very special in the way of cream tarts, and made exclusively for royalty!

Almost mechanically she set her fork to the tart — and realized at once that indeed it was something very special — very exclusive. For as the whipped cream parted under the silver edge it revealed that a folded square of paper no larger than a sixpence had been secreted in its lusciousness.

Anne Louise raised her eyes from the plate. The low sunny room with its preposterous green panels and fiercely-patterned carpet and curtains swam in her view. She had found a square of paper in a cream tart! *She had found a square of paper in a cream tart!*

Monsieur Perponcher stood by the door, as if making a final scrutiny of the arrangements; but his gaze — anxious and enquiring — was bent on her. She gave him the faintest perceptible nod of assurance, and he vanished. On the other side of the table, nearly hidden from sight by the massive hot-water urn, Miss Talfourd was still busied, snorting approval the while, as the aroma of the brew rose to her frosty nose.

Anne Louise drew her plate as close as she could to the edge of the table. She turned an indifferent regard on the view through the open casement. Across the wide green valley, above the surge of trees on the farther hills, glittered the gilded weathercock surmounting the cupola of Ehrenberg castle — that dusty palace-prison full of dusty old people, governed by an unspeakably horrible old woman. Was that little square of paper lying so close to her fork to be the passport to freedom? — that little square of paper which suddenly came to link the world of Now with the world of Then, the world of Daniel, and Washy, and Seven (with his long nose and cleft chin) and flaming ships, and —

How was she to secure that paper safely, without attracting Miss Talfourd's attention? Should she take it into her mouth with a forkful of cream — and then extract it into her handkerchief? Should she knock her fork clumsily to the floor? Should she engage Frosty-Face's attention, and pick it out of her plate while so doing?

She inclined to the latter method as the most dignified, but thought it might be difficult.

Said Miss Talfourd —

'I really believe that Perponcher has listened to my adhortation, and has had the merest suspicion of Congou mixed with the usual. I shall be surprised in that case if it is not positively supernacular to-day — supernacular!'

She passed a cup across the table : and somehow during the proceedings Anne Louise's fork fell to the floor.

None of the curtseying ladies who witnessed the Duchess of Limburg's passage through Perponcher's spacious shop to the grand-ducal carriage would for a moment have imagined that that princess held concealed in her lace-fringed handkerchief a clandestine letter from a young man.

They admired her oyster-coloured bonnet with green ribbons ; they debated the exact shade of biscuit moiré of her dress with its oyster trimmings and green sash ; they questioned the source of her very short silk gloves of palest yellow. Eagerly was she being discussed before ever the grand-ducal horses had clattered away with her — and with the juiciest piece of scandal that had passed under the very noses of Ehrenberg gossips for many a long year. . . .

Standing in the window of her bedroom Anne Louise read Washy's five-hundred-dollar letter. It was written in a laborious microscopic hand, and enclosed in a tiny square of waxed paper.

It ran —

'I am here with Daniel. I shall stay to help you for ever if necessary. Only tell me what I can do, and I will do it, I am moving into rooms at Perponcher's to-morrow. Miss Perp. will see you get my letters and arrange for your replies. She is a stunner and will do all she can. We have seen you often, but could never tell whether you noticed us or not. We are very well, and hope you are. Daniel sends his love. We have heard nothing of Mr. Tempest. Always your servant, Washy.

P.S.—The Perps are very anxious that you should destroy every letter you get as soon as you've read it.'

She suddenly found that her eyes were blinded with tears ; shook her head angrily as if by the gesture to disown them ; caught her breath in an uncontrollable sob. She was not given to such weakness : it brought home to her now the newness and the strangeness of this Anne Louise who stared with blurred vision at the distant wall of woodlands : it rather frightened her.

Dear, dear Washy! . . . No longer was she a lonely prisoner in a sentinelled castle in a strange land. She had a friend! Already were the seeds of conspiracy being sown! Already escape was being planned! A kaleidoscopic vision of rope ladders, cloaked figures, waiting carriages in dark lanes, galloping horses, passed and re-passed across the mirror of her imagination.

The weeks of disappointment were come to their end. Washy had not merely found her: he had found a way *to* her.

It had been indeed, heart-rending that, following the dawn visit of Washy and Daniel to her castle prison, there was nothing which she could do at all to establish contact with them except to make the town of Erhenberg the objective of her daily drive.

Accordingly every afternoon she and Miss Talfourd had rolled in state down the mile-long dusty avenue between the pines, across the valley, up over the grey stone bridge into the long main street that led to the market-place with its crowded stalls, jutting storeys, and jumble of red roofs and steep gables.

Every afternoon, too, she had been able to prolong the visit by desultory shopping — a comb, ribbons, a thimble, some other trifling need that must be supplied. Miss Talfourd was by no means averse to that pattern of entertainment, and carefully noted down every item of expenditure — for Anne Louise was trusted with no money — on a little ivory tablet with a small gold pencil which had belonged to her dear mother.

Twice Anne Louise had been rewarded. Once she had seen Daniel most perilously hanging out of a window in an upper story of the *Englischer Hof*; and on the other occasion she had passed the two of them in her carriage while they were walking toward the town-gate above the bridge — and had glanced at them with an indifference she did not feel.

Those had been red-letter occasions in a dreary procession of days that were as indistinguishable from one another as the grains of sand which sift through an hour-glass.

Life had been a monotony of unimportant occurrences. An occasional visit to the Grand Duchess during her morning sobriety: rather ceremonial calls on the court ladies — to drink over-sweet port and eat unwanted cakes, in stuffy rooms with heavy curtains and crowding furniture: once to see Ottilie Dedel's pale-faced, long-nosed children in their home — to find them eating a dish of live yellow slugs, seething in sugar, for the good of their lungs. Then the jerky little ceremonial — like a parade of marionettes — at dinner time. The hour of small-talk in the Mirror Gallery — stilted enough except when the subject of the Grand Duke was discussed with bated breath: 'He's a hunchback, Madam, and his mother hasn't seen him for twenty years!' Clack — clack. 'He raped an old woman last week, Adalbert told me!'

Buzz — buzz. 'Her Highness won't have him declared insane because then there'ld be a Council of Regency, and she wouldn't have things all her own way.' Sh — sh. 'They say he . . . She said he . . . I heard he . . .!'

And finally the day would be inevitably rounded off with a game of spelicans with Miss Talfourd — a grave, earnest game on the vast monastic table in the vast archiepiscopal boudoir. In the course of time, indeed, Anne Louise developed as keen an eye and steady a hand as Frosty-Face herself, and could extract the worst situated little spear of ivory from the jumbled heap on the polished surface under the moderator lamp without disturbing the rest. Miss Talfourd was greatly attached to the pastime. Dear Papa had played it every night of his life except, of course, Sundays — and Saturdays which were 'Sermon nights.' . . .

Then Miss Talfourd had heard about Perponcher's upper room. . . .

And so it was that this evening, escorted by the Court Chamberlain with white wand, Highness led the procession of dusty old ladies and dusty old gentlemen to dinner with a heart that sang. Happy princess to have for allies only three miles away a very young man and a very small boy! — to have tucked deep in her corsage a little magic square of paper that had travelled to her in a cream tart!

Washy's letter was the beginning of a most involved and exciting correspondence benevolently aided, read, and censored by Nanette Perponcher.

That mirific girl explained very simply to Washy that for a wealthy young American to linger purposelessly in a minor capital like Ehrenberg was to arouse suspicion.

'There must be some reason that you stay so long, Monsieur Washy — some attraction!' she said one afternoon while they sat at a little green table under the cherry-trees, eating bright red jellies and drinking a bright green liquid which Daniel liked very much.

'Some attraction, Miss Perp?' echoed Washy, puzzled.

'We must think of something to explain your so long visit to Ehrenberg. Otherwise people will talk, and the authorities may start to watch!'

Washy had not thought of that: he meditated the problem.

'I'll take the waters every morning!' he said with a sigh, thinking of the muddy beverage which was to be drunk in a damp little spa room in a grim little glade on the outskirts of the town.

Nanette laughed.

'You must have a better excuse than that, Monsieur Washy,' she said. He meditated afresh. He sighed again —

'Daniel and I have come here to learn German?'

Daniel looked very serious.

'There must be an attraction — a real attraction, why you should continue to stay in so small a town. *Me*, for example!'

Daniel looked relieved: Washy looked puzzled.

'You?'

'Me! . . . Is it that I could not be an attraction?' asked Nanette with some slight chagrin. 'It is only for — what you say ? — the good of the cause.'

Washy looked at her. Even the most faithful servant of a fairy-tale princess must ungrudgingly admit the loveliness of that face in which gravity and laughter were always at odds.

'You! . . . An attraction! . . . I *should* think so!' he said with unqualified admiration.

'It is settled then!' said Nanette. 'You shall look at me frequently. You shall touch my hand — by accident! . . . And I will look at you — like this!'

So devastating a look it was that she shot at him from under long lashes that a couple of ladies at a near-by table put their heads together and whispered between surreptitious glances; and a young gentleman in a tight-buttoned green coat, who had been sitting a few paces away, rose and stamped angrily out of the garden.

Thus was Ehrenberg satisfied. Even if Herr Hiob Herschel, son of that important official the Grand-Ducal Upper-Appeal-Court-Vice-President, was not.

Both Anne Louise and Washy soon discovered, however, that it was one thing to carry on a secret correspondence, and another altogether different to plan an escape. Not merely had Anne Louise no money, but she was never left to herself for a moment, except when she went to bed; and even then Miss Talfourd lay in the ante-room.

An ally within the castle, too, appeared essential — and lacking. She had sounded Nicholson, who had regretfully, politely, but flatly refused her assistance. No promise of fabulous wealth could move the woman.

'But you didn't mind drugging Baroness Holfender?' protested Anne Louise.

Nicholson was silent. She pleated her apron. Her eyes were on the ground.

'I'ld not dare do it again, your Highness,' she said at last. 'Not anything else! *They* suspected something *then*. I don't know why. *They* . . .'

ANDROMEDA

And broke off being unable to bear repeating — or even thinking about — the horrific fate of which *they* had warned her if she should think to connive at or abet prison-breaking by her mistress.

'Tell the woman,' had said the Grand Duchess, dismissing the matter thus easily, 'that the police know of a nice brothel near the barracks where she might be usefully employed — under supervision.'

It was Nicholson, too, who brought home to Anne Louise the profound difficulties of an escape — who told her of the rigid control that had always been exercised at the castle gates. It was impossible to enter or leave the building except by the immense forecourt, the Court of Honour, or by the equally large Garden Court at the back. There was a police control, as well as sentries, at the entrances during the day-time. At night the gates were locked, and might but be opened on the production of a pass signed personally by the Court Chamberlain. It was obvious that escape could only be effected during the morning walk or the afternoon drive: yet on the before-lunch excursion they were always accompanied — at a few yards distance — by a large and wooden young officer, while later in the day Major von Prutz, with his dark bitter face, was never out of sight or earshot.

'I've bought horses and a fine little travelling carriage,' wrote Washy in one of the letters which would suddenly materialize at Perponcher's — in a tart, under a plate, or in the current number of the *Wiener Zeitschrift* — 'Samuel's come, and I've got another man, an old soldier who served in the French cavalry with Bonaparte. He will do *anything* & Miss Perp says he's thoroly reliable. I've found out that the nearest place on the frontier is fifteen miles away. Once we get across we can take breath. Miss Perp says that tho' there are guard-posts nobody worries about your papers or asks for them. So all you've got to do is to make the opportunity and say the word "Go!" Daniel has been sick. He is all right now. I think Miss Perp makes him eat too many buns.'

Anne Louise meditating over this letter by the light of her bedside candle, found little comfort in it.

Her curtains were pulled wide, and rustled in a small night wind: somewhere in the woodland an owl cried. Otherwise there was no sound. Anne Louise fancied that the castle slept — under the crescent moon which rode high in a pale and cloudless sky — as though enchanted, so that the only movement within its walls would be the slow mounting of the dust through long ages; as though the inhabitants had wearied themselves to sleep by their dusty little processions through endless corridors, by their dusty little dinners, by their dusty

318

little vices, by the dusty games of chess, by the Berlin woolwork and small-talk with which each wearisome evening was spun out almost to an eternity.

A most intense desire for escape — for freedom — seized her, and grew until it became a physical pain, an unbearable anguish. It was impossible that she should support any longer the unmeaning round of the day — of the week — of the month, and (might it not be?) of the year. In the squalor of the hold of the lost *Joan Dearlove* there had been life and service. Here life itself took on the aspect of death, and she herself was the only living thing in a castle full of ghosts, whose ruler — lying as though coffined in her vast bed — had forgotten everything but the desiccated memories of meaningless fornications. Better ever the purposefulness of the violence and hardship to which Seven had directed her course, than this existence of triviality in which she was imprisoned by the chill anger or for the chill purposes of the chill marriage-broker in Brussels, with his gold tooth-clamp, his trebly-soled boots, his black wig and ravaged countenance of an elderly Apollo.

Why could not Washy do something? Why could not Washy speed up rescue? Why . . .? And chided herself for disloyalty to so true a friend; found herself speculating how Seven would have set to work.

Seven! — Had those ridiculous red socks of his ever been mended? Perhaps he had darned them himself. He was quite capable of doing so. . . .

The next day at Perponcher's she had a note from Washy. It said:

'Miss Perp's thought of something. *You will have a visiter in a day or two.* The sort you'd least expect!'

CHAPTER V

'THY PITY UPON ALL PRISONERS AND CAPTIVES...'

APART from Anne Louise's complete refusal to have anything to do with her 'Schema of Study', Miss Talfourd had only three complaints against life in the otherwise agreeable Grand Duchy of Ehrenberg — the dearness of white cotton stockings at three shillings the pair; the gross over-charging of her hairdresser ('I only used to pay two francs — one shilling and sevenpence — in Paris!') and the fact that she was unable to partake in any form of religious exercise approximating those inculcated and approved by the Church of England. Ehrenberg was overwhelmingly Roman Catholic in faith — 'And idolatrous flummery is what I call it, compared with the theopneustic simplicity of our ritual!'

It was, accordingly, with much gratification that she received a letter from Mr. Brand, the British Minister, introducing an acquaintance of long standing, the Reverend Humphrey Cobbold, at one time English chaplain at the Court of Hanover, who proposed to spend some time in the country collecting the materials for a monograph on religious disunity in Germany.

'A most amiable person,' said she to Anne Louise, after Mr. Cobbold had paid a morning call. 'A little difficult to tell his age. Exceptionally handsome and well-dressed — most intelligent — and, of course, a gentleman. One of the Hampshire Cobbolds. He was at College with Mr. Brand.'

Anne Louise was not interested. She had procured a small book bound in green Russia leather with gilt edges, and in it was compiling a full and true history of the Life and Adventure of Anne Louise, Duchess of Limburg and Princess of Lecques, in the form of letters of singularly philosophical cast addressed to an imaginary friend, Octavia.

'Mr. Cobbold was most anxious to pay his respects to your Highness in person,' said Miss Talfourd sitting down and taking up her crochet. 'He said that he ventured to think that he might be of some assistance!'

' "Assistance" !' echoed Anne Louise, leaving her quill in the ink-pot and turning to regard Miss Talfourd from her hard seat at a writing-table (of very ecclesiastical appearance) in one of the windows. ' "Assistance"!'

But Miss Talfourd was placidly hooking green silk loop to green silk loop — she was very fond of dark green, and Anne Louise often wondered if she ever found herself crocheting her dark green mittens into the dark green purse upon which she was engaged.

'*Spiritual* assistance, my dear!' explained Miss Talfourd. 'After all, you and I are the only Protestants in the castle — excepting Ottilie Dedel, of course. You always went to church at Severall ... Mr. Cobbold seems very sound — very orthodox — to me ... A great admirer of Kliefoth's sermons. I used to translate and read them to dear Papa in the evenings at home.'

It must have been Kliefoth's admirable sermons that turned the scale, because Anne Louise expressed forthwith her earnest desire to receive Mr. Cobbold. The sooner the better. To-morrow if possible.

Miss Talfourd, favourably impressed by this sign of grace, promised that a messenger should be sent at once to the gentleman. He *had* suggested that the day after to-morrow, being Sunday, they might like to have a little service at the castle. Should she get Baron von Stielerberg, the Court Chamberlain, to ask the Grand Duchess's permission for one of the smaller rooms to be turned into a chapel for the occasion? It would be so pleasant to have a dear old Church of England service. The Minister and Mrs. Brand could be asked — and the attachés — and one or two of the English residents and tourists for whom Mr. Brand could vouch personally.

'The sort you'ld least expect!' Washy's warning running in her mind, Highness enthusiastically supported the suggestion. ...

Miss Talfourd was well pleased with Mr. Cobbold's ministrations to the congregation of thirty who awaited him, on gilded chairs, in a lofty grey music-room ornamented with gigantic panels depicting gigantic Muses in symbolical poses. With a sentry standing without the folding doors to avert interruption, Mr. Cobbold ran through morning service with neat precision; doffed his surplice — in an anteroom — before preaching urbanely on the Miracle of Cana; and donned it again in order to give the benediction, while the Faithful — after two false starts by Ottilie Dedel at the organ — sang, rather tentatively, 'Sun of my Soul'.

As the congregation solemnly scuffled to their feet upon her entry and departure, Anne Louise was very conscious of an immaculate Washy and a cherubic Daniel in white peg-top trousers and a blue blouse with a frill round the neck — about which she felt certain there had been strained relations. Daniel winked at her as she passed down between the rows of chairs, and his lips moved in a silent greeting.

A little later, looking like a masquerading faun rather than a clergy-man, Mr. Cobbold sat opposite Anne Louise, little hands clasped and head a trifle bent so that chin rested upon exquisite folds of white neck-cloth. His whole attitude seemed to Miss Talfourd to be one of defer-ential attention. She had delicately withdrawn out of ear-shot so that Anne Louise's religious difficulties might be solved in private; from the distance she thought Mr. Cobbold might well have sat for the portrait of a young angel by one of the Italian masters, once you imagined him in flowing robes instead of the marvellous velvet-collared tail-coat which Stultz or Hayward must have made him.

Mr. Cobbold was saying in his delicate little voice —

'I really felt, your Highness, that my little address should have taken for its text the appeal in the Litany to the Lord — " 'Shew Thy pity upon all prisoners and captives!" '

He looked up at the princess as he spoke with a bright sidelong glance, with the merest suggestion of a smile of profound sympathy.

'Why?' asked Anne Louise bluntly. She must make sure of her interlocutor before committing herself.

Mr. Cobbold draped one little shapely leg over the other, and caressed a small shapely knee. He looked beautifully pensive as he answered obliquely —

'I have never undertaken the cure of souls in the parochial sense, your Highness. I do not think it is quite my métier. I sometimes fancy that I should not have entered the Church at all. But after I left the army . . . well, I was a younger son!' — And he shrugged his marvellously tailored miniature shoulders as though to indicate the fatalism with which younger sons should regard life. — 'The nearest I ever approached to it was when I was chaplain for a short time to the King of Hanover' — Again a sidelong glance in which he observed her reactions to that name of ill-omen; swiftly added — 'But His Majesty and I, alas! were incom-patibles, if I may say so! Still, there is much work in this world for a man of good will. And my cloth gives me special opportunities.' He coughed behind an elfin hand. 'Opportunities which I can employ without incurring the suspicion which would inevitably attach to a layman! . . . Now, a young friend of mine — a romantic young friend — a *mutual* friend, your Highness — '

Only by a slight lift of inquiring eyebrows did Anne Louise encour-age further confidence.

' — a Mr. Hallett, a young American.'

So this was Washy's co-adjutor — this exquisite little gentleman in black with the slightly flamboyant white neckerchief and the pearl buttons in his pleated shirt-front and the wide wristbands turned back over his cuffs, and the flushed olive face, who looked like an exquisite boy unless you were near enough to see the faint lines that were beginning to trace themselves at the corners of the bright black eyes! And even as she divined middle age beneath the mask of youth, so too did she guess at intrinsic hardness beneath a rind of soft speech.

As if he had guessed her discovery, he went on, in a low voice —

'Mr. Hallett is a romantic. His fellow-conspirator, Miss Perp — as he calls her — is another. Dear, delightful, *charming* romantics! But just a pair of children playing with gun-powder! *I* am a realist. You need to be a realist to play with gun-powder!'

Very true! That was what Anne Louise herself had felt. She looked at the little man with fresh interest, as she signified her concurrence by a nod.

'Now the business of which we have not spoken is romantic enough — as a theme! But to bring it to a successful conclusion it has to be treated like all other business — in the spirit of realism. It is not ... Hey-presto! And away! ... It is a working out of a time-table that shall be inviolable ... the allotment of definite duties ... the arrangement of every stage of a journey ... the readiness of what the theatre calls "properties" where you want them, and when you want them! Romance in fact, *must* be organized, if it is not to end in tragedy or disaster!'

'Yes!' said Anne Louise. Her spirits were rising. This elfin materialistic clergyman voiced her own misgivings about the conduct of affairs up to the present. She began to feel that he might organize an escape with the same precision with which he had performed morning service.

'It would take too long to explain how it came about that your young friend took me into his confidence. Do not think, however, that he disobeyed without justification the admonition of Solomon, Proverbs xxv — "Discover not a secret to another, lest he that heareth it put thee to shame!" ... Your Highness will agree that it would be a mistake to protract *private* conversation unduly.'

Anne Louise sat with hands decorously folded on rose damask lap; with head so decorously bent that she could watch the rise and fall of the white edging to the long opening of her bodice — and wonder whether the more rapid pulsation was observable by others.

'It would be as well to run no risks,' she said.

'As cold as a fish!' said Mr. Cobbold to himself, and asked himself whether such frigidity was a factor of any importance. Aloud he remarked —

'We — *We!* — must run no risks. On the other hand we must remember that time presses!'

It was true that time weighed heavily on her, but why should it particularly press on him — or Washy — or Miss Perp?

— Miss Talfourd, regarding almost affectionately the downcast head with the drooping ringlets of every shade of gold, congratulated herself upon the discovery of a spiritual guide so agreeable to her royal charge —

'The sooner everything can be arranged, the better,' said Anne Louise barely moving her lips.

'Yes!' said Mr. Cobbold easily. 'Especially when Baron Stockmar arrives in a week's time.'

'Stockmar? A week's time?'

Her voice trembled imperceptibily to any save herself.

'The Baron is accompanying the Coburg princes ... Ernest and Albert, your cousins, I believe ... to Brussels after their Italian tour. I thought your Highness would have known that they were staying here for a few days on the way!'

Mr. Cobbold omitted, incidentally, to say that the forthcoming visit of the Coburgs was the sole reason for his own stay in Ehrenberg. Neither did he mention the fact that Monsieur Perponcher was what might be termed a piece-work employee of the Hanoverian secret service.

Anne Louise realized instinctively that the coming of Stockmar foretold ill-fortune: that the dusty pageantry set in the vast monotony of Ehrenberg was but the prologue to some tenser drama.

She said —

'I *must* go! *Must!* ... You will help me? ... Please!' — Paused — 'I shall prove not ungrateful!'

Mr. Cobbold deprecated mention of gratitude by a neat shake of a neat head. He promised assistance by the soothing manner in which he patted his neat black knee. He tittered ever so slightly in appreciation of the neatness with which he had obtained his information —

'A messenger from King Leopold passed through Ehrenberg three days ago on his way to meet the baron. He stayed at my hotel, the Golden Eagle, for a night. I gathered something about your Highness's position from him. He will hardly recollect what secrets he imparted to me. He became — I regret to say — extremely intoxicated in the course of the evening. *Extremely* intoxicated! ... "Wine" indeed "is a mocker; strong drink is raging"!'

'Have you made any plans? Any at all?'

Her slim white fingers were inter-twisted; tightened so that the blood receded from them till the middle joints were become yellow as old ivory. Miss Talfourd — looking across the waste of black and white marble — decided that Highness was unburdening herself of a load of error.

'Everything is cut and dried, except for your actual escape from the castle. That must, of course, depend on circumstances. And circumstances will be most favourable during the commotions caused by the princes' visit. All that we conspirators ask, is that you shall place yourself unreservedly in our hands.'

'*It*,' she suggested, 'will be in about a week's time, then?'

'About a week,' he assented. 'But I will ask your Highness to receive me once before at least — perhaps twice, so that I may advise you of what we have decided!'

What '*we*' have decided! 'We' being those incredible conspirators whom she could imagine in secret conclave round a little green table under the cherry trees in Perponcher's garden — the eager, boyish Washy; Miss Perp with a face like that of a laughing madonna; the puckish Mr. Cobbold; and Daniel, listening gravely while he ate buns, or ices, or drank lemonade. She had caught a glimpse of such a convention of the original three plotters through a landing window once as she descended after tea: had even encountered them, presumably at the conclusion of a session, at a sudden turn of the stairs, and shown no recognition — not even the flicker of an eyelash — although gravely shaken by Daniel's stare and grin.

She asked a question that had vaguely puzzled her throughout the entire interview —

'May I ask why you are doing this for me?'

He had been about to rise. He paused, as though meditating his answer —

'It is my duty as a Christian to help a fellow-creature in distress,' he began: found that as a reason it sounded hollow: smiled — and though the curve of his lips was beautiful, the ruinous teeth he revealed were horrible. 'I suppose that besides being a realist, I am also a romantic! ... My tradition seems to lie with royalty — in affliction. I was in attendance on Queen Caroline during her trial in the House of Lords ... I escorted the Duchess Louise — mother of the young princes — to the Coburg frontier after their father, Duke Ernest, had divorced her ... She died a few years ago, and her second husband' — again he faintly tittered — 'has to take her coffin with him on his travels, or lose his annuity!'

No. She did not like the little man, but there was an air of complete efficiency about him. She gave him her hand. As he bowed low over it, he said, sufficiently loud to be heard by Miss Talfourd —

'That is a kind promise, Highness. If your Highness will receive me next Tuesday, I will bring the volume of Ogden's sermons with me. I always travel with it ... Is your dear father, Miss Talfourd — please remember me to him when you write — an admirer of Ogden? ... There is a wonderful message of comfort in his dissertation on the third verse of the hundred-and-forty-seventh Psalm: "He healeth those that are broken in heart: and giveth medicine to heal their sickness"!'

CHAPTER VI

CONVERSATIONS WITH A COUSIN

SOMEWHERE in the dark enchanted woods that surrounded the castle was a dark green pool. It had a stone verge stained with moss, and a wide girdle of overgrown grass set about with a colonnade of weather-beaten marble. Its water was of as dark a green as seaweed, and as dense as ancient beer, flecked with floating leaves and drowning pine needles: the herbage around it was but rarely scythed, and long, and starred with daisies and mooned with the seed-balls of dandelions.

Anne Louise loved the spot.

She spent half the morning there, on a marble bench, reading *Humphrey Clinker* — for the castle library had eventually produced further supplies of English literature than the *Account of the New Zealanders* — encased in the binding of a derelict copy of the works of Shakespeare.

The other half of the fore-noon was devoted to weeding and shearing and general salvage. She asked no assistance, bar a benevolent presence from Miss Talfourd: but Ottilie Dedel was always ready to assist with shears and spud.

They had arrived early on that July morning — so early that the long shadows of the forest on grass and verge were a luminous grey-blue, and the sunlight barring the water was barely gold.

Anne Louise had retrieved a pair of rusted clippers from a garden hut: regardless of her saffron gown, she travelled round the pool on hands and knees, clipping the ragged grass at the edge of the stone verge. Ottilie bent angularly double — a perpetual dewdrop hanging from the end of her bony nose — followed after with a small basket, garnering the debris. Miss Talfourd, more than a trifle disapproving, presided over the operation with spread skirts and stream of crochet, from a lion-ended marble bench —

A voice called —

'Eôs! Eôs! Come here, sir!'

Anne Louise sat up on her heels.

The handsomest young man that she had ever seen stood at the edge of the pool a little distance off. A greyhound came slowly and proudly toward him. Another waited at his side.

He wore a wide-skirted coat of dark blue and white trousers, and a white tall hat. He had the carriage and figure of a fairy prince, and his features were as beautiful and composed as those of a Greek god. His eyes were very blue: there was a faint pencilling of moustache upon his upper lip, and a still fainter line of golden down was shaded on the upper angle of his jaw.

This must be Albert of Saxe-Coburg-Gotha — Cousin Albert — whose career as husband of the Queen of England had been marked out for him from the cradle by Uncle Leopold: he was far too good-looking to be the elder, Ernest. There had been some mishap on the journey: the princes with Baron Stockmar, their mentor and master, had arrived late the previous night, and supped privately.

Anne Louise scrambled to her feet, and, perfunctorily dusting her hands, waited to greet him.

'You are Albert of Coburg,' she said in English. 'I am Anne Louise of Limburg . . . one of Uncle Leopold's misfits!'

His heels clicked together, and he bowed from the waist before taking her hand.

'I cannot imagine you as a misfit anywhere, cousin!' he answered: and, though he thus paid tribute to her, there was no shadow of expression in his voice or in his face. What he said was just a sentence; and the movement of his features was caused by the physical effort of speech and nothing else. He continued — 'My brother will pay his respects to you very shortly . . . Baron Stockmar asked me to make his apologies. He is confined to bed with one of his usual attacks. It started last night soon after we arrived. It usually takes him a week to recover.'

Anne Louise did not conceal her pleasure at the news. She would not have to suffer the ordeal of facing the baron and learning his and the king's plans for her — of confronting him with open rebellion, or of sullenly feigning acceptance — before she fled.

'Is his nose as red as ever?'

'Redder,' said Albert, as one stating an incontrovertible — but uninteresting — fact. 'It is very sad for him!'

They continued with polite and trite interchanges on the subject of the few people they knew in common.

'My aunt Kent — you met her, I suppose?'

Yes! Anne Louise had met his aunt, the Duchess of Kent.

'And Victoria?'

Yes! She had also met the Queen of England.

'And Victoria's half-sister, Féodore of Leiningen?'

Yes! She had met Féodore. And added maliciously —

'It is really difficult to believe that there is any relationship. Féodore is quite good-looking!'

She sensed rather than saw, that he gave her a rather puzzled glance.

So they walked together up and down the grass, exchanging cousinly platitudes and small-talk, followed proudly by the slim grey dogs. Their conversation might have been extracted from a hand-book on etiquette: their bearing was beyond reproach. Miss Talfourd watched them with deep approval —

'They are a very concinnous pair, my dear baroness!' she said. 'I could almost wish . . .'

Anne Louise, however, found the young prince wearisome beyond measure. He reminded her hideously of Leopold in his chill elegance, in the guttural excellence of his English, and even in his looks. Talking to him was like making conversation with an automaton capable of no response but one — the inevitably correct; with something that walked, and spoke, and ate, but was without idiosyncracy or emotion. She prayed that he would soon go: but he did not.

She was, in fact, destined to spend the greater part of the day in his company — thanks to the unparalleled exertions made by the Grand Duchess for the entertainment of her guests. For Highness even advanced her usual four o'clock sobriety by more than an hour, and rose from her bed — being hoisted to the floor by three men-servants wearing white-kid gloves; was upholstered in a tremendous gown of crimson velvet by her dressers, under the guidance of two ladies-in-waiting and the supervision of the old Mistress of the Robes; was be-wigged with a colossal red wig with corkscrew curls the size of rolling-pins; be-hatted in a confection of silver lace trimmed with wild roses, myrtle leaves, and pale pink ribbon.

Thus attired she drove out in the afternoon with Anne Louise and Albert and the nonentity Ernest, to visit a few of the nearer beauty spots. They journeyed in considerable state, and in a carriage so heavy that it required eight horses to draw it; the weight being due to the fact that it had been lined with iron plates in '31, after a Radical tailor had had the temerity to discharge a pistol point-blank at the great lady — with very faulty aim.

In the evening the Grand Duchess (in bright blue) presided at a banquet in honour of the visitors in the Hall of the Knights — a vast bare gallery painted coffee-colour with the pilasters picked out in green and gold, and very badly illuminated by more than a thousand candles. She sat directly under a life-size portrait of herself painted originally by

Schwinde in 1819, but having a new dress of the latest fashion over-painted on it every year so or by local artists.

By a great effort of self-control the old lady remained sober: by a still greater effort she restrained herself from telling her principal guests a few of her bawdiest stories — particularly one about their mother, which was incidentally quite untrue. She talked loudly through the concert which concluded the day's festivities.

Anne Louise saw Albert in four different changes of costume during the day: her dislike mounted with the sartorial crescendo that reached its climax in the dark green splendours of the Coburg uniform which he wore that evening. It was, accordingly, with angry resentment that she found him again the next morning trespassing on her privacy at the forest pool. She was barely polite, and contributed little to the discussion which he tried to initiate on the subject of the previous night's music.

Had she ever heard Mendelssohn play before?

She had not.

It was a piece of the greatest good fortune that he should be passing through Ehrenberg on his way to Dresden, was it not?

It was, indeed.

Did she care for the chorus from *St. Paul*, 'How lovely are the messengers'? He admired it very much.

As *her* Highness had no intention of caring for anything for which *his* Highness expressed a liking — she did *not* care for the chorus.

Presently he said abruptly — and she felt that there was some purpose, which she could not fathom, behind the question:

'Is anything ever heard nowadays of the Grand Duke — of Francis? He used to be a great patron of music, I believe.'

'What can there be to hear?'

'Is he better — or worse?'

'There are no bulletins. They still maintain polite fictions about him. They still keep him shut up somewhere. And he is still just sane enough to sign his name wherever he is told to. If he were declared a lunatic there would be a Council of Regency and the Grand Duchess would lose all her power!'

'He has been an imbecile for twenty years. It is sad!' said Albert in his most even tone.

She pictured him saying the same thing in the same tone when *she* had been a prisoner for twenty years, too. It angered her.

' "It is sad"!' she echoed in just his accents with lifted eyebrows. And then declared emphatically, 'It is *unbearably* sad!'

He ignored her mimicry. He explained the lack of vigour in his expression of polite regret —

'His . . . ill-health was due, I believe, to some irregularity in his private life!'

She took off her bonnet and tossed it on the grass with the gesture of a boxer hurling his hat into the ring.

'You mean — His madness was due to his immorality. That is what you really mean in plain language . . . The word "irregularity" is only correct in his case, if by it you imply conduct that is not regular to the average German prince — if by it you imply decency, honour, chivalry! . . . Do you know his story?'

If he was taken aback by her sudden violence, he did not show it. He merely said that he was unacquainted with the details.

She gave him the story — as she knew it — with angry emphasis.

'He fell in love with a little singer at the Opera here. She was the orphan daughter of a French officer. I don't know her history, or how or where he met her: he is a hunchback, you know, and never appeared in public if he could help it. Anyhow, he married her privately, and they had a baby — a little girl. His parents got to hear about it. They were furious: you see a prince can commit rape or adultery without comment, but he mustn't commit marriage. They didn't say anything, however, but sent him off on some sort of mission to Vienna. When he got back after a couple of months his wife and child had vanished. Eventually he traced them to Hanover — to find that they had died during a typhus epidemic in the poor-house. They had been buried like other paupers — in a plain deal box, without a single prayer being said over them! . . . And then he went mad!'

'It is a s— painful story,' he said; and, after a pause, went on to talk on safer subjects. They proceeded to arid discussion of places which they had visited in common. Anne Louise had once passed through the Coburg duchy. The only thing she had remarked about it was that all the toll-gates and posting-houses and public buildings had been painted with green and white stripes; whereas when you crossed the frontier at Frottstedt into Weimar you found them all orange and black.

'Ah! The dear Coburg!' said Albert; and Anne Louise thought to hear genuine emotion in his voice. She glanced at him quickly — to see that the chill perfection of his face had been suddenly made human by a smile. He was staring into the green water as though it were a magic mirror that reflected visions of his home. 'Wherever I go, and whatever I become,' he declared, 'I shall be always a true Coburger in my heart!'

She knew then that it was an acquiescent but not a willing victim that Uncle Leopold was sending garlanded for sacrifice on the steps of the Throne of England.

'If you feel like that why leave your country?'

It had been but a moment of sentiment on his part and he answered — realizing all her implications — in a voice devoid of expression —

'My duty.'

'To whom?'

For a moment he was puzzled how to reply. He paused, and then said —

'To my family.'

'To Uncle Leopold! . . . And why is it your duty?'

He was still fumbling for an answer when she continued, with yet another question:

'You know why I am here?'

He did not pretend ignorance; but she replied to herself.

'I am here — a prisoner: and you know it! — because I believe that I have the right to decide for myself whether I owe duty or not, and in what fashion that duty shall be paid. I have decided that I owe no duty. Therefore I will pay none. If a man says that you owe him ten thousand thalers, you demand proof of the debt. I demand proof of my debt, and there is none forthcoming.'

She saw now that his composure was a but a mask, for he wore a look of weary resignation.

'What can I do? My destiny was allotted me at birth — '

'Who allotted it? Not God . . . Uncle Leopold! There was a phrase I recollect in some old divine — "The Lord God is the Lord of Destiny, and He hath no viceroys!" '

He continued, regardless of her interruption —

'I was bred — educated — moulded — forged — sharpened for one purpose alone. Were that purpose to fail I should have no meaning. I have been a slave so long that only rarely do I feel the fetters.'

'But you must have some ideal,' said Anne Louise, picking up her straw bonnet from the grass, and swinging it by its strings.

He watched her with a kindling eye —

'Half of me would like to be at Rosenau — to live the life of a private gentleman — to walk in the woods and talk, just as we are talking now, but about other things. About music and art and books and philosophies. That half would like to shoot a little, and fish a little, and look after a small estate. I am a lazy man naturally, but they have so driven me on that now I am utterly confounded if every minute is not filled . . . I wonder if you understand? ... I wonder, in any case, why we are talking like this?'

Anne Louise pulled a thick dandelion stalk; broke off a section, and peered through the little tube as through a dwarf telescope.

'You and I are the two people in all the world who *can* "talk like this". We are in exactly the same position. We both have one would-be master ... one would-be "viceroy of our destiny". It would be surprising if we could not talk frankly to one another!'

'I will be even franker. It is more than probable that I shall fail of the purpose for which I have been created ... *She* — I am not disloyal — fears to be controlled. Because of that she may quite well never marry — like Queen Elizabeth. I think she fancies to model herself upon that queen. She goes her own way despite her ministers — despite her advisers — despite her mother — despite her friends — despite Uncle Leopold. She has successfully defied men who have had more than twice as many years' experience in statecraft as she has had months. England has become restive and disloyal. The methods of the Tudors are not suitable to 1839! Every slip she makes becomes a crime. Every slip is turned to political account! ... Ernest of Hanover is a dangerous and ambitious man: the men he employs are even more so ... What will be her fate unless she is soon controlled?'

'Could you control her?' she asked; looked at him appraisingly, and realized that beauty could be joined to strength.

He made no answer except by flushing, and returned her glance.

They started to walk back toward her ladies.

'Have you ever been in love, Anne Louise?' he said suddenly.

She considered the question.

'I suppose I have — a little bit!'

'With whom — if I may ask?'

Again she considered.

'I am really not quite certain ... And you?'

He shook his head.

'I have never been.' He paused and regarded her again, with a smile. 'But I — I could be!'

Looking sidelong at him, as they approached the others, she saw the animation fade from his face: saw his expression become one of a weary acceptance of destiny: saw that flicker away, too, so that his features were once more set to show nothing. ...

After luncheon he presented himself at her private apartments and proposed an expedition to the town to see the cathedral; the little roccoco opera-house built by the Grand Duke Francis Augustus; the fairy-tale jumble of tumble-down tower and court and peaked roof that constituted the Old Palace now used as the administrative buildings of the state as well as barracks for its miniature army; and the celebrated gate-house prison wherein were assembled such instruments of executive governance as thumb-screws, racks, headsman's swords, and scalping machines.

Anne Louise appreciated her afternoon. Albert talked intelligently on history, and art, and architecture: the tinted clay busts of great composers in the vestibule of the opera led to a battle — which she enjoyed — on the question of the rise of the Romantic School in music. Afterwards they had tea — chaperoned by Miss Talfourd — in royal privacy at Perponcher's, and watched the good Ehrenbergers promenade on the ramparts under lime trees humming with bees. Incidentally she there discovered a note in one of her gloves which caused her considerable thought when she was able to read it later.

Albert remained, at her invitation, in the Chinese Withdrawing-room until it was time to dress for dinner. He seated himself at a pianoforte, which was ordinarily hidden from view — presumably as being too secular an instrument — by an immense screen of stamped and gilded leather, and played snatches from Schubert, and Weber, and Meyerbeer to illustrate his arguments of the afternoon. Afterwards he sang in a low rather sweet voice some of the more sentimental *lieder*.

Miss Talfourd, writing home to Sister Sophy in Nottinghamshire a day or two later, said:

'There can be no question, my dearest, but that *My little Princess* has made a *capture*, although I greatly fear that it will not do her any good. Prince Albert of Saxe-Coburg-Gotha, who, according to common report, is to marry Queen Victoria — *when* she decides to wed, and *if* she does — is staying here on a short visit to the Grand Duchess. He is quite definitely *épris de* A.L. Everyone has spoken of him as a perfect *Iceberg*, particularly with the Ladies. But *with us* he is Animated, Amusing, Lively, Interesting — and yet the very module of correct behaviour and you may be sure that I watch with the eyes of a *Dragon*. We have the *jolliest* times. I am sure that Her Majesty, even if she has decided to be a second Queen Elizabeth as everyone says, would create what poor dear Charles used to term in his slangy but expressive way "*a terrible rumpus*" if she knew What Is Going On here. I do not think A.L.'s *Heart* is affected: She likes his company, his conversation, his friendship, but *no more*. She said to me this morning, "It is a change to talk to an intelligent man. Albert is the first I have met since I left Elsinore." I suppose she was thinking about that *extraordinary* creature

Mr. Tempest, of whom I have told you, and about whom she often talks.

'Stockings here are atrociously dear . . .'

One morning, on Albert's suggestion, they went riding through the columned labyrinth of the woods about the castle, until they emerged upon a narrow white road, which ran to the frontier — and freedom — between a wall of trees and steeply sloping meadows where the scented grass had been cut and lay in swathes in the sun, ash-coloured against the green-gold stubble. His equerry, Ottilie Dedel — no horsewoman — and the grooms, were far behind.

Anne Louise reined up. She straightened her shoulders, and looked along the valley, so golden after the darkling forest. There was no living soul in sight, although someone distant and unseen was whistling very sweetly, and an invisible dog barked, and the thin spire of man-made smoke mounted to the intensity of the blue sky from a thicket on the opposing hill.

'Albert,' she said — and he knew from her tone that she would say something of supreme importance — 'Albert, suppose I were to set spur to my horse and gallop away to freedom, would you ride after me — would you help to hunt me down?'

He studied her as she sat there on her grey mare. She wore a dark blue riding-habit: her tall hat with its absurd little veil hanging down behind was a trifle to the back of her head. She looked to him extra-ordinarily gallant, and adventurous, and young. To his imagination the ghostly towering pillars of the pines behind her had become the immense bars of a cage from which she had just escaped. His youth answered hers —

'Ride after you? Ride after you? . . . Why, Anne Louise, I would give the world to ride *with* you . . . Half of me at any rate would give the world . . . perhaps the best half! And the other half would stay reined in here, watching till you were out of sight, and praying for your escape.'

'*That* half of you — the Coburg half — would not hinder me? Would not obstruct? Would not think it its duty . . .? Would perhaps do a little to help if it were not itself compromised?'

'*That*' half of him had dwindled until it was in danger of vanishing as he answered with two words —

'Now? . . . Yes!'

And had a pang to think that perhaps in a moment she might be gone for ever from his life.

Her grey eyes were very honest as she answered him.

'It's for to-morrow . . . I'm to vanish during the State Ball. They asked me to make use of you . . . the people who are arranging everything. I could have done so without you knowing anything. But now I like you I couldn't do it without telling you.'

She saw the tiniest shadow — less than a shadow, perhaps — of suspicion cross his face; and smiled.

'Remember that I needn't have told you! . . . And have I used any allurements to win you to conspiracy? You cannot accuse me of having been particularly seductive!'

Recalling her chill response to his early approaches, his brow cleared and he, too, smiled.

Riding back, a little out of earshot of the rest, she told him something of the history of the past few months — of the escape from Severall; the disastrous journey that ended in Seven's house of Judgment; of the *Joan Dearlove*; of Seven himself, and Daniel, and Washy, and Captain Pedder.

'That fellow Tempest ought to be horse-whipped,' declared Albert, clutching his riding-crop the tighter.

'I hated him once,' she said, 'but now I know there was no personal feeling in what he did. As he had been trained for command so he would have me trained. So he would have dealt with — Victoria, if he had had the chance!'

He wondered whether Victoria would have survived the education. For a moment he toyed with fascinating speculations as to what would have happened had the Queen of England been kidnapped and sent an ocean journey in the steerage of an emigrant ship.

'He said that no one had the right to govern who had no personal knowledge of the life of the governed. He asked if I thought that a childhood spent in the seclusion of a palace was fitting education for the governance of millions of people who slept four in a bed, died of starvation in the streets, worked twelve hours a day and more, and had no possible escape from their misery except through the gin bottle.'

'He sounds extremely Radical!'

'If I had been going to marry a king, or a grand duke, or had been a sovereign in my own right, I think what he did would have made me a much better queen or whatever it might be!'

He seemed to be about to say something, and then thought better of it.

'I am certain, too, that if he knew about me now he would come and help.' She meditated for an instant. 'He wouldn't come for *mes beaux yeux*. Or out of chivalry. He would come from anger at having failed in a thing he had undertaken to do. Because he failed in a contract. He was like that. He was the proudest man I have ever known.'

'He was well-born?'

'His grandmother was hanged for theft. He was illegitimate. So was his father.'

'Good God!' said Albert, shaken to the core: he always was at any mention of sexual irregularity.

'How I hated him! We were both such very proud superior persons. I can see him now, looking at me through half-closed eyes, with his head a little bent, and the beginnings of derision on his face. Just despising me because I was born a princess, and proud. As I despised him for being born a bastard, and proud. Then after a while I began to see things from his point of view — I wonder if he will ever see mine? — to realize how his achievements had justified a pride which was only demonstrated if aroused by some baseless pride like mine. For when he wasn't with me he seemed to be the simplest, most considerate, and least proud of men. That rather hurt me, I think . . . If anything *should* go wrong on Tuesday, will you try to get his help for me?'

CHAPTER VII

SENSATIONAL OCCURRENCES AT A STATE BALL

THE State Ball took place on the next night.

More dusty servants, more dusty old ladies, more dusty old gentlemen than ever, scurried about the melancholy immensity of the stone warren of Ehrenberg Castle, engaged in incomprehensible preparations.

A single string of fairy-lights was set to adorn the iron palisade that caged the Court of Honour, the rim of its dreary fountain, and — somewhat sparsely — the length of the great avenue.

Neighbouring royalty was invited, and the entire social world of the Grand Duchy. The two fashionable hairdressers in the town were engaged six-deep, and no carriage was to be had for love or money at the posting-establishments. The provision of the buffet supper taxed the resources of Monsieur Perponcher; and a number of other similar establishments — less well able to stand the financial strain — wistfully provided enormous supplies of delicacies against problematical payment.

It was on the morning of the ball that Mr. Cobbold paid his respects again to the Duchess of Limburg. He had brought with him the promised volume of Ogden's sermons.

As he was about to enter the chilly precincts of her sanctuary, Prince Albert came out: he stood to one side with a profound bow that hid the transformation of his face from an angel's to that of a malevolent fairy.

Anne Louise was standing at one of the tall windows, looking out on lawns that were baking brown and yellow under the furnace of the sky. The distant vista of the lake showed something that did not appear to be water, but to be a sheet of white-hot metal. No breath of wind disturbed the woods. Miss Talfourd, bespectacled, in the remotest darkest corner of the room was fanning red face and bottle-green bosom and reading a three-week's old copy of the London *Morning Chronicle* — a paper of which she did not entirely approve.

He said, after respectful greeting —

'You understood the last note you received at Perponcher's?'

She had. At least she thought so.

'The wording was hardly such as I should myself have chosen,' he explained rather acidly, 'but Mr. Hallett insisted that if it was in any hand or any phraseology but his, you might become suspicious. Also it was compounded — that is the only word to describe the manufacture — by the full committee at which the small boy appeared to be a competent member!'

Anne Louise smiled. She could picture the proceedings — and sympathize with Mr. Cobbold. The letter had been more than usually mis-spelled and incoherent.

'What is vital,' he said in a low voice, 'is that you should have approached the Prince? You have?'

She nodded.

'He will do what he can. But of course he must not be implicated in any way.'

'Of course not, Highness. All that he has to do is to escort you from the ball-room. No suspicions will be raised by your absence if you are seen with him. His story is: — You felt faint from the heat. He accompanied you onto one of the balconies. You felt no better and asked him to take you to your apartments. He did so; rang for your woman, waited for her to come; as she did not — the bell-wire will be severed — returned to find your ladies! . . . Even a quarter of an hour's start is all we need!'

'The sentries — the inspection at the gates — the —'

He interrupted her.

'Everything has been arranged. Everything! All that is essential is for the time-schedule to be kept. Your Highness must be at the door of your suite at twelve o'clock precisely. The rendezvous at the cross-roads beyond the ruined chapel is for one.'

'Midnight? . . . One o'clock?' said Anne Louise. 'But the note I had the other day said I was to be at my door at one o'clock and that we should get to the cross-roads by a quarter to two!'

'We have had to advance the times to fit in the first stage of the journey properly.'

The solemn brass clock, domed like a cathedral, which stood on the chartulary chest showed that it was a trifle after eleven o'clock of the forenoon. Thirteen hours to go! In thirteen hours' time she would be exactly where she was all those aeons ago when she had sat waiting with Lovell in the yellow chariot in the stable-court at Severall!

Miss Talfourd's fan had dropped to the floor. The newspaper — rustling — followed it.

'What shall I take with me?' Anne Louise asked. She remembered, absurdly enough, that companion of her earlier travels, the invaluble Cyclopaedia of Mr. Partington.

'Nothing,' he answered, 'As a matter of fact a sub-committee of three has the matter of your outfit in hand . . . while I worked out plans of rather greater importance!' He smiled elfishly, and Anne Louise asked a question with raised eyebrow.

'The sub-committee was presided over by "Miss Perp" — how the young woman can bear being called so, I don't know! Its treasurer was Mr. Hallett. The boy Daniel was a very active and interested member.' He giggled and turned over the volume of sermons in his hand. 'They have bought everything for the female toilette that it is humanly possible to buy in Ehrenberg . . . everything! The boy insisted on personally selecting some very intimate articles of apparel for your Highness! . . . He apparently likes bright colours!'

He had an after-thought — 'A chaperone has been even engaged for your flight. An elderly and romantic-minded Englishwoman who has asked no questions. She will be waiting for you in the carriage.'

He was about to go when she asked him —

'You are coming to the ball yourself to-night?'

He nodded.

'I shall stay long enough to make sure that you have got away . . . Then I must busy myself laying false trails!'

'Thank you very, very much for all you have done, Mr. Cobbold. I am very grateful. If you will later tell me how I can show my gratitude — '

She gave him her hand. He bent very low over it before he touched her fingers with his lips. She chided herself that she recalled the ragged yellow teeth behind the cupid's bow of the mouth.

Miss Talfourd recovered consciousness with a sudden snort.

'In the interest of our discussion, Highness, I had almost forgotten poor Ogden,' said Mr. Cobbold evenly. 'Here it is! There is much of value and comfort in it . . . especially in time of perplexity. "That which was written was upright, even words of truth"!' . . .

There was a fanfare of silver trumpets from the gallery high up under the lofty roof.

At the proud notes the immense folding doors were flung wide by tall pages in the grand-ducal livery of scarlet and blue, and all the silent assemblage rustled and shivered and swayed into curtsey and bow. The sound was that of the dance of dead leaves; the sight that of a flower bed doing homage to a little wind.

Preceded by a backward-stepping chamberlain with long white rod of office, the Grand Duchess surged slowly on between the ranks of her guests, toward a large gilded elbow chair on a crimson dais backed by a crimson cloth-of-state and under a bullion-fringed canopy of the same colour. There were a number of other smaller golden chairs upon the wide platform.

Anne Louise, following in the leisurely procession of princes and princesses, was conscious of the splendour of the pageantry, but conscious only after the fashion of a traveller indifferently regarding hedgerow and field from the window of a swiftly moving coach. In three hours' time the gorgeous gowns and uniforms, the jewels and the orders would still be coruscant beneath the great glittering chandeliers that hung from the roof like stalactites of glass; the halberdiers would still be at their posts beside the dais; the Court Chamberlain in his gold-brocaded coat would still be standing behind the Grand Duchess's chair, holding his gold-knobbed staff — but not for her. In three hours' time —

She found herself on the dais, replying with banality to the banalities of a blond small-headed prince in a tight blue uniform who snuffled between every other word. But while the Duchess of Limburg, in orange satin, was making polite small-talk, Anne Louise, the fugitive-to-be, was asking herself such important and interesting questions as 'Shall I have time to put on some thicker shoes?'

She realized suddenly that the band in the high gallery had struck up, and that Albert was bowing before her. He wore the dark green Coburg uniform coat with heavy epaulettes and golden collar and sash, and white silk breeches and stockings. He was a perfect fashion-plate of a prince — and just as expressionless.

With him she opened the ball — a stately finger-tip-touching ceremony of a quadrille, during which they barely exchanged a word. After that she danced with Ernest of Saxe-Coburg-Gotha — a clumsy edition of his brother; with the small-headed prince; with a fattish, shabby, good-natured prince — the Heir-Apparent, she was told; with a thin general; with the British Minister; the non-royal partners being collected by the Court Chamberlain and produced for her, after consultation with the Grand Duchess.

She was glad when Albert presented himself before her again, as the violins swayed into the latest of Lanner's valses. As she went down the crimson-carpeted steps of the dais she glanced at the clock set in the balustrade of the musicians' gallery. It was half-past eleven o'clock.

Albert danced well, but without any token of enjoyment. Anne Louise felt sure he did everything well that he set his mind to, however much he may have disliked it. He said no word until they were half way down the great ball-room, and then suddenly spoke in a very low voice that was barely audible, even to her, amid the shuffling of feet, the murmur of conversation, and the wailing of the strings.

'You already feel the heat a little! . . . I want to talk to you, and there is very little time left. Let us go to the private buffet and out onto the balcony!'

The private buffet was a small white-panelled ante-chamber reserved for Highnesses and their immediate circle. The door was immediately by the dais. As Anne Louise and Albert approached, the Grand Duchess emerged. Her immense crimson bulk and vast white face filled the doorway, and hid her escort, an emaciated elderly princeling who had made an honest man of himself late in life by marrying — in approved German fashion — his plump young niece.

The buffet was deserted — had apparently been little frequented up to that time. There were, however, two empty champagne bottles on the long table spread with wines and viands, two empty tumblers, a seriously depleted bottle of sixty-year-old Courvoisier, and a somewhat dazed expression on the face of the scarlet-coated blue-breeched attendant.

'Cousin Theresa's third visit in less than two hours!' said Albert as they stepped out onto the balcony. 'I am certain no one else has come in here yet. Do you suppose she and that fellow have managed two whole bottles of champagne?'

'I should think so,' said Anne Louise. 'And even then the old lady will be behind her usual ration, if what Ottilie Dedel tells me is correct.'

'Good God!'

'A man I know . . . the father of a man I knew . . . used to drink a bottle of brandy every night of his life, and was none the worse for it,' said Anne Louise, anxious to show her knowledge of the world. She recollected Tog imparting that information while he knitted in his queer glassy den, and Daniel squatted by the fire, and rum punch was a-making, and they had been studying the fascinating problem of the internal combustion of habitual drunkards in the pages of Mr. Partington's Cyclopaedia — Would Cousin Theresa eventually explode and disintegrate into fatty ashes? — and Seven had come in and slammed his hat brim uppermost on the table. In perhaps an hour's time she would see Daniel: would she ever see Tog again — or Seven?

Albert had shaken off the topic of intemperance.

He said —

'I have been exploring this balcony. We can go along it as far as the music-room which is unlighted. The door opens into the corridor practically next to your suite . . . You've only half an hour more!'

342

The balcony was extraordinarily dark, for the castle rose like a cliff above, cloaking it in shadow. The ascending moon — invisible to them — had not yet topped the roofs, but the blackness of the sky was paling and silvering. Far below a few fairy-lights twinkled. Not a breath of wind stirred. The heat seemed little less than that of the day.

Anne Louise did not answer him at once. She stood holding fast to the balustrade as though to keep a grip on reality, and gazing onto the obscurity of the woods wherein already awaited her, perhaps, the magic chariot of freedom.

'In half an hour's time!' she said at last in an ecstacy. And again — 'In less than half an hour!'

'You have no qualms?'

'None!'

He was standing very upright, his hands behind his back. His face, turned toward her, was a mere blur; but something told her that his regard was one of great kindness. He said —

'Stockmar sent for me this evening. He told me what had been planned for you! I had had some inkling before, but was not certain . . . I am glad that you are going . . . *now!*'

Although she knew that in little more than thirty minutes she would have escaped for ever from that dusty mountain of hewn stone — from the constraint of body and soul which it represented — yet even then she shivered as one suddenly chilled.

'What is the plan?' she asked.

'To marry you to the Grand Duke — to Francis! A marriage in name only!'

'Francis?' she said incredulously. 'Francis? . . . But he is mad! It can't be!'

And dropped her fan with a clatter to the stone floor of the balcony. He stooped and picked it up before continuing —

'It is to be announced to-night — just before the main buffet doors are opened a little after twelve!'

Was it only twenty-nine minutes now? Even so there were twenty-nine minutes in which to be coldly furious, to be panic-stricken at the narrowness of escape.

'Oh God!' she cried. 'Why should they? It is a horrible thing! . . . Marriage with a madman! . . . With a hunchback! . . . No one would even try to imagine such a horror! . . . You must be wrong! . . . Why has no one said anything to me?'

And thought of chill Leopold who mated the Coburg breed like any farmer for his own frigid purposes — in Austria — in France — in

Germany — in Portugal — in England. Of the Grand Duchess, whose history was an abomination; whose mind was a corruption; whose soul did not exist.

'It is true,' said Albert. 'It is quite — quite true. I am certain ... Ehrenberg is a key-point strategically between North and South Germany. The Grand Duchess has hitherto come down neither for Austria nor for Prussia. She's been waiting for the highest bid. Uncle Leopold has always favoured Austria: he has his reasons for wanting to stand well with the Imperial Court. You are immeasurably the greatest heiress in all Europe. So he buys Ehrenberg for Austria, and Austria for himself, with you and your money.'

'How could they be sure that I should not make public protest?'

'Ask yourself if you could stand up before a thousand people and give Cousin Theresa the lie! ... In cold blood!'

She thought for a moment. Her quick imagination pictured the scene — herself in orange satin dress standing beside the seated Grand Duchess, one hand imprisoned on an arm of the gilded chair under large white fingers glittering with diamonds: she saw old von Stielerberg, the Court Chamberlain, standing sideways at the edge of the dais, holding his white rod of office as though it were a bishop's pastoral staff: saw a jumble of faces and uniforms and gowns and plumes and jewels and long noses and projecting teeth and flat noses and wigs and bald heads and staring-staring eyes — a caricaturist's nightmare of a crowd. She was honest even with herself. She knew that she could not have publicly given Cousin Theresa the lie. She said so.

'What do you think of your uncle now?' she added. 'First he tries to marry me to a blind man, and now to a lunatic ... Francis has not been seen in public at all for twenty years. No doctor can do him any good ... Perhaps they don't want a cure!'

He could not abandon in direct speech either his sense of duty or his honesty. He said nothing but —

'I am glad ... glad that you are going. Pray God you escape!'

'To escape from this ...' she indicated the black bulk of her prison looming over them with the merest backward jerk of her head, as she spoke in a low tense voice — 'will be something beyond words. To escape the foul thing they propose for me ... to escape to beggary ... to a hovel ... to the steerage of an emigrant ship ... to death ... would be an escape to Paradise!'

The great bell of the castle clock tolled the quarter thunderously over the song of the violins and the susurration of dancing feet and swaying dresses and rippling speech.

344

'Can we go, *now*?' she asked eagerly. 'I must change my shoes, and get a cloak.'

He felt a sudden pang at the thought that in a quarter of an hour's time he might be saying good-bye to her for ever.

'Let us show ourselves in the buffet window so that people shall see that we are here, before we go.'

Accordingly they stood for a few moments on the threshold of the tall french window, watching Ernest guzzle champagne with an exceptionally pretty girl — pretty girls were always poor Ernest's trouble, and eventually his downfall; watching Cousin Theresa's old crony guzzle old brandy in company with a scarecrow princess who looked like a parrot and was so poor that she was popularly supposed to live upon bird-seed.

The angular crimson and gold figure of the Court Chamberlain appeared in the doorway. He spied the figures in the window, and made his way to them bowing at each step as he crossed that sacred threshold, as if it were peopled not merely by guzzling royalty in the flesh but by the ghosts of generations of princes who had withdrawn there for deep refreshing.

He approached Anne Louise. Albert's supporting arm felt her tremble.

'Your Highness!' he began. 'Her Highness the Grand Duchess begs your presence in the ball-room at fifteen minutes past midnight, if your Highness would be so gracious.'

Highness was feeling the heat, but would be so gracious. Even as he backed formally from the presence, she turned to Albert, and her eyes were bright with fear, and her face suddenly very white.

'*Now*, Albert! *Now!*'

They stood for a moment more in the light that streamed out from the window. They receded from view: were swallowed up in shadows.

The Grand Duchess, who had been watching the dancing with a fixed and glassy stare and a wavering benevolent smile, had not been able for some time to recall why she was present at this function — or why, indeed, she had given it. With the stroke of the quarter past the hour, it all came back to her — Stockmar — Anne Louise — poor Francis! . . . Well, well, well! She had intended to speak to the child first, to give her Leopold's letter; but as she had no more say in the business than Francis, it was of no great matter that one had forgotten. An old woman could not be expected to remember everything! The child should think herself fortunate to have a bridegroom she need never see or concern herself about. What opportunities! Lucky, lucky girl! A proxy wedding; and Francis would sign the necessary documents and know no more about the business than the man-in-the-moon. The doctors said — as they had for twenty years — that he must not be disturbed by State affairs or even visited. Well, he hadn't been, and wouldn't be! . . . Everything would be for the best — especially Ehrenberg finances! . . . Now she had better get the thing over. She could always manage her voice; and as for her legs she could remain sitting.

Von Stielerberg, one tuft of hair standing on end like that of a cockatoo, posted himself at the edge of the dais, sideways so that he should not present his back to his sovereign. He raised a rheumaticky hand for silence as if bestowing a blessing.

'S-s-sh!' said the uniforms and gowns nearest the galaxy of golden chairs upon the crimson carpet; and the sound travelled across the crowded room carrying silence in its wake, until all the assembly were standing mute, staring expectantly at the heavy-faced old woman, the only seated figure in all the great room.

She had a big voice. It boomed the announcement across the room, accompanied by the customary platitudes — the glad assent of the lady's guardian, King Leopold — a mother's love — the blessing of the Almighty — love match — duty to the State. . . .

The condition of the Grand Duke Francis was no secret to anyone present, but after the first gasp of surprise a decorous hand-clapping echoed through the room.

Mr. Cobbold, standing withdrawn by himself in a corner whence he could watch clock and dais, clapped louder than any. He could not restrain himself from delighted giggles — from chuckles — from open laughter. What a gift! What a surprise packet! How beautifully this new piece fitted into his pattern! His face was that of a juvenile fallen angel.

He must amend what he had written. It would be quickest told in postscripts. He looked at the clock — twenty-three minutes past the hour: he had just time! He saw von Stielerberg bend with a worried expression to the Grand Duchess's ear. He could have screamed, could have shrieked with mirth, could have rolled on the polished floor hugging himself with unbearable pleasure . . . He went with dancing step about his unholy business.

CHAPTER VIII

KISSES FOR MR. HALLETT

THE cathedral clock was striking midnight as Washy said his whispered farewells to Miss Perp and Daniel at the private gate of the cherry-tree garden of the Establishment Perponcher. The wicket opened on a dark little lane unillumined as yet by the moon. Samuel stood a short way off at the bridles of a couple of horses, and a pistol bulged either side-pocket of the light riding-coat which Washy wore.

'I can't think why you want to go now, Washy-wash!' complained Daniel. 'You'll be there at least an hour too soon. And old Cobbold particularly said . . .'

This argument, coupled with pleas that he should be allowed to accompany the rescue party, had been raised by Daniel in the early forenoon, and had continued ever since. Washy shook a sage and decided head:

'Cobbold's not in charge of this expedition. I am. And I mean to be there in plenty of time to prepare for any eventuality . . . You've got to stay and look after Miss Perp until I come back and fetch you!'

Miss Perp stood very close to Mr. Hallett in the dark entry.

'Daniel!' she said suddenly, 'I have left a silver flask with cognac in it in the sitting-room. I forgot it. It may be useful. Will you fetch it — please?'

As the gentle patter of his feet died away along the garden path, she put a hand up to Washy's coat.

'Monsieur Washy,' she said. 'You *will* come back?'

'Of course I will . . . I've got to fetch Daniel,' he answered in a matter-of-fact way.

'Is that all you will come back for?'

He stood looking down on her pearly face and shining eyes. It dawned on him at this instant of parting, how lovely she was — how desirable she was — how (and he hesitated to admit it even to himself) attainable.

'You will not come back,' said Miss Perp. 'You will ride away with this beautiful princess of yours, and kiss her and marry her, and live happy ever after. Is it not so?'

He shook his head.

'Sure, she would never dream of me!' he answered her. 'For me she is like a fairy-tale princess, as you say. But like all fairies you can't touch her, or kiss her, or marry her! — That sounds poetry, but it's true . . . I don't think of her in the way you say at all. I think of her like something lovely and good in a vision. Like going to church. I can worship her, and admire her, and love her, without any hope of ever doing more than touching her hand — without ever touching her hand. It sounds silly, I guess?'

'No,' said Miss Perp. 'It doesn't! . . . She will not even kiss you her thanks?'

He shook his head again.

'Washy!' she said in a very low voice — in plea, in urgent prayer. 'Washy!' And no more. Her hands tightened upon the lapels of his coat as though to pull his face down to hers.

'Why, Perps!' said Washy; and his lips met hers as Daniel's tiptoe tread sounded along the path. . . .

But Washy was fated, after all, to be kissed by a princess that night.

For barely an hour later Anne Louise kneeled beside his dead body on an empty moonlit road running through the dark forest. There was a pistol in his lifeless hand, and blood dabbled his ruffled fair hair.

She kissed him on the lips as one kissing something very holy.

She did not attempt to move him from the spot where he had fallen, for fear that she should make of that gallant figure but a dishevelled and shapeless heap.

She brought herself to search his pockets — found a purse of gold. He would have wished her to have it: and with it and his pistol in her hand she stood for a little looking down on him, the tears streaming unheeded on to her cheeks.

'Good-bye, dear Washy,' she said, and turned out of the moonlight, and plunged back again into the blackness of the forest from which she had but just emerged.

Although so short a time had elapsed between the two kisses bestowed on Mr. Hallett, yet it had been crowded with events that appeared to happen with the shocking speed of a nightmare, and to succeed one another with the continuous precision of the ranks of a marching army.

The first full and unexpurgated narrative was told by Prince Albert of Saxe-Coburg-Gotha a week later, when the apparent insanity of the episode was shown to be a deplorable sanity.

Under his escort Anne Louise had left the ball-room, and gone to her apartments to get shoes and cloak. The prince had said good-bye and turned to go when someone flung himself fiercely at his back. Before he could call out, a gag had been thrust between his teeth; his hands had been fastened behind him, and he was being hurried down strange dark lanes and alleys within the castle. It was so swiftly done that all three stages of his capture appeared to be simultaneous.

It had struck him as curious that they met no one on their course, although from various entries there came the sounds of bustle, and voices, and the clatter of dishes. He was certain that they passed the great kitchen because of the bright red light that beat on to a dark passage through a door that was just ajar, and because of the mingled smells of cooking.

They emerged into a small dimly-lighted court excavated in the great bulk of the castle. A tilt-cart with a hood over the driver's seat stood before the door. All along the wall were ranged tubs and barrels full of refuse. The smell was indescribable, and the flag-stones slippery with cabbage-stalks and other débris of the kitchens.

In the light of the lantern set above the door he saw that two of his captors wore the dirty white cotton coats of kitchen porters, and that a third was habited in the crimson and blue livery of a royal lackey. Then he was suddenly pulled backward into a large wicker basket and the lid clapped shut on top of him. In the next instant it had been projected into the interior of the covered cart, and the swill tubs apparently were being loaded after it.

It was the fact that he should thus have been manhandled by scullions which above all angered him — the fact that the wearer of princely coronet, the bearer of a coat-of-arms with so many quarterings, should have been tumbled by kitchen knaves into a wash-basket like so much dirty linen!

The loading operations were still proceeding when he was aware of fresh voices, low and urgent. He caught two sentences —

'Your Highness is Müller's sister, Lieschen, who has been smuggled into the castle to catch a glimpse of the dresses! . . . But it is unlikely that any questions will be asked.'

And then they had started on a nightmare journey. He was unable to give any accurate idea of its duration. His discomfort had been so great that he might very conceivably over-estimate it! . . . Perhaps it lasted half an hour — perhaps an hour . . . Eventually, however, the jolting ceased, and after a while someone opened the basket and roughly helped him out. The moment he set foot to ground the cart was rapidly driven off.

He found himself at a forest cross-ways, very dusty and white, between black precipices of fir-tree under the high moon.

Halted as closely in the shadows of the road-side as possible was a large closed carriage with four horses, the postilions at their heads. Anne Louise stood by the carriage door, her wrist being held by a man in dark attire whom he had never seen before. Confronting her was another, small and exquisitely dapper, with a flushed dusky face; who bowed as he talked, and scraped as he talked, and gesticulated with small hands — wrist-banded with white — as he talked. He had seen him once before, and knew him to be the Judas Iscariot, Cobbold.

'Your Highness will perceive,' Mr. Cobbold was remarking in a gay fluting voice, 'that I have been at some pains to provide you with a more acceptable lover than that planned for you by your guardian and the Grand Duchess of Ehrenberg!'

Anne Louise looked round as he spoke, and saw Albert for the first time.

'Albert!' she said in a breathless voice. 'What does this mean? What . . .?'

Cobbold broke in —

'His Highness is as much mystified as yourself. He will eventually, I think, be as pleased as your Highness. With every respect to her Majesty the Queen of England, there can be no comparison between the bride *I* have chosen for him and the bride of his *uncle's* choice!'

Some unseen person behind pushed Albert toward the group in obedience to a gesture by Cobbold.

Anne Louise looked from Cobbold to the man who held her slim wrist, to Albert with his hands strapped behind his back, to the postilions, to two men who stood a little farther off with the reins of four or five restless horses looped over their arms. She appeared to be trying to convince herself that this was not reality but some nightmare from which she would immediately wake.

'Are you mad, Mr. Cobbold?' she said at length; but her tone was that of one who was only half-convinced that she herself was not mad.

'Far from it, Highness,' he answered. 'I am deputizing for the little God of Love! I am Mercury! I am Cupid! But I am not mad! . . . It is all very simple. I have taken pity on you. "Here", say I in my capacity of *deus ex machina*, "are a handsome young couple about to be forced into loveless matches! They were positively created for one another. They yearn for one another's embraces. And one another's embraces they shall have! In wedlock or out of it!" As you are perhaps, aware, I am in Holy Orders. A little ceremony can be arranged as a preliminary to the billing and cooing! Or not — just as you prefer. I am glad to say that I am broadminded!'

'This foul joke . . .' began Anne Louise; but Cobbold interrupted with —

'I am glad to assure your Highness that this is no joke . . . The carriage waits. The love-nest has been made ready — very secure and very secret! The escort is here to see that the love-birds attain it. The warming-pan is in the bed. It will soon only remain to recite the epithalamium and draw the curtains!'

Albert had stood fretting at his gag, anger at abduction heightened by grave doubts regarding the cleanliness of the handkerchief that muzzled him. Now at Cobbold's insolence he forgot all else. He sprang in attack — a foolish gesture for which his guard was prepared: was tripped up even as he leaped; fell heavily face downward in the dust; was hauled to his feet at once, and held. And Cobbold went on, ignoring the incident —

'The spot I have chosen is so secluded and remote that you need fear no rude intrusion on your transports, whatever search may be made. But I greatly fear that wide publicity will inevitably follow your Highnesses' decision to risk all for love. It is on account of this, and because no lady's reputation will survive a night or so spent locked alone in a bedroom with an ardent and good-looking young man, that I should recommend her Highness to consider seriously whether the little ceremony I suggested should not take place. It would make an honest woman of her — Oh, hideous phrase! — in the eyes of the world!'

'If . . .' said Albert, 'I can ever lay my hands upon your filthy little carcase I will shred the flesh off it. I will . . .' But no word of his mouthing escaped the gag, and his efforts at speech merely served vastly to amuse Mr. Cobbold.

'Tut!' said the little man, smiling. 'Tut-tut! The excitement of anticipation overwhelms you. We must go. Already desire grows high. I can see that her Highness is recalling the beautiful verses from the Song of Solomon:

"A bundle of myrrh is my well-beloved unto me; he shall lie all night betwixt my breasts
My beloved is unto me as a cluster of camphire in the vineyards of En-gedi.' "

Once again Albert hurled himself upon the little man, tearing himself from the grip on his strapped wrists, and bringing Cobbold to the ground beneath him. For a moment they rolled together in the dust, and then the other extricated himself, rose as nimbly as a cat, and fell a-kicking the prostrate prince, screaming with anger.

It was at this moment — Albert (green and gold uniform quenched in dust) rolling in the road by the off front wheel of the carriage; Cobbold with distorted face viciously kicking at him; all the satellites turned to watch with detached interest; Anne Louise straining in the grasp of her captor — that the tempo of the scene suddenly quickened to cataract speed. There was an explosion of events.

A young man suddenly emerged, whistling, from the dark wall of forest opposite. He was followed by a groom, leading a pair of horses.

Albert, lying on his back, could see him standing fore-shortened in the middle of the road in the intense brightness of the moon, tall hat a little on the back of his head, and mouth ajar as he stared.

There was immediate and dead silence, broken only by the jingle of harness and the fidgeting of horses.

'What . . .?' began the newcomer.

'Washy! Help!' cried Anne Louise, suddenly twisting herself out of her guardian's grasp in that moment of surprise, and running toward him.

A pistol appeared with surprising suddenness in Hallett's hand. He waved the girl past him to the shelter of the forest, and walked the few yards to the wordless group by the carriage. Dark-cloaked, Anne Louise was already invisible among the trees when he reached the silent men and spoke.

'What does all this mean, Mr. Cobbold?' he asked.

'It means . . .' said Mr. Cobbold, hand at the skirt of his tight-waisted riding-coat. 'It means that you are an hour early for your engagement here . . . It means — ' And he was utterly unable to deny himself the melodrama ' — Death!'

With that word he fired from his hip, and the young man had fallen backward without a word or a cry while still the forest echoed to the violence of the sound.

There was a sort of sigh and rustle among those who saw the murder. Cobbold licked his lips with a pointed tongue tip. He tossed the useless pistol into the carriage, and stepped forward a pace from its shadow into the moonlight. As he did so he levelled another pistol in his left hand and fired again.

Hallett's groom had already turned to fly, casting loose the led horses. He swayed clawing at the air when the bullet struck him, sagged to a heap on the road, toppled over into the ditch.

'A good shot!' said Mr. Cobbold approvingly. 'Thirty yards if it is an inch! . . . Now find that girl!'

'I didn't bargain for murder!' said the man who had held Albert. His voice was shrill and frightened. 'I didn't bargain for murder! I didn't have nuthin' to do with it! And I ain't goin' to have no more! Wot about you, Simmonds?'

'That was plain bloody murder . . .'

'Nonsense!' said Cobbold, and he sniggered as he spoke. 'Nonsense, you bloody milksops. We can't afford any witnesses . . . Find that girl, and look sharp about it, Smith! . . . Simmonds, help me get this fellow into the carriage!'

'Plain bloody murder,' repeated Simmonds. 'And plain bloody murder I won't abide! And I reckon these Dutchies won't either! My neck's my own, and I ain't goin' to risk it for no one!'

The men with the horses had come up, and one of the postilions deserted his place. Albert rolled under the carriage out of the way of heavy feet and hoofs: he had found that the strap about his wrists had somehow broken, and so was able to release himself from the gag. There was a confusion of speech, partly English and partly German — curses, high-pitched threats, angry protests. Then followed a sudden scuffle, and someone ejaculated fiercely —

'No, you don't . . . By God, you don't!'

And Simmonds said —

'It's all right, pal, the little bastard only had a brace! He ain't got nuthin' to fire. Pile 'im in, and let's go!'

The carriage quivered on its springs over Albert's head with a renewal of struggle in its interior, and the battle was still going on when the vehicle moved off, and he found himself lying on his back staring up at the moon. Another moment and the entire cavalcade was out of sight.

He got to his feet, dusted tatterdemalion uniform, ascertained that Washy and his man were unquestionably dead, picked up a small purple leather portfolio which Cobbold had been carrying, went to the forest verge and called Anne Louise's name — at first in a low voice, and afterwards more loudly. But no response came from the dark depths. To search for her by himself would be utterly hopeless. So he caught one of Washy's horses, and galloped furiously away.

It was not until some twenty minutes afterwards that Anne Louise had cautiously re-appeared. Her hiding-place had been in a thicket, overlooking a black and sullen pool in the denseness of the trees, too far for her to distinguish who had called.

CHAPTER IX

THE HOUSE BEYOND THE WORLD

EVEN in the chaos of her thoughts Anne Louise recalled the direction in which she must travel. Along the fringe of the forest she followed the moonlit road that led to the frontier and to freedom. The going was easy upon the carpet of pine-needles in the cloister of the great trees, darkly vaulted overhead, with arches of silver to the highway.

She was more afraid than she had ever been, more alone, and more sorrowful . . . A man had died in her cause — two men!

As she went cloaked and hooded through the forest, like a shadow within a shadow, she was overwhelmed and numbed as never before by the magnitude of disaster.

She had given Washy nothing but the affection of the sort she had bestowed on Daniel . . . and he had died for her! She had treated him as a sentimental boy . . . and he had been a knight errant! He had worn wonderful coats of exotic cut in blues and greens and violets, and sprigged waistcoats, and cravats that had not always been the perfect match . . . when he should have worn hauberk and helm!

For some reason she recalled Washy's saddened face at the discovery that one of his neck-cloths did not meet with approval. Then the tears suddenly streamed down her cheeks; she was shaken by an uncontrollable fit of sobbing; she abandoned herself to weeping.

She sat down at the foot of a tree to recover; and, when she felt better, assessed the situation.

The frontier could not be more than eight or nine miles away: therefore in three hours' time she ought to be in Bavaria. Washy's purse, on investigation, proved to contain twenty-five rix-dollars — more than one hundred pounds in English money: therefore she had nothing to worry about on the score of cash. She had Washy's pistol, too, which was loaded, judging from the fact that it was at half-cock and the percussion cap in place: therefore she was not utterly defenceless. The immediate objective was to get across the border, and find some friendly cottage, farm, or inn. Until then it was futile to make further plans: the one essential thing was to escape the vast dusty mausoleum of Ehrenberg, the huge old woman whose soul had corrupted before her body, the mad bridegroom, the fallen-angel face of Mr. Cobbold, the shadow of Uncle Leopold. To escape — even if it meant using the pistol on herself.

She put the purse in the bosom of her dress — and remembered Sarah Liddell as she did so: tore the wide hem off her under-petticoat, since she had no handkerchief; and then, with the pistol in her hand under her cloak, rose to her feet and journeyed on.

She ran — she walked — she stumbled — interminably through the forest as it darkened with the declining moon, and then as it grew grey with daybreak.

She was fatigued almost past endurance: in the haze that clouded her mind all sorts of reasonless pictures flashed — Seven encountering the stowaway Daniel in the *Joan Dearlove* after anchor had been weighed and the ship was curtseying under spread of sail to the sea; encountering him and laughing instead of blaspheming — Seven dragging the wet-faced man along the deck as if he had been a sack of rubbish — Seven's horrified reception of the embrace of Mrs. Horatio Vyvyan — Seven heaving the singed and dreadful body of Pedder from out of the very furnace mouth. Had she misjudged Seven as well? Was there something of knight errantry about him, too?

She toiled on mechanically, her eyes on the ground. . . .

Had she been walking for one hour — two hours? How long was it since she had stepped off the crimson dais to dance the opening quadrille with Albert? . . . What had happened to Albert? . . . What had been the motive behind Cobbold's extraordinary conspiracy? — For how should Anne Louise tell that she (once a pawn in the Belgian King's chill plans for England) had been used that night to further fierce conspiracy for Victoria's next heir, that half-blind brooding figure, the King of Hanover?

She went on. . . .

Had she been walking for two hours — three hours? How long was it since she had seen Washy lying dead in the road, face turned up to the moon, and pistol in his hand? . . . Why did not dead men shut their eyes? . . . Washy should have a tomb like any knight, in a chantry in some great church — should lie in alabaster effigy, hands folded in prayer, awaiting the Trumpet Call to the Last Tournament. There should be an inscription in Latin, or in French, the language of chivalry — 'Ici gît le Sieur Washington Hall . . .'

She nearly fell over a projecting root, and the stumble awakened her to a realization of the present — the chill silence and the sombre twilight of the great crypt of the forest; that the aisles of it stretched as far as the eye could see in every direction; that, somehow, she was lost. . . .

It was a long while later when she came to a region of much younger growth, where the shafts of the trees were slim and close together, the dark roof low overhead, and the ground full of rabbit burrows and strewn with dead twigs. A few tall foxgloves spattered the dusk, and in the distance a band of golden-green showed like the line of light through a trap-door that has been left ajar.

She dragged herself toward it; through knee-high fern and a high wall of bracken, into a slanting meadow above a valley lit by sunrise.

Far below a stream wound between trees that cast the long blue shadows of early morning. On the farther slope a few white farms nestled in hollows amid bright orchards or protected by dark copses; the grey smoke of them rose in thin spirals to a pale and cloudless sky. Beyond the valley wall rose far greater hills, rounded, purple with distance and scarred with bare patches of limestone as if the snows of winter yet lingered toward their crests.

A mile away, to Anne Louise's left, a ruined castle was outlined against the sunrise, flat as though cut out in cardboard. To her right a road sloped downward with the meadow, bordered by a high stone wall in which, mid-way, there was a door.

She stumbled toward it, driven on by the knowledge that she must find out where she was, and impelled, too, by the hope that here — just as well as anywhere else — might be obtained the help she eventually must secure.

The latch rattled and the door creaked as Anne Louise opened it.

A long smooth lawn, bisected by a flagged path, stretched to a low and friendly house with green shutters. There was a tall lime tree on either side of the path, and the high walls — for it was a very secret garden — were rich with white roses. The luminous shadows of early morning lay on the grass; sunrise shone in the upper windows; the tattle of birds was the only sound.

So withdrawn and still was the house, so secluded its garden, that, with the shutting of the door behind her, it was as if Anne Louise passed out of the world of conflict and of violence, and — indeed — of everyday things, into the close of fairydom. It was, perhaps, because of this that she threw back her hood and unclasped the cloak that had hidden her flame-coloured dress, as she stepped across grass frosted with dew.

The house door was shut, but to the left of it french windows were open on to the lawn that lapped the sills.

She entered without hesitation.

Entered a small room lined with books from floor to ceiling, but for a dark sea-scape in gilded frame over an English fireplace. A table of figured walnut stood in the midst of the thick Turkey carpet, and tapestried wing arm-chairs were set on either side of a grate filled with fir-cones. The room was bright with pale sunshine: from the subdued tapestry of its several thousand books a faint savour (perhaps that of old and fine leather) mingled with garden scents which came in on an inquisitive and whispering breeze.

Anne Louise sat down in one of the arm-chairs, very upright, the cloak fallen from off her shoulders, silver pistol incongruous on the shimmering stuff of her lap. She awaited the coming of her involuntary host or hostess . . . Presently her head nodded . . . Her hand released its clasp of the deadly thing which it had clutched so long . . . She was suddenly asleep. . . .

A long time passed.

A robin came to the threshold and looked in . . . A grave-faced man-servant, in a sleeved waistcoat of white entered, bearing a tray; perceived sleeping princess as he set his burden down upon the table; surveyed her with startled expression for an instant; withdrew on silent feet . . . So presently there came a little red-faced plump gentleman with very bright grey eyes, and scanty and ruffled grey hair, and vivid crimson silk dressing-gown — rather like the robin, he was, on the whole — who surveyed her, too. His bird-like glance travelled from the golden disorder of her ringlets and the pallor of the charming half-hidden face, to the pistol on her lap, to the dusty hem of that wonderful spreading gown of flame satin, to the dustier tips of small shoes. His expression was very kind.

He tiptoed to the door, drawing the grave-faced man-servant after him. Only when he was safely outside did he speak, and then in a most subdued whisper.

'Higgins,' he said in English, 'that young lady is very young. A very young, young lady! A child! . . . Lay another place for breakfast, Higgins! And be as silent as — as — as a pole-cat! Is a pole-cat silent, Higgins? . . . As silent as a dormouse! . . . A dormouse *must* be silent. Another place for breakfast! And a great deal more breakfast — more bacon, more eggs, more muffins, more cream, more raspberries, more coffee, more everything. And silence will be your second name as you lay it, Higgins, or I will call down the curse of Donar, Perkunas, the Black Dog, and the three hundred and fifty-four devils of Lerida! And tell your wife to make ready the pink room . . . See she puts a pin-cushion in it — and a "tidy". Now, Higgins, in the name of Beltane . . .'

Anne Louise awoke — to the pistol on her lap — to a sunlit library that had been transformed into an English breakfast-room — to the presence of a little red-faced gentleman, who was peeping at her over the rim of a large willow pattern cup, above a sheaf of manuscript propped against a large silver coffee-pot — to a most enticing aroma of coffee and hot bread and bacon and raspberries. The snowy cloth was crowded with dishes, and on a side-table between the two windows more dishes kept hot over little spirit lamps.

It was so English a scene that she spoke in that language as she tried, simultaneously, to rise from her chair and to secrete that preposterous pistol in the interstice of the upholstery between side and seat.

'I beg . . .' she began; but was allowed to proceed no further.

'*I* beg, madam,' said the little gentleman — whose red face was so shiny that it looked as if it had been buffed up by hand — 'I *do* beg, Madam, that you will not distress yourself with explanations. Leave them till you have breakfasted! Leave them until you like! Don't make them at all.'

He shot up as he spoke, coffee-cup in one hand, muffin — with a large semi-circular bite out of it — in the other. He spoke most earnestly.

'This intrusion . . .' began Anne Louise, endeavouring to behave in what she conceived to be a correct manner for an invading female.

'My dear young lady,' said the little gentleman in an even more excited manner than before, 'there has been no intrusion! If you have come here for safety or for help, as I imagine, I will now assure you of it. I will guarantee it! I will swear it by my Hippocratic oath! Anyone who thinks otherwise will have to deal with Morgan Tudor. With Morgan Tudor!'

So there was a good fairy — with a very red face — in that secret fairy house at the edge of the dark forest!

'I can't . . .' said Anne Louise.

'*Now*, madam!' said Dr. Tudor warningly, 'I thought that we had agreed that there should be no explanations at all — certainly none until you have breakfasted . . . I did not have the meal laid in another room, because as a physician I was convinced that the spectacle of an elderly gentleman at breakfast would be a nice normal thing for a young lady who has undergone a good deal of strain to wake up to. I was convinced that the sight and smell of breakfast would be in themselves restorative . . . Now I daresay that you would like to — er — shake off — the dust of travel, first. And then you will honour us with your company. Kidneys and bacon! Scrambled eggs! Fresh trout! Coffee! Tea! Muffins! Honey! Raspberries! We'll ring for Mrs. Higgins! You'll like Mrs. Higgins!'

He had set his hand to the little silver bell on the table when Anne Louise said desperately —

'Whoever comes you'll not say . . .'

Dr. Tudor played a perfect fantasia upon the bell.

'My dear young lady,' said he, 'you have come to the one house in Germany where we know how to keep secrets. If *you* have secrets, so have *we*! We are more secret than the tomb. We are not of this world at all. When you entered our precincts you left the world behind as utterly as Graelent did when he followed his fairy lady across the deep river . . . So far as you are concerned we will all suffer from ablepsy, aphonia, and amnesia — speaking as a medical man!'

A plump elderly woman in rustling black dress of bombazine, with a white cap with lappets that entirely hid her hair, took Anne Louise to a small rose-pink bedroom. 'The bed'll be aired by time you've had breakfast, Miss,' said she. . . .

When Anne Louise returned to the morning room, fresh supplies of provender had arrived: there did not appear to be a vacant spot anywhere on the surface of the table.

Dr. Tudor was depressed by her failure to do justice to the fare — by a mere sipping of coffee, and a crumbling of dry toast: he quoted, in support of his various arguments, dietetic maxims from the Book of Iago ap Dewi, the School of Salerno, and the remains of the Physicians of Myddfai.

He was a cheerful, garrulous little fellow, whose face had the colour, of a ripe cherry; with a shining buttony nose, and shining blue eyes, and shining yellow teeth, and a chin as shining as if it had been bees-waxed after shaving — all nestling in a shirt-collar that was much too high and much too wide for him, and girded about by a blue-and-white spotted neck-cloth with a tremendous bow.

By a great effort Anne Louise forced herself to display interest in his prattle. Her tired mind, however, only grasped a tithe of what he said . . . He and Frank were writing a book — had been for many years . . . Now where had Frank got to? He was never in time for breakfast by half an hour, poor fellow! . . . It was a history of medical practice in Western Europe from the earliest times to the present day . . . Two volumes had already been published, and brought them up to the eleventh century.

A little clock chimed nine . . . Now *where* was Frank? Later than ever!

She would never guess what he had been reading when she awakened! . . . It was Sir Charles Scarburgh's personal account of the treatment of

Charles the Second in his last illness. Wonderful remedies they employed in those days! What did she think of forty drops of the Spirit of Human Skull as a prescription?

Skulls — death — why did dead men's eyes stay open ? — ran the course of Anne Louise's thoughts.

If Frank didn't come soon he would really have to send and make sure that he was getting up!

Anne Louise set her cup down in its saucer with the careful attention of one uncertain of sobriety. A sense of unreality flooded her mind: this pleasant room was but a mirage, Dr. Tudor but imagined, and his voice — and her's as she answered him — but the echo of the noises of the world penetrating her dreams.

'There has been a great depreciation in the standing of a physician since the olden days,' said Dr. Tudor, helping himself lavishly to the fat red raspberries. 'In the time of Howell Dda, the doctor to the royal household sat at meat near the king, and he lodged with the court chamberlain. Yet in my young day, I remember, the Countess of Dudley was so proud that she would never speak to her medical man directly, even if he were taking her pulse. Her orders were passed on to the poor worm by her maid! . . . Now what in the name of Galen and Aesculapius has become of Frank?'

This could not be real! Or was it? . . . Had she stepped into a magic circle that had thrown up its invisible barrier against the prowling ghosts without — the chill ghost of Uncle Leopold; the gibbering shadow of a mad bridegroom; that vampire of dead lusts surging on its gilded bed in the dusty castle, heaving like the mass of live slugs in yellowing sugar, which she had seen Ottilie's children eat.

'Dear old Willis used to say to me,' went on Dr. Tudor, '— but of course you won't know of him! Very celebrated in his day. He was doctor to George the Third when the old king went mad . . .'

'Mad . . .?' said Anne Louise. And again, 'Mad!'

'My dear young lady!' protested the doctor. He seized the bell and rang it furiously, interjecting below his beath: 'It is too bad of Frank! It really is!' — went on, 'Surely you knew that George went completely off his head in his later years! . . . Willis did all he could for him. A very great doctor!' He paused, and added with considerable pride — 'I was trained under him, at his asylum at Greatfield.'

Anne Louise, suddenly awake, was about to ask a question when the grave-faced Higgins appeared.

'Is —' began Dr. Tudor; halted in mid-speech; meditated; continued '— is *he* getting up?'

'His Highness is coming downstairs now,' said Higgins.

Anne Louise had risen to her feet. She swayed so that she must needs support herself with fingertips on table. Her face had become grey.

' "Highness"? ' she said. That was all.

There was a footfall outside the door.

Said Dr. Tudor in a flurried manner —

'My dear, your little secret — whatever it is — is safe with us. Ours must be safe with you. Must be! *Must* be! . . . The Grand Duke —'

As the door opened Anne Louise sighed, and slid to the floor.

In the tremendous confusion forthwith created by Dr. Tudor, there entered a slim man, with a keen intelligent face that was pink and beautifully shaven, with a thatch of curly iron-grey hair crowning a head sunk deep into his shoulders — sunk so deeply that he seemed to have no neck. A hunchback.

'Frank, my dear fellow, there's a girl here, and she's fainted!' said Dr. Tudor. 'Higgins, fetch your wife! And, Higgins, fetch the sal volatile! Help me up with her, Frank! You take her feet — I'll take her head! . . . God bless my soul, isn't she a pretty thing?'

Between them they set her gently in one of the arm-chairs.

The Grand Duke of Ehrenberg looked at her in silence.

'My girl would have been about her age,' he said wistfully.

BOOK SIX

PERSEUS

★

CHAPTER I

THE MAN WHO DIED TWICE

The sky was paling into night, and twilight rose in the valley like the rising of phantasmal waters, as Seven came homeward over the rim of barren hills from which the glamour of sunset was swiftly being withdrawn. He rode down toward orchard and spinney and sloping meadow that were shadowless, and from whose verdure all defined colour fast receded.

So it was already dusk when he came to the whitewashed cottage which he had given Sarah Liddell immediately he had returned from Elsinore. The little house stood back from the road at the end of a grey small garden, against a wall of young pines: it was grey, too, in the evening, and a smudge of grey smoke from its single chimney stained the pallid greenish sky above the trees.

He dismounted; left his weary horse to crop the long grass at the road-side; walked up the narrow path to the door, and knocked on it with the handle of his crop.

'Sally-ally!' he called. 'Sally-ally, are you in?'

A heavy tread sounded within the house, and a moment later Sarah Liddell greeted him at the door.

Outwardly she appeared unchanged from the Sarah Liddell of the *Joan Dearlove* and before; immense red face framed in battered straw hat tied under chin with faded handkerchief; immense and shapeless body hummocking stained red gown. She held in her hand an iron ladle of which she did not let go for a single instant.

But if thus externally she was not altered, yet her manner was very different from what it had been. There was about her a restraint wholly alien to her nature, and the old lusty good-humour had departed from her speech.

It was not that she was not grateful. The tears of gratitude, indeed, glistened in her eyes as she thanked him for all he had done. She stood on the flagged floor of her kitchen (in which daylight and candlelight were nicely balanced) and pointed out, with the ladle, the completeness with which her new home had been equipped — from shining crockery on shining dresser, to red fringe for high mantel-shelf and oak windsor chair beside the cheerful fire. There was even a side or two of bacon hanging from the hooks on the beams that crossed the low ceiling, and a black kitten curled on the rag rug before the hearth. Seven fancied that Tog — who had been responsible for the equipment — must have devoted at least two of his household slates to memoranda regarding the outfit.

No, it was not that she was not grateful. It was rather as though she paused uncertain on the verge of some unexpected confidence; or was, perhaps, overwhelmed by the sense of her indebtedness.

'Mr. Sep . . .' she began at length. 'I think . . .'

Then suddenly the garden gate slammed. There was a strange scuffling noise, and the rattle of little squeaky wheels along the path. A loud voice bellowed something. She cast an agonized look on Seven as she went to the door.

Captain Henry Pedder was outlined in the opening. Or, rather, a trifle more than half of Captain Henry Pedder; for he had no legs, and his great trunk — not quite upright on the short stumps — was borne on a small stout tray mounted on little iron wheels. His shoulders were bowed so that the palms of his great hands — encased in padded leather gloves — rested on the threshold. He looked, most tragically, like a giant frog. His head was thrust forward, and, out of the square red-scorched face, eyes that were almost yellow glared at Seven.

Repulsion and pity fought within Seven as he said —

'Evening, Cap'n. I have just come to see how you and Sarah are getting on. I am glad . . .'

But Pedder had leaned forward like a rower tugging at his oars; with one stroke of his hands he propelled himself five or six feet into the room with a hideous screeching and clatter of the little carriage. At a second stroke he had passed Seven standing by the candle on the scrubbed white table, and was making for a door in the far dark corner of the room. He said no word. Seven noticed that the wheeled tray served him, too, as trouser pocket, for a short clay pipe and pewter tobacco box danced off it in the fury of his travel. The man had gone beyond a loudly slamming door before Seven could retrieve the jetsam and restore it.

Seven straightened himself up.

'Why in the name of all that is merciful do you put up with a fellow like that, Sally-ally?' he asked.

'He's got no one else, Mr. Sep!' she answered, bent over an iron pot that gave forth a fragrant steam from its seat among the glowing coals.

'But he has no claim on you!'

'No one has greater, Mr. Sep!'

'Turn round, Sally! I can't talk to your behind . . . What do you mean?'

'He — he's — my son, Mr. Sep!'

She suddenly stood erect, and turned to him; and, before he had recovered from the surprise, added:

'. . . And your brother! . . . Your half-brother, Mr. Sep!'

There had been no need to add that. With her first words he had recollected their conversation in the *Joan Dearlove*, and realized that she must have 'obliged' after all: realized the full truth, and knew that at long last he had encountered another of the experiments in flesh and mind and soul that his father had carried out. This dreadful remnant of a man was not merely brother to him in blood, but brother in experience. Just as the piteous wreckage was all that was left of the great heathen who had ruled men with his fists and taken women according to his lust; so had the swaggering giant on the poop of the *Joan Dearlove*, with his cruelties and insatiable desires, been the wreckage of a spirit and a brain that had been tested beyond their strength. He was filled with compassion.

Sarah Liddell went on, in a low voice, watching the door in the dark far corner:

'Now I am a-feared, Mr. Sep! Very greatly a-feared! For he that was my baby is a bitter bad man — as well you know!'

'Afraid of what, Sally?'

'A-feared for *you*!'

'For me?' echoed Seven in some surprise.

'When we were in Elsinore and I told him who I was and why I would look after him, he fell a-cursin' his father. Cursin' and roarin' like Apollyon himself. He broke the table at his bedside with a blow of his fist, Mr. Sep, and all his gruel was spilled on the floor. And he threw himself about the bed until his wounds opened afresh. Just like he was being torn by a devil inside of him! He cursed God, and me that bore him — p'raps he was right! — and the day he was born, and those (as he said) what supplanted him . . . So I said naught about you, Mr. Sep; but when we got here — and where else could I go? — he began to ask questions, and go down to the public-house, and ask more questions. And little as folk here know about Mr. Fielding or you, yet he learnt enough to guess everything. The night he made certain of it all, he came back drunk — not loud drunk, but boastful drunk! . . .'

She broke off; and paused; and concluded briefly — 'He's a dangerous, dangerous man — even now — Mr. Sep!'

'But he can have no grudge against me,' said Seven. 'I knew nothing about his history before to-night. I never saw him in my life until you told me about the *Joan Dearlove* and I took passage with him . . . What is his name?'

'Two!' said Mrs. Liddell. 'Two Pedder is what you'll find him in the parish register at Crickhowell. Born April 7th, 1794 . . . That's where Mr. Fielding sent me with my old mother — Pedder was her maiden name — when my belly began to swell . . . And a nice job the master had with parson about it! An *on*-Christian name is what the old man called it. In the end the baby weren't baptized at all . . . They say, don't they, that the unbaptized can't —' And she halted, hesitating to utter suggestion of the irrevocable damnation of her son.

'But that's no reason why he should bear ill-will to me!'

'He was the only one that lasted out six years but you, Mr. Sep.'

The daylight had faded now so that nothing was distinguishable through the low windows; and she lit another candle in a brass candle-stick on the mantel-shelf, and drew short red curtains before the lattices, shutting out the ghosts of nightfall. She went on talking the while:

'It was in the seventh year he failed. He'd been broke by what he had gone through, Mr. Sep. He'd become hard and reckless and lost to decency. All the great sum he had — six hundred pounds it was, I think — he spent with evil women. On drink, and gamin', and horse-racin', and more women. At the end he hadn't a groat — not a penny; and was in rags. Mr. Fielding gave him another hundred pounds and sent him away. He'ld have nothing more to do with him — would never see him again — would never answer a letter. He only spoke of him to me once. He just said one day, "Well, Sarah, it's domino with your boy!" And it was! He didn't know that I knew already.'

They were facing each other now, Seven leaning back against the table, head a little sunk, tapping a muddy riding-boot with his whip; Sarah Liddell before the hearth, turning over and over the ladle which she held in both her hands.

'How *did* you know?' he asked.

Her face became a yet deeper red.

'I had to sign a paper before he was born, saying I'd no claim on the baby if it was a boy. But I couldn't forget. When I came back here again afterwards I found where the master kept the letters and papers about all his children . . . I was the only one he'ld trust to dust his room . . . I used to see all the reports. They came every six months. Dreadful things they were! There was one little child that went mad; and one that died; and one ran away; and one sort of sank in the mud

and just vanished; and one was caught in some machinery and killed.
He was too tired to escape. They said they thought he wanted to die!'
'Oh, God!' said Seven.
'And my boy died, too! Just as surely as if he'd been caught in
the machinery, or drowned, or killed by disease. That' — and she
indicated the door through which Pedder had gone, by a nod of her
head — 'isn't my boy! My boy is dead. He was murdered by his father.
That isn't my boy! . . . *My* boy wouldn't come back o' night from the
public and boast of the dreadful things he'd done! Of the women he'd
wronged! Of the men he'd killed —'
She broke off. On the bare boards overhead came the rattle of the
little iron wheels of Pedder's carriage. Easily and gently the wheels
ran over the floor, as if — so to speak — he were just paddling along.
She explained: 'There's a low bank opposite the back of the house
at the far end, and he's put a gangway from it to the upper floor. He
can roll up it to his bedroom. He can't manage the stairs. They are
very steep . . .' Continued in a yet lower voice: 'And he *has* killed
men, Mr. Sep! *And* women, too! From what Mr. Reid's told me I know
it's no lie!'
Remembering the *Joan Dearlove*, Seven could well believe it. He
nodded agreement; and then asked —
'Was it just coincidence, Sally, that you went aboard the *Joan
Dearlove*, or did you know it was his ship?'
'I knew he called himself Henry Pedder and had stayed at sea,
from letters in the master's desk . . . Then last Christmas, Joe — I'd
told him everythin' — read a piece in the paper saying how the barque
Joan Dearlove, master, Cap'n Henry Pedder, was going to load slate
for Ameriky after being repaired. I hadn't seen my boy for three and
thirty years. So I asked Joe if we could go to Ameriky — and he was
willin'. He could earn a livin' anywhere — he was a very handy man
with his hands, was poor Joe.' She reverted to the subject of the son-
who-was-not-her-son. She said: 'Three times he tried to kill his own
father! Three times! The third time he murdered by mistake some
harmless old man. It was in a house in London!'
So that was how and why old grey-headed Quilter had died over his
Anacreon all those years ago! He remembered, as though it were but
yesterday, his father talking to two men in red waistcoats, who had
come from the Bow Street Police-Office, in that long upper room
looking on to tree-tops and clouds. 'H'any h'ideas, sir, h'as to the
h'offender?' one had asked — a slow-spoken Cockney, whose jaws
moved as though he were some ruminating animal, even when he was

silent. 'None', had replied his father with cold finality; but he — watching the older man — had guessed him to know or suspect the identity of the assassin.

'And now he makes the most dreadful threats against you, Mr. Sep! There's murder in his heart. He says you robbed him of his birthright. Sometimes he screams and raves like one possessed . . . Only yesterday he told me that he'd come within an ace of roastin' you alive!'

Seven suddenly found himself chilled by the malignity of the creature that was his brother.

'That's partly true, Sally-ally,' he said soberly. 'Late on Monday night when everybody was in bed Reid smelled something burning, and got up, and found the backstairs well alight . . . But how could he have done it?'

'I don't know. But do it he did. And worse he will do yet. You'll have to find some way of stopping him, Mr. Sep. You can't be on your guard night and day, week in and week out . . . It's horrible for a mother to curse the day . . .'

Something sang past his head so that he felt the wind of it upon his cheek — something called Death, that spilled its destruction harmlessly enough upon a white and red china dog on the mantelshelf, shivering it to pieces; something that sprang from a sudden violent noise and was followed by utter silence and bitter-smelling smoke.

In one rapid movement he swung round, and faced the direction whence Death had flown toward him.

Against the back wall of the house a steep staircase mounted away from him, without either bend or break, to the floor above. In the upper dusk he could see the half-man leaning so far out over the stairs — supported by the grip of one great hand upon a baluster — that his legless body seemed to hover in the air over them like a brooding gargoyle. In his other hand he held a long and smoking pistol.

So swiftly then did the tragedy — if tragedy it was — take place, that it was over before it was well begun.

With a screech of fury Pedder flung the useless weapon from him so that it crashed on to the iron-grey flags of the kitchen floor. He tried to regain his balance. Seven heard the scraping of the wheels on his little trolley upon the boards.

Sarah Liddell said something that he did not catch; and then in a swift straight rush — astonishing in one of her size and age — had swept up the stairs. She seemed to gather up her son in her course, because for a moment he saw her looming upright in the darkness of the stair-head and steadying, erect against herself, that hulk of what had been a man, which came but little higher than her waist.

She called (he thought) 'May God have mercy upon you!'

And then, before he could cry, or struggle, or clutch at safety, Pedder was hurled from the stair-top.

He appeared to dive over the first few stairs, and then shot helplessly headlong down the rest as though down a slide. The bumping of his fall was accompanied by the clatter of his trolley. There were, perhaps, thirteen or fourteen stairs, and he crashed over the last on to the flags upon his brow with a thud, and a rattle — and a crack.

From the manner in which the great body strove to ride over its own neck and then collapsed, Seven knew that his brother was dead. He did not need to look.

Sarah Liddell came slowly down. He saw that she still held the iron ladle in her hand. She paused over the dusty huddle at the stair-foot for a moment, and then went back to her place by the fire.

'There was no other way, Mr. Sep,' she said. 'And my son was dead long ago! . . . My little son! . . . My very little son!'

He saw that the great tears were streaming down her cheeks.

'*That* wasn't my son, Mr. Sep. It's something he left behind when he died years and years ago. Something he left behind when his father killed him.'

'Yes, Sally. Just what's left of a body — and nothing more!'

'You see, Mr. Sep. I found out from his father's papers where he was sent when he was a little boy. And once or twice I got away and travelled all night and walked ten miles on the chance of seein' him. It was a Sunday, the first time; and after I'd waited an hour I saw him come out of the big double green gates of an old house on his way to church . . . I should have known him anywhere. He had a little green short jacket with flat pewter buttons, and a white shirt with a frilled ruff round the neck, and white pantaloons, and a wide black hat; and he carried a big prayer-book and walked ever so prettily between two little misses in sprigged muslin. I sat as close to him as I could in church and heard him piping up in the psalms. One of them was — "I will cry unto God with my voice: even unto God will I cry with my voice, and he shall hearken unto me." But God didn't hearken unto him, poor lamb! . . . And another time I crept into the garden and hid among the bushes. And there he was, walking up and down the lawn talking about old ancient history and dead kings and queens to an old parson, with his little hands cupped behind his back — just

like his father used to do — and his fair hair all blowing in the wind . . .
My little boy! *Mine!*'

Seven was most extraordinarily moved. It was the child that had
baptized his umbrella 'Excalibur' who answered:

'That little boy died long ago, Sally-ally! And is walking to church
across the fields of Paradise between two seraphs in sprigged muslin.
And is talking theology to elderly archangels in the gardens of the
Golden City . . . You can die and yet leave your body behind you,
Sally-ally! There are lots of bodies walking about to-day without
there being anybody alive in them.'

'There would have been no rest for you, and no safety, Mr. Sep,
if I hadn't . . .'

He made no answer, but turned and looked down on the dusty
heap which once had been a little boy who had sung the psalms lustily,
and talked history with an ancient parson, and worn a small green coat
with pewter buttons. Poor little boy who had been killed by his father's
experiments, and had left such dreadful wreckage to become still
worse! The hatred which he had felt long ago against that father welled
up afresh. Here was one victim — where were the others? . . . In their
graves or sunk hopelessly and irredeemably — as Sally had said — 'in
the mud'.

'Mr. Sep,' said Sarah Liddell suddenly . . . 'am I a — murderess?'

Seven recalled himself to decisive speech — to decisive action.

'No,' he answered briefly. 'You have probably saved my life. *This*
fell downstairs accidentally — as well he might. You think that he
had been drinking this evening . . . I am going to send for the doctor.
He will make things easy for you, and when he has been, you shall
come to Judgment. Reid shall fetch you. There is no need to say more
than I have said . . . Open the doors so that the smell of powder is
blown away.'

He bent down and picked up the pistol from the floor, balanced it
for a minute in his hand, and then thrust it into a side-pocket.

He approached her: he kissed her wet cheek: he took the ladle from
her hand.

'God bless you, Sally-ally,' he said. 'Sit down now, and help will
be with you very soon . . .'

In the doorway he turned and looked back into the shadowy room.
She was still standing on the same spot, staring at that which was
hidden from him by the table, seeing not the husk of a half-man on
the floor but the tousle-headed boy debating history with a parson on a
rectory lawn of long ago.

He rode back through the pitchy darkness. His horse's hoofs echoed on the hollow of the hump-backed bridge near his gates, and he pulled up by the lighted windows of the little inn that abutted on the hurrying stream. He dismounted and walked along the echoing dark passage to the bar.

As he had expected, two of his stablemen, with pint mugs beside them, were playing cards by the light of a dip. They rose when they saw who it was stood over them.

'Howell,' he said calmly, 'saddle a horse and ride down into Tregyb and bring back Doctor Morgan at once. That fellow at Sarah Liddell's has broken his neck, I think. I suppose he was drunk!'

It was of a brother that he spoke thus easily, he told himself: of a brother killed but a bare half hour ago by the woman who had borne him.

Howell extricated bandy legs from betwixt settle and table.

'Bruck his neck, has he, y'r honour?' he said. 'Inteet it iss no loss. In here he wass an hour or so ago, railing at the world and trinking gin as if he would trown himself in it. Yess-yess, a foul-mouthed fellow, inteet!'

Said the other man, anxious to add his quota of sensation —

'There hass been a foreign chentleman waitin' for y'r honour these last several hours. Since four o'clock. He did say to Mr. Tog that he did come across the width of England and Wales to see y'r honour!'

CHAPTER II

A TALE OF CONSPIRACY

THE foreign gentleman who had awaited him for so long had not been left to kick his heels in the desolate splendours of the bare reception rooms of Judgment. He had been gathered — a trifle puzzled — to the cordial bosom of the family, and there Seven found him upon his return. He was sitting very upright in an arm-chair beside a small clear fire, in Togarmah's snuggery.

Every one of the multitudinous pictures in the little room twinkled in firelight and candlelight — for Tog would have nothing to do with such innovations as gas — and the curtains and carpet and upholstery glowed deep red. A brass kettle sang upon the hob, and on the table were all the materials for rum punch as well as bread and cheese.

Tog faced the stranger across the hearth, short legs well thrust out, and slippered feet crossed at the ankle and resting on a footstool. Between them, opposite the fire, sat Lovell, a loose wrap about her, and her charming face bent over a book upon her lap. By the light from a pair of brass candlesticks on the mantelshelf and another most carefully arranged at a nice angle on the table behind her, she was reading aloud of Mr. Winkle's sporting exploits in the *Pickwick Papers* to the two men.

The entertainment was obviously much to Tog's taste; and it duly received the courteous — if slightly bewildered — attention of the visitor.

Although a little family scene such as this had been a nightly occurrence whenever he was at Judgment since his return from Denmark over six weeks ago, Seven still had the feeling on entering the room, that the pages of time had been turned back, and that once again he was breaking in on the pleasant gathering that he had interrupted with news of the *Joan Dearlove*. Each night for the period of the splitting of a second the figure of Lovell — so discreetly enveloped — became the slender figure of the princess, her mistress, and he almost looked to see the worshipping face of Daniel turned on the girl from his firelit cavern under the table.

At the sound of the opening door, Tog looked round over the rim of his silver-framed spectacles — he always put on his best glasses for occasions of ceremony; laid down on his knees green knitting with needles that were own cousins to a brace of marlin-spikes.

'You are very late, Sep!' he exclaimed . . . 'This, sir, is Mr. Tempest!'

The stranger rose to his feet. He was blond, tall, broad-shouldered, lean-flanked, excessively good-looking, and very young — although there was little that was boyish about his face except its contours, and his speech held the composure of a man well-habituated to the world.

'I must apologize for this intrusion on you, sir,' he said in excellent — though harsh — English, to the dark tall man in the dark dress who stood halted in the doorway, regarding him without vestige of expression. 'In my view, however, the matter about which I must speak with you is urgent — most urgent. I have come a long way to see you — a very long way. I have also run greater risks than I care to think about in so doing.'

'May I ask your name?' said Seven.

'Mr. Cash can tell Mr. Tempest,' replied the other, 'that names sometimes are unimportant!'

He spoke almost in a tone of reproof, as though unaccustomed to such demand.

Until that instant Seven had merely thought the visitor to be one of his foreign correspondents who had posted on from London to see him — as happened on occasion. His reference to the name which had been produced on the spur of the moment for Pedder in the Aleppo Merchant Inn, linked the newcomer with the *Joan Dearlove*, with Anne Louise, with Daniel, with Margarethe Thirkelsen — more especially with Anne Louise. No word of her had there been since that morning when Mr. Peel, at her behest, had hastened apology and offer of help to him at the House of Gertrude Englishwoman. Daniel — his agents had traced to the capital of the South German Grand Duchy of Ehrenberg, where that small boy appeared to be playing the part of chaperone to his abductor during a protracted siege of the leading pastry-cook's daughter.

'May I venture to inquire whether your business is with Mr. Cash or with Mr. Tempest?' asked Seven.

'Up to the present Mr. Cash's part in the matter of which I would speak, has been merely that of — of travelling companion. It is Mr. Tempest who made a contract . . . which I am informed has not yet been fulfilled!'

In the silence which followed, Tog stirred in his chair. He addressed the girl sitting so quietly near him.

'You had better run away now, Penny-my-dear,' he said. 'There's business to be talked.'

As she rose obediently with her book, he rose also — green knitting clutched against his person in somewhat ludicrous caricature of Venus hiding nudity — so that he might return the grave little bow she gave the gentlemen as she left the room. Then he, too, made preparations for departure.

'I should like my friend to hear what you have to say,' said Seven to the young man. 'He is acquainted with all Mr. Cash's travels — and with Mr. Cash's fellow-traveller. Stop here, Tog!'

The visitor made a small stiff bow of assent, and sat down again, methodically parting the tails of his blue coat as he did so. He sat very upright, his chin held even higher than was necessary to clear the points of his high collar which was wrapped about with a black cravat. There was something of the pattern-book about him.

'I have come here at considerable inconvenience and risk,' he began anew; and spoke as one who, despite his youth, did not approve of inconvenience and felt that the taking of risks was almost an unheard of and disreputable procedure.

'Yes?' said Seven, in a tone implying that the statement had been made before and would not bear repetition.

The other flushed a little; and, when he continued, his alien accent had become a little more pronounced.

'For various reasons it was thought well that I should come to England as quickly as possible. Thus I have undoubtedly arrived ahead of the mails from South Germany. You will not have yet seen this in England, I imagine, sir!'

From a green morocco leather pocket-book he produced a small piece of paper which he handed to Seven, who had seated himself in Lovell's chair, and was lounging with his long-booted legs stretched toward the brightness of the fire. It was a fragment from a German newspaper, and badly printed in eye-tiring Gothic type.

'Can't read German — or speak it!' said Seven, rejecting the snippet; and appeared, without so saying, to thank the Almighty for the inability. He lied, in fact, because he did not propose to make things easier than need be for any bumptious German.

'It is a cutting from the *Ehrenberger Post* printed on the afternoon on which I left the Grand Duchy. It says . . .'

'Ehrenberg?' said Seven thoughtfully. 'Ehrenberg! . . . Just a moment! Mix the punch, Tog! . . . I could do with a drink . . . And with something to eat!'

He cut himself a slice of bread and a wedge from a large flat cheese with raised lettering on its upper crust — a 'Resurrection' cheese pressed between broken gravestones from Llanfihangel. He ate inelegantly whilst Tog mingled a savoury brew of sugar and rum and lemon and hot water.

Their visitor watched proceedings without a flicker of expression, and then averted his gaze as though the sight were more than he could bear.

He waited almost ostentatiously until Seven should be disengaged. 'Go on!' said Seven.

'This is what the newspaper says,' said the young man, and in an emotionless voice began a rapid and fluent translation of the paragraph, which ran:

HORRIBLE TRAGEDY IN THE EHRENBERG FOREST. Early this morning Ernst Schmidt, a charcoal burner, aged 42, while proceeding to work in the Ehrenberg Forest, found the dead body of Mr. Washington Stephen Hallett . . .

'Hallett!' ejaculated Seven, a piece of cheese poised half-way to his mouth. 'Hallett! . . . Go on sir!'

. . . a young and wealthy American, lying in the road near the ruined chapel of St. Hubert, about a league and a half from the village of Mariedorf. The body was already cold, and there was a bullet wound, apparently inflicted at close range, in the region of the heart.

Researches by police agents have proved the crime to have had robbery as its motive, as Mr. Hallett is known to have been in possession of a large sum of money of which there is now no trace. His negro servant, Samuel Berwick, was also found dead in a ditch by the road-side. He had been apparently shot in the back of the head as he tried to make his escape from the murderers. Notification has been sent to the Bavarian authorities, as there is little doubt but that the miscreants have already crossed the frontier. Investigations are proceeding rapidly.

Mr. Hallett had apartments in the house on Rampart-street of Mr. Town Councillor Perponcher. He was making a leisurely tour of Europe in the company of his young ward, a boy of ten or eleven years of age . . .

'That boy, sir, is in actual fact a relation or ward of yours, I believe,' suggested the stranger.

'He is, sir . . . How long is it since you left Ehrenberg?'

'A week this afternoon.'

'Then I shall probably hear from my agent to-morrow. He has full power to act on my behalf in regard to the child . . . I am obliged to you all the same for taking such trouble to advise me of the position that has arisen.'

'Agent! . . . Your agent!' echoed the other. 'You have then an agent in Ehrenberg?'

He had folded away the newspaper cutting, and was extracting some other document from the green pocket-book as he spoke. He paused in the midst of the operation, and flashed a look at Seven in which there was more than a hint of suspicion.

'If your — ward — were abducted, as was mine, would you not think it most reasonable to employ an agent to discover his whereabouts? The child, Daniel, was traced by one of my men over a month ago, when Hallett ceased perambulating Europe, and apparently settled down to woo the local baker's daughter. I took no steps to recover possession of him because I had assured myself that he was very happy . . .'

'And I'll tell you what's more, Sep,' said Tog stirring his tumbler of punch with a brisk cheerful clinking sound. 'You did nothing about it because you not merely knew no harm would come to the child, but you felt that the success of the conspiracy might cause infinite pleasure to its instigator!'

Seven said nothing in reply. He sat silent staring into the yellow fire. Out of the past his ears caught the echo of Anne Louise's appeal in his bedroom in Eisinore — 'There will be no more experiments? — *Or on Daniel?*'

Amid the play of flame-light and shadow on his long face, the younger man thought to catch the flicker of a smile about his lips. What he saw, however, so far encouraged him that he proceeded to extract a paper from his pocket-book, which he tossed on to the table. He sipped in a disapproving manner the glass of punch that Togarmah had set on the cupboard top at his right elbow, and fell a-coughing as if unused to so strong an elixir. When he recovered he went on —

'I did not come, of course, merely to give you information about the boy. That could have been safely done by post. *And* without trouble to myself. What I have come about is a certain lady . . .'

'If you are talking to Mr. Cash,' said Seven, 'I may tell you that he always referred to that lady as Anne Louise. If to Mr. Tempest, then she is the Duchess of Limburg. There is no reason why she should be anonymous in this house and this company.' He turned his head a little. The stranger's pocket-book lay close by, directly under the candlestick on the red tablecloth. He continued: 'Incidentally, if you desire to keep your own anonymity you had better not leave about a pocket-book newly stamped with the Coburg arms. I'm no herald, but I have good sight and it is not difficult to identify three rampant lions and a crowing cock. I saw them once on something that belonged to Anne Louise . . . I suppose you're some relation?'

'I realize now that in this house and this company,' said the young man very formally, repeating Seven's own phrase, 'there can be no harm in my saying that I am a relation — a cousin. I am Albert of Coburg and Gotha . . . I need not ask you to keep my visit secret!'

'The only person who is likely to give it away,' remarked Seven caustically, 'is yourself!'

The prince flushed again. When he continued his accent had further worsened, although his speech remained grammatically correct, and its precision was unimpaired.

'You have heard, sir, of the ostensible reason for the death of Mr. Hallett — who was a very gallant gentleman! There are, perhaps, not more than half a dozen people in Europe who can tell you what really happened, or what conspiracy lay behind his murder a week agô in the forest road . . . I have here a letter — one of a number of letters of similar tenour. It is addressed to a Mr. Postlethwaite who is the resident correspondent in Munich of *The Times* newspaper of London. The others — in my possession, too — are also addressed to the representatives of various newspapers, such as *The Morning Herald* and *The Morning Chronicle*. Another was intended for Mr. James Bradshaw, who is Tory Member of Parliament for Canterbury.'

'It would almost appear that you have been engaged in robbing her Majesty's mails!'

'They were the contents of a portfolio picked up in the road immediately after the murder of Mr. Hallett!' he answered curtly. The jest was obviously offensive to him. 'I will read you the letter to Postlethwaite —

"Ehrenberg: Wednesday, July 17th,
2 a.m.

"Dear P.— Here's a piece of news, barely an hour old, which will make your wig curl; and I can vouch for its accuracy because I was present. Her Highness the Duchess Anne Louise of Limburg has eloped with his Highness Prince Albert of Saxe-Coburg-Gotha, the destined bridegroom of her Majesty Queen Victoria!

"The discovery was made shortly before one o'clock this morning during the course of a State Ball given at the Castle of Ehrenberg, when the youthful royal pair were found to be missing, and search made for them. It was ascertained that, taking advantage of the confusion attendant on this brilliant function, the couple had slipped away, smuggled themselves out of the castle in a tradesman's van, and then galloped off in a carriage which had been awaiting them in a secluded corner of the forest that surrounds the palace.

"Emissaries were sent after them immediately by the Grand Duchess of Ehrenberg, acting for their guardian King Leopold of the Belgians; but as the frontier is only fifteen miles away the runaway lovers are probably long since out of reach. It is thought that they are most likely to address their course to Italy, where the Prince has been recently touring and has had every opportunity of finding a love-nest for himself and his lady.

"It has been remarked lately that Prince Albert was greatly *épris*, and had on various occasions bewailed the matrimonial path marked out for him by his family. The Princess, already the heroine of a very remarkable escapade, is known to be the greatest heiress in Europe. Whether they are wedded as yet or not, my dear P., I can't say, but don't mind wagering that they are bedded. . . ." '

'Ah!' snarled Tog, and bit savagely at his cheroot and threw the resultant ruin into the fire with almost as much ferocity as if he were stoning the writer.

' ". . . Yours ever, C." And then there's this post-scriptum — "I find, on reading what I have written, that I have not mentioned the fact that just before the discovery of the elopement the Grand Duchess in person had announced to the assembly the forthcoming nuptials of the Princess with the Grand Duke of Ehrenberg, Francis. A piquant sauce for as good a dish of scandal as you are ever likely to have set before you! . . . Forgive the scrawl. I am writing this in the carriage on my way to Hanover." '

'Exactly how much truth is there in this precious document?' asked Seven.

He had risen while the letter was a-reading, and prowled round the room, straightening pictures on the wall, examining others to see if they were foxed. He put the question across his shoulder as he stood bent over a large musical-box set on a small table in a corner. He had been tinkering with the toy at intervals for days. Now he raised the lid, and made some adjustment with a screw-driver as he spoke.

Said Albert, addressing his back in precise tones —

'Exactly none!'

'There must have been something to serve as a basis for it. You can't spin any sort of story you like, and expect the world to believe it without witnesses or evidence. The man who wrote that letter knew his business, I'll dare swear. He could prove what he said — or prove something that looked precious like what he said.'

'Just so,' answered Albert, declining to address Seven's back again, and speaking across the hearth to the intent Togarmah. 'He *would* have been able ostensibly to prove his story but for Mr. Hallett . . . That's why Mr. Hallett died!'

Seven released a spring. With a whirring and a grinding noise the little brass barrel of the musical-box began to revolve. A thin sweet jingle of tune rippled out — a small plaintive echo of a childhood air — a forlorn dancelet for baby ghosts —

> *Schöne Jungfer hübsch und fein*
> *Komm mit mir zum Tanz herein . . .*

Even as Albert spoke, so he recalled Washy, as he had seen him, lying fallen in the moonlit road, with tumbled hair and a pistol in his hand; and the tinkling music wove itself into the texture of his thoughts as though it were a dirge for the dead boy.

Seven, satisfied with the result — whatever it was — of the adjustment, moved a lever marked 'Repeat' so that for the next five minutes their speech had tristful accompaniment from the musical-box. It outraged Albert.

Said Seven, facing round —

'You have now shown us, or told us, what did *not* happen, sir. Only one incontrovertible fact remains — and that is that Mr. Hallett is dead. Suppose now you tell us precisely what *did* happen — and why!'

Albert disliked Seven's tone; he disliked Seven's manner; he abominated the musical-box: but he had set himself a certain task, and he went forward with it — although his bearing became more aloof, his speech if possible more formal.

'Mr. Hallett employed agents to keep him in touch with the princess's movements after she left you. They were so successful that he arrived in Ehrenberg only twenty-four hours behind her. He eventually established communication with her, and set to work at once to plot her escape. Then unfortunately he came into contact with an agent of the King of Hanover named Cobbold, who seemingly threw himself heart and soul into the conspiracy.

'The man Cobbold knew ... it is surprising how much, and how many people, he knew! ... that my brother and I were to pay a visit of a few weeks to Ehrenberg. At his suggestion my sympathy was secured and my help enlisted, although it was clearly understood that I was not to be implicated in any way. ...'

He went on to describe the events leading up to the moment when he had escorted Anne Louise from the ball-room to her door, while the musical-box wheezed, clucked, and fell silent on — maddeningly enough — an incompleted air. He had to halt his narrative perceptibly while his mind supplied the missing notes.

He told the rest of the story in staccato sentences to a profoundly intent audience. Only once did Seven interrupt, and that was to say suddenly and seriously — winding the musical-box afresh as he spoke —

'I should be glad, sir, to hear at a later date your reactions to Mr. Cobbold! They should be violent!'

It was then, as the faint melancholy tune tinkled out again, that Albert realized that perhaps he could like the strange dark man who had watched and listened without a word, and had made no comment except vicariously through that ironic and tinnient lament.

'They *are* violent,' said Albert, and continued his tale of the death of Washy, the frustration of Mr. Cobbold, and the disappearance of Anne Louise. When he had not been able to find her, he had galloped back to the castle as fast as his horse could set foot to ground; changed his uniform, and reappeared at the ball. It seemed the best thing to do for her sake as well as his own.

Seven nodded his approval.

'What did you say about it?'

'I told the truth — with omissions. I saw no reason why I should mention her plan of escape — or Hallett's or Mademoiselle Perponcher's parts in it. I was not supposed to know! ... That's not quite true!' — he corrected himself — 'I told the full story to one of her ladies, Miss Talfourd. She was very sympathetic. Her English morality' — he spoke the phrase as if the last word were almost but not quite synonymous with 'hypocrisy' — 'was jarred to revolt by the proposed marriage ... I thought Anne Louise might need a friend. I had heard about you from her; and it was Miss Talfourd who told me where to find you!'

Seven nodded further approval.

'So she escaped in the end?'

Albert shook his head.

'Just before I left I was told that she had been found wandering in the forest, and had been brought back and put to bed. They told me that she was very dazed.'

Seven sat himself down once again on the chair before the fire.

'Tog,' he said, 'give the prince some more punch!'

He remained for a long while silent, with legs outstretched, staring at — without seeing — a print of the Grand Jubilee Cricket Match played at Lord's on July the tenth, 1837.

At last —

'And what was behind this curious affair?'

Albert extracted another document from his pocket-book; handed it to Seven.

'This is another letter from Mr. Cobbold's mail-bag. It and the rest had been obviously written in advance. They were presumably to have been despatched by special couriers as soon as it was certain that the plot had succeeded.'

Seven unfolded the epistle. It was in the same neat small writing as the letter to Postlethwaite of *The Times*, and was addressed to the ultra-Tory member of Parliament for Canterbury, James Bradshaw, who had already been involved in a duel owing to his indecent attacks on the young Queen of England. One or two sentences had obviously been inserted by the writer after he had completed the original missive. Seven read it aloud, for the benefit of Togarmah —

' "Ehrenberg: July 17th, 1839.

"My dear Bradshaw, — A most extraordinary event which will undoubtedly have a very profound effect upon politics and policies has occurred here to-day, and I send you special and early word of it so that you may make use of the information as soon as possible. Prince Albert of Saxe-Coburg-Gotha, destined husband of your *favourite* Victoria, has to-night eloped with the Princess Anne Louise of Limburg, whose forthcoming marriage to the Grand Duke of Ehrenberg was actually on the eve of announcement. This is not just rumour and report, but a fact known to hundreds here as the elopement took place during the course of a State Ball.

"It needs no exceptional imagination to realize how this news will be received at Buckingham Palace, or Windsor Castle, or wherever our obstinate young Autocrat is. There will be many others beside yourself who will have small sympathy with the hurt to pride occasioned by this flagrant rejection of her charms (?) by one whom she has been always brought up to look upon as her peculiar property.

"There are only two sequels possible to this news. In the first place,

Vicky from injured susceptibilities may throw herself into the arms of the first eligible straight off, in order to show that she doesn't care. *And the only eligible* — who is also extremely personable — *in the country* at the time is Prince George of Cumberland, Crown Prince of Hanover! That would suit our book very well!

"The other alternative is that it will strengthen her more than ever in her frequently expressed determination never to marry. If you add to her ardent desire to be a second Elizabeth, this violent shock to her womanly self-respect — the Queen of England jilted! — and the growing obsession that she would infallibly die in child-birth, you have the almost inevitable certainty of a spinster Queen. And you know as well as I do — if not better — that the country will not stand much longer the tantrums, the obstinacy, the scandals, the political partisanship, the rule by foreign *camarilla*, that has marked the two years' reign of this young woman whom even her ministers cannot control. Unless she gets married soon, and involved in the cares of a family, and learns subjection to a sensible husband, every political observer knows that her days on the Throne are numbered. . . ." '

'Is that all true?' asked Seven, breaking off.

'I should say,' replied Albert judicially, stirring his punch with a less disapproving air than hitherto, 'that it is an exceptionally level-headed view of the situation.' He hesitated; but the brutality of the letter appeared to have encouraged him to frank disclosure. He went on — ' The Tory party is openly disloyal and regrets that Cumberland did not inherit the Crown. The Radicals are of course against her, and, with her decline from popularity, many of the Whigs are deserting the colours . . . I know that my uncle takes a very gloomy view of the situation, and that even the Prime Minister, Lord Melbourne, suffers from qualms!'

'So that was the milk in the coconut!' said Tog, putting down his knitting and scrubbing his hand through the short badger-grey bristles of his head. 'A pretty bloody plot, dom it! . . . But my interest — and your interest, Sep? — is in what happened to An — her Highness the Princess Anne Louise.'

'It was on her behalf that I came here!'

'Why here?'

'I gathered from her that there was no one else whom she thought capable of giving her aid. She said to me once that she thought you might help her . . . not from chivalry, nor for her *beaux yeux*, but because you disliked leaving a piece of business half-completed.'

'Well, what do you want me to do?' remarked Seven with a grim smile. 'Do you want me to declare war on your precious uncle, or on the Grand Duchess of Ehrenberg?'

He drank off his punch, and held the tumbler toward Tog for refilling.

'Apart from the question of my self-pride,' he continued, 'can you give me any adequate reason why I should further concern myself with the fate of the young woman?'

'Yes,' said Albert rather pompously, and shifted his regard from the remarkable tartan outfit of Mr. Togarmah Smith — who, spectacles at end of short nose, was watching him admiringly — to the saturnine face of Seven. 'You are directly responsible for her present position. But for your interference she would have been now in the comparative safety of the castle of Lecques. Or in any of a hundred other places whence she could have defied King Leopold. Your fantastic theories have been her ruin, if you will permit me to say so. To educate her for a throne you send her to sea for six weeks or more without a female companion, in the chaperonage of yourself, a small boy, and a young man of no principles! Do you think any reputation would survive that?'

Togarmah, watching Seven, shifted uneasily, warningly. But the master of Judgment did not lift his gaze from hot coal and crumbling log.

'The Grand Duke of Ehrenberg does not appear to complain,' Seven said at length, almost defensively.

'The Grand Duke of Ehrenberg is a lunatic. A hunchback. He has been shut away for twenty years!'

'My God!' said Seven; and rose to his feet in one quick jerk. 'What is this story?'

Albert had risen, too, and they confronted one another across the hearth. Regarding the two faces — fair, composed face with cold blue eyes; dark face with mobile features and eyes that might suddenly flash into swift interrogation or anger or sardonic amusement from under their shrouding lids — Togarmah felt that the prince had never been younger than he was; that Seven would never be older.

'The match was felt to be a very suitable one by those who promoted it,' said Albert drily. 'Both for reasons of diplomacy and finance. Using extreme terms the parties, in their view, are — a mad prince too foolish to complain, and a bad woman who should be too wise to complain! . . . All very suitable!'

'The dirty filthy bastards!' said Tog. He cast his knitting on the floor. He seized his glass of punch, and crashed it down on the elbow of his chair, with such violence that the tumbler shivered and the hot liquid poured on to his trouser leg. He paid no attention — nor to the fact that his spectacles had travelled off his nose on to his lap. 'The filthy swinish pimps!' said Tog. 'The dom'd bloody incestuous whore-mongers!' said Tog. 'She was the sweetest little creature —'

'God help her!' said Seven.

'Why not you?' countered Albert, who had obviously not altogether approved Tog's stream of invective.

' — Or you, for that matter?'

'I have done everything I can ... More than I should ... I am not a free agent ... She is your responsibility —'

'I do not necessarily accept that responsibility.'

'You'll be a dirty lousy dog if you don't,' said Tog. 'You'll not be fit for a gentleman to live with, if you don't! And I'm dom'd if I will! I'ld rather make my living cleaning night-stools in Bedlam than stay, if you don't! I'ld rather be a tout for superannuated prostitutes in St. Giles' than stay, if you don't! I'ld —'

'You cannot really accuse me of setting fire to her ship in mid-Atlantic!'

'No,' replied Albert, 'but I can accuse you of sending her across the Atlantic quite unnecessarily. She would have, for instance, been per-fectly safe in Holland. There's no love lost between my uncle and the Dutch King — as everybody knows ... I say that you are directly responsible for her present troubles.'

'And, again, I disclaim responsibility!' declared Seven doggedly — not so much to Albert and Tog as to Seven-Daniel.

'Then you *are* a dirty dog, Mr. Tempest,' said Tog bouncing to his feet. 'A dirty, treacherous dog. And I give you my notice here and now. And I'll go to-morrow — blast you!'

'You always were in love with her, Tog,' said Seven, outwardly un-moved. 'Now I wonder if —'

He stared directly, and with speculation, into the young prince's eyes: for some moments the two men stood silent, holding one another's regard.

The door opened, and Lovell appeared. She was carrying a small flat basket full of keys, and a large slate covered with grey pencilling and headed — 'Household Duties: Thursday.'

It was the official closing of the session.

Togarmah made a sort of gesture of renunciation toward keys and slate. He rose; and his knitting again dropped to the floor with the movement.

'I shall be going to-morrow,' he said. 'You'll probably like to look through my boxes! They *always* examine servants' boxes when they go ... You'd better see that there are no spoons — or the best silver caddy! ... Penny!' — he raised his voice to the deaf girl — 'Will you come and keep house for me? ... Good!'

Lovell — very puzzled — smiled at him the confiding smile of a child: watched him stamp out of the room: departed, too, with keys and slate.

Said Seven, when she had made her little bow from the doorway and gone —

'To-night's news is, then, that Anne Louise is to marry a madman, and that Lovell will probably do the same!' ...

He stood over the dying fire in the empty room, elbows resting on the mantelshelf, staring at first one absurd print and then another.

His father! For what wreckage of soul and body had he not been responsible! He thought of Pedder — the little boy in the green jacket who had sung so lustily in church and talked history to the parson! — ravening about his ship. Of those other brothers who had been remorselessly destroyed and had utterly vanished. He thought then of himself — as he had once been: as he was now, warped, egotistical, ironic. Of his supreme contempt for other people's opinions: of his supreme belief in himself. Of Daniel, who was to have gone the way of — himself or of Pedder? Of Anne Louise — whose destiny he had tried to mould according to his theories; whose life he seemed to have broken.

Then suddenly he knew quite well that he was no demi-god — that beneath the outward mask of chill divinity that he never doffed, even to himself, there was the frightened, questing, very human spirit of the child who had watched Excalibur burn and cursed his father; of the boy who had passionately loved the wretched lad, Tod, transported so many years ago for poaching a rich man's rabbits; of the youngster who had comforted and caressed that unhappy girl, Daniel's mother.

He knew that he loved Daniel with a very human love — and hungered for the child's affection in return.

He knew that Margarethe Thirkelsen's magic could never have succeeded, had it not been for his real self — a human, lustful, childish self. He recalled the phrase in one of the books he had found in her room: 'It is impossible to hypnotise a subject against his will.' That was true. Deep down within him, ignored and unheeded by his consciousness, his true self had staged revolt — had leaped to surrender.

Thinking back now, he felt some grim amusement at his inward chagrin when Margarethe heard with utter indifference of his impending departure. She had displayed no more interest in her paramour of a night, than in any other of her guests.

Anne Louise! He saw her bright mutinous face, framed in the enchanting ringlets that held so many shades of gold — the short straight nose — the powdering of freckles — the short upper lip pouting into a smile as she royally received the adoration of Daniel. Saw her unquenchably gay — except with him — cobbling old clothes; reading gravely out loud the most preposterous information from the pages of Mr. Partington; nursing a sick child; standing un-panicked on the poop of the *Joan Dearlove* as the ship flamed in a great bouquet of fire under the vault of night; coming with dancing step down an alley in Elsinore, in Quakerish grey, between worshipping Washy and worshipping Daniel.

Now Washy was dead! And Anne Louise was to be bride of a madman — bride of a hunchback ... For six years had he been his father's serf, but Anne Louise's serfdom might endure for sixty ... He dared not to think of it — dared not — dared not! ... But he did.

He set his hand to the red-tasselled bell-pull. He pulled so violently that he could hear the distant jangling of the bell resounding through the silent sleeping house: waited a minute, and then tugged more violently even than before.

He realized that whoever answered would in all probablity have to shrug some clothes on. In the window was a small mahogany escritoire with a stained green leather top, strewn with spikes upon which Tog kept the household accounts meticulously filed. He seated himself at it; found a sheet of paper in a drawer, and set himself to write a letter quickly, decisively, while he waited.

As he wrote an idea struck him ... He smiled rather grimly at the fantastic notion ... Continued writing ... Set down his pen and thought with furrowed concentration for a minute ... It was not so fantastic ... It was possible ... Practicable ... Flawless! He burst into roars of laughter.

There was a bumping at the door by-and-by, and Mr. 'Snorker' Reid made his appearance. Although he had changed his occupation to that of a house-servant (of indeterminate duties) he still wore a pair of excessively nautical bell-bottomed trousers, into which the tails of a white cotton night-shirt were tucked. He waited beside the desk, the grey down on his queer wedge-shaped head fluffed up from the pillow, and his queer triangular mouth more acutely triangular than ever in his efforts to suppress yawns.

'Snorker,' said Seven, 'one of the men must saddle up and be gone post to London with this letter within half an hour. He must arrange on the road for relays for me. The post-chaise is to be got ready. It'll be light in two hours time. I shall leave then.'

'Aye-aye, sir!' said Snorker. 'Where you goin', cap'n?'

'To recover my self-respect,' said Seven: and was aware of the advent of Tog, garbed in a shabby red flannel dressing-gown and a crumpled night-cap with a tassel as long as a Chinaman's queue.

'I mentioned two madmen to you a little while ago,' said Mr. Tempest easily to Mr. Smith. 'I now know of a third! . . . I want you to help me in my lunacy, Tog! Now, listen. . . .'

CHAPTER III

PERSEUS SETS OUT

SEVEN covered the two hundred and five miles from his house of Judgment to London in precisely twenty hours. At ten minutes past eleven he was being ushered upstairs to his first-floor sitting-room at Osborne's Hotel, in the Adelphi, by a very small and very ancient waiter, in whom garrulousness and sleepiness strove so that his babble of conversation sounded like the bedtime twittering of a treeful of sparrows.

'Dreadful weather — very!' said the waiter. 'Most unseasonable . . . Tiring journey, I daresay, sir? . . . Come far, sir? . . . Mind the corner stair! . . . Very uneven — very! . . . Worst of these old houses . . . Here we are, sir! . . . The identical room as mentioned by Mr. Dickens in *Pickwick Papers*. A very gentlemanly gentleman, Mr. Dickens — although they *do* say . . .'

He opened the door of a large room papered in dark red, whose principal features were an enormous mahogany sideboard backed by a mirror which multiplied its large flock of plated toast-racks, muffineers, cruets, entrée dishes, biscuit-boxes, and sugar sifters; a round table spread for supper with a chicken, a raised pie, an uncut ham, and a bottle of burgundy; and a fat little grey-haired gentleman in black with with a white neck-cloth, and a fat pale face.

'So you've come yourself, Quilter!' said Seven, much pleased. 'Sit down, and have some supper — or, if you won't, at any rate help me with the burgundy!'

'A small glass, I thank you . . . There are some papers to be signed and others for you to see if you are going to be away any length of time, Mr. Tempest,' said Quilter in a high light voice. 'I did not care to send one of the clerks . . . In this morning's foreign mail there is an advice from Sauerwein in Ehrenberg stating that he would be leaving for England by diligence with the boy in two days' time. He asks for funds to be sent to Paris. Send him fifty pounds? Very good, sir! . . . Here are the letters of credit you asked for, as well as a circular letter of Messrs. Herries. Also your passport — the fee of two guineas is sheer robbery! I've booked your berth on the Antwerp packet. Your carriage must be there at dawn for shipping — the boat sails at sunrise.'

Seven glanced at a letter which awaited him on a salver.

'Carriage can go,' he said. 'Have to put off my own departure until the next day. Got an appointment with Melbourne in the morning, I see . . . I've kept you up for nothing.'

The fat little man deprecated apology, and Seven studied the papers as he ate. Presently he looked up —

'So once again you plan a journey for me, Quilter,' he remarked.

' "Once again", sir?'

'It is a long time since you booked those outside seats on the night mail for South Wales!'

'I often wondered whether you remembered,' said Mr. Quilter with a faint smile. 'It will be twenty-six years ago in November! . . . I shall never forget seeing him burn your umbrella. If ever murder looked out of a child's eyes, it looked out of yours!'

'There were others who did more than *look* murder!'

'Yes, indeed,' said Mr. Quilter reflectively, twisting the fourth button from the top of his roll-collared coat — presumably a habit allowed for by either his tailor or his female belongings, since, although its thread was a great deal longer than any of the rest, that particular button had never been known to come off. 'There were times — if I dare say so — when *I* could almost have contemplated his murder with something approaching equanimity!'

In Seven's opinion, Mr. Quilter could not have contemplated the slightest breach of good manners with equanimity, far less so serious an interference with the Decalogue.

He said without further preamble —

'Well, your father's murderer has paid the penalty. Late payment — but in full!'

Quilter was sitting at the table facing him across chicken and ham, and pie, and salad. He set down, with a steady hand, the glass of wine he had been raising to his lips.

'A violent end, I should opine, Mr. Tempest?' he said in a tone which held no emotion but that of interest.

'Very violent!' said Seven.

'Your father always said that your brother would end as he lived — that there was no sense in hastening the process!'

'So you, as well as he, knew that it was Pedder who killed your father in mistake for mine?'

'Certainly, Mr. Tempest. You see, I was as much in your father's confidence as I am, I am glad to say, in yours . . . But Mr. Quilter was not my father — he was, so to speak, a stepfather!' He paused for a minute, and his pale face flushed. 'There can be no harm in saying, now, that he married my mother just before I was born . . . To — to give me a name . . . He was very fond of her in a gentle old-fashioned way . . . She died when I was still an infant.'

Seven reflected that he had known Quilter in positions of responsibility for nearly nineteen years, and intimately — as his personal adjutant — for the ten years since his father's death: and yet had been unacquainted until the moment with any single particular of his private life — whether he was married or single, where he lived, or what was the mode of his living on the large salary that he drew.

'I wonder why you told me that?' he meditated out loud.

Quilter transferred his attentions from the pendulous button to a neat gold pencil-case, which he slowly revolved in white plump fingers with the most meticulously kept nails. His reply at first appeared to be inconsequent —

'Mr. Fielding did me the honour of consulting me whether, or not, he should voice to the authorities his suspicions as to the murderer's identity — suspicions that almost amounted to a certainty. He did so for two reasons . . . One — that the murdered man was my stepfather. The other — that the unhappy murderer was . . . my brother!'

Seven set knife and fork down on plate.

'You felt that to have a brother publicly executed as well as a grandmother was a trifle too much! I agree . . . Greetings, brother!'

He rose and stretched across the table a hand which the other shook warmly.

'I am One,' said Quilter. 'Only I have christened myself by the scriptural appellation of Onesimus. A trifle less eccentric nomenclature than a plain numeral . . . My adopted nephews and nieces — dear creatures! — insist on calling me Onny!'

The two men stood confronting one another — tall dark man with cleft chin and inquiring eyebrows; little pale fat man with pale hair and pale face and pale eyes. They were utterly dissimilar.

'I didn't know that any had survived but me,' said Seven.

'I didn't survive,' said Onesimus. 'I refused to play. Wherever I was sent, I ran away; and went on running away.'

'But where to — ?'

'To the old doctor in Nottinghamshire who brought me up . . . My — our father gave me up in the end. He had me paraded before him; called me "an insolent and obstinate shrimp" — I have never been physically impressive — and "scratched" my entry for the Fielding stakes, as one might say. In other words he set me to a clerk's job in the counting house. And there I remained. But as I grew older he used me more and more in his confidential business, so that in that respect at least I have lost little!'

'He appears to have treated you unusually gently.'

'Gently!' said Onesimus in a strange voice. 'Gently? . . . You could not possibly conceive what he did.' Again he flushed — only this time far more deeply. 'He conceded my intelligence; but he considered my physique deplorable and my courage to be nil. As to a certain extent he had recognized my existence and status, he considered himself justified (he said) in declining to allow his stock to be perpetuated through my means . . . He — took steps — to avert — that contingency!' . . .

Thought Seven, turning over and over a plated fork between his fingers —

> This is a hideous story . . . But even so, is it as monstrous a thing to sterilize a son as to surrender a niece to the physical possession of a bridegroom she may loathe — to someone horrible — to something abhorrent?

He sickened at his thoughts.

> On this assessment the chill Moloch, in whose shadow Anne Louise lay bound for sacrifice, was a more devouring and more remorseless god even than was he who had devoured Quilter and Pedder and the others. . . .

The interview with that urbane and elegant gentleman who was Prime Minister of England took place in an atmosphere of the greatest informality and friendliness.

My Lord was about to go riding, in a prune-coloured coat and tight strapped trousers of almond green. He lounged on a sofa in a lofty drawing-room that was all mirrors, chandeliers, and windows; one languid arm trailed over sofa-back, and one languid foot nestled indolently among brocade cushions. He had a handsome weary face with dark eyes under straight thick eyebrows, and an expression of lazy benevolence.

'It isn't a question of English domestic or foreign politics, so *I* can offer you no help,' said my Lord Melbourne. 'And I am certain her Majesty will not be inclined to interfere. Between ourselves, Mr. Tempest, she has already complained to me once or twice that her uncle, King Leopold, was inclined to think that he "ruled the roast" in regard to her affairs. She has put him in his place — very gently, very firmly, very decidedly!' He permitted himself a slight smile that held both affection for Majesty and admission of Majesty's firmness and decision.

'Accordingly, as you may imagine, she cannot very well concern herself in a matter which is entirely his business, and none of her's. Or that I should recommend her to do so.'

'Even in such special circumstances?'

'To what circumstances do you refer?'

Seven stood on his heels on the low marble curb of the fireplace, his hands resting on his hips.

'In spite of the Reform Act you probably realize that I could — if I chose — control the elections in three boroughs? . . . That is the first circumstance!'

'I thought,' said my Lord with distinguished urbanity, 'that it was four boroughs! . . . Without any disrespect, Mr. Tempest, to the most charming little creature — Should one call a queen a "charming little creature", even if she is so? — it still would be easier for you to control the free and independent electors of your three-four boroughs than for me to control one small lady — bless her! — even if I wanted to, in this case!'

'The second circumstance may possibly have weight with your lordship', said Seven brutally. 'It might persuade your lordship to suggest to her Majesty the suitability of a letter of remonstrance to her uncle . . . Do you think that a young woman — a mere girl — should be forced into marriage with a person of disordered intellect? . . . The Grand Duke of Ehrenberg has been — unbalanced, I am told, these last twenty years!'

My Lord was silent. His grey romantic head was averted, as if he would not look — as if he *could* not look — at the portrait, over the fireplace, of a girl. A portrait in a great gold frame. Of a girl with close curls, masquerading as a page in satin; a girl with a pointed chin and very wide eyes, holding in her hand — as Eve might have held the apple to Adam — a cluster of great purple grapes. That girl had been Byron's mistress (or hadn't she?) and had tried to obliterate the memory of his forgetting in a so foolish and half-hearted attempt at suicide; had run away from home like the mad, wild thing she was; had become a pitiful, tippling, unbalanced creature. Had been his wife, Caroline, a 'person of disordered intellect!'

A mad mate! . . . Even the recollection was unendurable. If such had been his agony, what must it be for a young girl to be tied irrevocably to a lunatic?

'I knew nothing of this,' he said slowly.

'Why should you? . . . But now you know — what then?'

Melbourne sat up with a jerk; thought; shook his head.

When he spoke again his voice was no longer lazy — was regretful — carried conviction —

'I assure you, Mr. Tempest, that I have seen a letter which the Queen wrote to her uncle last night. It will make him extremely angry. Very angry, indeed! Very, very angry! H.M. certainly won't be able to ask any favours for a long time to come . . . If I can help you personally in any way, I will . . . Shall I give you an introduction to the King? He doesn't like me — it's mutual — but . . .'

'Don't need it,' said Seven. 'He knows *me*. My House advanced him a million sterling for arms after the revolution of '30. He'll know me a great deal better soon. Too well for his liking, I should fancy . . . I've got a very sharp weapon. As the Queen can't help, I'll use it. His squeals will be heard from Laeken to Downing-street!'

He spoke with concentrated ferocity. What might be happening even now to Anne Louise? The parallel between her case and Quilter's recurred to his mind: he questioned again whether the ruthlessness of his father had actually been as great as the ruthlessness of her uncle . . . Marriage with a madman!

'I will make him squeal indeed!' asseverated Mr. Tempest, and my Lord, watching him from eyes that so misleadingly looked slumbrous, decided that such might well be the case. . . .

At dawn Seven boarded the Antwerp packet.

By midnight they had completed the passage from Thames to Schelde, and he found his carriage and a courier waiting for him at the quayside.

Soon after a fog-dimmed sunrise he reached Brussels, wearied by a five-hour journey over bad roads, through a monotony of mud and rain and a landscape in which breaking day revealed no beauty, but only the tokens of an almost insect industry.

By noon a very small dapper officer had called on him with the King's reply to his curt demand for an interview. It was equally curt: it made an appointment for that afternoon. At three o'clock accordingly Seven Tempest was received by Leopold, King of the Belgians, in the bleak royal study in the palace at Laeken.

It was an apartment so bare, so chill, so impersonal, that the outer panels of the door might well have borne an inscription in white paint:

Private
Belgian Kingdom Ltd.
Coburg Marriage Market Ltd.
Office of H.M. the General Manager

The walls were painted stone-colour; the few chairs had drab covers; the carpet was of a dull green ornamented with brown discs;

393

the curtains were dead white; the tables and desks — like those in a counting-house — were so high that it was impossible to write on them unless standing or seated on a tall office stool.

In the hour between luncheon and the coming of Mr. Tempest, Managerial Majesty — in the plainest of black coats with plain black stock — had been engaged with his English correspondence, just arrived. One letter left him horrified and furious; and, since there was none to see, he permitted a handsome frosty face to reveal feelings in a whitening and pinching of nostrils of Grecian nose; in a contraction of level brows under elegantly high forehead.

He leaned against a tall desk in the window, stropping a small mother-of-pearl pen-knife upon his tightly trousered thigh, and grinding his teeth (until the dry squeak of molar against molar warned him how destructive was such process to dental enamel) whilst he read the missive for a second time.

The letter was from Victoria of England to her '*Dearest* Uncle'. There was chatter about family, and chatter about nothing at all, studded with a stray emotional word or two in German; and lots of under-scoring, and lots of capital letters and exclamation marks; and then two devilish sentences in the fine angular girlish writing — two sentences that suggested the downfall of the plans upon which he had been engaged for so long.

'The whole subject of marriage is an odious one,' wrote the Queen's Most Excellent Majesty, 'and one which I hate to decide about. At any rate I shall certainly not marry for two or three years.'

Two or three years! Years in which she would continue her head-strong folly, and the agents of Ernest of Hanover would continue their campaign for her throne by whatever means they thought fit! Years which would see completed the destruction of his influence with her!

Victoria was in revolt all along the line. She had refused to help him against the Dutch; she had politely told him to mind his own business when it came to English politics; now she casually threatened destruction to his greatest scheme of all.

He cursed out loud, and stropped the little blade the faster on his leg. He would have liked to give Victoria the same medicine as Anne of Limburg.

Once before had his ambition to rule England been frustrated — by the death of his first wife, that plump, laughing, and obedient creature, the Princess Charlotte of Wales, the Queen-to-be. Then he had woven his web afresh: had mated his sister with the Duke of Kent — a large,

394

bald, impecunious fool, who had had the grace to die almost immediately. Whence Victoria.

From her cradle he had planned that she should sit on the Throne of England as his deputy, his agent, his viceroy. To make this assurance doubly sure, from the cradle he had also planned that she should wed his brother's son, Albert, the immaculate, the beautiful, the submissive. To these ends, twenty years of scheming, persuading, threatening, cajoling!

And now *this*!

He pulled a white china bell-handle violently. An unseen door opened: someone slid quietly into an alcove entirely screened by thick white curtains, and, thus hidden from sight, proceeded to play soft piano music — slipping from a Handel minuet into Mozart, into Schumann . . . An invisible David discoursing soothing music to a Coburg Saul!

Thus comforted, Uncle Leopold's meditations proceeded more happily.

Albert! — A good boy! An obedient boy! A malleable boy!

Well, Albert must pull the chestnuts out of the fire! He stood to win a lot. It was several years since Victoria had seen him, and in the interval he had become almost too good-looking to be true. Uncle Leopold had a pretty sound knowledge of feminine psychology — he had dealt in the marriage market for a good many years — and he was prepared to wager that the moment Victoria saw Albert all her decisions would melt like snow in summer.

But where the devil had Albert got to? He should have reached England before this on the great matrimonial campaign; yet there was no word of, or from him.

It was at this juncture that Seven Tempest arrived in the managerial office.

Majesty, still lounging against the high desk in the window, replied to his brief bow with the briefest possible nod; rang the white-handled bell again; remained silent until the music had ceased, and the invisible pianist had returned whence he came — an angry little David who never once had been beheld by Saul in five years of playing.

The General Manager of Coburg Marriage Market Ltd. came straight to business —

'Your letter to me states that you are not merely aware of all that happened at Ehrenberg, but that you are in a position to inform me of further machinations against my family. I should be glad to hear what you have to say.'

Seven had not been invited to sit down.

There was a high writing slope, with a clerk's stool before it, against the wall under a very large map of Europe. Seven set his tall hat upon the desk, perched himself easily upon the stool, heels on the rungs. He wore a shabby dark green coat, with no trace of wristbands, and a most careless cravat. He might have been the representative of a rival firm dropped in to discuss a possible deal in cotton-seed, or coal.

He delayed response to the request for information until he should have surveyed — with hostile eyes — Anne Louise's Moloch. A sallow, tall Moloch, with lines of ill-temper etched about mouth and nose — with obvious black wig — with astonishingly thick shoes for so elegant (if plain) a costume — a querulous, fidgety, bitter-faced Moloch! He realized that that other orgulous viceroy of destiny, his father, had been a far greater man: that he had been a Creator — of vast industries, of employment, of a people's wealth; not for himself, but as though he were the very Life Force itself. Knew, too, that *this* man was a Devourer, seeking along devious roads, and through the huckstering of flesh and blood, naught but his personal aggrandizement.

When at length he spoke it was as one speaking to an equal.

'I'm not going to beat about the bush, sir. You are probably a busy man' — he said this with an air of concession — 'and I most certainly am. I will cut out tact, and diplomacy, and manœuvring for position. I will just say outright what I mean —'

'And after this preamble?'

Said Seven, meeting frosty gaze in frosty face —

'The Duchess of Limburg is *not* going to marry the lunatic you have chosen for her.'

Leopold's expression and attitude altered by not one whit. He still lounged against the desk, long elegant legs crossed at the ankles.

'Really?'

'You will note that I don't appeal on her behalf. I just say that she is not to.'

'I had noted that!'

'Good! You will write cancelling the proposed contract, and give the princess permission to leave at once for Lecques, or wherever she chooses to go.'

'Really!' said Leopold again, and waited further enlightenment, tapping nonchalantly on his front teeth with a gold pencil.

'Otherwise — otherwise —' remarked Seven, wondering when that slightly blurred Apollo would break out into fury, or whether he never did so, but just froze; '*Otherwise*, your other and more important marriage scheme will just collapse like a sand castle.'

'You appear to take a good deal of interest in the matrimonial arrangements of my family.'

'Just at the moment.'

'You are not proposing, by any chance, to enter it yourself?'

Seven entirely ignored the remark. He tilted the high stool on to its two back legs, and so sat gently rocking himself to and fro, supported by his elbows upon the desk behind. The representative of the rival firm of Tempest and Limburg was about to show his hand — and a strong hand, too.

He said nonchalantly —

'You may be interested to know that in order to make certain of your compliance with my very reasonable request I have abducted your nephew, Albert. Far more efficiently than those who botched the job at Ehrenberg!'

The King said nothing for a minute. He regarded his varnished toes meditatively, with no more token of emotion than if he were considering a quotation for cotton-seed or coal.

'The kidnapping of Prince Albert of Saxe-Coburg-Gotha would almost appear to be becoming a habit,' he remarked. 'May I ask whence he was abducted this time?'

'From a balloon while he was crossing the Channel,' said Seven informatively.

So cold were the dark eyes which were turned on him then that Seven found himself comparing them to the eyes — not of a snake, which to his knowledge he had never seen, but — of a basalt statue caught by a high North light.

He proposed to give away nothing which would reveal Albert's surreptitious visit to Judgment: he amended his statement —

'Actually he was found disguised as an old woman in the cellar of a greengrocer's shop in High Street, Marylebone.'

Leopold never cared to recollect those impecunious days when he had lodged with such a tradesman in that desirable locality. He said with cold ferocity —

'You have committed a penal offence. Punishable in England by transportation for life.'

'I did not say that the abduction had been accomplished in England. . . . This is all utterly beside the point. The only fact that concerns you really, is the fact that I have got the prince.'

'Blackmail?'

'Blackmail!'

'What is to prevent me having you arrested here and now?'

The face of the General Manager of the Coburg concern was not a pretty sight: scored with the bitter lines of anger, it seemed to have frozen into a mask.

'Nothing,' responded Seven easily, 'except that it will not help you to find your nephew . . . Wouldn't you like to know where he is? . . . Well, I will tell you. He's in a ship in port. But what ship, and what port, are my little secrets. And we have worked out a preliminary voyage for him — to Australia? — To Chile? — To Java? And he'll start quite soon, unless — '

'This is monstrous — '

'Not so monstrous as the thing you proposed to do to a young girl!'

'Do you presume — '

'Yes,' said Seven, 'I do! . . . Let me tell you this quite plainly. Unless you do as I have suggested, Albert will be whisked off into space for an indefinite time. And time is the all-important factor in your little game. Unless you can produce Albert very, very shortly, your plans for the matrimonial conquest of England are going to be sunk — a matter of supreme indifference to me, but *not* to you. The King of Hanover is not being idle — as you well know!'

Leopold was a realist. He had the choice between dropping a useful minor policy at Ehrenberg — of getting a good price for a shop-soiled article! — and seeing his most cherished plan crash into appalling wreckage. If Albert were detained too long, or compromised, at this critical juncture — ! Besides there was another circumstance. . . .

He made his choice with frosted dignity.

The General Manager and his business acquaintance then debated the deal in detail; they haggled about niceties; they argued provisos; they tussled over the question of securities for the fulfilment of contract.

A secretary came — went. And then another. Leopold, standing at his desk, signed his name; thrust the document across to Seven, who had risen and stood in the window looking out on to the dank park.

Seven read the papers, pushed one back again, and pocketed the other, nodded, picked up his hat.

'What do you make out of this?' asked the General Manager of Coburg Marriage Market Ltd. as the younger man turned to go.

'Precisely my travelling expenses,' answered the agent of the House of Limburg. . . .

Outside the office door Mr. Tempest in an absent-minded manner donned his hat; and, thus indecorously covered, stalked through the corridors of the palace, lips pursed in a whistle, which, if it had not been soundless, would have been tuneless — for he had no ear for music.

Tuneless and soundless that whistle may have been, but it echoed as loudly in his ears as the bugles of a conqueror trumpeting victory in the enemy stronghold.

He — Seven Tempest — had beaten the Coburger. He had chopped off the tentacle of the octopus that had wound itself about Anne Louise of Limburg. He was the Perseus who had freed Andromeda — the knight errant who had rescued the damsel in distress — and . . . *and* the business man who had not failed to fulfil his contract.

He got into his carriage, and flung himself sprawling in its dark green depths. As they drove through the dripping park, and past a dreary lake with a few miserable swans, on the first stage of the long journey south and east to Ehrenberg, he was smiling very grimly.

Uncle Leopold had made several miscalculations — and not the least when he had fancied that Albert would be the blind instrument of his will. Uncle Leopold would receive some unpleasant surprises when and if that young man won the maiden heart of the Queen of England.

He recalled with intense amusement the youthful earnest face of the prince as — nightcapped and nightshirted — he sat on the edge of his bed at Judgment absorbing with interest and restrained approval the details of the very plan which had just been carried to so successful an issue.

CHAPTER IV

THE MISSING ANDROMEDA

THE thin mists of dawn were withdrawing from the valley. The land-scape was very still and almost shadowless, beneath a high cloudy sky seamed with a faint gold — so faint a gold as to be little more than silver — and with runlets of a blue that was only just not grey.

After four days of ceaseless travel, Seven at last had reached the many-arched stone bridge beyond which the huddled walls and roofs and pointed gables of Ehrenberg rose up sharply, above the glassy river and wide water-meadows.

Country carts full of farm produce were already creaking their way to the town: a blond unshaven official in shabby green uniform yawned stupendously, and nodded the carriage permission to pass through the resounding arch of the great gate-house beyond the bridge: a clock struck the hour, and its jangle echoed through the empty streets: the postilion sounded a *tarantara* on his absurd little horn — they swung right-handed through a narrow street of overhanging houses, came out under the lime-trees upon the ramparts, and pulled up at the ancient and historic hostelry of the Swan-with-Three-Necks.

It was an inn which fattened on the present by reason of the past; for it was a perfect mausoleum of dinners and déjeuners and beddings of the famous, whose names — from Prince Eugene of Savoy to the Emperor Napoleon — were recorded on a tombstone-like slab of marble in the entrance hall.

Two yellowed plaster busts of royal clients, with august noses and periwigs, were also the only ornaments of the bare private sitting-room to which Seven was ushered.

He flung himself down at a little table in the window while a drowsy waiter fetched coffee and rolls.

The sun had risen by the time he had breakfasted; but the mists returned, and, through the gap between the leafy masses of the limes, there was a vista of the valley drenched in a golden haze, of long and luminous shadows, and of a shimmering wood of young birch-trees on the hills opposite.

Little as he knew of court life, Seven yet felt that it must still be far too early to visit royalty — even if that royalty were Anne Louise. He filled in time by undertaking an unusually elaborate toilette; rather